A RIVER
ENCHANTED

A RIVER ENCHANTED

A NOVEL

ELEMENTS OF CADENCE - BOOK I

REBECCA ROSS

HARPER Voyager

An Imprint of HarperCollinsPublishers

A RIVER ENCHANTED. Copyright © 2022 by Rebecca Ross LLC. All rights reserved. Printed in the United States of America. No part of this book may be used or reproduced in any manner whatsoever without written permission except in the case of brief quotations embodied in critical articles and reviews. For information, address HarperCollins Publishers, 195 Broadway, New York, NY 10007.

Harper Voyager and design are trademarks of HarperCollins Publishers LLC.

Designed by Paula Russell Szafranski
Map design by Nick Springer / Springer Cartographics LLC
Wave illustrations © perori / Shutterstock.com

ISBN 978-0-06-305598-8

TO MY BROTHERS—

CALEB, GABRIEL, AND LUKE,

WHO ALWAYS HAVE THE BEST STORIES

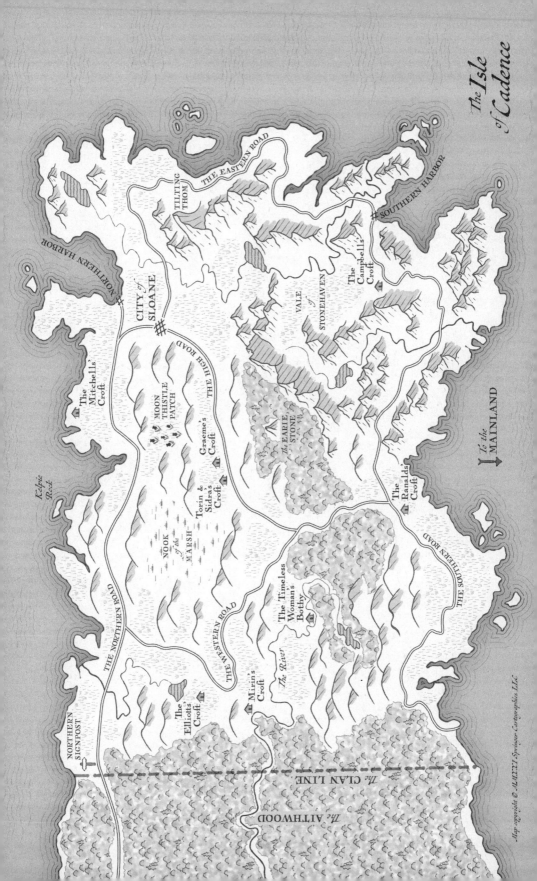

The Isle of Cadence

NORTHERN HARBOR

SOUTHERN HARBOR

THE EASTERN ROAD

TILTING THOM

CITY of SLOANE

The Mitchell's Croft

THE HIGH ROAD

MOON THISTLE PATCH

Graeme's Croft

Torin & Sidra's Croft

NOOK of the MARSH

Kelpie Rock

THE NORTHERN ROAD

THE WESTERN ROAD

The Elliott's Croft

NORTHERN SIGNPOST

Mirin's Croft

The River

The Timeless Woman's Bothy

The Campbell's Croft

VALE of STONEHAVEN

The Earie Stone

The Ranald's Croft

THE SOUTHERN ROAD

To the MAINLAND

The Clan Line

THE CLAN LINE

The Aithwood

Map copyright © MMXXI Springer Cartographics LLC.

PART ONE

A Song
for Water

CHAPTER 1

~~~~~~~~~~~~~~~~~~~~

I t was safest to cross the ocean at night, when the moon and
stars shone on the water. At least, that's what Jack had been
raised to believe. He wasn't sure if those old convictions
still held true these days.

It was midnight, and he had just arrived at Woe, a fishing
village on the northern coast of the mainland. Jack thought the
name was fitting as he covered his nose; the place reeked of
herring. Iron yard gates were tinged with rust, and the houses
sat crooked on stilts, every shutter bolted against the relentless
howl of the wind. Even the tavern was closed, its fire banked,
its ale casks long since corked. The only movement came from
the stray cats lapping up the milk left for them on door stoops,
from the bobbing dance of cogs and rowboats in the quay.

This place was dark and quiet with dreams.

Ten years ago, he had made his first and only ocean crossing. From the isle to the mainland, a passage that took two hours
if the wind was favorable. He had arrived at this very village,
borne over the starlit water by an old sailor. The man had been

weathered and wiry from years of wind and sun, undaunted by the thought of approaching the isle in his rowboat.

Jack remembered it well: his first moment stepping onto mainland soil. He had been eleven years old, and his initial impression was that it smelled different here, even in the dead of night. Like damp rope, fish, and woodsmoke. Like a rotting storybook. Even the land beneath his boots had felt strange, as if it grew harder and drier the farther south he traveled.

"Where are the voices in the wind?" he had asked the sailor.

"The folk don't speak here, lad," the man had said, shaking his head when he thought Jack wasn't looking.

It took a few more weeks before Jack learned that children born and raised on the Isle of Cadence were rumored to be half wild and strange themselves. Not many came to the mainland as Jack had done. Far fewer stayed as long as he had.

Even after ten years, it was impossible for Jack to forget that first mainland meal he had partaken of, how dry and terrible it had tasted. The first time he had stepped into the university, awed by its vastness and the music that echoed through its winding corridors. The moment he realized that he was never returning home to the isle.

Jack sighed, and the memories turned to dust. It was late. He had been traveling for a sennight, and now he was here, defying all logic and ready to make the crossing again. He just needed to find the old sailor.

He walked one of the streets, trying to whet his recollection as to where to find the dauntless man who had previously carried him over the water. Cats scattered, and an empty tonic bottle rolled over the mismatched cobbles, seeming to follow him. He finally noticed a door that felt familiar, right on the edge of town. A lantern hung on the porch, casting tepid light over a peeling red door. Yes, there had been a red door, Jack recalled.

And a knocker made from brass, shaped like an octopus. This was the fearless sailor's house.

Jack had once stood in this very place, and he nearly saw his past self—a scrawny, windswept boy, scowling to hide the tears in his eyes.

"Follow me, lad," the sailor had said after docking his boat, leading Jack up the steps to the red door. It was the dead of night and bitterly cold. Quite the mainland welcome. "You'll sleep here, and then come morning you'll take the coach south to the university."

Jack nodded, but he hadn't slept that night. He had laid down on the floor of the sailor's house, wrapped in his plaid, and closed his eyes. All he could think of was the isle. The moon thistles would soon bloom, and he hated his mother for sending him away.

Somehow, he had grown from that agonizing moment, putting down roots in a foreign place. Although truth be told, he still felt scrawny and angry at his mother.

He ascended the rickety porch stairs, hair tangling across his eyes. He was hungry, and his patience was thin, even if he was knocking at midnight. He clanged the brass octopus on the door, again and again. He didn't relent, not until he heard a curse through the wood, and the sound of locks turning. A man cracked open the door and squinted at him.

"What do you want?"

At once, Jack knew this wasn't the sailor he sought. This man was too young, although the elements had already carved their influence on his face. A fisherman, most likely, by the smell of oysters, smoke, and cheap ale that spilled from his house.

"I'm looking for a sailor to carry me to Cadence," said Jack. "One lived here years ago and bore me from the isle to the mainland."

"That would be my father," the fisherman replied harshly. "And he's dead, so he can't take you." He made to shut the door, but Jack set his foot down, catching the wood.

"I'm sorry to hear that. Can you guide me?"

The man's bloodshot eyes widened; he hacked up a laugh. "To Cadence? No, no I can't."

"Are you afraid?"

"Afraid?" The fisherman's humor broke like an old rope. "I don't know where you've been the last decade or two, but the clans of the isle are territorial, and they don't take kindly to any visitors. If you *are* fool enough to go and visit, you'll need to send a request with a raven. And then you'll need to wait for the crossing to be approved by whichever laird you're seeking to bother. And since the lairds of the isle are on their own time frame . . . expect to wait a while. Or even better—you can wait for the autumnal equinox, when the next trade happens. In fact, I would recommend you wait until then."

Wordlessly, Jack withdrew a sheet of folded parchment from his cloak pocket. He handed the letter to the fisherman, who frowned as he glanced over it by lantern light.

Jack had the message memorized. He had read it countless times since it arrived the previous week, interrupting his life in the most profound of ways.

Your presence is required at once for urgent business. Please return to Cadence with your harp upon receipt.

Beneath the languid handwriting was his laird's signature, and beneath it was the press of Alastair Tamerlaine's signet ring in wine-dark ink, turning this request into an order.

After a decade with hardly any contact with his clan, Jack had been summoned home.

"A Tamerlaine, are you?" the fisherman said, handing the letter back. Jack belatedly realized the man probably was illiterate but had recognized the crest.

Jack nodded, and the fisherman studied him intently.

He endured the scrutiny, knowing there was nothing extraordinary about his appearance. He was tall and thin, as if he had been underfed for years, built from sharp angles and unyielding pride. His eyes were dark, his hair was brown. His skin was pallid and pale, from all the hours he spent indoors, instructing and composing music. He was dressed in his customary gray shirt and trousers, raiment now stained from greasy tavern meals.

"You look like one of us," the fisherman said.

Jack didn't know if he should be pleased or offended.

"What's that on your back?" the fisherman persisted, staring at the one bag Jack was carrying.

"My harp," Jack replied tersely.

"That explains it then. You came here to be schooled?"

"Indeed. I'm a bard. I was educated at the university in Faldare. Now, will you carry me to the isle?"

"For a price."

"How much?"

"I don't want your money. I want a Cadence-forged dirk," the fisherman said. "I would like a dagger to cut through anything: ropes, nets, scales . . . my rival's good fortune."

Jack wasn't surprised by his request for an enchanted blade. Such things could only be forged on Cadence, but they were created with a steep price.

"Yes, I can arrange that for you," Jack said after only a moment of doubt. In the back of his mind, he thought of his mother's dirk with its silver hilt, and how she kept it sheathed at her side, although Jack had never once seen her use it. But he knew the dagger was enchanted; the glamour was evident when one didn't look directly upon the weapon. It cast a slight haze, as though firelight had been hammered into the steel.

There was no telling how much his mother had paid Una

Carlow to forge it for her. Or how much Una had, in turn, suffered for rendering the blade.

He held out his hand. The fisherman shook it.

"Very well," the man said. "We'll leave at daybreak." He went to shut the door again, but Jack refused to remove his foot.

"We must go now," he said. "While it's dark. This is the safest time to make the crossing."

The fisherman's eyes bugged. "Are you daft? I wouldn't cross those waters at night if you paid me a hundred enchanted dirks!"

"You must trust me on this," Jack answered. "Ravens may carry messages to the lairds by day, and the trade cog may glide on the first of the season, but the best time to cross is at night, when the ocean reflects the moon and the stars."

When the spirits of the water are easily appeased, Jack added inwardly.

The fisherman gaped. Jack waited—he would stand here all night and all of the next day if he had to—and the fisherman must have sensed it. He relented.

"Very well. For *two* Cadence dirks, I will carry you across the water tonight. Meet me by my boat in a few minutes. It's that one, in the berth on the far right."

Jack glanced over his shoulder to look at the darkened quay. Weak moonlight gleamed on the hulls and masts, and he found the fisherman's boat, a modest vessel that had once been his father's. The very boat that had originally carried Jack in his first crossing.

He stepped down the stoop, and the door latched behind him. He momentarily wondered if the fisherman was fooling him, agreeing to simply get Jack off his porch, but Jack walked briskly to the quay in good faith, the wind nearly pushing him down as he strode over the damp road.

He lifted his eyes to the darkness. There was a wavering

trail of celestial light on the ocean, the silver path the fisher-man needed to follow to reach Cadence. A sickle moon hung in the sky like a smile, surrounded by freckles of stars. It would have been ideal if the moon was full, but Jack couldn't afford to wait for it to wax.

He didn't know why his laird had summoned him home, but he sensed it wasn't for a joyous reunion.

It felt as if he had waited an hour before he saw a firefly of lantern light approaching. The fisherman walked hunched against the wind, a waxed overmantle shielding him, his face trapped in a scowl.

"You had better be good to your word, bard," he said. "I want two Cadence dirks for all of this trouble."

"Yes, well, you know where to find me if I'm not," Jack said, brusquely.

The fisherman glared at him, one eye bigger than the other. Then, conceding, he nodded at his boat, saying, "Climb aboard."

And Jack took his first step off the mainland.

The ocean was rough at first.

Jack gripped the boat's gunwale, his stomach churning as the vessel rose and fell in a precarious dance. The waves rolled, but the brawny fisherman cut through them, rowing the two of them farther out to sea. He followed the trail of moonlight as Jack suggested, and soon the ocean became gentler. The wind continued to howl, but it was still the wind of the mainland, carrying nothing but cold salt in its breath.

Jack glanced over his shoulder, watching the lanterns of Woe turn to tiny flecks of light, his eyes smarting, and he knew they were about to enter the isle's waters. He could sense it as if Cadence had a gaze, finding him in the darkness, fixating on him.

"A body washed to shore a month ago," the fisherman said, breaking Jack's reverie. "Gave us all a bit of fright in Woe."

"I beg your pardon?"

"A Breccan, by the woad tattoos on his bloated skin. His blue plaid arrived shortly after him." The man paused in his speech, but he continued to row, the paddles dipping into the water in a mesmerizing rhythm. "A slit throat. I suppose it was the work of one of your clansmen, who then dumped the misfortunate soul in the ocean. To let *us* clean up the mess when the tides brought the corpse to our shores."

Jack was silent as he stared at the fisherman, but a shiver chased his bones. Even after all these years away, the sound of his enemy's name sent a spear of dread through him.

"Perhaps one of his own did it to him," Jack said. "The Breccans are known for their bloodthirsty ways."

The fisherman chuckled. "Should I dare to believe a Tamerlaine is unbiased?"

Jack could have told him stories of raids. How the Breccans often crossed the clan line and stole from the Tamerlaines during the winter months. They plundered and wounded; they pillaged without remorse, and Jack felt his hatred rise like smoke as he remembered being a young boy riddled by the fear of them.

"How did the feud begin, bard?" the fisherman pressed on. "Do any of you even remember why you hate each other, or do you simply follow the path your ancestors set for you?"

Jack sighed. He just wanted a swift, *quiet* passage over the water. But he knew the story. It was an old, blood-soaked saga that shifted like the constellations, depending on who did the retelling—the east or the west, the Tamerlaines or the Breccans.

He mulled over it. The current of the water gentled, and the hiss of the wind fell to a coaxing whisper. Even the moon hung lower, keen for him to share the legend. The fisherman sensed it as well. He was quiet, rowing at a slower pace, waiting for Jack to give the story breath.

"Before the clans, there were the folk," Jack began. "The earth, the air, the water, and the fire. They gave life and balance to Cadence. But soon the spirits grew lonely and weary of hearing their own voices, of seeing their own faces. The northern wind blew a ship off course and it crashed on the rocks of the isle. Amid the flotsam was a fierce and arrogant clan, the Breccans, who had been seeking a new land to claim.

"Not long after that, the southern wind blew a ship off course, and it found the isle. They were the Tamerlaine clan, and they too established a home on Cadence. The island was balanced between them, with the Breccans in the west and the Tamerlaines in the east. And the spirits blessed the work of their hands.

"In the beginning, it was peaceful. But soon, the two clans began to have more and more altercations and scuffles with each other, until whispers of war began to haunt the air. Joan Tamerlaine, the Laird of the East, hoped she could stave off conflict by uniting the isle as one. She would agree to marriage with the Breccan laird as long as peace was upheld and empathy was encouraged between the clans, in spite of their differences. When Fingal Breccan beheld her beauty, he decided that he, too, wanted harmony. 'Come and be my wife,' he said, 'and let our two clans join as one.'

"Joan married him and lived with Fingal in the west, but as the days passed Fingal continued to delay on formally reaching a peace agreement. Joan soon learned that the ways of the Breccans were rigid and cruel, and she couldn't adapt to them. Disheartened by the bloodshed, she strove to share the customs of the east, in hopes that they might also find a place in the west, granting goodness to the clan. But Fingal became angry with her desires, thinking she would only weaken the west, and he refused to see Tamerlaine ways celebrated.

"It wasn't long until the peace was hanging on by a fragile thread and Joan realized Fingal had no intention of uniting the isle. He said one thing but enacted another behind her back, and the Breccans began to raid the east, stealing from the Tamerlaines. Joan, longing for home and to be rid of Fingal, soon departed, but she made it only as far as the center of the isle before Fingal caught up with her.

"They quarreled, they fought. Joan drew her dirk and cut herself loose from him—name, vow, spirit, and body, but not her heart, because it was never his. She bestowed a tiny nick upon his throat, the very place where she had once kissed him in the night, when she dreamt of the east. The small wound swiftly drained him, and Fingal felt his life ebb away. When he fell, he took her with him, forcing his own dagger into her chest, to pierce the heart he could never earn.

"They cursed each other and their clans, and they died entwined, stained in each other's blood, in the place where the east meets the west. The spirits felt the rift as the clan line was drawn, and the earth drank the mortals' blood, strife, and violent end. Peace became a distant dream, and that is why the Breccans continue to raid and steal, hungry to have what is not theirs, and why the Tamerlaines continue to defend themselves, cutting throats and piercing hearts with blades."

The fisherman, leaning toward the tale, had ceased rowing. When Jack fell silent, the man shook himself and frowned, returning to his oars. The sickle moon continued its arc across the sky, the stars dimmed their fires, and the wind began to howl now that the story was over.

The ocean resumed its billowing tide as Jack set his eyes on the distant isle, his first glimpse of it in ten long years.

Cadence was darker than night, a shadow against the ocean and the starry sky. Long and rugged, it stretched before them like a sprawled dragon sleeping on the waves. Jack's heart stirred at the sight, traitor that it was. Soon, he would be walking the ground he had grown up on, and he didn't know if he would be welcomed or not.

He hadn't written to his mother in three years.

"You're a deranged lot, that's what I think," the fisherman muttered. "All this nonsense and talk of spirits."

"You don't revere the folk?" Jack asked, but he knew the answer. There were no faerie spirits on the mainland. Only the patina of gods and saints, carved into the sanctuaries of kirks.

The fisherman snorted. "Have you ever seen a spirit, lad?"

"I've seen evidence of them," Jack replied carefully. "They don't often reveal themselves to mortal eyes." He inevitably recalled the countless hours he had spent roaming the hills as a boy, eager to snare a spirit amid the heather. Of course, he never had.

"Sounds like a bucket of chum to me."

Jack made no reply as the vessel glided closer.

He could see the golden lichens on the eastern rocks, luminescent. They marked the Tamerlaine coastline, and Jack's memories surged. He remembered how things that grew on the isle were peculiar, bent to enchantment. He had explored the coast countless times, to Mirin's great frustration and worry. But every girl and boy of the isle had been drawn to the whirlpools and eddies and secret caves of the coast. In the day and in the night, when the lichen glowed, golden as leftover sunlight on the rocks.

He noticed they were drifting. The fisherman was rowing, but they were angled away from the lichen, as if the boat was hooked to the dark stretch of western coast.

"We're sailing into Breccan waters," Jack said, a knot of alarm in his throat. "Here, row us to the east."

The fisherman heaved, directing the boat the way Jack instructed, but their progress was painfully slow. Something was wrong, Jack realized, and the moment he acknowledged there was trouble, the wind abated and the ocean turned glassy, smooth like a mirror. It was quiet, a roaring silence that raised his hackles.

Tap.

The fisherman ceased rowing, his eyes wide as full moons. "Did you hear that?"

Jack lifted his hand. *Be quiet,* he wanted to say but held his tongue, waiting for the warning to come again.

Tap. Tap. Tap.

He felt it in the soles of his shoes. Something was in the water, clicking its long nails on the underside of the hull. Testing for a weak spot.

"Mother of gods," the fisherman whispered, sweat shining on his face. "What is making that racket?"

Jack swallowed. He could feel his own perspiration beading his brow, the tension within him taut as a harp string as the claws beneath continued tapping.

The mainlander's scorn had caused this. He had offended the folk of the water, who must have gathered in the foam of the sea to hear Jack's legend. And now both men would pay for it with a sinking boat and a watery grave.

"Do you revere the spirits?" Jack asked in a low tone, staring at the fisherman.

The man only gaped, and then a flicker of fear crossed over his face. He began to turn the boat around, rowing with great heaves back to Woe.

"What are you doing?" Jack cried.

"I go no further," the fisherman said. "I want nothing to do with your isle and whatever haunts these waters."

Jack narrowed his eyes. "We had an agreement."

"Either jump overboard and swim your way to shore, or you'll be coming back with me."

"Then I suppose I'll have your dirks forged three-quarters of the way. How would you like that?"

"Keep your dirks."

Jack was speechless. The fisherman had almost hauled them out of the isle's waters, and Jack couldn't go back to the mainland. Not when he was so close to home, when he could see the lichen and taste the cold sweetness of the mountains.

He stood and turned in the boat, carelessly rocking it. He could swim the distance if he left his cloak and leather satchel of clothes behind. He could swim to the shore, but he would be in enemy waters.

And he needed his harp. Laird Alastair had requested it.

He quickly opened his satchel and found his harp within, hiding in a sleeve of oilskin. The saltwater would ruin the instrument, and Jack was struck by an idea. He dug deeper into his bag and found the square of Tamerlaine plaid, which he hadn't worn since the day he left the isle.

His mother had woven it for him when he was eight, when he had started to get into fistfights at the isle school. She had enchanted it by weaving a secret into the pattern, and he had been delighted when his nemesis was rewarded with a broken hand the next time he tried to punch Jack in the stomach.

Jack stared at the scrap of seemingly innocent plaid now. It was soft when draped on the floor but strong as steel when it was put to use guarding something like a heart or a pair of lungs. Or in this desperate case, a harp about to be submerged.

Jack wrapped his instrument in the checkered wool and

slid it back into its sleeve. He needed to swim to shore before the fisherman dragged him farther away from it.

He shed his cloak, embraced his harp, and jumped overboard.

The water was bitterly cold. The shock of it stole his breath as the ocean swallowed him whole. He broke the surface with a gasp, hair plastered to his face, chapped lips stinging from the salt. The fisherman continued to row farther and farther away, leaving a ripple of fear on the surface.

Jack spat in the mainlander's wake before turning to the isle. He prayed the spirits of the water would be benevolent to him as he began to swim to Cadence. He set his eyes on the glow of the lichen, trying to pull himself to the safety of the Tamerlaine shore. But the moment he treaded the ocean, the waves rolled and the tide returned with a laugh. He was drawn under, jerked by the current.

Fear coursed through him, pounding in his veins until he realized that he broke the surface every time he reached for it. By the third lungful of air, Jack sensed the spirits were toying with him. If they wanted to drown him, they would have done it by now.

Of course, he thought, struggling to swim as the tide pulled him under again. Of course, his return wouldn't be effortless. He should have expected this sort of homecoming.

He scraped his palm on the reef. His left shoe was ripped from his foot. He cradled his harp with one hand and stretched out the other, hoping to find the surface. Only water greeted him this time, rippling through his fingers. In the dark, he opened his eyes and was startled when he saw a woman, darting past him in the water with gleaming scales, her long hair tickling his face.

He shivered and nearly forgot to swim.

The waves eventually had enough of him and coughed him

out on a sandy stretch of beach. That was the only mercy they gave him. On the sand, he spluttered and crawled. He knew instantly that he was on Breccan soil, and the thought made his bones melt like wax. It took Jack a moment to rise and gain his bearings.

He could see the clan line. It was marked by rocks that sat in a row like teeth on the beach, running all the way into the ocean, where their tops eventually descended into the depths. It was roughly a kilometer away, and the distant glow of the lichen beckoned him to hurry, *hurry*.

Jack ran, one foot bare and frigid, the other squishing in a wet shoe. He wove around tangles of driftwood and a small eddy that gleamed like a dream about to break. He crawled under a rock arch, slipped over another boulder that was crinkled with moss, and finally reached the clan line.

He hefted himself over the rocks damp from sea mist. With a gasp, he stumbled onto Tamerlaine territory. But he could finally breathe, and he stood on the sand and made himself inhale, deep and slow. One moment, it was quiet and peaceful, save for the rush of the tide. The next? Jack was knocked off his feet. He hit the ground, harp flying. His teeth went through his lip, and he struggled beneath the weight of someone manhandling him.

He had forgotten all about the East Guard in his desperation to reach Tamerlaine land.

"I have him!" called out his attacker, who actually sounded more like a zealous lad.

Jack wheezed but couldn't find his voice. The weight on his chest lifted, and he felt two hands, hard like iron manacles, latch themselves to his ankles and drag him across the beach. Desperate, he reached out to recover his harp. He had no doubt that he would need to show Mirin's plaid to prove who he was, since the laird's letter had been in his cloak, now abandoned in the rowboat. But his arms were too heavy. Fuming, he relented to being toted.

"Can I kill him, captain?" the lad who was dragging Jack asked, all too eager.

"Maybe. Bring him yonder."

That voice. Deep as a ravine with a trace of mirth. Terribly familiar, even after all these years away.

Just my fortune, Jack thought, closing his eyes as sand stung his face.

At last, the dragging ceased, and he lay on his back, exhausted.

"Is he alone?"

"Yes, captain."

"Armed?"

"No, sir."

Silence. And then Jack heard the crunch of boots on the sand and sensed someone looming over him. Carefully, he opened his eyes. Even in the dark with nothing but starlight to limn the guard's face, Jack recognized him.

The constellations crowned Torin Tamerlaine as he stared down at Jack.

"Hand me your dirk, Roban," said Torin, to which Jack's shock morphed into terror.

Torin didn't recognize him. But why should he? The last time Torin had seen and spoken to him, Jack had been ten years old, wailing, with thirteen thistle needles embedded in his face.

"Torin," Jack wheezed.

Torin paused, but the dirk was in his grip now. "What did you say?"

Jack held up his hands, sputtering. "It's me . . . Jack Tam . . . erlaine."

Torin seemed to turn into rock. He didn't move, blade

poised above Jack, like an omen about to fall. And then he barked, "Bring me a lantern, Roban."

The lad Roban scampered away, then returned with a lantern swinging in his hand. Torin took it and lowered the light, so it would spill across Jack's face.

Jack squinted against the brightness. He tasted blood on his tongue, his lip swelling almost as much as his mortification, as he waited.

"By the spirits," Torin said. The light finally receded, leaving splotches in Jack's sight. "I don't believe it."

And he must have seen a trace of who Jack had been ten years ago. A malcontent, dark-eyed boy. Because Torin Tamerlaine threw his head back and laughed.

"Don't just lie there. Stand up and let me get a better look at you, lad."

Jack reluctantly obeyed Torin's request. He stood and brushed the sand from his drenched clothes, wincing as his palm burned.

He delayed the inevitable, afraid to look at the guard he had once aspired to be. Jack studied his mismatched feet, the cut on his hand. All the while, he felt Torin's gaze bore into him, and eventually he had to answer it.

He was surprised to discover they were now the same great height. But that was where their similarity ended.

Torin was built for the isle: broad shouldered and thick waisted, with sturdy, slightly bowed legs and arms corded with muscle. His hands were huge, his right one still casually holding the dirk's hilt, and his face was cut square and anchored with a trim beard. His blue eyes were set wide, and one too many spars had left his nose crooked. His hair was long and bound back by two plaits, blond as a wheat field, even at midnight. He wore the same garments Jack remembered him by:

a dark woolen tunic that reached his knees, a leather jerkin studded with silver, a hunting plaid of brown and red draped across his chest, held fast by a brooch set with the Tamerlaine crest. No trousers, but not many men of the isle bothered with them. Torin sported the customary knee-high boots made from untanned hide, shaped to his legs and held in place by leather thongs.

Jack wondered what Torin thought of him in return. Perhaps that he was too skinny, or looked weak and scrawny. That he was too pale from sitting indoors. That his clothes were drab and terrible, and his eyes jaded.

But Torin nodded his approval. "You've grown, lad. How old are you now?"

"I'll be twenty-two this autumn," said Jack.

"Good, good." Torin glanced at Roban, who stood nearby, scrutinizing Jack. "It's all right, Roban. He's one of us. Mirin's boy, in fact."

That seemed to shock Roban. He couldn't have been older than fifteen, and his voice cracked when he cried, "*You're* Mirin's son? She speaks of you often. You're a bard!"

Jack nodded, wary.

"It's been a long time since I've seen a bard," Roban continued.

"Yes, well," Jack said, with a twinge of annoyance, "I hope you didn't break my harp at the clan line."

Roban's lopsided smile dimmed. He stood frozen until Torin ordered him to recover the instrument. While Roban was gone, humbly searching, Jack followed Torin to a small campfire in the maw of a sea cave.

"Sit, Jack," Torin said. He unbuckled his plaid and tossed it across the fire to Jack. "Dry yourself."

Jack caught it awkwardly. He knew the moment he touched the plaid that this was one of Mirin's enchanted weavings. What secret of Torin's had she woven into it, Jack wondered with irritation, but he was too cold and wet to resist it. He draped the checkered wool around himself and stretched his hands out to the fire.

"Are you hungry?" Torin asked.

"No, I'm fine." Jack's stomach was still roiling from the voyage across the water, from the horror of being on Breccan soil, from nearly having every tooth knocked loose by Roban. He realized his hands were shaking. Torin noticed as well and extended a flask to Jack before he settled across the fire from him.

"I noticed you arrived from the west," Torin said with a hint of suspicion.

"Unfortunately, yes," Jack replied. "The mainlander rowing me to the isle turned coward. I had no choice but to swim, and the current brought me to the west."

He took a bracing sip from the flask. The heather ale was refreshing, stirring his blood. He took a second swallow and felt steadier, stronger—owing, he knew, to consuming something that had been brewed on the isle. Food and drink here boasted flavor tenfold over mainland fare.

He glanced at Torin. Now that they were in the light, he could see the captain's crest on his brooch. A leaping stag with a ruby in its eye. He also noticed the scar on Torin's left palm.

"You've been promoted to captain," said Jack. Although that was no surprise. Torin had been the most favored of guards from a very young age.

"Three years ago," Torin replied. His face softened, as if his old recollections were as close as yesterday. "The last time I saw you, Jack, you were yea high, and you had—"

"Thirteen thistle needles in my face," Jack finished drolly. "Does the East Guard still hold that challenge?"

"Every third spring equinox. I have yet to see another injury like yours, however."

Jack stared at the fire. "You know, I always wanted to be one of the guard. I thought I could prove myself worthy of the east that night."

"By falling on an armful of thistles?"

"I didn't *fall* on them. They were *shoved* into my face."

Torin scoffed. "By whom?"

By your lovely cousin, Jack wanted to reply, but he remembered that Torin was fiercely devoted to Adaira and most likely thought she was incapable of being so fiendish.

"No one important," Jack replied, despite the glaring truth that Adaira was the Heiress of the East.

He almost asked Torin about her, but thought better of it. Jack hadn't envisioned his childhood rival in years, but he now imagined Adaira as wed, maybe with a few bairns of her own. He imagined she was even more beloved than she had been as a youth.

Dwelling on her reminded Jack there was a gap in his knowledge. He didn't know what had been happening on the isle while he was away, steeped in music. He didn't know why Laird Alastair had summoned him. He didn't know how many raids had occurred, if the Breccans were still a looming threat when the ice came.

Emboldened, he met Torin's stare. "You meet every stray who crosses the clan line with instant death?"

"I wouldn't have killed you, lad."

"That's not what I asked."

Torin was quiet, but he didn't break their gaze. The firelight flickered over his rugged features, but there was no regret, no hint of shame in him. "It depends. Some stray Breccans are truly fooled by the spirits' mischief. They misstep and they mean no harm. Others are scouting."

"Have there been any raids recently?" Jack asked, dreading

to learn if Mirin had been lying to him in her past letters. His mother lived close to western territory.

"There hasn't been a raid since last winter. But I expect one will come soon. Once the cold arrives."

"Where did this most recent raid happen?"

"The Elliotts' croft," Torin replied, but his eyes were sharp, as if he were beginning to piece together the lack of Jack's knowledge. "You're worried about your mum? Mirin's farm hasn't been raided since you were a lad."

Jack remembered, although he had been so young he sometimes wondered if he had dreamt it. A group of Breccans had arrived one winter night, their horses turning the snow muddy in the yard. Mirin had held Jack in the corner of their house, one hand pressing his face into her chest so he couldn't see, the other wielding a sword. Jack had listened as the Breccans took what they wanted—winter provisions and livestock from the byre and a few silver marks. They broke pottery, overturned piles of Mirin's weavings. Quickly they went, as if they were underwater, holding their breaths, knowing they had only a moment before the East Guard arrived.

They hadn't touched or spoken to Mirin or Jack. The two of them were inconsequential. Nor had Mirin challenged them. Calm she had been, inhaling long draws, but Jack remembered hearing the beat of her heart, swift as wings.

"Why have you come home, Jack?" Torin asked quietly. "None of us ever thought you would return. We assumed you had created a new life for yourself, as a bard on the mainland."

"I'm only here for a brief visit," Jack replied. "Laird Alastair asked me to return."

Torin's brows arched. "Did he now?"

"Yes. Do you know why?"

"I think I know why he's summoned you," Torin said.

"We've been facing a terrible trouble. It's been weighing heavily on the entire clan."

Jack's pulse quickened. "I don't see how I can do anything about the Breccans' raids."

"It's not the raids," Torin replied. His eyes were glazed, as if he had seen a wraith. "No, it's something much worse than that."

Jack began to feel the cold creep into his skin. He was remembering the taste of isle-bred fear, how it felt to be lost when the land shifted. How storms could break at a moment's notice. How the folk could be benevolent one day, and malevolent the next. How their capricious natures flowed like a river.

This place had always been dangerous, unpredictable. Wonders bloomed alongside dreads. But nothing could prepare him for what Torin said next.

"It's our lasses, Jack," he said. "Our girls are going missing."

~~~~~~~~~~~~~~~~~~~~~~~~~~~~~~~~~~~

CHAPTER 2

Sometimes Sidra saw the ghost of Torin's first wife sitting at the table. The visits occurred when one season ended and another began, when change could be felt in the air. Donella Tamerlaine's ghost liked to bask in the morning light, dressed in leather armor and plaid, watching as Sidra stood in the kitchen by the fire, cooking breakfast for Maisie.

Sometimes Sidra felt unworthy, as if Donella were assessing her. How well was Sidra caring for the daughter and husband she had left behind? But most of the time Sidra felt as if Donella was simply keeping her company, so fastened was her soul to this place, to this ground. The women—one dead and one living—were connected by love and blood and soil. Three cords that were so interwoven that Sidra was not surprised that Donella appeared to her and her alone.

"I have to send Maisie to school this autumn," Sidra said as she stirred the parritch. The cottage was quiet, dusted with dawn, and the wind was just beginning to howl its morning gossip. When Donella was silent, Sidra glanced at her. The ghost sat in her favorite chair at the table, her tawny hair flowing down her shoulders. Her armor was incandescent in the light, a breath away from being wholly translucent.

Donella was so beautiful it sometimes made Sidra's chest ache.

The ghost shook her head, reluctant.

"I know," Sidra said with a sigh. "I have been teaching her letters and how to read." But the truth was, all of the isle children were required to attend classes in Sloane when they turned six. Which Donella knew, despite being dead for the past five years.

"There is a way to delay it, Sidra," Donella said. Her voice was faint, a tendril of what it had once been when she was alive, although Sidra had not even been an acquaintance to her then. The two women had taken very different paths in life, and yet it had strangely led them both to the same place.

"You think I should begin teaching her my craft?" Sidra asked, but she knew it was what Donella was thinking and it took her by surprise. "I always assumed that you would want Maisie to follow your legacy, Donella."

The ghost smiled, but her demeanor was melancholy, even as the sunrise illuminated her. "I don't see the sword in Maisie's future, but something else."

Sidra slowed her stirring. She inevitably thought of Torin, who was stubborn as an ox. On their wedding night, they had sat across from each other on their bed—fully clothed—and conversed for hours about Maisie and her future. How they would raise her together. He wanted his daughter to go to school on the isle. She would be taught everything: how to wield bow and arrow, how to read and write, how to whet a sword, how to count her numbers, how to knock a man to the ground, how to mill oats and barley, how to sing and dance and hunt. Not once had Torin mentioned Maisie learning Sidra's craft of herbs and healing.

As if sensing her doubt, Donella said, "Maisie has already learned from watching you, Sidra. She enjoys tending the garden at your side. She likes to help you when you make your salves and tonics. She could become a great healer beneath your instruction."

"I enjoy her company," Sidra admitted. "But I'll have to talk to Torin about it." And she didn't know when she would see him next.

What she did know was Torin's dedication to the East Guard. He preferred the night shift, and he slept during the day in the dark, quiet bowels of the castle because he wanted to be in the barracks with the other guards. She understood his commitment, the thoughts that dictated his mind. Why should he, even though he was captain, be sleeping at home when his guards were sleeping in the barracks?

Occasionally, he ate his dinner with her and Maisie, which meant it was their breakfast. But even then, his love and attention were given to his daughter, and Sidra did everything he had married her for—to keep the croft and help him raise his child. Every now and then, before the moon had fully waxed and waned and when Maisie was visiting her grandfather on the croft next to theirs, Torin would come to her. Their couplings were always spontaneous and brief, as if Torin only had a few moments. But he was always gentle and attentive to her, and sometimes he lingered with her in the bed, tracing the wild tangles of her hair.

"I think you will see him again sooner than you think," Donella said. "And he will not deny you anything, Sidra."

Sidra was stunned by that idea, thinking the ghost was exaggerating. But then Sidra wondered, *Well, when have I ever asked Torin for anything?* And she realized that she rarely did.

"All right," she said. "I'll ask him. Soon."

The front door blew open. Donella evanesced and Sidra,

startled, whirled to see none other than Torin enter the cottage, windblown and ruddy. His tunic was damp from dew, his boots coated in sand, and his gaze found her instantly, as if he knew exactly where she would be—by the fire, stirring his daughter's breakfast.

"Who were you talking to, Sid?" he asked, frowning as his eyes swept the room.

"No one," she said, flustered. Torin had no idea she could see and speak with Donella, and Sidra didn't think she would ever be brave enough to tell him. "You're home. Why?"

Torin hesitated. She had never questioned *why* he was visiting. Of course, if he was here, he was hungry after working all night. He wanted his dinner and to hold his daughter.

"I thought I'd sup with you and Maisie," he said, his voice lowering. "And I have a visitor with me."

"A visitor?" Sidra dropped her spoon, intrigued. If she had been listening to the wind that morning, she might have heard the gossip it bore over the fells. But she had been preoccupied with the ghost of Torin's first love.

She walked around the table, the draft stirring her unbound hair, and only stopped when a young man entered the cottage, his shoulders hunched in apparent discomfort. He held something in his arms; it looked like an instrument hiding in an oilskin sleeve, and Sidra's heart leapt in joy until she noticed how disheveled he was. He had Torin's plaid draped across his shoulders, but his garments beneath were plain and hung from him like an ill-fated fortune. He cast a long shadow, one made of worry and resentment.

But these were the moments Sidra lived for. To aid and heal and unravel mysteries.

"I know you," she breathed with a smile. "You're Mirin's son."

The stranger blinked and straightened, astonished she had recognized him.

"Jack Tamerlaine," Sidra continued, recalling his name. "I'm not certain if you remember me, but years ago, you and your mum visited my family's croft in the Vale of Stonehaven, to purchase wool. My cat had gotten herself stuck in the old elm tree in our kail yard, and you were kind enough to climb up after her and bring her safely down to me."

Jack still appeared bewildered, but then the lines marring his face eased and a hint of a smile played on his lips. "I do remember. Your cat nearly scratched my eyes out."

Sidra laughed, and the room instantly brightened. "Aye, she was a cranky old tabby. But I did care for your scratches afterward, and it seems I did a fair job at it."

The chamber fell silent. Sidra was still smiling, and she felt Torin's gaze. She turned her attention to him only to see he was regarding her with pride, and it surprised her. Torin never seemed to pay any heed to her skills of healing. That was her work, as the East Guard was his, and they kept those pieces of themselves separate. Save for those rare moments when Torin needed stitches or to have his nose reset. Then he submitted, albeit begrudgingly, to her hands and care.

"Come inside, Jack," Sidra invited, seeking to make Jack feel welcome, and Torin shut the front door. "I'll have breakfast on the table in a moment, but in the meantime . . . Torin, why don't you find Jack something to wear?"

Torin motioned for Jack to follow him into the spare chamber. Most of Torin's garments were at the barracks, but he kept his finest raiment at the cottage in a chest lined with juniper boughs—tunics and jerkins and the rare set of trousers, as well as several plaids.

Sidra hurried to set the table, drawing forth her reserves, which she always kept within reach in case Torin unexpectedly joined them. She set down boiled eggs and crocks of butter and sugared cream, a wheel of goat cheese and a pot of wildflower honey, a plate of cold ham and salted herring, a loaf of bread and a jar of currant jelly, and lastly, her pot of parritch. She was pouring cups of tea when Torin reemerged into the main chamber, holding Jack's instrument as if it might bite him. Sidra opened her mouth to ask him how Jack had come into his care when the bedroom door banged open and out bounded Maisie, her brown curls tangled from sleep, her bare feet slapping on the floor.

"Daddie!" she cried and jumped into Torin's arms, mindless of the instrument.

"There's my sweet lass!" Torin caught her with one arm, a broad smile on his face. Maisie settled on his hip, wrapping her arms and legs about him, as if she would never let him go.

Sidra walked to them, carefully taking Jack's instrument from Torin, listening as father and daughter spoke to one another in their singsong way. Torin asked about the flowers Maisie had planted in the kail yard, how her writing lessons were progressing, and then came the moment Sidra was waiting for.

"Daddie, guess what happened."

"What happened, sweetheart?"

Maisie glanced over his shoulder to meet Sidra's gaze, smiling roguishly. *Spirits below, that smile,* Sidra thought, her heart welling. She felt her love for Maisie so strongly she couldn't breathe for a moment. Even though the lass was not made from her own flesh and blood, Sidra imagined Maisie had been spun from her spirit.

"You lost your front tooth!" Torin said in delight, noticing the blank spot in Maisie's grin.

"Aye, Daddie. But that's not what I was going to tell you." Maisie set her smile on him, and Sidra braced herself. "Flossie had her kittens."

Torin's brow rose. He looked straight to Sidra. A father who sensed he was standing in a bog.

"Did she now?" he said, but he continued to stare at Sidra, knowing she had set this convenient trap for him. "How wonderful, Maisie."

"Yes, Daddie. And Sidra said I must ask you if I can keep them all."

"Sidra said that?" Torin, at last, glanced back to his daughter. Sidra could feel her cheeks getting warm, but she set Jack's instrument in his chair and resumed her tea pouring. "She loves her cats, doesn't she?"

"I love them too," Maisie said vibrantly. "They are so cute, Daddie! And I want to keep all of the kittens. Can I, can I *please*?"

Torin was silent for a beat. Again, Sidra could feel the heat of his gaze on her as she moved from teacup to teacup.

"How many kittens are there, Maisie?"

"Five, Daddie."

"*Five?* I . . . I don't think you can keep them all, sweetheart," Torin said, to which Maisie let out a whine. "Listen to me, Maisie. What about the other crofts that need a good cat to guard the kail yards? What about the other lasses who don't have any kittens to hold and love? Why don't you share? Give four kittens to other lasses and keep one for yourself."

Maisie slumped, scowling.

Sidra decided to add her input, saying, "I think that is a great plan, Maisie. And you can always go and visit the other kittens."

"Do you promise, Sidra?" Maisie asked.

"I promise."

Maisie smiled again and wiggled her way down from Torin's arms. She sat in her chair, eager for breakfast, and Sidra turned back to the fire, to set her kettle on the hook. She felt Torin approaching, then heard him whisper into her hair, "How are you ever going to have a guard dog here if the croft is overrun with cats?"

Sidra straightened, felt the air pull between them. "I've told you, Torin. I need no guard dog."

"For the hundredth time, Sid . . . I *want* you to have a dog. To guard you and Maisie at night when I am away."

They had argued about this for an entire season now. Sidra knew why Torin was so insistent. Every warm night that passed only heightened his anxiety about a potential raid. And if it wasn't the Breccans sparking his worries, it was the malevolent folk. Trouble had been wandering the isle lately, in the wind and the water and the earth and the fire. Two young girls had gone missing, and she understood why he was so persistent. Neither she nor Torin wanted to see Maisie at risk of being ushered away by a faerie spirit. But Sidra didn't believe a guard dog was the solution.

A dog could scare spirits away from a yard, even the good ones. And her faith in the folk of the earth ran deep. It was because of that devotion that Sidra could heal the worst of wounds and illnesses in the east. It was why her herbs, flowers, and vegetables flourished, empowering her to nourish and heal the community and her family. If Sidra dared to bring a dog into the fold, it might convince the spirits that her faith in them was weak, and she didn't know what sort of consequences that would lend to her life.

She had been raised believing in the goodness of the spirits. Torin's faith had steadily crumbled over the years, and he hardly spoke a kind word about the folk these days, intent on judging them all by the malicious few. Anytime Sidra broached the subject of the spirits with him, Torin turned cold, as if he were only half listening to her.

She wondered if he blamed the spirits for Donella's untimely death.

Sidra turned to meet his gaze. "I have all the guard I need."

"And what am I to say to that?" he uttered, low and angry. Because he was rarely there, he knew she wasn't speaking of him.

"You take offense where there is none," she said gently. "Your father is next door. If there is any trouble, I will go to him."

Torin drew a deep breath, but he didn't say another word about it. He only studied her, and Sidra had the prickling sensation that he could read her face and the slant of her feelings. A moment passed before he stepped away, conceding this battle for now. He sat in his straw-backed chair at the head of the table and listened as Maisie chattered about the kittens, but his eyes lingered on Sidra, as if he were seeking a way to convince her about the dog.

She had almost forgotten about Jack until the spare chamber door squeaked open, and Maisie, glancing at the visitor, stopped talking midsentence.

"Who are you?" she blurted.

Jack seemed unruffled by the girl's bluntness. He came to the table, found his chair with the instrument waiting, and sat, stiff as a board in Torin's clothes. The plaid was heavy and awkward, fastened at his shoulder. The tunic could have fit two of him within its generous size. "I'm Jack. And you are?"

"Maisie. That's my daddie and that's Sidra."

Sidra felt Jack look at her. "Sidra," not "Mum" or "Mummy." But she had never made any pretense to Maisie of being her mother, no matter how young and tender the girl was. That had been part of Sidra's bargain with Torin: she would raise Maisie and love her wholeheartedly, but she would not lie and pretend she was the girl's blood mother.

Every spring, Sidra would take Maisie and a handful of flowers to Donella's grave, and she would tell the lass about her mother, who had been lovely and brave and gifted with the sword. Even though it sometimes left a lump in Sidra's throat, she would tell Maisie the story of how her father and mother had trained and sparred on the castle grounds, first as rivals but later as friends and then lovers.

"And how did *you* meet Daddie?" Maisie would always ask, savoring the stories.

Sometimes Sidra would tell her, sitting in the sunshine and long grass, and sometimes she would save that particular saga, which was not nearly as dashing as the ballad of Torin and Donella.

But that was a story for another day.

"What's that?" Maisie asked, pointing to Jack's instrument.

"A harp."

Sidra realized that Jack was favoring his left hand. "Are you wounded, Jack?"

"It's nothing," Jack replied, just as Torin said, "Yes. Can you tend to him, Sid?"

"Of course," Sidra said, reaching for her basket of healing supplies. "Maisie, why don't you show your father the kittens?"

Maisie was delighted. She took hold of Torin's hand and tugged him out the back door. With their departure, the house was quiet again. Sidra approached Jack with her basket of salves and linen.

"May I tend to your hand?"

Jack turned his palm skyward. "Yes. Thank you."

She drew her chair close to his and began her ministrations. Gently, she washed away the sand and dirt and was just beginning to fill the cut with her healing salve when Jack spoke.

"How long have you and Torin been together?"

"Almost four years now," Sidra replied. "I married him when Maisie was just a year old." She began to wrap his hand with linen, and she could sense the queries rising in him. He was a wanderer who had just returned home, struggling to arrange the pieces of the isle together. Sidra continued, for his sake, "Torin was first married to Donella Reid. She was a fellow member of the guard. She passed away after Maisie's delivery."

"I'm sorry to hear that."

"Yes. It was a difficult loss." Sidra envisioned Donella and realized Jack was sitting in the ghost's chair, the sunshine pouring in from the window on the far wall. Before, the light had shone through Donella's visage, but it gilded Jack now. He looked just like Mirin, Sidra thought. Which meant he must not favor his mysterious father at all. A father the gossips were still hungry to speculate about.

"There," Sidra said, finishing her care. "I'm going to send you off with this bottle of salve and honey. You should dress your wound morning and night for three days."

"Thank you," said Jack, accepting the offering. "How can I repay you for your kindness?"

Sidra smiled. "I think a song would suffice, once your hand has recovered. Maisie would love to hear your music. It's been a long time since we have enjoyed such a luxury."

Jack nodded, carefully flexing his fingers. "I would be honored."

The back door swung open, and the windstorm that was Maisie and Torin returned. Sidra noticed that Torin had a few fresh scratches on his knuckles, from the kittens, no doubt, and a peevish gleam in his eyes. Also from the kittens.

"Let's eat," he said gruffly, as if he were in a hurry.

Sidra sat, and they began to pass dishes around the table. She observed that Jack ate very little, that his hands shook, that his eyes were bloodshot. She listened as Torin spoke of the isle and realized that Jack didn't know any of the current news. He meekly asked about Laird Alastair, about the crops and the guard and the tension with the west.

"I often worry about my mum, living so close to the clan

line alone," he said. "It's good to hear things have been peaceful here."

Sidra paused, but she met Torin's gaze. *Does Jack not know . . . ?* She was opening her mouth to say it, but Torin cleared his throat and changed the subject. Sidra relented, realizing if Jack didn't know, it wasn't her place to inform him, even though she now worried about him finding out later.

As soon as the meal was over, Torin rose.

"Come, Jack," he said. "I'm heading to the city and can walk you there. Best to see the laird first and then your mum, before the wind carries any further gossip about you."

Jack nodded.

Maisie began her chore of carrying cutlery and cups to the wash barrel, and Sidra followed the men to the threshold. Jack walked the path through the kail yard, down to the road, but Torin lingered.

"I hope four of those kittens have found their new homes by the time I return," he said, partly teasing.

Sidra leaned on the doorframe, the wind tangling her dark hair. "They're too young to be separated from their mother."

"How much longer then?"

"Another month, at least." She crossed her arms and met his steady gaze with one of her own. She was testing him, of course. To see when she could next expect him to come to her. To see how much time she had to prepare her argument for keeping Maisie home.

"That's a long time," he stated.

"Not really."

But he looked at her as if it were. "Perhaps you and Maisie can begin to find people who want the kittens."

"Of course," said Sidra with a smile. "We will make the most of our time."

Torin's gaze dropped to her mouth, to that wry tilt of her

lips. But he turned without another word, walking the path between the herbs only to pause at the gate, running his hand through his hair. And while he didn't glance back at her, Sidra knew.

He would return to her long before a month had passed.

Jack remembered the way to the city of Sloane, even after ten years of absence, but he politely waited for Torin to join him on the road, his stallion clomping behind him. The two men walked in companionable silence, Jack uncomfortable with the way Torin's garments swallowed him. Inwardly, he grumbled, but he also was grateful. The raiment was resilient against the wind, which was blowing from the east, dry and cold and full of whispers. Jack closed his ears to the gossip, but once or twice he imagined he heard *The wayward bard is here.*

Soon, everyone would know he was back on the isle. Including his mother. And that was one reunion Jack was dreading.

"How long do you plan to stay?" Torin asked, glancing sidelong at him.

"For the summer," Jack replied, kicking a pebble from the road. Although he honestly wasn't sure how long he would be forced to be here. Torin had mentioned that two girls had vanished in the past fortnight, and Jack still didn't see how he was needed for something like that, as terrible as it was. Unless Laird Alastair wanted Jack to play his harp for the clan as a way to mourn the losses, but Torin said he still had faith the girls would be found whenever the spirits ceased their mischief and surrendered them back to the mortal realm.

Whatever the laird needed him for, Jack would do it quickly and then return to the university, where he belonged.

"You have responsibilities on the mainland?" Torin queried, as if sensing Jack's thoughts.

"I do. I'm in the midst of my teaching assistance and hope

to become professor within the next five years." That is, if this time away on Cadence didn't ruin his chances. Jack had worked long and hard to be in the position he held, teaching up to one hundred students a week and grading their compositions. Unexpectedly taking a term off would now open the door for another assistant to steal his classes and possibly replace him.

The mere thought made his stomach churn.

They passed the croft of Torin's father, Graeme Tamerlaine, the laird's brother. Jack noticed the kail yard was beset with brambles and the cottage looked dismal. The front door was framed with gossamer. Vines snaked across the stone walls, and Jack wondered if Torin's father still lived there, or if he had passed away. And then he remembered that Graeme Tamerlaine had become a recluse in his old age and rarely left his croft. Not even for feast days in the castle hall, when all of Eastern Cadence gathered to celebrate.

"Your father . . . ?" Jack asked, uncertain.

"Is quite well," Torin said, but his voice was firm, as if he didn't want to speak of his father. As if the dilapidation of Graeme Tamerlaine's croft was the norm.

They walked onward as the road rose and fell with the lay of the hills, which were green from spring storms. Foxglove grew wild in the sun, dancing with the wind, and starlings soared and trilled against a low swath of clouds. In the distance, the morning fog began to burn away, revealing a glimpse of the ocean, endlessly blue and sparkling with light.

Jack soaked in the beauty, but he remained guarded against it. He didn't like the way the isle made him feel alive and whole, as if he were a part of it, when he wanted to remain a distant observer. A mortal who could come and go as he pleased and suffer nothing for it.

He thought of his classes again. His students. A few of

them had burst into tears when he shared the news that he had been called away for the summer. Others had been relieved, as he was known to be one of the strictest of teaching assistants. But if a pupil was going to take his class, he wanted to ensure they had grown in skill by the end of it.

His thoughts were still centered on the mainland when he and Torin reached Sloane. The city was just as Jack remembered. The road had been transformed into smooth cobbles winding between the buildings, houses built close to each other, their walls made of stone and cob with thatched roofs. Smoke rose from the forges, the market brimmed with activity, and the castle sat in the heart of it, a fortress made of dark stones dressed in banners. The sigil of the Tamerlaines snapped from the parapets, betraying which wind blew that afternoon.

"I think a few people are happy to see you, Jack," Torin said.

Caught off guard by that statement, Jack began to pay attention.

People were noticing him as he passed. Old fishermen sitting beneath canopies, mending their nets with gnarled hands. Bakers carrying baskets of warm bannocks. Milkmaids with their swinging pails. Lads with wooden swords, and lasses toting books and quivers of arrows. The blacksmiths between strikes on their anvils.

He didn't slow his pace, and no one dared to stop him. Most of all, he didn't expect to witness their excitement, their smiles as they watched him pass.

"I have no idea why," Jack said dryly to Torin.

As a boy, he had been disliked and mistreated because of his status. If Mirin had sent him into town to buy some bread, the baker would give him the burnt loaf. If Mirin asked him to bargain for a new pair of boots in the market, the cobbler would give him a used pair with worn leather thongs that would break before the winter snows had melted. If Mirin gave him a silver mark to buy a honey cake, he would be given the sweet after it had fallen on the ground.

Bastard followed him in whispers, more than his own name. Some of the wives in the market would study Jack's face to compare against their husbands', wondering and suspicious despite the fact that Jack was an unforgiving reflection of his mother and unfaithfulness was rare in Cadence.

When Mirin began weaving enchanted plaids, the people who had snubbed Jack suddenly became a little kinder, because no one could rival Mirin's handiwork, and she suddenly knew everyone's darkest secrets while they had yet to learn hers. But by then he had begun carrying every slight around like a bruise in his spirit. He had provoked fights at school, broken windows with rocks, refused to bargain with certain people when Mirin sent him to the market.

For him, it was bizarre now to acknowledge how eager the clan was to see him, as if they had been waiting for the day he would return home as a bard.

"This is where I leave you, Jack," Torin said when they reached the castle courtyard. "But I suppose I'll see you again soon?"

Jack nodded, stiff with nerves. "Thank you again for breakfast. And the clothes. I'll have them returned as soon as I'm able."

Torin waved away his gratitude and led his horse into the stable. Jack was admitted into the castle by a set of guards.

The hall was lonely and quiet, a place for ghosts to gather. Thick shadows hung in the rafters and in the corners; the only light streamed in through the arched windows, casting bright squares on the floor. The trestle tables were coated in dust, the benches tucked beneath them. The hearth was cold and swept clean of ashes. Jack remembered visiting with Mirin every full moon to feast and listen to Lorna Tamerlaine, Bard of the East and the wife of the laird, play her harp and sing. Once a month, this hall had been a lively place, a place for the clan to come together for fellowship after a day of work.

The tradition must have ceased with her unexpected death five years ago, Jack thought, sorrowful. And there was no bard on the isle to take her place, to carry the songs and legends of the clan.

He walked the length of the hall to the steps of the dais, not realizing the laird was standing there, watching his approach. A grand tapestry of moons, harts, and mountains covered the wall in glorious color and intricate detail. Alastair seemed woven into the tapestry until he moved, catching Jack by surprise.

"Jack Tamerlaine," the laird said in greeting. "I didn't believe the wind this morning, but I must say the sight of you is much welcome."

Jack knelt in submission.

The last time he had seen the laird had been the eve of his departure. Alastair had stood beside him on the shore, his hand on Jack's shoulder as he prepared to board the sailor's boat to cross over to the mainland. Jack hadn't wanted to appear afraid in his laird's presence—Alastair was a great man, in stature and character, imposing even though he was prone to smile and quick to laugh—and so Jack had boarded the sailor's boat, holding in his tears until the isle had faded, melting into the night sky.

This was not the man who greeted Jack now.

Alastair Tamerlaine was wan and gaunt, his clothes hanging loose from his narrow frame. His hair, once dark as raven feathers, was bedraggled, a dull shade of gray, and his eyes had lost their luster, even as he smiled at Jack. His thunderous voice was hoarse, made from shallow breath. He looked weary, like a man who had been at battle for years without respite.

"My laird," Jack said in a wavering tone. Was this the purpose of his summoning? Because death stalked the ruler of the east?

Jack waited, bowing his head as Alastair drew close. He felt the laird's hand on his shoulder, and he lifted his eyes. His shock must have been evident, because Alastair let out a rasp of laughter.

"I know, I am much changed since you last saw me, Jack. Years can do that to a man. Although time on the mainland has been good to you."

Jack smiled, but it failed to reach his eyes. He felt a flare of anger at Torin, who should have mentioned the laird's health that morning at breakfast, when Jack had inquired after him.

"I have returned, sir, as you have asked me to. How may I serve you?"

Alastair was quiet. He blinked, a crease of confusion in his brow, and in that swell of silence, Jack was overcome with dread.

"I wasn't expecting you, Jack. I didn't ask you to return."

The harp in Jack's arms became a millstone. He continued to kneel, gazing blankly up at the laird, his thoughts scattering.

It hadn't been Alastair, although his signet ring had been used in the letter.

Who summoned me?

As tempted as he was to shout his frustrations into the hall, he remained silent. But a glimmer of movement answered him.

From the corner of his eye, he saw someone emerge onto the dais, as if she had come from the moonlit mountains of the tapestry. Tall and slender, she wore a dress the color of storm clouds, and a red plaid shawl framed her shoulders. Her raiment whispered as she moved, drawing closer to where he knelt.

Jack's gaze was riveted to her.

Her face, freckled and angular, with high cheeks that

carved into a sharp jaw, evoked not beauty but reverence. She was flushed, as though she had been walking among the parapets, challenging the wind. Her hair was the color of the moon, bound in an array of braids that were pinned together as a crown. Tucked within them were small thistle blooms, as if stars had fallen upon her. As if she held no fear of their sting.

He saw a shadow of the girl she had once been. The lass he had chased over the hills one chaotic spring night and challenged for a handful of thistles.

Adaira.

She stared at him, still on his knee, as he stared at her. His shock burned away, replaced by indignation that blazed so fiercely he couldn't breathe when he thought about what he had surrendered to come home. His title, his reputation, the culmination of years of dedication and hard work. Gone like smoke in the breeze. All this he had given up not for his laird, which he could justify, but for *her* and her whims.

She sensed it in him—the heart of the wild boy who had chased her, now older and harder. His mounting ire.

Adaira responded with a cold, victorious smile.

CHAPTER 3

J ack Tamerlaine," Adaira greeted him. Her voice was nothing like he remembered; if he had heard it in the dark, he would have assumed she was a stranger. "What a surprise to see you here."

Jack said nothing. He didn't trust himself to speak, but he refused to break their gaze, as she seemed eager to make him do.

"Ah, I forget the two of you are old friends," Alastair said, pleased. He held his arm out to his daughter, and she drew even closer, so close that her shadow almost spilled over Jack in his obedient stance.

"Indeed," said Adaira, breaking her stare with Jack to bestow a softer, genuine smile upon her father. "I should reacquaint him with the isle, since he has been away for so long."

"I don't think—" Jack began to protest, defiant, until Alastair looked at him with an arched brow.

"I think that is a wonderful plan," the laird said. "Unless you oppose it, Jack?"

Jack did oppose it. But he shook his head, swallowing his words, which caught like thorns in his throat.

"Excellent." Adaira turned that sharp smile upon him again. She had noticed the twist in his voice—the discomfort she had inspired. She didn't seem to care. No, she seemed to welcome it, and she motioned for Jack to rise, as if she held the power to command him. And yet, didn't she? She had made him break his prior commitments to rush home.

He might have been on the mainland for the past decade, forming himself into the mold of a bard and forgetting his ties to Cadence. But in that instant, looking at Adaira, he remembered his upbringing. He felt the last name he wore like a cloak—the only name that would claim him, even at his very worst—and he knew that his deepest allegiance was to her and her family.

He stood.

"I hope you can grace my hall with your music soon, Jack," Alastair said, stifling a deep, wet cough.

"It would be an honor," Jack replied. His concern heightened when Alastair pressed a knuckle to his lips, his eyes shut as if his chest ached.

"Go and rest, Da," Adaira said, touching his arm.

Alastair regained his composure and lowered his hand, smiling at his daughter. But it was a weary smile, a façade, and he kissed Adaira's brow before he departed.

"Come with me, Jack." Adaira turned and strode through a secret door, one he would have never noticed. Incensed, he had no choice but to chase after her through branching corridors, his eyes boring into those fair braids of hers and the thistles she wore like jewels.

I should have known it was her.

He almost let out a scathing laugh but stifled it just as Adaira led him into the inner garden. He came to a sudden halt on the moss-spangled flagstones, nearly bumping into her. Once, she had been taller than him. He was pleased to discover he had a full hand width of height on her now.

He watched with heavy-lidded eyes as she faced him. They were silent, the air fraught between them.

"You didn't know it was me," she said at last, amused.

"You didn't even cross my mind," he replied in a clipped tone. "Although I should have known you would have no shame in forging your father's signature. I take it you also stole the signet ring from his hand? Did you do it while your father slept? Or did you drug him? You were very thorough with your crime, I must say, or else I wouldn't be standing here."

"Then what a relief that I went to such lengths," she said, so calmly it threw him off balance. He realized she was bringing out the worst in him; he was acting as if he were eleven again, and the shock of that made him fall into a furious silence, worried he would say something he would regret. That is, until she added, "I wouldn't have called you home if I didn't have a purpose for you."

"You speak of purpose?" he countered, stepping closer to her. He could smell the faint trace of lavender on her skin. He could see the ring of hazel in her blue eyes. "How dare you say such a thing to me, when you've dragged me away from my obligations and my duties? When you have interrupted my life without remorse? What do you want with me, Adaira? What do you *want*? Tell me so I can do it and be gone from here."

She held her composure, intently staring at him. It almost felt as if she could see through him, beyond flesh and bones and veins, down to his very essence. As if she was measuring his worth. Jack shifted away, uncomfortable with her attentiveness and her silence. How cold and placid she was in the face of his smoldering wrath, as if his reaction was unfolding as she planned.

"I have much to tell you, Jack. But none can be spoken in the open, where the wind might steal the words from my lips," she said, inviting him to keep pace with her as she began to walk the winding garden path. "It's been a while since I last saw you."

He didn't want to reflect on that final moment between them, but it was inevitable, because she was looking at him, daring him to dredge it back up. And she had brought him *here*, to the garden, where it had happened.

The last time he had seen Adaira had been the night before he left Cadence. Mirin was speaking with Alastair and Lorna at the castle, and Jack had wandered, morose and angry, into the starlit garden. Adaira had also been there, of course, and Jack had reveled in hurling pebbles at her through the roses, startling and then irritating her until she had found his hiding place.

But she hadn't responded as he expected, which had been to run away to tattle on him. She had taken hold of his tunic and challenged him, and they had wrestled amongst the vines and flowers, crushing the blooms and muddying their clothes. Jack had been surprised by how strong she was, how viciously she fought, as if she had been waiting for someone to match her. Her nails drew his blood, her elbows bruised his ribs. Her hair stung his face.

It had roused strange feelings within him. Adaira had fought as though she knew exactly how he felt, as if they were mirrors of each other. But that was ridiculous, because she had everything he didn't. She was adored, and he was reviled. She was the clan's joy, while he was the nuisance. And when he remembered that, he had striven to triumph in the match, pinning her beneath him on the garden path. But he drew back when he saw his fury reflected in her eyes. It was then she had said to him—

"Your parting words to me were that you 'despised my existence,' and that I 'sullied the Tamerlaine name,' and that you hoped that I 'never returned to the isle,'" Jack drawled, as if those words had meant nothing to him then. For some strange reason, they made him ache now, as if Adaira's farewell had seeped into his bones. But then again, he had never been one to forgive and forget easily.

Adaira was silent as she walked, listening to him.

"I'm sorry for the words I spoke that night," she said, catching him by surprise. "And now you know why I had no choice but to forge my father's order, because you would have never returned for me."

"You're right," he said, and her eyes narrowed. He wasn't sure if her mistrust was sparked by his honesty or the fact that he was agreeing with her. "I would have never returned for you alone, Adaira."

"As I just said," she spoke through her teeth.

At last, Jack thought as he slowed his pace. At last he had roused her temper. He said in a smug tone, "But only because I have built a life for myself on the mainland."

Adaira paused on the path. "A life as a bard?"

"Yes, but there's more to it than that. I'll soon be a professor at the university."

"You're teaching now?"

"Hundreds of students a term," he replied. "Endless music has passed through my hands over the past decade, most of it my own creation."

"That's quite the accomplishment," she said, but he noticed how the light in her eyes dimmed. "Do you enjoy teaching?"

"Of course I do," he said, although sometimes he also thought that he hated it. He was not one of the adored assistants, and every blue moon he dreamt of casting off all the expectations that sat heavy on him. Sometimes he imagined becoming a traveling bard who drank lore and spun it into song. He imagined gathering stories and reawakening places that were half dead and forgotten. And he wondered if remaining at the university, held within stone and glass and structure, was more akin to being a bird, held captive in an iron cage.

But these were dangerous thoughts.

It must be the isle blood in him. To crave a life of risk and little responsibility. To let the wind carry him from place to place.

Jack suddenly dashed these reveries, worried that Adaira might see them in his expression. "So now you can understand why it was very difficult for me to leave my life's work for a mysterious purpose. And I want to know why you summoned me home. What do you want with me, heiress?"

"Let me first say this," she said, and Jack braced himself. "You are a bard, and I am not your keeper. You are not tethered to me. You are free to come and go as you please, and if you want to leave the isle tonight and return to the mainland, then leave, Jack. I will find another to fulfill my request."

She fell silent, but Jack sensed there was more. He patiently waited for it.

"But if I am honest," Adaira continued, holding his gaze, "I need *you*. The clan needs you. We have been waiting ten long years for you to return home to us, and so I would ask you to stay and aid us in our time of need."

Jack was astonished by her words. He stood frozen, staring at her. A terrible voice within him whispered, *Leave*. He thought of the winding corridors of the university, full of light and music. He thought of his students, their smiles and their determination to master the instruments he set into their hands.

Leave.

It was tempting, but her words were far more enticing. She claimed that she needed him in particular, and he was curious now. He wanted to know why, and he took a step forward, following her once again.

She led him into a small inner chamber, devoid of windows. A room in which to discuss sensitive topics, he knew, as there was no chance of the wind stealing the words spoken there. A host of candles burned on a table, and flames crackled in the hearth, shedding light. Jack stood by the closed door as Adaira approached a table and poured them each a dram of whiskey. When she brought the drink to him, he hesitated, even as the firelight caught the glass, casting her hand in amber.

"Is this a peace offering or a bribe?" he asked, brow arched.

Adaira smiled. It was genuine, crinkling the corners of her eyes. "A bit of both, perhaps? I thought you might enjoy a taste of the isle. I hear mainland fare is quite dull."

Jack accepted the offering, but then he realized she was waiting for him to make a toast.

He cleared his throat and said, a bit gruffly, "To the east."

"To the east," she echoed, clinking her glass with his. And she waited until he had taken his first sip of the whiskey, which curled down his throat like a flame of ancient fire, to add, "Welcome home, my old menace."

Jack coughed. His eyes watered and his nose burned, but he held himself together and merely winced at her.

This is not my home anymore, he almost said, but the words melted when she smiled at him again.

Adaira moved to sit in a leather chair, pointing to an empty one across from hers. "Have a seat, Jack."

Whatever she had to ask of him must be truly wretched if she had to ply him with whiskey and order him to sit. Jack relented, sitting on the edge of the cushion, as if he might need to bolt at any moment. He laid his harp across his lap, weary from toting it around.

She was gazing at him again, her fingertip tracing the rim

of her glass. He took that quiet moment to study her in return. In particular, her hands. There were no rings on her fingers. But sometimes partners didn't wear rings to signify their
vows. Sometimes they broke a golden coin and each wore a half
of it around their neck, and so Jack's eyes traveled upward. Her
dress was cut square, exposing the valleys of her collarbones.
Her throat was bare; no necklace hung about it. He presumed
Adaira was still unwed, which surprised him.

"You're exactly how I imagined you to be, Jack," she said,
and his eyes snapped back to hers.

"I haven't changed?" he asked.

"In some ways, yes. But in others . . . I think I would know
you anywhere." She downed her whiskey, as if the confession
had made her feel vulnerable. Jack watched as she swallowed,
uncertain how to reply.

He kept his face poised as he drained the rest of his drink.

"More?" she asked.

"No."

"Your hand's bandaged. Are you hurt?"

Jack flexed it. The pain from the cut had faded consider-
ably, thanks to Sidra's care. "Just a scratch. The folk of the sea
weren't very welcoming."

Adaira rolled her lips together, as if she wanted to say something else but decided against it.

"Should you tell me now, heiress?" Jack asked. His stomach
was beginning to ache, wondering why Adaira needed him.

He wanted to get this over with and be gone.

"Yes," said Adaira, crossing her legs. He caught a glimpse
of her calf, the mud on her boots. "I suspected you enjoyed
your life on the mainland since you never visited us here, and
as you have many responsibilities at your university . . . let me
be frank. I don't know how long I will need you."

"Surely you have *some* idea," he said, tamping down his

irritation. He lived by a schedule and hated to imagine floating through time. "A week? A month? If I'm not back in time for the autumn term, I'll lose my position at the university."

"I truly don't know, Jack," Adaira replied. "There are many factors at play, ones beyond my control."

Jack's first assumption was that she had called him home to play for her father, since the laird looked gravely ill. Which meant that Adaira was about to ascend as laird herself. Jack felt a pang of awe, imagining her crowned.

His eyes traced the thistle blossoms, tucked within her braids.

"You saw Torin earlier, yes?" Adaira asked.

Jack frowned. "I did. How did you—?"

"The wind," she said, as if he should remember how it gossiped. "Did my cousin tell you about the two lasses who have gone missing?"

"Yes. But he didn't provide much detail, other than that he believes the spirits are at fault."

Adaira glanced across the room, her face solemn. "Two weeks ago, eight-year-old Eliza Elliott went missing on her walk home from school. We searched acres of land, from the school to her family's croft, but we found little trace of her. Only a few places in the grass and heather, where it looked like she walked, only to vanish." She paused, her eyes returning to his. "I'm sure you remember the ways of the isle, Jack."

He did.

He remembered the perks as well as the dangers of straying from Cadence roads. The roads were pathways that resisted enchantments. The spirits couldn't influence the roads, but they could toy with the grass and rocks and wind and water and trees of the isle. They could turn three hills into one, and one hill into four, but even then, there were ways of knowing the lay of the land, and which parts of it were prone to shift, and which landmarks remained fixed. Many children who didn't know that secret map had gotten lost for hours if they wandered from the road.

"You believe the folk have tricked her?" Jack questioned.

Adaira nodded. "Not a week after her disappearance, another lass went missing. Annabel Ranald. Her mother says she went to tend to the sheep one afternoon and never returned. She is only ten years old. And we searched all the way to the northern coast. We searched their croft, every cave and loch, the hills and the glens, but there is no sign of her, save for a trail in a patch of heather that ends abruptly. As it was with Eliza's disappearance, like a portal had opened to them."

Jack raked his hand through his hair. "This is troubling, and I'm sorry to hear of it. But I don't know how I can help in this endeavor."

Adaira hesitated. "What I am about to tell you must remain between us, Jack. Do you agree to hold this confidence?"

"I agree."

And yet she still faltered, doubtful. It irked him, and he said, "You don't trust me?"

"If I didn't trust you, I wouldn't have called you home for this," she countered.

He waited, all of his attention bent upon her, and she released a deep sigh.

"When my mum was still living, she used to tell me the most vivid stories," Adaira began. "Stories about the spirits, about the folk of the earth and the water. I enjoyed her tales and held them close to my heart, but I never thought too deeply about them. Not until after she had died and my father fell ill and I realized I was about to be alone, the last of my blood. Not until Eliza Elliott went missing.

"Torin and I both went to my father, to seek his advice. For it was evident to us that someone in the clan must have done something to upset the spirits, and the folk had taken one of our own to punish us for it. My father instructed Torin to continue searching the east with his mortal strength—his eyes and his ears and his hands, to be ready at any moment for a spirit portal to open and lead him to the other side. But after Torin was dismissed, my da spoke to me alone. He asked me to recount one of my mum's stories, the legend of Lady Ream of the Sea, which my mum often sang to us in the hall.

"So I did, although I hadn't thought of my mum's stories in years, for the pain they bring me. And yet even as I thought of Ream rising from the foam of the tides, I still didn't grasp what my father was hoping I would understand on my own. It took me a few more stories before I saw it."

She paused. Jack was transfixed. "And what was that, Adaira?"

"That in my mum's stories and songs . . . she could describe the spirits in perfect detail. How they looked in appearance. How their voices sounded. How they moved and danced. As if she had *seen* them manifested."

Jack instantly thought of the woman in the sea, how her hair had tickled his face. He shivered. "And had she?"

"Yes," Adaira whispered. "It was something only she and my father knew. A bard can draw the spirits in their manifested forms, but only with a harp and their mortal voice. Old knowledge passed down on the isle for many years, kept hidden by the laird and bard out of respect for the folk."

"Why would your mother need to sing for them?" Jack said, his palms beginning to perspire.

"I asked my father this very question, and he told me that it was a way to ensure our survival in the east. We remained in good favor with the spirits, he said, because her worship pleased them, and they in turn ensured that our crops grew twofold, and the water ran clean from the mountains into the lochs, and the fire always burned through the darkest and coldest of nights, and the wind didn't carry our words over the clan line to our enemies."

Jack shifted. He felt the weight of her words. He knew why she had summoned him now, and yet he wanted her to say it to him. "Why have you called me home, Adaira?"

She held his gaze, her face flushing. "I need you to play one of my mother's ballads on your harp. I need you to invite the spirits of the sea to manifest, so I may speak with them about the missing lasses. I believe they can help me find Annabel and Eliza."

He was silent, but his heart resounded like thunder and his mind spun like leaves caught in a whirlwind.

"I have a few concerns about this, Adaira," Jack said.

"Tell me then."

"What if the spirits answer the music, but they are malevolent toward us?" he asked. For while he worried about his own well-being, he was even more concerned about hers. She was the sole heiress, the only child of the laird. If something befell her, the east would be bewildered. Jack didn't want that on his hands, to witness the spirits of the sea drown her.

"We'll play at night. When the moon and stars shine on the water," Adaira said, as if she had anticipated that he would ask this.

When the spirits of the sea are easily mollified.

Jack's dismay didn't ease; he recalled the sound of fingernails tapping on the hull of the fisherman's boat, seeking a weak spot. The dim figure of the woman in the water, laughing at him as he desperately swam to shore. Did he truly desire to reel that spirit to him like a fish on a hook? To sing up that dangerous being?

So he tried once more and asked, "What if they don't come to the sound of my music, my voice? What if they remember their fondness and respect for your mum and refuse to answer me, a bard who has been ousted by the clan?"

"You were never ousted by us," Adaira said, intently watching him. And then she whispered, "Are you afraid, Jack?"

Yes, he thought, desperately. "No," he said.

"Because I will be there with you, at your side," she said. "My father was always with my mother when she played. I won't let anything befall you."

It was strange how much he believed her in that moment, given their troubled history. But her confidence was like wine, softening him. He could see why the clan adored her, followed her, worshiped her.

"Perhaps this will grant you clarity," Adaira continued. "My da explained it to me like this: My mother couldn't play with a skeptical heart. The folk came not just to hear the music, but to be adored by her. Because that is what they desire from us. Our praise, our faith. Our trust in them."

Jack's initial reaction was to scoff. How could he praise the beings that were stealing girls? But he swallowed his retort, remembering Mirin's old stories. Not all spirits were bad. Not all spirits were good. To be safe, it was wise to fear them all.

He didn't want to believe what Adaira was telling him, and his mainland opinions rose up in his mind. But then he thought, *If she's right and the spirits relinquish the lasses, I can return to the university within the week.*

"Very well," he said. "I will play this for you and for the clan. For the two missing lasses. Where is your mother's music?"

Adaira rose and led him to a southern turret of the castle, up a stairwell, and into a spacious chamber Jack had never seen before.

The walls were carved deep with shelves, crowded with illuminated books, and the floor was black-and-white-checkered marble, polished so fine it caught his reflection as if he stood on water. Three large windows let in rivers of sunshine, and there was an oaken table, covered in parchment, inkpots, and quills. In the center of the room was a grand harp, exquisitely crafted. The strings gleamed in the light, aching to be played.

Jack walked to it, unable to take his eyes from the instrument. He knew who it had once belonged to. As a boy, he had listened to her play it in the hall. Reverently, he traced the shoulder of the harp, and he thought of Lorna.

"This harp has been well maintained," he said. He had expected to find it dust ridden, its frame cracked by the weight of strings. "Do you play?" And he couldn't explain why the mere thought of Adaira sitting at this harp, her fingers rendering music, made his breath catch.

"Very little," Adaira confessed. "Years ago, my mum taught me how to care for the instrument, how to pluck a few scales. Unfortunately, the music never took to my hands."

Jack watched as she sorted through heaps of parchment on the table, eventually bringing a few sheets to him.

It was a ballad, "The Song of the Tides." And even though the notes and lyrics were silent on the parchment, waiting for breath and voice and fingers to rouse them to life, a warning swelled within him the longer he entertained the music in his mind.

Something about it felt dangerous. He couldn't fully describe it, but his blood recognized the threat swiftly, felt the bite of its unsung power. Chills swept over his skin.

"I'm going to need some time to prepare," he said.

"How much time?" Adaira asked.

"Give me two days to study it. That will give my hand time to heal, and I should be ready to play by then."

She nodded. He couldn't tell if she was pleased or disappointed with his answer, but he sensed a fraction of the weight she was carrying as the Heiress of the East.

He didn't envy her status or her power as he had once.

"And where will I be playing this?" he asked.

"On the shore," Adaira replied. "We can meet at midnight, two nights from now, at Kelpie Rock. You remember where to find it?"

It was the place where they had once swum for countless hours as children. Jack wondered if Adaira was choosing it because the rock held strong memories for them both. He vividly recalled bobbing on the waves as a lad and racing her to the shore, eager to beat her.

"Of course," he said. "I haven't forgotten my way around the isle."

She only smiled.

Jack was carefully folding Lorna's music into his harp case when Adaira said, "I suppose you are eager to see Mirin?"

He bit back a sarcastic retort. "Aye. Since you're done with me, I'll be heading that way to visit her."

"She'll be overjoyed to see you," Adaira stated.

Jack said nothing, but his heart felt like stone. When he had first arrived at the mainland school, his mother had written him once a month. He had gone to a broom closet and wept every time her words had arrived. Reading of the isle roused his longing to return home, and he often skipped his music classes, hoping his professors would send him back. They hadn't, of course, because they were determined to see him flourish there. The wild isle-born lad who would have had no proper last name if not for the generosity of his laird.

As the years passed, Jack had finally given himself up to the music, falling deeper and deeper into that world, and Mirin's letters had become more and more infrequent, until they only arrived annually, when the leaves turned gold and the frost fell and he had aged another year.

"I have no doubt," Jack said, and this time the sarcasm bled into his voice.

Adaira must have noticed, but she didn't make a remark. "Thank you for your help, Jack," she said. "Would you also be able to meet with me again tomorrow at noontide?"

"I don't see why not."

Adaira tilted her head, gazing at him. "You are *quite* overjoyed to be home, aren't you, my old menace?"

"This place was never my home," he said.

She made no reply to that comment, but her eyes softened. "Then I'll see you tomorrow."

He watched her leave. He stood in the music chamber for a few minutes more, to soak in the solitude.

The light was beginning to fade. He felt how late the hour was, and he knew he couldn't delay the inevitable.

It was time for him to see Mirin.

Jack once reveled in the swiftness of hill travel. As a boy, he had been quick to learn which summits flattened and which ones multiplied, which rivers changed course and which lochs vanished, which trees moved and which ones held steady. He knew how to find his way back to the road should the folk succeed in tricking him.

But it might have been foolish of him to think that would still be the case a decade later.

The isle looked nothing like he remembered. He pressed west as he walked the fells, Torin's boots wearing blisters on his heels, and suddenly the land around him was wild and endless. He might have once loved this place and its many faces, but he was a stranger to it now.

One kilometer stretched into two. The hills turned steep and merciless. He slipped on a slope of shale and cut his knees.

He walked for what felt like hours, searching for a road, until afternoon gave way to evening, and the shadows around him turned cold and blue.

He had no idea where he was as the stars began to burn.

The southern wind blew, carrying a tangle of whispers. Jack was too distracted to pay attention, his heart beating in his throat as a storm broke overhead. He pressed on through mud puddles and streams.

It would be easy for a young lass to get lost here, he thought.

He reminded himself how much he had grown to hate this place and its unpredictability, and he eventually came to a halt, drenched and angry.

"Take me!" He dared the spirits who were toying with him. The wind, the earth, the water, and the fire. He challenged the glens and the mountains and the bottomless trickling pools, every corner of the isle that sprawled before him, gleaming with rain. The fire in the stars, the whisper of the wind.

If they had ushered the girls away for their own amusement, why did they hesitate with him? He waited, but nothing happened.

The gale chased the clouds, and the sky teemed with constellations again, as if the storm had never been.

Jack trudged onward. Gradually, he began to recognize his surroundings, and he found the western road once more.

He was almost to Mirin's.

His mother lived on the edge of the community, where the threat of a raid was constant, even in summer. Despite the risk the Breccans posed, Mirin had insisted on remaining there. She had grown up an orphan until a widow took her as an apprentice, to teach her the craft of weaving. This house and land were hers now, her only inheritance, the widow having long since perished.

Jack could soon see firelight in the distance, escaping through closed shutters.

It drew him off the road, where he found the narrow path that wound to Mirin's front yard as easily as if he had walked it yesterday, the grass whisking against his knees. The air smelled sweet from bog myrtle and sharp from smoke, which streamed from the chimney, smudging the stars.

All too soon, he reached the yard gate. Jack stepped inside it, his eyes sweeping the ground in the dim light. He could see row after row of vegetables, ripe from warm days. He remembered all the hours he had knelt in this soil as a boy, tilling and planting and harvesting. How he had complained about it, opposing everything Mirin had asked him to do.

He was stricken with nerves as he approached her door.

There was an offering for the folk of the earth on the threshold—a small bannock, now soggy from the rain, and two acorn cups of jam and butter. Jack took care not to bump them, unsurprised that the pious Mirin had set out a gift.

He knocked, shivering.

A moment passed, and he began to consider sleeping in the byre beside the cottage. Or even in the storehouse with the winter provisions. He was about to retreat when his mother answered the door.

Their gazes met.

In that frozen second, a hundred things tore through Jack's mind. Of course, she wouldn't be happy to see him. All the heartache he had given her as a wild boy, all the trouble, all the—

"*Jack*," Mirin breathed, as if she had been waiting all day for him to knock.

She must have heard the wind speak of him. Jack felt a rush of guilt that he hadn't come to see her first.

He stood awkwardly before her, uncertain what to say, wondering why his throat felt narrow at the sight of her. She was still as trim as she had been in the days before, but her face appeared gaunt, her cheeks hollow. Her hair, which had been the same shade as his, boasted more silver at her temples.

"Is it really you, Jack?" she asked.

"Yes, Mum," he said. "It's me."

She opened the door wider, so the light would spill over him. She embraced him so tightly he thought he might snap, and he was overwhelmed by her joy.

He had spent countless years resenting her for the secrets she kept. For never telling him who his father was. But the knot in his chest began to ease the longer she held him. He sagged in crushing relief at her warm response, but his harp remained between them, as if it were a shield.

Mirin drew back, eyes glistening. "Oh, let me look at you." Radiant, she studied him, and he wondered how much he had changed. If she saw herself in him now, or maybe a trace of his nameless father.

"I know, I'm too thin," he said, flushing.

"No, Jack. You are perfect. Although I must dress you in better garments!" She laughed in delight. "I'm so surprised to see you. I wasn't expecting you to visit until you had finished your teaching assistance. What brings you home?"

"I was summoned by the laird," Jack replied. Not quite a lie, but he didn't want to bring up Adaira yet.

"That is good of you, Jack. Come in, come in," she beckoned. "It looks like the storm caught you."

"Yes," he said. "I got lost on the way here, or else I would have arrived sooner."

"Perhaps you shouldn't travel by hill for a while," Mirin said, shutting the door behind him.

Jack only snorted.

It was strange how his mother's cottage hadn't changed. It looked exactly the way it had the day he left.

The loom still commanded the main chamber. It had been here before the cottage, the loom built from timber harvested from the nearby Aithwood. Jack's attention drifted away from it, touching the stretch of rug made of woven grass, the clutter of mismatched furniture, the baskets of dyed yarn and folds of freshly woven plaids and shawls. The hearth was adorned with a chain of dried flowers and a family of silver candlesticks. A cauldron of soup simmered over the fire. The ceiling rafters were dappled from Jack's slingshot; he looked up at the small dents in the wooden beams and fondly remembered how he had sprawled on the hassock, shooting at the ceiling with river stones.

"Jack," Mirin said, stifling a cough.

The sound of that wet cough roused bad memories for Jack, and he looked at her. She was wringing her hands; her face suddenly looked pale in the firelight.

"What is it, Mum?"

He watched her swallow. "There's someone I want you to meet." Mirin paused, glancing at his old bedroom door, which was closed. "Come out, Frae."

Jack was frozen as he watched the bedchamber door swing open. Out walked a young lass, barefoot and shyly beaming, her long auburn hair tamed by two braids.

Jack's initial thought was that she was Mirin's apprentice. But the girl came right to Mirin, wrapping her arms around his mother in a terribly familiar way. The little stranger smiled up at Jack, her eyes brightly curious.

No. No, this cannot be . . . His heart beat wildly with shock the longer he beheld the lass.

His gaze rose to Mirin. His mother was unable to hold his stare; her hand trembled as she stroked the girl's copper braids.

And then came her words, words that pierced Jack like a sword, and it took everything within him not to double over as Mirin said, "Jack? This is your younger sister, Fraedah."

~~~~~~

CHAPTER 4

Jack's bones were leaden as he stared at the girl, his sister—
his sister—and somehow managed to say, "It's nice to meet
you, Fraedah. I'm Jack."

"Hello." Frae smiled, her cheeks marked by two dimples.
"You can call me Frae, actually. All of my friends do."

Jack nodded. His face felt hot; he couldn't swallow.

"Mum told me I have an older brother who's a bard," his sister continued. "She said you'd return soon, but we didn't know
when. I've dreamt of meeting you!"

Jack forced a smile. It felt more like a grimace, and he narrowed his eyes at Mirin, who was finally looking at him, a
pained expression on her face.

"Frae?" she said, clearing her throat. "Why don't you go and
sleep in my room tonight? You can see Jack tomorrow at breakfast."

"Yes, Mum," Frae replied in a dutiful tone, her arms falling
away from Mirin's waist. "Good night, Jack."

He didn't respond. He couldn't find the words in time, even

as she grinned once more at him, like he was a hero in a story she'd been hearing about for years.

Frae slipped into Mirin's bedchamber, latching the door behind her.

Jack stood, quiet as stone, staring at the place where she'd been.

"Are you hungry?" Mirin asked, tentatively. "I left soup on the fire for you."

"No."

He had been *starving* up until that moment. Now his stomach was churning, his appetite gone. He had never felt more uncomfortable or out of place in his life, and his eyes swept toward the front door, seeking an escape route. "I can sleep in the byre tonight."

"What? No, Jack," Mirin said firmly, standing in his path. "You can have your old room."

"But it belongs to Frae now."

Frae. His little sister, whose entire existence Mirin had kept concealed from him. He gritted his teeth, felt the sting of his palm as his fingers curled inward.

Before his mother could speak again, Jack hissed, "Why didn't you tell me about her?"

"I wanted to, Jack," Mirin replied in a low voice. She seemed to worry Frae might overhear them. "I wanted to. I just . . . I didn't know how to tell you."

He continued to regard her, coldly. He wanted to leave, and Mirin must have sensed it.

She stretched out her hand to him, gently touching his face.

He flinched, even as he longed to see and feel her love for him. The love he had seen in her hands when she had touched Frae's hair. Effortless and natural.

He felt the years that had been lost between them now, like a limb torn away. Time that could never be regained, time that had encouraged them to grow apart. Mirin might have given him life and raised him the first eleven years, but the mainland professors and their music had shaped him into who he was now.

Mirin's hand fell away. Her dark eyes glistened with sorrow, and he worried she was about to weep.

His throat was still aching, but he managed to say, "I would appreciate some dry clothes, if you have them."

"Yes, of course," Mirin said, her posture easing with visible relief, as if she had been holding her breath. "*Yes*, I have clothes ready for you. I always hoped you would return, and so I . . . in here, Jack. . . ." She strode into his bedroom.

Jack stiffly followed.

He watched as Mirin opened the wooden trunk at the foot of the bed. She withdrew a stack of perfectly folded garments. A fawn-colored tunic and a green plaid.

"I made these for you," she said, staring down at the raiment. "I had to guess how tall you'd be, but I think I imagined right."

Jack accepted the clothes. "Thank you," he said, the words clipped. He was numb with shock and irritated from wearing Torin's oversized, drenched clothes all day. He was hungry and tired and overwhelmed by the knowledge of Frae, by the request Adaira had made of him.

He needed a moment alone.

Mirin must have sensed it. She left without another word, closing the door behind her.

Jack sighed, dropping his guise. His face grooved in pain, and he closed his eyes, drawing in long, deep breaths until he felt strong enough to survey his old room.

A candle burned on his writing desk, washing the stone walls in faint light. His childhood storybooks were lined up in a row; he wondered if Frae had read them by now. He was surprised to find his slingshot still hanging on a nail in the wall, alongside a small tapestry that must have belonged to his sister. A reed mat covered the floor, and the bed sat in one corner, draped in his childhood blanket. Mirin had woven it for him, a warm covering to ward off the chilly nights of the isle.

His eyes traced it, catching on something unexpected near the pillow.

Jack frowned and stepped closer, realizing it was a bouquet of wildflowers. Had Frae picked these for *him?* Surely not, he thought. But he couldn't help but assume that his mother and sister had been waiting for him to arrive all day. Ever since they heard of his presence on the wind.

He set his harp down.

He disrobed and dressed in the clothes Mirin had made for him. To his shock, they fit him perfectly. The wool was warm and soft against his skin, and the plaid came around him like an embrace.

Jack lingered in his room a moment longer, struggling to dissolve the emotion he was feeling. By the time he had regained his composure and returned to the common room, Mirin had a bowl of dinner waiting for him.

This time he accepted it as he sat in a straw-backed chair by the fire. The soup smelled of marrow and onions and pepper, of all the green living things Mirin grew in her garden. He let the steam ease before he began to eat, savoring the rich flavors of the meal. The taste of his childhood. And he swore for a moment that time rippled around them, granting him a glimpse of the past.

"Have you come home for good, Jack?" Mirin asked, sitting in a chair across from his.

Jack hesitated. His mind was still reeling with questions about Frae, with answers he was keen to learn. But he decided to wait. He could almost fool himself, thinking it was the old days. When Mirin had told him stories by the hearth.

"I'll be returning to the mainland in time for autumn term," he said, despite Adaira's warning.

"I'm glad you're home, even if it's just for a spell," Mirin said, lacing her fingers together. "I've been curious to hear more about your university. What is it like there? Do you enjoy it?"

He could have told her many things. He could have started at the beginning, recounting how in those early days he had hated the university. How learning music had come slowly to him. How he had wanted to smash his instruments and return home.

But perhaps she already knew that, from reading between the lines of the letters he had written her.

He could have told her about the moment when things changed, in his third year, when the most patient of professors had started to teach him how to play the harp and Jack had found his purpose at last. He was told to take great care with his hands, to let his fingernails grow long, as if he were becoming a new creature.

"I like it just fine," he said. "The weather is pleasant. The food is average. The company is good."

"You're happy there?"

"Yes." The reply was swift, reflexive.

"Good." Mirin said. "I didn't want to believe Lorna when she told me that you would prosper on the mainland. But how right she was."

Jack knew the Tamerlaines had funded his education. The university was expensive, and Mirin alone could not have afforded it. He still sometimes wondered why he was chosen, out of all the other children on the isle. Most days he surmised that he was chosen because he was fatherless, troublesome, and wild, and the laird thought instruction far from home would tame him.

But perhaps Lorna had hoped Jack would return as a bard, ready to play for the east. As she had once done.

He didn't want to dwell on such things. And it was time for him to address Mirin directly. He set his bowl aside and turned from the fire to face her.

"How old is Frae?"

Mirin drew in a deep breath. "She's eight."

Eight. Jack felt the truth like a blow, imagining it. All those years he had been on the mainland, lost in music, he had had a little sister at home.

"I assume she's my half-sister?" he asked.

Mirin was wringing her pale hands again. She glanced at the flames. "No. Frae is your full-blooded sister."

The revelation was both a pain and a relief. Jack struggled to know which feeling to feed, eventually voicing the very thing that had driven a wedge between him and his mother. "I take it Frae knows who our father is then?"

"No, she doesn't," Mirin whispered. "I'm sorry, Jack. But you know I can't speak of this."

She had never apologized for anything before. It shocked Jack so much he decided to let the old argument ebb, and he acknowledged what was truly bothering him now.

He had a little sister, living on an isle where girls were vanishing.

This was a grave complication to his plans, which had been to play for the water folk and then bolt. He did not see how he could leave, unless he had some reassurance that both Mirin and Frae would be safe after he departed.

"I hear there's been trouble on the isle," he said. "Two lasses have disappeared."

"Yes. The past fortnight has been tragic." Mirin paused,

tracing the bow of her lips. "Do you remember the old stories I used to tell you? Those bedtime tales as old as the land?"

"I remember," he said.

"It was my greatest fear. That you would roam the hills and be tricked by a spirit. That you would never come home one day, and there would be no trace of you. So I told you those stories—to stay on the roads, to wear flowers in your hair, to be respectful of fire and wind and earth and sea—because I believed they would protect you."

The stories had been frightening, entertaining. But stories were not made of steel.

"I've been told one of the missing girls is Eliza Elliott," he continued, watching his mother's reaction closely. "The Elliotts' croft is only six kilometers from here, Mum."

"I know, Jack."

"What measures are you taking to ensure Frae isn't next?"

"Frae is safe here with me."

"But how can you be *certain* of that?" he demanded. "The folk are mercurial, even on their best days. They can't be trusted."

Mirin laughed, but it was full of scorn. "You truly plan to instruct *me* on the spirits, Jack? When you have always been irreverent toward their magic? When you have been gone from this place the past decade?"

"I've been gone because you sent me away," he reminded her tersely.

Her offense waned. She suddenly appeared older to him. She appeared frail, as though the shadows in the room might break her, and he glanced at the loom.

"You're still weaving enchanted plaids, Mum." He sounded accusatory, even as he strove to soften his voice.

Mirin said nothing, but she held his gaze.

Her gift of weaving enchanted plaids was none other than

the magic of the earth and water spirits: it began in the grass and the lochs, which gave the sheep sustenance, which trickled into the softness of their wool, which was sheared and spun and dyed into yarn, which Mirin took in her hands and wove upon her loom, turning a secret into steel. She was a vessel, a conduit for the magic, and it passed through her because she was devout. The spirits found her worthy of such power.

But that power came with a price. To weave magic drained her vitality. This truth had roused an icy fear in Jack's chest when he was young and imagined her dying and abandoning him. He found that chill was even worse now that he was older.

"The clan needs them, Jack," she whispered. "It's my craft and my gift."

"But it's making you *ill*. Gods below, you have Frae now! What would happen to her if you passed?"

Would his sister be given to his care? Would she go to the orphanage in Sloane? The very place where Mirin had begun?

Mirin rubbed her brow. "I'm fine. Sidra has been providing me with a tonic that helps my cough."

"Ceasing the enchantment is something you should be seriously considering, Mum. In addition to that, I think you should surrender this croft because of how close it is to the clan line, and move to the city where you'll be saf—"

"I'm not giving up this croft," his mother said. Her voice was like flint, slicing his words. "I earned this place. It's mine, and it will one day be Frae's."

Jack exhaled. So Mirin was teaching Frae her craft of weaving. This day continued to get worse and worse, and he felt as if his fingers were tangling more threads than he could handle. "You haven't taught her how to weave enchantments, have you?"

"When she comes of age," Mirin snapped. He knew she was angry when she rose and began to extinguish the candlesticks on the mantle. Their conversation was over, and he watched the flames die beneath her fingertips, one by one. He wondered if she was regretting his visit.

I should have stayed on the mainland, he thought with an inner groan. But then he wouldn't have known of Frae's existence, or about the missing lasses, or how much the clan that had once shunned him as a bastard now needed him.

Mirin snuffed the last candlestick. Only the fire in the hearth remained, but she pierced Jack with a stare that made him freeze.

"Your sister has been very excited to meet you. Please be kind to her."

Jack's mouth fell open. Did Mirin think him a monster?

She didn't give him a chance to respond. His mother retreated to her room, leaving him alone and bewildered by the dying flames.

He woke with a start. The hearth had gone dark; the embers glowed with the memory of fire, hissing a small thread of smoke. For a moment, Jack didn't know where he was until his eyes adjusted, taking in the familiarity of his mother's cottage. Something had woken him. A strange dream, perhaps.

He leaned his head back against the chair, staring into the darkness. The night was silent, save for that strange noise again. A sound like a shutter being shifted and rattled. A sound drifting from his old bedchamber.

Jack stood. Gooseflesh rippled on his arms as he walked into his room. He listened as the shutters moved, as if someone was trying to open them and enter the chamber. The chamber that was now his little sister's.

His blood began to pound as he approached the window. He stared at the shutters until they seemed to blend into the wall and shadows. Rushing across the room, he forgot about the discarded clothes he had left crumpled on the floor. They caught his feet like a snare, and he stumbled and fell forward against his desk with a clumsy bang.

At once, the shutters became silent until Jack flung them open, furious and terrified. He saw nothing, his gaze sweeping the moonlit yard. And then a ripple of shadow caught his eye, but by the time he shifted his focus, it was gone, melting into the darkness. Jack wondered if he was hallucinating, and he trembled, contemplating pursuit. But what sort of weapon could wound a spirit? Could steel cut the heart of the wind? Could it divide the ocean's tide? Could it make the spirits cower and bend to mortals?

He was just about to slip out the window when a strong northern gust blasted against his face, howling into the room. He winced at the sharpness of its breath, even if there were no voices within it.

"Jack?"

He startled and turned to see Mirin standing on his threshold, a rushlight in her hand.

"Is everything all right?" she asked, looking to the open window beyond him.

The wind continued to hiss into the room, stirring the tapestry on the wall, overturning the books on the desk. Jack had no choice but to latch the shutters, which began to rattle again.

Perhaps he had only imagined the intruder. But the night had felt calm and still a moment ago.

Jack struggled to slow his breath, to blink away the wild gleam in his eyes. "I heard a noise at the window."

Mirin's gaze flickered to the shutters. A flash of silver caught the firelight at her hip, and Jack saw that she was wearing her enchanted dirk, sheathed at her waist.

"Did you see anything?" she asked in a wary tone.

"A shadow," Jack replied. "But I couldn't discern what it was. Is Frae . . . ?" His voice trailed off.

"She's in bed," Mirin replied, but she exchanged a worried look with Jack.

They quietly walked into the main bedchamber. Mirin's candle cast a ring of faint light into the room, gilding the tangles of Frae's auburn hair as she slept.

Jack felt a pinch of relief and returned to the threshold. Mirin followed, long enough to whisper to him, "It must have been the wind."

"Yes," he said, but the doubt left a sour taste in his mouth. "Good-night, Mum."

"Good-night, Jack," Mirin said, shutting the door.

Jack climbed into his childhood bed. The blanket wrinkled beneath him. He forgot about Frae's flowers until he heard them crinkle by his ear. He took them gently in his hand and closed his eyes, trying to convince himself that the night was serene, peaceful. But there was something else, lurking at the edges. Something sinister, waiting to rise.

He couldn't sleep when he thought of it.

A spirit had come for his sister.

CHAPTER 5

Jack was up at dawn, anxious to locate Torin and tell the captain about the strange rattle at the shutters. He had every intention of sneaking away from Mirin's croft before she woke, but it seemed his mother anticipated his attempt to do so. She was waiting for him in the common room, working at her loom, a pot of oats bubbling over the fire.

"Will you join us for breakfast?" she asked, keeping her focus on her weaving.

Jack hesitated. He was about to utter an excuse when the front door opened and in walked Frae with a burst of cold morning air. A basket of eggs hung on her arm, and she brightened at the sight of him.

"Good morning," his sister said, and then she seemed to grow shy. She walked to the table and fidgeted with the teacups, trying her best not to look at him.

Jack couldn't slip away. Not with Frae's demure gaze and Mirin's rigid stance, as if they both expected him to bolt and were furiously hoping he would remain.

He sat at the table and watched Frae's smile widen.

"I made you some tea," she said. Then she whispered, "You do like tea, don't you?"

"I do," Jack replied.

"Oh, good! Mum said you probably did now, being on the mainland, but we weren't sure of it." Frae took a mitt and unhinged the kettle from its hook over the fire and carefully poured Jack a cup of tea. He was baffled, taken off guard by how eager she was to serve. How confident Frae was, how easily she knew her way around the kitchen and the croft. He clearly remembered being eight and begrudging every single chore Mirin had set upon him, stomping and whining when he had to gather the eggs and set the table and wash the dishes afterward.

No wonder she had been so eager to give him up to the mainland.

"Thank you, Frae," he said, taking the warm cup in his hands.

Frae set the kettle down and brought him a pitcher of cream and a pot of honey, then hurried to set the rest of the table, humming as she went. Mirin eventually joined them, carrying the cauldron of oats with her. She filled their bowls with parritch, and Frae finished her tasks by setting out bacon and mushrooms, boiled eggs, fruit, sliced bread, and a crock of butter.

It was a feast. Jack worried they had made it just for him.

Their first meal together was awkward. Mirin was quiet, as was Jack. Frae kept parting her lips as if she wanted to say something, but then, too nervous to speak it, filled her mouth with oats instead.

"Do you go to school in the city every day?" Jack asked his sister.

"No, just three days a week," she said. "The other days I'm here with Mum, learning her craft."

Jack's gaze slid to Mirin. Mirin met it beneath her lashes, but her eyes were guarded. Their argument last night hung between them like gossamer.

"Have you seen Adaira yet?" Frae asked.

Jack nearly choked on his tea. He cleared his throat and attempted a smile. "I have, actually."

"When did you see the heiress?" Mirin was the one to now cast an inquisitive glance at him, and Jack ignored it, reaching for a slice of bread.

"I saw her yesterday morning."

"Were you friends with her?" Frae continued, as if Adaira were a spirit herself to be worshiped. "Before you left for school?"

Jack spread a hunk of butter on his bread. Mirin scowled at his excess. "I suppose you could say that." He took a huge bite, hoping talk of Adaira would end.

But his mother continued to watch him closely, seeming to realize who, indeed, had asked him to return. He hadn't studied Lorna's ballad at all the night before, as he was supposed to have done, and he still felt a sting of worry when he imagined playing that eerie music.

"Will you eat supper with us tonight?" Mirin asked, breaking off his stormy thoughts. She cradled her teacup in her long fingers, breathing in the steam.

Jack nodded, noticing his mother had scarcely eaten a bite of her parritch.

"You're probably very busy today, aren't you?" Frae's voice rose an octave, betraying how anxious she still was to speak to him.

Jack met her gaze. "I do have a few things to accomplish today. Why do you ask, Frae?"

"Nothing," his sister blurted, and shoveled another spoonful of parritch in her mouth, blushing.

It was apparent she wanted to ask him something and was

too afraid to voice it. Jack had only been a brother for less than a day in his mind, but he wanted her to feel comfortable enough to speak to him, to not be timid when she was with him. He realized he was frowning.

He softened his expression as he looked at Frae. "Is there something you need help with?"

Frae glanced at Mirin, who was staring at her parritch until she sighed, raising her eyes to Jack's.

"No, Jack. But thank you for offering."

Frae's shoulders stooped. Jack sensed that his mother and sister were reluctant to ask him to do anything. Chagrined, he decided he would have to unearth their needs another way. Without asking or making them ask.

Frae rose from the table first. Gathering the empty dishes, she carried them to the wash barrel. When Mirin made to rise and join her, Jack surprised himself by taking the bowl right out of her hands.

"Let me," he said, and Mirin, in her shock, relented. She looked so tired and worn, and her bowl was still full of parritch. It worried him.

He joined Frae at the wash barrel, and she gave a little gasp when he began to dunk the bowls beneath the water.

"This is *my* chore," she said. As if she would fight him for it.

"Do you know what, Frae?"

She hesitated and then said, "What?"

"This used to be my chore too, when I was your age. I will wash and you can dry. How does that sound?"

She still looked perplexed, but then Jack handed her a freshly washed bowl, and she took it and began to wipe it dry with a rag. They worked in rhythm with each other, and when the table was clear, Jack said, "Will you take me on a tour of the yard, sister? It's been so long since I was home, I don't remember where everything is."

Frae was ecstatic. She threw the door open, grabbed her shawl when Mirin chided her to, and led Jack through the kail yard. She pointed out every single vegetable and herb and fruit they were growing, her voice as sweet as a bell that never ceased ringing. Jack patiently listened, but he was gradually taking them in the direction of the northern face of the house, where his shutters sat open to welcome the sunlight.

He studied his window, as well as the strip of grass that stretched between it and the fence. There was nothing to indicate someone or something had approached last night. Again he wondered if he had dreamt it all, but he stayed at the window, unable to ignore his disconcerted musings.

"Frae? Has someone ever knocked on your bedroom shutters before? In the middle of the night?"

Frae stopped walking. "No. Why?" And then she gasped and rushed to say, "Oh! I'm so sorry to have taken your room! I hope you aren't angry with me!"

Jack blinked, surprised. "I'm not angry at all, Frae. I don't need a room anymore, to be honest."

Her copper brows quirked as she began to fiddle with the ends of her braids. "But why? Don't you want to remain here with us?"

Why did her inquiry meet him like a spear? He suddenly didn't want to disappoint her, and Jack had never cared about such things before.

"I don't mind sharing a room with Mum," she added, as if that would convince him to stay. "Truly."

"Well . . . I *do* have to return to my school," he said, watching her hopeful expression fall. "But I'll be here all summer."

The promise spilled from his mouth before he could think better of it. Before he could remind himself that a part of him still hoped to leave by the end of the week. He couldn't break his word now, not when he had given it to Frae.

Summer was a long time in a child's mind. Frae grinned and bent down to pick a few violets from the grass. Jack watched as her dainty fingers traced the petals, pollen smearing like gold on her skin.

"I found some wildflowers on my bed last night," Jack said. "Did you pick them for me, Frae?"

She nodded, her dimples flaring in her cheeks again.

"Thank you. It was a thoughtful gift."

"I can show you where I picked them!" she cried, and he was shocked when she reached for his hand, as if she had held it countless times before. "It's this way, Jack. I know where all the best flowers grow."

She tugged on his arm, completely unaware that a piece of him had melted.

"Wait a moment, Frae," he said, kneeling before her so their gazes would align. "Will you promise me something?"

She nodded, her trust like a knife in his side.

"This will probably never happen, but if you ever hear the shutters rattle like something is trying to open them, knocking on them, promise me that you will not answer it," Jack said. "You will wake Mum and stay with her."

"Or I could come wake you, right, Jack?"

"Yes," he said. "You can always come to me if you are afraid or uncertain about something. And even when you are in the yard, I want you to make sure that you tell Mum where you are, and that you remain near her, within sight of the cottage. Always take someone with you to pick flowers. Can you promise me that also?"

"I promise. But Mum has already told me such."

"Good," he said. But within, he told himself, *I have to stay here until this mystery of the missing lasses is solved. I have to see this through, even if it takes longer than summer.*

"Is that what happened to Eliza and Annabel?" Frae asked

with a somber expression. "Did a spirit knock on their windows?"

Jack hesitated. He didn't want to scare her more than necessary, but he remembered Adaira's words from the day before. One girl had gone missing on her walk home from school. The other, while tending the sheep in the pasture. He thought back on the stories Mirin had once told him. Legends where spirits—often benevolent ones—thrived in the yard and were even welcomed inside, such as when a fire was lit in the hearth. But he had never heard of one approaching a house and forcibly entering. Not that it was impossible, as the spirits often accepted the gifts left for them on porches and thresholds, but it seemed that even the most dangerous of beings preferred to be in the wild, where their powers were strongest.

"I'm not sure, Frae," Jack said.

"Mum says the spirits in our yard are good. As long as I am home or stay on the roads or at school, the folk can't trick me. They watch over me, especially when I wear my plaid."

Jack's eyes drifted to Frae's shawl, which she had knotted crookedly over her collarbones. He noted its shimmer of enchantment. The shawl was green from summer bracken and nettles, with a vein of madder red and lichen gold. Colors of the earth spirits, harvested and crushed and soaked to make dyes. He wondered what secret was woven into that pattern, and for once he was glad of Mirin's skill.

He smiled at his little sister, hoping to ease her worry. "Mum's right. Now show me where the best flowers grow."

Torin was walking the nook of the marsh, searching for the missing girls, when he spotted Jack standing beside a crown of rocks, waiting to speak with him. Torin took his time. His clothes were wrinkled stiff from the rain, and his eyes bleary from a long night, but he continued to comb through the wet grass. His boots squelched, startling meadow pipits in their morning foray as his guards fanned out behind him. Eventually he reached Jack and the shadows of the rocks. Torin noticed a flower was tucked into Jack's dark hair, but he said nothing of it.

He had finally met Frae then.

"No sign of either lass?" Jack said.

Torin shook his head. "Not a trace."

"I think you should search the western hills, up by my mum's croft."

"Why is that?" Torin knew he sounded skeptical, but all he could think of was how the spirits had been thwarting him. The wind had blown away any markings in the grass. The storm had broken, impeding him at every turn, and even now the rain sat in puddles, destroying any evidence of where the lasses might have wandered off to.

He feared the worst—that he would not be able to find either girl. The conversation he had had with Eliza's mother last week still rattled in his skull, like broken bones.

Why would the folk take my daughter? Can I strike a bargain with them to get her back?

Torin had been speechless, uncertain what to say to the desperate woman. But it had turned his thoughts toward more dangerous, risky contemplations.

Jack was quiet, waiting for Torin's attention. The wind carved a path between them, but there were no whispers within it that morning.

"I heard something strange last night," Jack began, and Torin's focus sharpened. He listened as Jack told him about the shutters rattling, the shadow that had fled into the hills.

"You saw them?" Torin demanded. "What did they look like? Which manner of spirit was it? Earth? Water?"

"I saw a *shadow* moving," Jack corrected. He paused, hesitant. "I couldn't determine how it was built. But it has me wondering . . . are the spirits becoming bolder? Have they been approaching houses with the intention to enter, uninvited?"

"It's rare, but I've heard stories of them doing so in the past," Torin replied. "And if it truly was a spirit knocking on your window last night . . . it's a sign they're growing cold and cruel. To steal a lass directly from her home."

Jack frowned. "Could it mean that there is trouble brewing in the spirit's realm?"

"Perhaps," Torin said. "But there's no true way of knowing, now, is there? If they refuse to manifest and speak directly to us, we can only wonder." He sighed, motioning for his guards to gather. "If you think something might be hiding in the west hills, we'll search there."

Torin began to chart his course by the rising sun, heading toward Mirin's croft, but Jack stopped him.

"You don't think it was a Breccan scout, do you, Torin?"

Torin paused, let his guards pass by him before he responded. "If it was a Breccan, I would know. No one crosses the clan line without my knowledge." And he flexed his left hand, the one that bore the scar.

Three years ago, Alastair had named Torin the Captain of the East Guard. After the ceremony, Torin had held out his hand, and the laird had cut his palm with his sword—steel enchanted with awareness. The pain had run deep, deeper than any other blade Torin had ever felt. It sank into his bones and relentlessly ached, as if his hand had been cleft in two. He had carried that pain and walked the edges of Eastern Cadence—her rugged coastline, her border between west and east—letting his blood drip on the earth and the water. Just as the Captain of the East

Guard had done before him. No one could step foot on Eastern Cadence without him feeling it.

His blood was bound to the land.

He could have told Jack that the last scout he had intercepted had been on the southern shore of Cadence, near the place where Roban had confronted Jack the other night. But Torin didn't.

He didn't tell Jack it had been a Breccan warrior who had attempted to swim his way over, who foolishly believed that Torin couldn't feel a trespasser in the eastern tides. He didn't tell Jack that the Breccan had been armed and viciously fought Torin in the sand, or that Torin had interrogated the scout in the same cave where he had given his plaid and heather ale to Jack in welcome. He didn't tell Jack that when the Breccan had remained silent, giving none of his plans away, Torin had killed him and dumped his body in the ocean.

No, he hadn't told anyone of that night. Not even Sidra.

He parted ways with Jack, following the trail his guards had forged up the hill. And Torin had to finally ask himself . . . *What?* What was he was searching for? A ribbon, a shoe, a shred of clothing? A physical trace that would lead him somewhere? A door that opened to another realm? A manifested spirit who would be helpful and guide him to the girls? A body? His initial search for Eliza and Annabel had been unsuccessful, but perhaps that was because he was relying on his physical limitations.

When he reached his guards on the road, Torin sent them ahead to Mirin's with orders to search her land. He trailed behind, his eyes sweeping the thick grass and the deer trails, and he was almost to Mirin's croft when he came across a glen he had never encountered before. A narrow, deep valley with a river flowing along its floor, trickling over rocks.

He paused, wondering if this river would lead to a portal.

Ever since he was a lad, Torin had longed to uncover one, to pass through a doorway that would usher him into the spirits' domain.

Feeling compelled to search this glen, Torin slid down the steep bank and walked in the shallow currents. He followed its winding path, his eyes peeling the rocks and dangling roots for a hidden door. Water was seeping into his boots when he unexpectedly came upon a bothy built on the stony bank. It was small and rugged, almost unnoticeable if one didn't look closely, built of woven branches and vines. A hole in its mossy roof let out puffs of smoke.

He stopped in the river, uncertain as to who occupied it. The hair rose on his arms the longer he regarded the bothy, as if this place was holy ground where spirits gathered. He cautiously moved forward, hand on the hilt of his sword, and knocked on the driftwood door.

"Come in," a voice beckoned him, smooth and melodic. A young woman's voice.

When Torin pushed the door, it creaked inward, but he remained on the threshold. He had never seen a spirit manifested. He had only ever heard their whispers on the wind, and felt their warmth in the fire, and breathed their fragrance in the grass, and drunk their generosity in the water from the loch. So he didn't know what to expect as his eyes adjusted to the dim light.

"Are you afraid?" the woman said with a laugh. He still couldn't see her in the shadows. "Come inside. I'm not a spirit, if that's what you fear."

He cautiously entered the bothy, stooping to avoid hitting his head on the mossy lintel.

There was a small peat fire burning in a ring of stones. A tiny table held a collection of books, a cauldron of parritch, and a bowl of blackberries. A shelf was crowded with carved figurines. A basket of branches sat beside a rocking chair, and in the chair was a woman, ancient and silver haired, her gnarled hands whittling a slender piece of wood.

Torin stared at her, confused, but her eyes remained on her work. The confident whisking of her knife and the wood shavings that fell with her motions. It almost looked as if she was carving a reflection of him . . .

"Ah, it is the esteemed Captain of the East Guard," the woman said, glancing at him and recognizing his plaid and crest. Again, her voice was young and vibrant. "You were not expecting me to look like this, were you?"

He was silent, disturbed.

"Old and weathered, you would call me," she continued, "with a voice that does not match how I appear."

"Who are you?" Torin asked.

She finally ceased her whittling, piercing him with a set of watery blue eyes. "You wouldn't know me. I don't belong in your time, captain. That is why my body has aged, but my voice has not."

"Then what time are you from? How did you come to live on this river?"

She nodded to her shelf of figurines. "Choose one, and I shall tell you. This is my penance for a vow I broke, long ago: I must tell visitors my story before I may answer a question of theirs in return, for this glen is cursed, beckoning only those who are in great need. But choose wisely, captain. A figurine as well as a question, for my voice will last only so long before it fades."

Torin wanted to ask her about the missing girls but held the words back, heeding her warning. He turned to the shelf, gazing at the collection. There were more than he could count, a variety of women, men, and beasts hewn from all types of wood. But his eyes were drawn to one figurine in particular. Her hair was long, unbound, studded with flowers, and one hand rested over her heart, the other reaching out with invitation.

Torin gently took her within his hand, vividly remembering the day he had married Sidra. The wildflowers that had crowned her. How he had found stray petals in her hair hours after the ceremony, when she sat in his bed and they drank wine and talked late into the night.

He inhaled a sharp breath. "Has my wife been here?" And he turned to show the beautiful figurine to the woman.

She cackled. "Are you wed to Lady Whin of the Wildflowers?"

"This is a spirit?" Torin studied the figurine more closely and saw that flowers also bloomed from her fingertips. "I didn't realize the folk looked so similar to us."

"Some of them do, captain. Some of them don't. And remember . . . take care with your questions. I am only beholden to answer one, after my tale has been spun."

"Then tell me your story," he said.

She was quiet for a long moment. Torin watched as she continued to cut into the wood, another figurine coming to life in her hands.

"I was Joan's handmaiden," she began at last. "I went with her when she married Fingal Breccan. I accompanied her into the west."

Torin's eyes widened. He knew the legend of his ancestor, who had sought to bring peace to the isle. Joan Tamerlaine had lived two centuries ago.

"In the days before the clan line, it was beautiful," the woman said. "The hills were cloaked in heather and wildflowers. The streams ran cold and pure from the mountains. The sea was full of life and abundance. And yet a shadow lay over it. The Breccans often sparred amongst themselves, keen to prove which family was stronger. You had to sleep with one eye open, and trust was scarce even among brothers and sisters. I witnessed more bloodshed than I ever had before, and I eventually couldn't bear to live there. I asked Joan to release me from my vow of service, and she did, because she understood. Every night, we dreamt of the east, homesick.

"I left and she remained. But when I returned home, I wasn't welcomed by my family. They cast me away for breaking my vow to Joan, and I wandered, destitute, until I came to a loch in a vale. I knelt and drank and soon noticed something else, deep within its waters. A glimmer of gold.

"I was hungry and weary; I needed that gold to survive. I plunged into the water and began to swim to the bottom. But every time I thought I was almost there, when I stretched out my hand to capture the gold, it evaded me, sinking a little deeper. Soon, I could feel my chest smoldering—I was almost out of air. And just before I changed my course, the spirit of the loch met me. She kissed my mouth, and suddenly I could breathe in the water, and I continued to swim, defiant of my mortality, deep into the heart of the loch. Greedy and desperate for that promise of gold."

She fell quiet, her hands pausing in their work. Torin stood transfixed by her story, the figurine of Lady Whin cradled in his palm.

"But you never got the gold," he murmured.

The woman met his gaze. Her voice was changing, becoming raspy and frail, as if her confession was aging it. "No. I came to my senses and realized the loch was bottomless, and soon I would lose myself within it and the games the loch spirit played. I turned and swam back the way I had come, so exhausted I almost didn't reach the light. When I broke the surface, I realized a hundred years had passed while I had been treading the deep." She resumed her whittling, emotionless. "The family I knew was dead, long buried. Joan, too, was dead, I learned. She had died entwined with the Breccan laird, their blood staining the earth. She had cursed the west as Fingal had cursed the east. The magic of the spirits was unbalanced now because of their strife and the clan line.

"Magic would henceforth flow bright in the hands of the Breccans. They could harness enchantments with no conse- quences to their health, weaving magic into plaids, hammering charms into their steel. But the folk would suffer from their magic. The crops would grow sparse in the west. The water would be murky. The fire would burn dim, and the wind would be harsh. The Breccan clan would then be a strong yet hungry clan, belonging to a solemn land.

"In turn, magic would flow bright in the spirits of the east. And while the Tamerlaines would have to suffer in order to wield it, their gardens would flourish, their water would be pure, their winds would be balanced, and their fires would be warm. The Tamerlaine clan would then be a prosperous but vulnerable people, belonging to a lush land."

Torin was quiet, soaking in her story. He knew of the curse. It was why the Breccans had no resources come winter, and why so many Tamerlaines required the medical attention of his wife.

He glanced at the woman, wondering how many questions he could ask before her voice fully faded.

"Do the spirits of the isle come here to visit you then?" he asked.

"Occasionally. When one is in need."

"You didn't happen to see one with two young lasses, did you?"

"What would a spirit want with a mortal bairn?" she countered.

Torin felt his impatience rise. "Is there a way to call the spirits? To make them manifest?"

"If there is," the woman said, her words almost undecipherable, "I don't know it, captain."

He sensed her time had ended; her voice was spent. He wanted to ask her more about the spirits, but he would have to do it another time, when her voice had been replenished.

How will I find my way back to this place? he wondered, knowing this glen was cursed to shift and change. He studied the figurine of Lady Whin once more. Perhaps it could be a guide to him. It was uncanny how much it reminded him of Sidra.

"May I keep this?" he asked.

The woman gave him a curt nod, her attention focusing on her work, as though he were no longer present.

Torin left the bothy, the door closing behind him on its own. He tucked the figurine into his pocket, thinking Maisie would love it, and began to walk up the river before he paused, listening as the water's babble changed.

Torin glanced over his shoulder and froze. It was just as he had feared.

The river had altered its course by a handbreadth, and the timeless woman's bothy was nowhere to be seen.

Torin had just emerged from the glen and was heading north when he caught sight of Roban, sprinting toward him through the heather.

Torin knew something was wrong. He felt a pit in his stomach as he ran to meet the young guard.

"What is it, Roban?" Torin asked. But he already knew the answer.

He saw the sweat dripping from Roban's brow, the sheen of panic in his eyes. His worn edges from searching day after day, night after night, with nothing to show for it.

"I'm afraid it's happened again, captain," the boy panted. "Another lass has vanished."

CHAPTER 6

Sidra walked the streets of Sloane, a basket of healing supplies hanging from her arm. Each door she passed held an offering on its threshold for the spirits. Appeasements and manifest prayers in the shape of carved figurines and small stacks of peat, so the fire could dance and burn, and chimes made of fishing line and glass beads, so the wind could hear its own breath when it passed by. There were small bannocks and cups of milk for the spirits of the earth, and salted herring and jewelry strung with shells for the water.

Desperation hung like fog, and Sidra let her thoughts roam to dark places.

She thought of the two lasses, Eliza and Annabel. Two girls now unaccounted for, and Sidra imagined them being claimed by the folk. She wondered if a girl could become a tree, no longer aging in mortal ways but by seasons. Could a girl become a wildflower patch, resurrected every spring and summer only to wilt and fade come the sting of frost? Could she become the foam of the sea that rolled over the coast for an eternity, or a flame that danced in a hearth? A winged being of the wind, sighing over the hills? Could she be returned to her human family after such a life, and if so, would she even remember her parents, her human memories, her mortal name?

Grief welled within Sidra as she returned her attention to the city thoroughfare. She came to Sloane twice a week, to make a round of visits to her patients there. Her first appointment was with Una Carlow, and Sidra followed the song of a hammer striking an anvil.

She arrived at Una's forge and stood in the sun for a moment, watching the blacksmith work in her shop. The air was thick with the tang of hot metal, the sparks flying as Una hammered a long blade of steel. Sidra could feel every strike in her teeth until Una finally quenched the blade in a tub of water, the steam rising with a hiss.

Una withdrew the sword and handed it off to her apprentice, who was red faced and perspiring from pumping the bellows. Sidra thought of how the fire always burned at the forge, how its embers never fell cold and docile. If anyone was intimate with Cadence fire, knowing its temperament and power and secrets, it was Una.

As such, Una was one of the only blacksmiths in the east who wasn't afraid to hammer enchantments into her steel. She could take a secret and an ingot, melt them together over a blistering fire, and shape them as one on her anvil. Once an enchanted blade was complete, she always fell ill with a fever and was sometimes unable to leave her bed for days.

"Sidra," the blacksmith said in greeting, removing her thick leather gloves. "How are you and Maisie?"

"We're well," Sidra replied, but she felt the true meaning of Una's question. "She's with Graeme for now. I'm thankful that he's able to watch her while I'm away on visits."

"Good," Una said, joining her at the edge of the forge.

"And how are your two children?" Sidra reached into her basket to find the tonic she had made for Una's vitality. "It's been a while since I've seen them."

"Growing up too fast," Una replied with a smile. "But they're content. When they're not at school they're either here with me or spending time with Ailsa at the stables, keen to learn all of my wife's horse secrets."

Sidra nodded, wholly understanding the caution, even though Una and Ailsa's son and daughter were adolescents now. Old enough to heed the strict rules parents were suddenly doling out with the disappearances.

As she set the tonic jar on Una's outstretched palm, the blacksmith surprised her by saying, "Do you ever wonder if we are unknowing participants in a spirit's game? If they move us like pawns on a board and glean pleasure from provoking our heartaches?"

Sidra hesitated. She looked deep within herself and knew the answer was *yes*. She had thought as much. But her devout nature had instantly stamped out those dangerous wonderings; she worried that the earth would sense that disbelief in her when she worked the kail yard, when she crushed the herbs to make healing salves.

"It's a troubling thought," Sidra said. "To think they gain pleasure from tormenting us."

"Sometimes, when I watch the fire burn in the forge," Una continued, "I imagine what it would be like to be immortal, to hold no fear of death. To dance and burn for an endless era. And I think how dull such an existence would be. That one would do anything to feel the sharp edge of life again."

"Yes," Sidra whispered. She was too paranoid to say anything more, and the blacksmith sensed it.

"Don't let me keep you," Una said. "Thank you for the tonic. I've been commissioned to make an enchanted blade tomorrow, so this will help me bear the effects."

Sidra bid Una farewell and continued on her route. The day unfurled just as she had expected until a cold burst of northern wind blew through the city. She paused, watching it twine with smoke, overturn baskets in the market, rattle shutters and doors.

Sidra's black hair tangled across her face as she stood in the center of the street.

And that was when she heard the faint whisper, like a rush of wings.

The wind brought news.

Jack waited for Adaira at the castle. It was noontide, just as she had requested for their meeting, and a servant had brought him to the music turret, telling him the heiress would be with him directly. Impatient, Jack passed the time by walking the length of the bookshelves, selecting a few volumes to sift through. He found a book brimming with music that he swiftly recognized. These were the ballads of the clan. The songs Lorna once sang on feast nights.

Jack smiled as he read the notes. He fondly remembered these songs; they had shaped his childhood, those wild days roaming the heather and exploring the sea caves. And he was pleased to discover that even years later, this music still roused a warm nostalgia within him. It drew him back to those moments in the hall, when he had savored listening to these songs. Long before he ever dreamt of becoming a bard or dared to imagine that he would one day learn the secrets of instruments.

He eventually shut the music book and set it back on the shelf. It was riddled with dust. Realizing he must have been the first person to touch the volume in years, he suddenly felt sad, thinking of how quiet the east had become without Lorna.

He walked to the harp in the center of the room, but refrained from playing. He noticed the table was cleared; all of the papers and books that had been piled upon it yesterday were gone save for a sealed letter.

Curious, Jack took a closer look at the parchment. The letter was addressed to Adaira, and it bore the crest of two swords in a ring of juniper. The Breccans' sigil.

He recoiled from it, alarmed. Why would the western clan write to her?

He paced the room, trying to cast his thoughts about the letter aside, but his worries lingered. What could the Breccans want from her? It was strange that the first thing that crossed his mind was that they wanted to marry her.

Jack came to a stop before the balcony doors, disconcerted when he remembered the legend of Joan Tamerlaine, dying entwined with Fingal Breccan. Did the Breccans dream of peace again after so many years of strife?

He wondered if the isle could be made whole again, but thought it impossible.

An hour had passed on the sun dial. Where was Adaira?

The view overlooked the thoroughfare of Sloane, and as Jack's gaze skimmed the street he realized there was some sort of commotion happening below. People were gathering together in the market. A few men started running, and vendors began to close their stalls early. It looked like school was even released spontaneously; young girls and boys were being escorted home.

Jack looked for Frae amongst the dispersing students, but there was no sign of her bright russet hair. *She's with Mirin today,* he recalled, the tension in his shoulders easing. *She's safe, at home.*

He continued to watch the activity in the streets. He decided to leave—after all, Adaira had stood him up—and he hurried through the courtyard to the market.

"What's happening?" he asked one of the women who was closing her bakery.

"You didn't hear the news?" she replied. "Another lass has gone missing."

"Who?" Jack demanded.

"I'm not sure yet. Several names have been mentioned, but we're waiting for it to be confirmed by Captain Torin."

At once, Jack's stomach dropped, his blood ran cold, and his thoughts scattered like broken glass. On the mainland, he had been afraid of nothing but failure. Failing a class, failing to graduate, failing to please his lover. His fears had only pertained to himself and his own performance. Now he realized how self-absorbed he had been all those years. He was swiftly learning ever since he had returned home that he couldn't live on music alone, that he cared about and needed other things, even if their appearance in his life came as an utter shock, like bulbs blooming after a long winter. He felt his greatest fear come to life within him, a fear that had been born only days before.

Frae could be missing.

He didn't waste another moment.

Jack sprinted along the road. He refused to stop, even when his breath turned to fire in his lungs and a stitch pulled in his side. He ran all the way to Mirin's croft and vaulted over the yard fence, and he thought his heart had melted when he burst through his mother's front door.

He halted, his boots leaving a track of mud on the floor. Mirin stood at her loom, startled and wide eyed as she turned to behold his dramatic entrance. And there was Frae, sprawled on the divan, reading a book with flowers tucked in her braids.

He stared at his little sister, as if he didn't trust his own eyes, and he trembled as he shut the door. He felt a rush of relief, followed by a twinge of guilt, to know it wasn't Frae but another nameless lass.

"Jack?" Mirin asked. "Jack, what's wrong?"

"I thought . . ." He couldn't speak. He swallowed and battled his breath. "I heard another lass went missing."

"Which lass?" Frae cried, shutting her book.

"I'm not sure. No names have been shared yet." Jack hated the fear that crept over Frae's expression. "Perhaps it's only a rumor, and not true at all. You know how the wind gossips."

Mirin's gaze shifted to her daughter. "It'll be all right, Frae."

Jack was stricken as Frae's face crumpled, on the verge of tears.

He didn't know what he would do if she wept, but it made something in him ache. At the university, he had come to learn there were moments when words were not enough, and he strode into his bedroom. His harp still sat in its sleeve, waiting to be freed.

He carried the instrument back into the common room and sat in a chair across from Frae. A few tears had trickled down her cheeks, but she wiped them away when she realized what he held.

"Would you like to hear a song, Frae?"

She nodded vehemently, pushing stray hair from her eyes.

"I would be honored to play for both you and Mum," Jack said, resisting the temptation to glance at Mirin, who was lowering the shuttle of her loom. "But I must warn you, Frae . . . this is my first time playing on the isle. I might not sound nearly as good as I do on the mainland."

This was his first time playing in *Mirin's* presence was what he truly meant to express. He was worried that she wouldn't be impressed by the craft he had spent years mastering. But Mirin, who never left her loom in mid-weave for anything, stepped away and joined them, sitting next to Frae on the divan.

"Then let us be the judge of that," Frae replied with a sniffle. Her lashes were damp, but her tears had ceased. She watched with rapt attention as Jack withdrew his harp. Its first time breathing the air of the isle.

He had earned this harp in his fifth year of study. Constructed from a willow that had grown beside a maiden's grave, its wood was light and resilient, its sound sweet, chilling, and resonant. Carvings of vines and leaves had been burned into the sides, simple adornment compared to other harps his fellow students had earned. But this harp had called to him long ago.

As Jack tuned the pins, he examined the thirty brass strings, and he thought about all the hours he had spent on the mainland playing this instrument, coaxing sad, wistful ballads from its heart. Out of the three classes of music a harp could make, Jack preferred the lament. But he didn't want to add to Frae's sorrow. He should play either for joy or for slumber. Perhaps a mix of both. A song framed on hope.

His old plaid was draped over his knees as he continued to tune the harp, and the fabric caught Mirin's eye.

Jack leaned the harp against his left shoulder.

"What shall I play for you two?" he asked.

They were speechless.

"Anything," Frae eventually said.

Jack felt an echo of pain when he realized his sister didn't know any old ballads. She had been only three when Lorna passed away, far too young to remember the bard's music. And Jack inevitably thought of the ballads he had read through earlier that day, song after song that he had grown up listening to. Frae's childhood had been robbed of that music.

He began to play and sing one of his favorites—"The Ballad of Seasons." A lively and happy tune of spring that melted into summer's verse, which was smooth and mellow. And that in turn became the staccato fire of autumn, which descended into the sad yet elegant verse of winter, because he couldn't resist the sorrow. When he finished, his last note fading in the air, Frae burst into enthusiastic clapping and Mirin wiped the tears from her eyes.

Jack thought he had never felt so content and full.

"Another one!" Frae begged.

Mirin caressed her hair. "It's time to weave, Frae. We have work to do."

Frae sagged, but she didn't complain. She followed Mirin to the loom, but her eyes traced the harp in Jack's hands with longing.

He could keep strumming, he realized. He could pluck notes while they wove.

Jack played song after song while Mirin and Frae worked at the loom. All the ballads he wanted his sister to know. A few times, Frae became distracted, her eyes wandering toward his music. But Mirin didn't chide her.

The afternoon had deepened by the time Jack set down his harp. Thunder rumbled in the distance, and wind rattled the shutters. The scent of rain was heavy in the air as Jack reached into his harp case and took out the parchment Adaira had given him the day before.

He didn't know the girls who were missing. He didn't know what would happen when he played this bewitching music, if the spirits would answer him or not. But he had always desired to prove himself worthy of the Tamerlaines. To be wanted, to feel as if he belonged.

Music had once given that to him. A home, a purpose.

As Mirin and Frae wove, Jack began to fervently study "The Song of the Tides."

It was Catriona Mitchell, and she was only five years old.

The youngest daughter of a fisherman and a tailor, she had been helping her father mend nets by the quay when she went to play with her older siblings on the northern coast. None of them recalled seeing her wander away, but Torin had found a trace of her footsteps on the sand, just before the high tide rolled in.

He followed her trail. She had been alone on the coast before choosing to climb a knoll, where it became harder for Torin to follow her path. He examined the grass and the rocks, wondering what had prompted the child to leave her siblings on the sand.

A flash of red caught his eye.

Torin crouched, at first fearing it was blood, until he moved the grass aside and saw it was only a flower. Four crimson petals, veined with gold. It was beautiful, and he had never seen anything like it before.

He frowned as he studied it. He knew the eastern landscape well; he was familiar with the plants that flourished on this side of the isle. Yet this flower was odd and out of place, as if a spirit had purposefully left it here to be found.

He wondered if it marked a portal to the other side.

Gently, he scooped it into his palm. The blossom had been lying on the ground, already sheared, and he wondered if this had been what Catriona had seen, what had prompted her to climb the knoll.

Torin searched the area again, combing for evidence of where she had gone next. He succeeded in finding a few small steps heading to the hills of the isle. Her bare feet had crimped the grass, but then it was as though she vanished. There was no further trace, no sign of footsteps, save for another loose red flower, sitting like a drop of blood on the ground.

Torin recovered it, careful not to crush the petals in his hands. He searched the dirt, the nearby stones, the tussocks of grass, for a small doorway. Surely, the spirits had opened a portal, inviting her into their domain. Where else would she have gone?

He felt a strange tug in his stomach. It was fear, something he had learned to tame long ago, but he decided that he needed to see Maisie with his own eyes.

He gave his guards orders to mark the trail and continue scouring the area for more footsteps and doorways, and he rode home.

He was relieved to find Sidra at the kitchen table, herbs spread before her like a map he could never read. She was preparing tonics for her patients, and her sable hair was caught in a messy braid.

She glanced up the moment he entered.

"Torin," she breathed. "Do you have news?"

He hated the hope in her eyes. He shut the door behind him. "It's Catriona Mitchell. She's been missing since this morning. I've found a partial trail, as well as something that I need your assistance on."

At once, Sidra set down her pestle and met him in the center of the room. He carefully retrieved the two red flowers from his leather pouch, setting them into her waiting palm.

"Can you identify this flower for me?" he asked, hopeful.

Sidra studied the flowers. A frown pulled at her brows. "No. I've never seen such flowers before, Torin. Where did you find them?"

He explained, suddenly feeling exhausted and defeated. Another lass gone, on his watch. Another girl vanished, leaving behind a strange flower in her wake.

Catriona Mitchell was only five years old. The same age as Maisie.

Torin's eyes lifted. He could see into the bedroom, because Sidra had left the door open. Maisie was fast asleep on the bed.

Torin walked closer, to lean on the doorframe and watch his daughter sleep. His chest ached.

"Torin? Do you want to rest for a while?" Sidra asked quietly.

He sighed, turning back to his wife. She was reaching for the kettle and had set out a plate of treacle biscuits. The last time he had properly eaten was at this table, when he had brought Jack home.

"No, I don't have time," he whispered, fearing if he woke Maisie he wouldn't be able to leave.

Sidra set down the kettle, looking at him with worried eyes. He began to walk back to the door, but he paused, glancing at the red flowers she had set down on her wooden cutting board. The blossoms were stark against the collection of her other herbs, keen to be noticed.

"I don't know what to do, Sid," he said. The confession tasted like ash in his mouth. "I don't know how to find these lasses. I don't know how to make the spirits give them up. I don't know how to comfort these families."

Sidra came to him. She wrapped her arms around his waist and Torin leaned into her, if only for a moment. He closed his eyes and breathed in the scent of her hair.

"I'll see what I can uncover about these flowers, Torin," she said, easing back so she could meet his weary gaze. "Don't give up hope. We'll find the girls."

He nodded, but his meager faith had fully crumbled over the past few weeks.

Not knowing what to believe anymore, he kissed Sidra's knuckles and left.

The sun was bright, but the clouds to the west had started

to bruise. A storm was brewing, which would make it very difficult to find any further trace of where Catriona had wandered to.

Torin was about to mount his horse when his gaze was caught by the hill to his left. It was cloaked with heather, and a walking path cut up the middle. It led to his father's croft next door, and Torin decided he owed Graeme a visit.

It had been a few years since Torin had properly called on his father. He rarely visited because the memories lingered like ghosts in his childhood home and he and his father had always harbored different opinions. Their estrangement had been sparked when Torin and Donella handfasted in secret.

You're acting like a fool, Torin, Graeme had said when he realized his son's plans. *You need to ask Donella's parents before you give her your vow.*

Torin, twenty and besotted, hadn't cared for Graeme's advice. He and Donella did what they wanted, and it had indeed caused a stir in the clan. It had almost ruined Torin's chances of being promoted to captain.

After Donella perished, Torin's days had become bleak, like a winter that never seemed to end. Maisie had been a baby, squalling in his arms, and Torin had finally carried his daughter to Graeme, desperate.

Help me, Da. What am I supposed to do? She does nothing but cry. I don't know what to do.

The words had poured out of Torin's mouth, and he had wept, finally, like he had broken a dam. He hadn't wept when Donella bled to death after the birthing. He hadn't wept when he watched her shrouded body find its final rest in her grave. He hadn't wept when he held Maisie for the first time. But all the tears had broken free the moment he set his daughter into his father's arms and confessed his ineptitude.

How had this happened to him? Donella was gone, he had

a child and no inkling how to raise her, and he was alone. This was not the path he had ever envisioned for himself.

Graeme had held Maisie, just as shocked by Torin's weeping as Torin was himself. Bleary and heartsick, Torin had sat in his father's chair in the common room. Graeme had then said words he didn't want to hear, words that made him rigid.

Your daughter needs a tender hand, Torin. Find her a mother. A woman of the isle who can help you.

Find her. As if she grew on a tree. As if she were fruit to be picked.

With Donella buried and dead only three months.

Furious, Torin had snatched Maisie from Graeme's arms and departed, vowing he would never return to his father for help.

That evening a raven had brought a note to Torin's door. He knew it was his father's doing; Graeme had refused to leave his croft ever since Torin's mother abandoned them.

Warm the goat milk. Test it on your wrist to ensure it's not too hot before you feed it to her. Walk and sing to her when she cries. Make sure she sleeps on her back at night.

Torin had ripped Graeme's note to pieces and burned it in the hearth. But he did as his father had instructed. Slowly, Maisie cried less, but she still was far more life than Torin could handle. And then, a few months later, he had met Sidra in the valley.

He ascended the hill now, desperate once more. He made it to the crest, reaching his father's kail yard. It was overcome with weeds, even though Sidra came once a week to tend to Graeme's garden. Torin noticed the roof needed mending, the shutters hung crookedly, there was a bird's nest in one of the eaves, and the rain barrel looked foggy. All seemed broken and disheveled—that is, until Torin approached his father's door.

Then the weeds retreated with a whisper, exposing the stone

pathway. The despondent vines that grew up the side of the house turned into honeysuckle climbing a trellis. Wildflowers bloomed amid the kail and herbs. The gossamer melted away, and the shutters were straight and recently painted.

Watching the cottage and yard change with his presence gave Torin pause. He was humbled, thinking of all the times he had judged the croft and his father's past decisions from the road. The disrepair, the messiness. Why couldn't his father take care of things? And yet all along it was beautiful and orderly; Torin had simply been unable to see it.

He wondered if Sidra saw past the glamour, and when he noticed how tidy the rows of vegetables were, he knew she did. She had probably seen the heart of this place from the beginning.

The folk of the earth guarding this yard must be very shrewd.

"Sidra? Sidra, is that you again?" Graeme called from within before Torin had even knocked. The yard must have given his presence away. "Tell Maisie I have her ship ready. Come inside, come inside! I was just about to make some oatcakes . . ."

Torin let himself in. The common room was messy, and this time it was not glamoured. His father had an overwhelming collection of things. There were piles of books, heaps of loose papers, waterlogged scrolls from another era set in haphazard stacks. Five pairs of fancy mainland boots with laces, hardly worn, and a jacket the color of fire, lined with plaid. Jars of golden pins, a jewelry box that held his mother's abandoned pearls. A map of the realm pegged on the floor, because the walls were already crowded with drawings and musty tapestries and a chart of the northern constellations. All were possessions from Graeme's former life, when he had been the ambassador to the mainland.

Torin wound through the maze, coming to the large table

by the hearth, where Graeme sat waiting. In his hands was a clear bottle, holding an intricate little ship.

"*Torin.*" Graeme almost dropped the glass. His mouth hung open, and he stood, startled. "Are Sidra and Maisie with you? I finished the ship for her. See? She and I have been working on it together, when Sidra brings her to visit."

"It's only me," Torin said, and he couldn't help himself: he soaked in the sight of his father.

Graeme looked softer, older than he had five years ago. He had always been tall and broad, just like his brother Alastair. But whereas Alastair was dark headed and vibrant and given to swords, Graeme was fair and reserved and drawn to books. One brother had risen as laird, the other as his support, his representative to the south.

Graeme's beard was silver now. His hair was caught in a messy plait. His clothes were wrinkled but clean. The lines at the corners of his eyes said that he must have been smiling more often than not, most likely when Sidra and Maisie visited.

He was a great contrast to his brother. Alastair had become so gaunt and wan over the years that Torin wondered if Graeme would even recognize his brother if he saw him.

"Why have you come?" Graeme asked, as politely as he could.

"For advice."

"Oh." Graeme carefully set down Maisie's ship-in-a-bottle, and his hands moved over the sea of clutter on his table. Bottles waiting to be filled, tiny iron instruments, slivers of wood, tins of paint, pieces of cloth. *This, then, is how he fills his days,* Torin thought. "Here, sit . . . sit there. Do you want tea?"

"No."

"Very well. How can I advise you then?"

"Another lass has gone missing," said Torin. He felt that

beat again, thrumming in his pulse. Time was running out. "This is the third one in three weeks. I found a small trail of footprints, but there is no further trace of her save for two red flowers, as if her blood turned into petals. I've been searching for days and nights now. I've searched the sea caves and eddies, the glens, the mountains, the shadows between fells. The girls have vanished, and I need to know how to make the folk return them."

"The spirits?" Graeme frowned. "Why would you do that?"

"Because the spirits have taken this child, just as they took the other two lasses. They are slipping the girls through portals I cannot see."

Graeme was pensive. He let out a slow breath and said, "You blame the spirits."

Torin shifted his weight, impatient. "Aye. It is the only explanation."

"Is it?"

"How else would a bairn completely vanish?"

"How else, indeed."

"Are you going to answer me or not? Surely you have some thread of knowledge about spirits in all of . . . of *this*." Torin waved his hand to the stacks of books and papers. Most of it was mainland trash, but even so, Graeme Tamerlaine had once known everything. He had been full of wondrous stories, of spirits and mortals alike. He could have been a druid if he had set his heart on it.

Graeme raked his fingers through his beard, still lost in his thoughts. "We see what we want to see according to our faith, Torin. Spirits or no."

Torin felt his pride flare. His father always knew what to say to irritate him, humble him. To make him feel as if he were eight years old again.

"Faith or no, I know spirits can wreak havoc when they wish," Torin said. "Just this morning, I spoke with a woman who looked to be ninety but whose voice was that of a young maiden's. When she was a lass, she saw a gleam of gold in the bottom of a loch and swam down to claim it, only the loch was endless, the trick of a water spirit. And when the lass returned to the surface, a hundred years had passed. Everyone she had known and loved in her life before were dead and gone, and she has no place here."

"A sad tale, indeed," Graeme said, sorrowful. "And one you should take caution from, as your answer lies within the lesson she endured."

"What? That the spirits take delight in tricking us?"

"No, of course not. There are many of the folk who are good, who give us life and balance on the isle."

"Then what is my answer, sir?"

Speak plainly, Torin wanted to demand, but he held his temper behind his teeth, waiting for his father to explain.

"If you seek a portal, a passage that will lead you into the spirits' realm," Graeme began, "you need one of two things: an invitation, or your eyes opened."

Torin mulled that over before saying, "But my eyes *are* open. I know this land, even with its capricious nature. I have combed through every glen, every cave, every—"

"Yes, yes, you've seen with your eyes," Graeme interrupted. "But there are other sights, Torin. There are other ways to know this isle and the secrets of the folk."

Torin was silent. He could feel a flush creeping over his face; his breath hissed through his teeth. "How, then, shall I open my eyes? Since I doubt an invitation would be extended to me."

Graeme said nothing, but he started to search through a

pile of old books. Eventually he found one and set it into Torin's palm.

Torin was inwardly hoping it held a map of some sort. A chart of fault lines and hidden doors in the east. He was vastly disappointed. The book was handwritten and incomplete, half of it missing, and its pages were worn and crinkled, some peppered by ash stains, some smudged by water, as if it had passed through many hands.

He struggled to read one of the pages, but his irritation waned when he recognized a name. Lady Whin of the Wild-flowers. He was tempted to reach for the wooden figurine, still hiding in his pocket, as he read about the earth spirit.

Lady Whin of the Wildflowers was never one to boast
But when Rime of the Moors woke late from winter's chill
She challenged him outrightly for the strath by the coast
And Rime, steady and proud, deemed her words fair
Thinking he could beat her with the last moon of Yore
When the heart of the cold beat bright in the air

"These are nursery stories," Torin said, turning the page only to find it smudged, but he was confident Whin had outwitted Rime. "Where's the other half of the book?"

"Missing," Graeme said, pouring himself a cup of tea.

"You have no idea where it is?"

"If I did, don't you think I would have recovered it, son?" Graeme added a hearty splash of milk into his tea, meeting Torin's gaze over the rim of the cup as he sipped. "Take it, Torin. Read it. Perhaps the answer you need rests within those pages. But I expect you to return this book to me in a timely manner. That is, unless Sidra and Maisie want it. Then they can keep it."

Torin arched his brow, only mildly offended. He noticed the slant of sunlight on the floor, realizing he had stayed much longer than he had intended.

"Sidra and Maisie thank you for the book then." He lifted it as a toast, despite the fact that this visit had been a waste of his time. As he wound his way back through the clutter, Torin was surprised that Graeme accompanied him to the door.

"It once belonged to Joan Tamerlaine," said Graeme. "It was written before the clan line was formed."

Torin paused at the gate, frowning. "What are you talking about?"

"The book in your hand, son."

Torin glanced down at it again. "This was *Joan's?*"

"Aye. And it's in the west."

"What is?"

"The other half of the book." His father shut the door without another word.

Jack sat at his desk that night, studying Lorna's ballad by firelight. He had come to know her notes well. They hummed in his thoughts, eager to be played, and he was just about to extinguish his candle when his shutters rattled.

He froze.

He had no blade to defend himself. His eyes darted around the room, landing on his old slingshot. He rose and grabbed it, although he had no river rocks to shoot, and he pushed open the shutters with a burst of anger.

There was a caw, a flap of dark wings.

Jack's breath loosened when he realized it had only been a raven. The bird retreated before circling back, then landed on his desk with an indignant screech.

"What do you want?" he asked, noticing the roll of parchment that was fastened to its leg. He gently unraveled it, but the bird continued to wait, and Jack read:

> *Forgive me for missing our meeting today. As you might*
> *imagine, I was swept away by Catriona's disappearance. But*
> *I still desire to speak with you, my old menace. Let me come to*
> *you this time. Tomorrow evening at Mirin's, before you play for*
> *the spirits.*

There was no signature, but only one person called him "old menace." Adaira must be expecting a reply, because her raven still waited, watching him with beady eyes.

Jack sat at his desk and wrote:

> *Your apology is accepted, heiress. My sister will be thrilled to*
> *see you tomorrow. My mother will insist on feeding you. Come*
> *hungry.*

He began to sign his name but thought better of it. With a wry tilt on his lips, he wrote:

> *—Your one and only O.M.*

He rolled it up and bound the parchment with twine to the raven's leg. The bird took flight with a flap of dark blue wings.

Jack dreamt of the spirits of the sea that night. He dreamt of opening his mouth to sing for them and drowning instead.

CHAPTER 7

H old the slingshot like this," Jack instructed Frae. They stood in one of the croft's paddocks, in the crook of the river. The air was cool with evening and smelled of the nearby Aithwood—sweet sap and sharp pine and damp oak. The wind was tranquil, the hillside spotted with wild orchids.

Adaira should be arriving soon.

"Like this?" Frae asked.

"Yes, that's right. Take up a river stone and place it in the pocket." He watched as Frae found her stone and pulled back on the pouch, aiming for the target he had built out of the byre's old wood. It seemed to take her forever to let it go, and the rock sailed past the target, to her disappointment.

"I missed," she mumbled.

"I missed in the beginning too," Jack reassured her. "If you practice every day, you'll soon hit the target."

Frae took up a rock and shot again. It was another miss, but Jack only encouraged her to try it once more, to shoot until all of the river rocks they had gathered were gone, lost in the long grass of the paddock. As they walked to retrieve them, Jack studied the river. It flowed through the western portion of Mirin's property, wide but shallow, melodious and brimming with perfect slingshot rocks.

"Mum has probably already said this to you," he began. "But you know that you should never draw water from this river, don't you?"

Frae watched its currents, seemingly harmless as it reflected the hues of sunset. "Yes."

"Do you know why, Frae?"

"Because it flows from the Breccans' land. But I can gather rocks from it, right? For your slingshot?"

He met her gaze and nodded. "Yes. Just the rocks."

"Have the Breccans ever poisoned it before, Jack?" Frae asked, bending to pick up the stones. "The river, I mean."

He hesitated until she looked up at him. Her eyes were mirrors of his—wide set and dark as new moons. Only hers still shone with innocence, and he wished more than anything she could remain that way. Full of hope and wonder and goodness. That she would never know the sharp, jaded ways of the world.

"No," he replied. "But there's always the chance that they might."

"Why would they want to do that, Jack?"

He was quiet, rolling his lips together as he gathered his thoughts. "It's hard to understand, I know, sister. But the Breccans don't like us, and we don't like the Breccans. We've been at odds with them for centuries now."

"I wish it could be different," Frae said with a sigh. "Mum says the Breccans are hungry when winter comes. Can't we just share our food with them?"

Her words brought Jack to a stop as he imagined an isle that was united. He could hardly fathom it.

Frae paused, looking up at him. She held the slingshot in one hand and rocks in the other. A few wilted flowers were tucked into her hair.

"I wish it could be different too," he said. "Perhaps one day it will be, Frae."

"I hope so."

They walked back to their starting point to have another practice round. He wanted Frae to have a weapon and to know how to use it. He wanted her to carry this slingshot with her everywhere.

She aimed and fired, hitting the corner of the target.

"I did it!" she cried, and Jack was clapping when another voice spoke.

"Excellent shot, Frae."

Jack and Frae both turned to see Adaira standing a few paces away, watching with a smile. She was dressed in a dark red gown, an umber cloak shielding her back. Her hair was loose and brushed into silk, the long waves reaching her waist.

Jack almost didn't recognize her. She looked otherworldly at first glance as the sun continued to set, limning her in gold.

"Heiress," Frae said in an awed tone. "I can't believe you're here! I thought Jack was teasing me."

Adaira laughed. "No teasing. I'm honored to spend the evening with you, Frae."

"Would you like to shoot the slingshot?" Frae asked. She sounded nervous, and Jack's heart warmed.

"I would love to." Adaira stepped forward.

Frae handed her the weapon and picked out the perfect stone for her. "It's actually Jack's. He's letting me use it for now."

"Oh, I recognize it," Adaira said, glancing at him.

Indeed, he thought, holding her gaze for a beat. He had been a terror with his slingshot in the old days.

Adaira's attention returned to Frae. "Can you show me how to use it?"

Jack watched, arms crossed, as his little sister showed Adaira how to hold it, how to aim, how to set the stone in the pouch. Adaira took her first shot, nailing the target.

Jack arched a brow, impressed.

Frae jumped up and down, cheering. A slow, satisfied grin broke across Adaira's face.

"That was quite fun," she said, handing the slingshot back to Frae. "Now I see why your brother loved it so much."

Jack only snorted.

"Frae!" Mirin called from the crest of the hill. "Come help me finish supper."

Frae's shoulders slumped as she brought the slingshot to Jack.

"Why don't you keep it for now," he said. "That way you can practice whenever you feel like it."

Frae appeared shocked. "You're certain?"

"Very. I have no need for a slingshot these days."

That restored Frae's excitement. She bounded up the hill, proudly showing it to Mirin as the two of them returned to the house.

Jack continued to stand beside Adaira in the crook of the river. The stars were beginning to dust the sky when she spoke.

"She seems quite fond of you, Jack."

"Does that come as a surprise?" he countered, bristling.

"No, actually. But I confess that I'm jealous."

Jack studied her profile. She was gazing at the river, as if mesmerized by its dance. Adaira smiled, but it was inspired by sadness. "I always wanted a sister. A brother. I never wanted to be the only one. I would give up my right to rule if it meant I could have a horde of siblings."

Jack fell quiet, but he knew exactly what thoughts were in

her mind. She was thinking of the castle graveyard. The three little graves beside her mother's. A brother and two sisters, born years before her. All three had been stillborn.

Adaira, the last child of Lorna and Alastair, was the only one to survive.

"Do you know what the clan says of you, Adaira?" Jack began softly. "They call you our light. Our hope. They claim even the spirits bend a knee when you pass. I'm surprised flowers don't grow in your footsteps."

That coaxed a slight chuckle from her, but he could still see her melancholy, as if a hundred sorrows weighed her down. "Then I have fooled you all. I fear that I am riddled with flaws, and there is far more shadow than light in me these days."

She met his gaze again. The wind began to blow from the east, cold and dry. Adaira's hair rose and tangled like a silver net, and Jack could smell the fragrance within its shine. Like lavender and honey.

He thought that he would like to see those shadows in her. Because he felt his own, brimming in his bones and dancing in solitude for far too long.

"Is there somewhere I can speak to you in private?" she asked.

He knew she was referring to the wind. Whatever she had to say to him, she didn't want the breeze to carry her words, and Jack glanced up the hill toward Mirin's cottage. He could take Adaira to his room, but he didn't think that would quite feel right, with Mirin and Frae both in the kitchen. But then he had a better idea, and he motioned for Adaira to follow him up the hill.

He took her to the storehouse, a round, stone building with a thatched roof where Mirin's winter provisions were kept. The space smelled like dust, golden grains, and dried herbs as he and Adaira stood face-to-face in the dim light.

"You've been searching for the lass," Jack said.

Adaira sighed, briefly closing her eyes. "Yes."

"Have there been any signs of where she might have gone?"

"No, Jack."

"I'm worried about Frae," he said before he could swallow the words.

Adaira's expression softened. "As am I. Are you prepared to play tonight, as we originally planned?"

Jack nodded, even though his heart began to pound with anticipation. His dreams from the night before surged in his mind. He stared at Adaira and thought, *I've dreamt of drowning at the spirits' hands, and what if your fate is now twined with mine?*

"What is it?" she whispered in a husky tone.

He wondered what she saw in his eyes before he glanced away, shaking his head. "It's nothing. I'm as ready as I'll ever be, given that I'm more mainlander than islander these days."

Adaira bit her lip. Jack sensed she had a retort to his comment.

"What is it, heiress?"

"You said something to me the other day, Jack," she began. "You said, 'This place was never my home.'"

Jack stifled a groan. He didn't want to talk about this, and he raked his hand through his hair. "Yes. What of it, Adaira?"

She was quiet, studying his face as if she had never seen him before. "Do you truly believe such words? Do you wholeheartedly claim the mainland as your home?"

"I had no choice but to make it my home," he said. "You know this as well as all the others in the clan. My nameless father never claimed me. And I wanted, more than anything, to belong somewhere."

"Did it ever cross your mind that we were waiting for you to return, Jack? Did you ever think of us, and that maybe we longed for you to come back and fill the hall with music again?"

Her words stirred his blood, and that frightened him. He scowled, felt the coldness creep across his face as he regarded her.

"*No*. I never once thought that. I believed the clan was glad to be rid of me."

"Then we have failed you," Adaira said. "And for that, I'm sorry."

Jack shifted his weight. A question was nipping at his thoughts. He didn't want to voice it, but holding it in soon felt unbearable. He asked, "Do you know why your parents sent me to the mainland? Out of all the other children to give this chance to . . . why me?"

"I do. Don't you realize I know all the secrets of the east?"

Jack waited. He didn't want to beg, but Adaira was letting this silence draw out far too long for his liking. "Why then, heiress?"

"I can tell you, Jack. But I will have to take you back in time to do so," she said, tucking strands of hair behind her ear.

Again, she was quiet, watching his impatience rise.

"Then take me back," he requested, tersely.

"I'm sure you remember that night," she began. "The night you and I clashed at a particular thistle patch. The night you chased me across the hills."

"The night you shoved a handful of thistles into my face," he corrected dryly. Of course, they would see this story from different perspectives. But standing so close to Adaira now, breathing in the waning light of a summer evening and listening to the isle's wind howl beyond the door . . . he remembered that night vividly.

Jack had been ten, eager to prove himself worthy of the East Guard. The moon thistle challenge was held every three years, to determine which aspiring recruits knew the lay of the isle, as well as the danger of magical plants.

He had taken the time to scout the hills the day before, to find the perfect patch of moon thistles. And when Torin had blown the horn at midnight, commencing the challenge, Jack had dashed to his secret patch, only to discover that Adaira had beaten him to it. She had harvested nearly all of the thistles and when she broke into a run, he had chased her, thinking they could split them. Instead, Adaira had turned around and shoved the thistles into his face.

The pain had been unbearable. Like fire, trapped beneath his skin. Jack had instantly floundered in the grass, wailing until Torin found him and dragged him home to Mirin. But the worst had yet to come. Moon thistles were enchanted plants. A prick from their needles promised a nightmare later, in sleep. Jack had suffered through thirteen terrible nights after Mirin had drawn all the spindles from his swollen face.

A hint of a smile played over Adaira's countenance. Jack watched the corners of her lips curve.

"I still remember those nightmares you gave me, heiress," he said.

"And you think *you* were the only one bewitched by moon thistles, my old menace?" she countered. "This is the other side of the story you have yet to learn: I ran home, because you gave me no other choice. You ruined my chances of joining the guard. And when I arrived at my bedchamber, I realized my palms gleamed with thistle needles." Adaira held up her hands, studying them as if she still felt the sting. "So many I couldn't count them all, nor could I extract them myself. I went to my mum, because she often remained awake, late into the night. When I showed her my palms, my mum asked me, 'Who did this to you, Adi?' And I told her, 'The lad called Jack.'

"She began to remove them, needle by needle, and she said, 'You mean the lad who becomes quiet when my music floods the hall.' I didn't understand what she meant by that. But on the next full moon feast, I watched you when my mum sat on the dais and began to play her harp. I watched you, but I didn't see anything remarkable within you. Because you were not the only one who became quiet when she played. You were not the only one who hungered for her songs. All of us did. And yet she saw the flame within *you*. A light she had been waiting for. She knew what you would become before you did.

"Not many of us on the isle can wield music; it is its own mistress here, and it chooses who it will love. But my mother saw that mark on your hands, heard the songs you were destined to play before you had encountered your first note. And you can say that you were unclaimed here, but nothing could be further from the truth, John Tamerlaine. When you left for the university, my mother was content. As if she knew you would return a bard when the time was right."

Jack listened to her every word, but he stiffened when Adaira spoke of marks and light, and most of all when she addressed him by his given name, John. He had always hated the name Mirin had blessed his birth with and had soon chosen Jack for himself, refusing to answer to anything else.

"What are you saying to me, Adaira?" he asked, hating the way his voice broke.

"I am saying that my mother chose you as her replacement. She saw you as the future Bard of the East," Adaira said. "She died before she could see you return in your glory, but I know she would proud of you, Jack."

Jack didn't like this, the different angle on his history. He didn't like how Adaira's softly spoken words cut deep like a knife, cracking him open.

"So my future was never my own?" he asked. "There was no choice as to where *I* wanted to reside come the end of my education?"

Adaira flushed in the twilight. "No, of course you have a choice. But can I tempt you, Jack? Can I tempt you to stay with the clan for longer than the summer? Perhaps a full turning of the year? The hall has been quiet for so long now, and we have been trapped in weeks of mourning and sorrow. I think your music would bring us back to life, restore our hope."

She was asking him to let his music trickle through the isle like a stream returning after a long drought. To play on the full moon feasts and at burials and on holy days and at handfastings. To play for the younger generations, such as Frae, who held no knowledge of the old ballads.

Jack didn't know how to respond to her.

His shock must have been evident, because Adaira hastened to add, "You don't have to give me your answer now. Or tomorrow even. But I hope you will consider it, Jack."

"I'll think about it," he said gruffly, as if he never would. Yet his mind raced. He thought of Lorna's music turret, with the bookshelves and the grand harp and the clan music, hidden in a dust-riddled tome. It reminded him of the letter he had seen on the table, addressed to Adaira. "I saw something yesterday, which I need to speak to you about."

"And what did you see, Jack?"

"The Breccans wrote to you. Why?"

She hesitated.

It struck him then that he had no right to know the things in her mind, the plans she was making. To be within her circle. But he felt an ache in his stomach, and while he had no idea where it came from, he realized that he longed to be in the confidence of someone who had walked hours, searching for missing girls. Who had told him her secret plans and trusted him with her late mother's music. Who had given him the chance to become something far greater than he had ever envisioned for himself.

"You sound displeased about this," Adaira said.

"Of course I'm *displeased*!" Jack said, exasperated. "What does our enemy want?"

"Perhaps I wrote to them first."

That brought Jack upright. "Why?"

"If I share the answer with you, I expect that you will keep it secret, for the good of the clan. Do you understand, Jack?"

He held her gaze, thinking of the other secrets they shared. "I may be your favorite old menace, but you know that I won't speak a word of it."

Adaira fell pensive, and he thought she would withhold her answer until she said, "I want to establish a trade between our two clans."

Jack gaped at her for a moment. "A trade?"

"Yes. I have faith that a trade will stave off winter raids, if we can peacefully give the Breccans what they need come the lean months."

Frae's words returned to Jack, her innocent voice echoing through him. *Mum says the Breccans are hungry when winter comes. Can't we just share our food with them?*

"And what will they give us in return?" Jack said. This trade would drain the Tamerlaines if they weren't careful. "We don't need anything of theirs."

"The one thing they have in abundance: enchanted possessions," Adaira replied. "They can weave and forge and create magical craft without consequence. I know it doesn't make sense for us to ask for their charmed blades and plaids if we want peace, but I also know that our people here are suffering for making those things. And I want to see that burden lifted."

She spoke of people like his mum. Like Una.

Jack was quiet, but he dreamt of the same things. He had always hated the way his mother sacrificed her health to make those uncanny plaids. One day she would push herself too far, too hard, and the cough she tried to hide would morph into a claw, ripping her up from within.

Furthermore, if a trade could be established between the two clans, then Jack would no longer have to worry about his mother's croft being raided. This very storehouse that he was standing in, which beckoned a Breccan like low-hanging fruit come winter, could be secure.

Adaira mistook his silence. "You disapprove, bard?"

He frowned at her. "No. I think it's a good idea, Adaira. But I'm worried that the Breccans don't want peace the same way we do, and that they might fool us."

"You sound like Torin."

Jack didn't know if that was meant as a compliment or not. Once, he had wanted to *be* Torin, and Jack almost laughed, thinking about how different he was now. "Your cousin disapproves of your idea?"

"He thinks establishing a trade will be a nightmare," Adaira replied. "The clan line presents the greatest obstacle—do we cross it into their territory, or do we allow them to cross into ours? Either way, Torin says it's 'bound to be something that goes awry and bloody.'"

"He's not wrong, Adaira."

Her brow creased. Jack studied her, watching the thoughts whirl through her. She was parting her lips to say more when they both heard Frae calling for them.

Jack peeked out the solitary window. He could just discern his sister walking in the backyard, shouting their names.

He didn't want Frae to see him and Adaira emerge from the storehouse. He waited until his sister turned to face the river before he opened the door. Adaira slipped out into the evening, with Jack close behind, and they approached the yard gate side by side, as if they had been walking the property.

"Here we are, Frae," Adaira said.

Frae whirled to face them. "It's time for supper," she said, touching the ends of her braids. "I hope you like winkle soup, heiress."

"It's my favorite," Adaira replied, reaching for Frae's hand.

Jack watched as a smile stole across his sister's face. She was awed to be holding the heiress's hand.

Warmed, he followed as Frae led them into the firelight.

Mirin had laid out a lovely spread for Adaira. The best plates and glasses, the oldest wine, and polished silverware that gleamed like dew. They had been cooking most of the day, preparing food for the Mitchell family in their time of grief, and the house was still heated from it, the air holding a trace of berries and the briny scent of the winkles Jack had gathered from the shore at low tide.

Frae had picked fresh flowers and lit the candles, and Jack settled in his customary chair. Adaira took the seat directly across from him. His mother was speaking, filling bowls with the soup, but Jack's mind was distant. He was thinking of all the things Adaira had just said to him. To play for the east. To stay the full turning of the year.

To trade with their enemies.

"I can't believe you're here in our house," Frae said.

Jack's reveries broke as he watched his sister shyly grin at the heiress.

"I know, it's been a very long time since I've visited," said Adaira. "But I remember when you were born, Frae. My da and mum and I came to see you for the first time."

"Did you hold me?"

"I did," Adaira replied. "You were the best bairn I ever held. Most children cry in my arms, but not you."

Mirin began to cough. The sound was deep and wet, and she tried to muffle it behind her palm. Adaira's smile faded, as did Frae's. Jack sat frozen as he watched his mother cough, her thin shoulders shaking.

"Mum?" he stood, fearful.

Mirin calmed and motioned for him to sit. But he saw the flash of blood on her palm, even as she seamlessly wiped it away on the underside of her apron. He had never seen her bleed after a coughing spell, and it chilled him. Her health must have steadily declined in the years he was away.

"I'm fine, Jack," Mirin said, clearing her throat. And then it was as if it had never happened. She took a sip of wine and guided the conversation away to other matters, engaging Adaira. Jack let out a long breath and returned to his chair. But he noticed once again that his mother hardly ate.

After supper, he cleared the table and washed the dishes, insisting that Frae and Mirin entertain Adaira by the hearth. He listened to the women talk as he dunked the plates in the wash barrel. Frae proudly displayed her slingshot to Adaira again before pointing upward and saying, "See all those divots in the rafters overhead? Jack made those."

He thought it was a good time to bring out the pie and set a pot of tea to boil.

"Did they teach you how to serve tea and cook at the university?" Mirin asked with amusement, watching Jack handle the kettle.

"They didn't," he replied, pouring a cup for Frae and Mirin. For Adaira. "But mainland fare is quite dry. So I asked the cook one night if I could use the kitchen after hours, to make my own food for the next day. He agreed, and so I began to cook for myself whenever my lessons gave me a moment to breathe. I remembered everything you taught me, Mum, even though I once disliked cooking. Cream and honey?" he seamlessly asked Adaira as he handed her a cup.

She was sitting on the divan beside Frae. Her fingers

brushed his as she accepted the tea, but her eyes were wide, as if she were battling shock, watching him serve tea. "Just cream," she said. He walked to the buttery in the corner of the kitchen to get the chilled glass of cream, then brought it to her.

"Jack? Jack, the *pie!*" Frae whispered between her fingers.

He winked as he returned to the kitchen for one of the two pies he and Frae had baked together that afternoon. One for them, and one for the Mitchell family. At first it had felt strange to bake for people he didn't know, until he remembered the old ways of the isle. For any event, be it joyful or sorrowful— a death, a marriage, a divorce, a sickness, a birth—the clan rallied and prepared food to express their love for those involved. Cottages became gathering places for hearty, comforting food whenever tears or laughter flowed. Jack had forgotten how much he liked that tradition.

He served Adaira the first slice and grinned when she cast a wary look his way.

"*You* made this?"

"Aye," he said, standing close to her, waiting.

Adaira took her spoon and poked at the pie. "What's in it, Jack?"

"Oh, what all did we dump in there, Frae? Blackberries, strawberries, pimpleberries—"

"*Pimpleberries?*" Frae gasped in alarm. "What's a pim—"

"Honey and butter and a dash of good luck," he finished, his gaze remaining on Adaira. "All of your favorite things, as I recall, heiress."

Adaira stared up at him, her face composed save for her pursed lips. She was trying not to laugh, he realized. He was suddenly flustered.

"Heiress, I did *not* put pimpleberries in there," Frae frantically said.

"Oh, sweet lass, I know you didn't," Adaira said, turning

a smile upon the girl. "Your brother is teasing me. You see, when we were your age, there was a great dinner in the hall one night. And Jack brought me a piece of pie, to say he was sorry for something he had done earlier that day. He looked so con- trite that I foolishly believed him and took a bite, only to realize something tasted very strange about it."

"What was it?" Frae asked, as if she could not imagine Jack doing something so awful.

"He called it a 'pimpleberry,' but it was actually a small skin of ink," Adaira replied. "And it stained my teeth for a week and made me very ill."

"Is this true, Jack?" Mirin cried, setting her teacup down with a clatter.

"'Tis truth," he confessed, and before any of the women could say another word, he took the plate and the spoon from Adaira and ate a piece of the pie. It was delicious, but only because he and Frae had found and harvested the berries and rolled out the dough and talked about swords and books and baby cows while they made it. He swallowed the sweetness and said, "I believe this one is exceptional, thanks to Frae."

Mirin bustled into the kitchen to cut a new slice for Adaira and find her a clean utensil, muttering about how the main- land must have robbed Jack of all manners. But Adaira didn't seem to hear. She took the plate from his hands, as well as the spoon, and ate after him.

He watched her swallow, and when she smiled at Frae, tell- ing his sister it was the best pie she had ever tasted, Jack felt a stab of vulnerability. It disquieted him, and he turned away with a frown and sought refuge in the kitchen. Mirin was there, viciously cutting into the pie.

"I can't believe you did such a thing to the laird's daugh- ter," she murmured, mortified. "People must think I let you run wild!"

The truth was that Adaira had never exposed him as the pimpleberry culprit, and so he had gone unpunished. Mirin had not known, because Alastair and Lorna had not known. Only he and Adaira.

"Go spend time with your company, Mum," he said, carefully taking the knife from her. "And if you're not completely ashamed of who I once was, enjoy a piece of pie."

Mirin sharply exhaled, but she softened as she watched him prepare two plates for her and Frae.

He remained in the kitchen, rewashing a few of the dishes, as if he had overlooked them earlier. But he listened as Adaira and his little sister laughed; he listened as Mirin told a story. This was how isle evenings were spent—gathered by the hearth, sharing lore and tea and laughter.

Eventually, he couldn't continue feigning there were dishes to be washed without attracting suspicion, and he turned to scrubbing the tabletop clean.

"Jack?" Frae suddenly cried. "You should play your harp for Adaira!"

He hesitated before looking at Adaira, only to find her gaze was already fixed on him.

"That's a lovely idea, Frae," she said. "But I should return home before the moon rises." She stood and thanked Mirin for supper and Frae for the pie. "I'll return soon for another slice," Adaira promised, and Frae blushed with pride.

"I'll walk you out," Jack said. He opened the door and stepped into the peace of the kail yard. The night was cool. He drank the moment of silence before Adaira joined him.

They walked to the gate, where her horse was tethered. Adaira turned to face him, and he noticed how exhausted she suddenly appeared in the starlight, as if she had been holding a mask over her face the entire evening.

"Midnight?" she said.

"Yes," he replied. "At Kelpie Rock, which I vividly remember how to find."

Adaira smiled before passing through the gate to mount her horse.

Jack stood among the herbs and watched her ride away, until she melted into the shadows of night. He stared into the dark space between the stars, measuring the moon. He had a few more hours until midnight. A few more hours until he played for the folk of the tides.

He returned inside. He asked Mirin to tell him a story of the sea.

"Another one!" Maisie said.

Sidra's eyes were heavy. She was lying in bed beneath the quilts, reading aloud by candlelight. Maisie wiggled closer to her side as Sidra yawned, attempting to close the tattered book Torin had brought home from Graeme's.

"I think it's time for bed, Maisie."

"No, another story!"

Sometimes Maisie had Torin's temperament. Orders flew out of her mouth, and Sidra had learned it was best to respond in a gentle way. She stroked Maisie's honey brown curls.

"There will always be time tomorrow," she said.

Maisie's face wrinkled, and she turned her head, fixing sad, imploring eyes on Sidra. "Just one more, Sidra. Please?"

Sidra sighed. "Very well. Just *one* more, and then I'm blowing the candle out."

Maisie smiled and settled down again, her head propped on Sidra's shoulder.

Sidra turned the page carefully. The spine of the book was weak; a few leaves were loose and smudged.

"That one!" Maisie said, her finger striking the page.

"Careful, Maisie. This is an old book." But Sidra's eyes were drawn to the same story. Flowers, a few illuminated with gold ink, illustrated the edges of the text.

"Long ago, it was a hot summer day on the isle," Sidra began. "Lady Whin of the Wildflowers walked the hills, searching for one of her sisters, Orenna. Now, Orenna was known to be one of the stealthiest of the earth spirits. She liked to grow her crimson flowers in the most unlikely of places—on hearthstones, in riverbeds, on the high, windy slopes of Tilting Thom—because she liked to eavesdrop on the other spirits, the fire, the water, and the wind. Sometimes she would glean their secrets and share them with her kind, with the alder maidens and the rock families and the elegant bracken of the vales.

"Whin and the Earie Stone had learned of her ways, and after receiving complaints from water and fire and threats from wind, they decided that Orenna must be approached. So Whin found her sister, who was coaxing flowers to bloom along the chimney of a mortal house.

"'You've angered the fire with your stealthy ways,' Whin explained. 'As well as the wind and the water, and we must maintain peace with our brethren.'

"Orenna appeared shocked. 'I only give my beauty to places that need it, such as this drab chimney.'

"'You are free to bloom in the grass on the hillsides, in the gardens of mortal kind, and among the bracken,' Whin said. 'But you must leave these other places alone and let the fire and the water and the wind tend to them.'

"Orenna nodded, but she didn't like to take correction from Whin, or the Earie Stone. The next day she grew her flowers on the highest summit of the isle, Tilting Thom. And while the mountain is still a subject of the earth, the wind commands that place with a mighty breath. The wind soon learned of her eyes in the cleft of the rock, how she watched their wings blow north and south, east and west. How she stole their secrets. They threatened to bring the mountain down, and Whin once again had to seek her sister.

"She found Orenna by the coast, coaxing flowers to grow at the bottom of gleaming eddies.

"'I have told you once, now twice,' Whin began. 'You can bloom amid the grass of the hillsides, in the gardens of mortal kind, and in the bracken, but nowhere else, sister. Your stealthy ways are causing strife.'"

"Orenna was full of pride. She was also full of knowledge now, having watched the ways of the other spirits. She knew Whin was crowned among the wildflowers, but Orenna thought she could rule better than her sister.

"'You are simply weak, Whin. And the other spirits know they can command you.'

"Well, the wind knew better, and carried those haughty words of Orenna's to the Earie Stone, the oldest and wisest of all the folk. He was incandescently angry at Orenna, and he called her to him. She had no choice but to obey, and she knelt when the Earie Stone looked at her.

"'You have chosen again and again to disrespect the other spirits, and so I have no other choice but to discipline you, Orenna. From hence onward, you will only grow in dry, heart-sick ground where the water may deny you, the fire may destroy you, and the wind can make you bend to its might. In order to bloom, you will have to give your life source; you will have to cut your finger on a thorn, and let your golden ichor flow like sap, down to the ground. And last of all, the mortal kind of the isle will learn your secrets by consuming your petals. This is your punishment, which may last as short as a day should you truly repent, or an eternity should your heart turn hard and cold.'

"Orenna was furious at the Earie Stone's justice. She thought herself strong enough to resist his verdict, but she soon discovered that her flowers could no longer bloom where she willed. Even the lush grass, who had always welcomed her, couldn't give her space to blossom, and she had to search the entirety of the isle to find a small patch of dry, heartsick ground in a graveyard. Even then, she couldn't bloom, not until she pricked her finger on a thorn and her blood ran, slow, thick, and golden, down to the earth.

"She bloomed, but she was much smaller than before. She was vulnerable, she realized, and the other spirits denied her company. Sad and lonely, she called to a mortal girl who was picking wildflowers one day. The girl was delighted, but soon ate the flowers and learned all of Orenna's secrets, just as the Earie Stone had foretold.

"Defiant, Orenna never repented but carved a life for herself in the ground she was given. She's still there to this day, if you are fortunate or misfortunate enough to find her."

Sidra fell quiet, reaching the end. Maisie had fallen asleep, and Sidra carefully slipped from the bed, tucking the blankets around her daughter. She carried Graeme's book and a rushlight into the kitchen and stood at the table. She had left all of her herbs and supplies out. Jars, salts, honey, vinegar, and an array of dried herbs. The two red flowers Torin had brought her were still where she had left them. They hadn't wilted, which foretold their magical essence, just like a moon thistle, and Sidra studied them in the firelight, occasionally glancing back over the legend.

She had encountered plenty of graveyards before, although she had never seen small, crimson flowers blooming amid the headstones. And if the Orenna flower couldn't bloom freely in the grass, then these two blossoms must have been dropped in the place where Catriona had vanished. Something or someone had been carrying them, perhaps to ingest the petals.

She would have to tell Torin about it at first light.

But she wondered . . . what would happen if she swallowed one?

Sidra wasn't sure, and she returned to bed with a shiver.

CHAPTER 8

Adaira was waiting for Jack on the shore. The air was cold, but the moonlight was generous, guiding him down the rocky path to meet her on the coast, his harp tucked beneath his arm. She was pacing on the sand— the only indication that she was anxious—and she had braided her hair, to keep the wind from toying with it. He couldn't discern her expression until he was almost upon her.

"Are you ready?" she asked.

He nodded despite the worry that nagged him. He drew his harp from its skin and settled on a damp rock. A small crab scuttled between his boots, and a few dead jellyfish lay scattered like purple blossoms. He positioned his harp on his lap, propping it against his left shoulder, just above his swift-beating heart. From the corner of his eye, he could see Adaira standing tall and rigid. The starlight illuminated her.

She doesn't seem real, but neither does this moment, Jack thought, with a tremor in his hands. He was about to play Lorna's ballad and draw forth the spirits of the sea. And it almost felt as if the ground beneath him quaked, just slightly, and as if the tide grew softer as its foam reached for his boots. As if the wind caressed his face, and even the reflection of the moon gleamed a little brighter in the rock pools. All of it—air and water and earth and fire—seemed expectant and waiting for him to worship them.

Jack played a scale on his harp, his fingers stiff at first. A memory rose, unbidden, a memory made on the mainland. He had been sitting in an alcove of the Bardic University with Gwyn, his first love, at his side watching his every move, her hair tickling his arm and smelling of roses. She had been scolding him for creating such sad songs, and he didn't tell her that he felt the most alive when he played for sorrow. Now it was strange how that moment felt old and bleached by the sun, as if it had happened in the life of another man, not Jack Tamerlaine's.

Knowing he couldn't play this strange music with such reservations and distractions, he strove to find a calming place within himself. To remember and fall back into a time when he was a boy and Cadence was all he had known. When he had loved the sea and the hills and the mountains, the caves and the heather and the rivers. A time when he had yearned to behold a spirit, face-to-face.

His fingers grew nimble, and Lorna's notes began to trickle into the air, metallic beneath his nails. He could hardly contain the splendor of them anymore, and he played and felt as if he were not flesh and blood and bone but made by the sea foam, as if he had emerged one night from the ocean, from all the haunted deep places where man had never roamed but where spirits glided and drank and moved like breath.

He sang up the spirits of the sea, the timeless beings that belonged to the cold depths. He sang them up to the surface, to the moonlight, with Lorna's ballad. He watched the tide cease, just as it had done the night when he returned to Cadence. He watched eyes gleam from beneath the water like golden coins; he watched webbed fingers and toes drift beneath the shallow ripples. The spirits manifested into their physical forms; they came with barbed fins and tentacles, with hair like spilled ink, with gills and iridescent scales and endless rows of teeth. They rose from the water and gathered close about him, as if he had called them home.

Jack saw Adaira take a step closer to him, her fear like a net. He almost missed a note; she was dividing his attention, even though she was a glimmer at the corner of his eye. She took another step closer, as if she thought he would be swept away, and he turned his head slightly to keep her in his sight. Because she was his only reminder that he was mortal and man, no matter what this music made him feel, that he wasn't a creature of the waters . . . as he suddenly yearned to be.

Adaira, he wanted to say to her, interjecting her name between the notes her mother had woven and spun. *Adaira* . . .

The spirits felt his attention shift from them to her. The woman with hair like moonlight, the woman made of sharp beauty.

Now that they beheld her, they seemed unable to forget her. Not even Jack's music could draw their attention away, and his heart began to falter.

"It is her," one of the spirits said in a waterlogged voice. "It is, it is *her.*"

They must think Adaira is Lorna, Jack thought. He was nearly to the last stanza, his hands were trembling, and his voice had turned ragged on the edges. How long had he been playing? The moon was lower, and the spirits refused to remove their scrutiny from Adaira.

Look at me, his fingers played between the notes he plucked. *Give your attention to me.*

Instantly, all the glimmering eyes returned to him. Ah, yes, they seemed to say. The mortal man still plays for us. They listened and softened once more as Jack crooned at them. All of the spirits in their manifest forms adored him.

Save for one.

It was the one spirit out of the dripping horde whose form most resembled a human woman. She stood thin and reedy on two legs in the heart of the gathering, the water lapping at her barnacled knees. Her skin was pale with a sheen of pearl, and her hair, like kelp, fell long and thick to clothe her body. Her face was angular, but she had an upturned nose, a mouth like a hook, and two eyes that were iridescent as oyster shells. She held a fishing spear in one hand, and her fingernails were long and black. She could almost pass for a human. But there were elements of her that exposed her as a spirit. Gills fluttered in her neck, and patches of golden scales adorned her skin. Traces of her magic that she couldn't disguise.

It was Lady Ream of the Sea. The one who had threatened to sink the fisherman's boat, who had darted past Jack and laughed with the tide when he had swum to the shore.

Jack studied the spirit, marveling, but Ream paid him no heed. She stared at Adaira.

The song reached its end.

For a moment, all was silent. The spirits wanted more; he could sense it. And yet he felt empty, sucked dry to his bones.

"Why have you summoned us?" Ream asked Adaira. Her voice was muted, warbled. It would sound clear and crisp beneath the water, Jack suspected. "Do you seek to ensnare and bind us with the mortal man's song?"

"No," Adaira said. "I seek your wisdom and insight, Lady of the Sea."

"About a mortal matter, I presume?"

"Yes."

Jack didn't move as he listened to Adaira describe the troubling events. She spoke of the missing children and told Ream there was no trace of where the girls might be, if they still lived. She spoke of the third girl who had vanished the day before after playing on the shore with her siblings. There was no suspicion in her voice, nothing that betrayed Adaira's belief that the folk of the tides were at fault.

"And what do we have to do with mortal children?" Ream questioned. "Your lives on land are far more amusing to us than beneath the water in our domain, where your skin prunes and you must remain in a bubble to survive."

So they *had* held mortals below at some point, Jack thought with a flash of alarm.

Adaira took a step closer to the water, unafraid. She held out her palms and said, "You dwell in the sea, a vast place that surrounds our isle. Have you seen nothing then? Did you not witness Annabel Ranald and Eliza Elliott disappearing? Did you not see Catriona Mitchell walk along the coast yesterday?"

The spirits began to exchange glances with one another. A few of them grumbled and shifted in the water, but no one answered. They waited for Ream to speak for them.

"If we saw or did anything, heiress, we cannot speak of it."

"Why is that?" Adaira's voice was cold. Her anger was rising.

"Because our mouths have been sealed from speaking truth," Ream replied, and her words were even more blurred than before, as if her tongue were caught. "You will have to seek your answers from those who are higher than us."

Jack rose, stiffly. At last, he drew the gaze of Ream, and she looked at him with her iridescent eyes.

"Who is higher than you?" he asked. He didn't know there was a hierarchy among the spirits. His mind began to spin, wondering how he could summon anything else from the water.

"Look around and above you, bard," Ream said to him. "We

are only greater than fire." She set her gaze on Adaira again and struggled to say, "Beware, mortal woman. Beware of blood in the water."

The spirits hissed in agreement, and the tide returned with vengeance. The ocean rushed forward, the tide pushing the waves far higher than it had before, and the spirits melted into the foam. Jack had no time to move, to reach for Adaira, as the waves swallowed them whole.

It's happening, he thought, clutching his harp, as he frantically kicked to find the surface. *The spirits are going to drown us.*

He felt fingers in his hair, a painful yank. He opened his eyes, expecting to dimly see Ream smiling with her pinprick cache of teeth, ready to drown him. But it was only Adaira. She took hold of his arm and guided him up to the surface.

As they clambered up the Kelpie Rock, they had to fight the draw of the tide before the waves pulled them both under again. It was a narrow, uncomfortable rock; they had no choice but to sit back to back, shivering from the cold, and wait for the tide to recede.

Jack remained silent as he picked threads of algae from his harp strings. But he was inwardly overcome, astounded at what he and Adaira had done. At the power of Lorna's ballad to summon all the spirits of the sea—the folk he had once heard about in the legends of his childhood. Faceless phantoms and mystical beings that rarely revealed themselves to mortals . . . he and Adaira had just *beheld* them. Conversed with them.

Summoned them.

He struggled to hold his rapture in check, but Adaira laughed and Jack couldn't resist smiling.

"I can't believe we just did that," she said. "You, actually. Not me. I did nothing but stand there."

"You spoke with them," Jack argued. "Something I could hardly find the wits to do."

"Aye. But still . . . it was different from what I expected." She shuddered, as if struck with both horror and excitement. "You did well, bard."

Jack snorted, but her compliment seeped into him. He was about to reply when he felt a strange ache in his head, just behind his eyes. He closed them, pressed the heel of his palm to his throbbing lids. The pain flickered like lightning, coursing down his arms to his fingertips. He gritted his teeth against it and hoped Adaira couldn't hear him gasp as the discomfort found a resting place in his bones.

He tried to breathe, deep and slow, but his nose was dripping now.

He touched the bow of his lips; his fingers came away with a dark, wet stain. His nose was bleeding, and his hand trembled as he pressed a corner of his wet plaid to it, hoping to staunch the flow.

"Jack? Did you hear me?" Adaira was saying.

"Mm." He suddenly didn't want her to know. He didn't want her to know he was in agony, that he was bleeding. But the truth hit him like an axe: playing for the spirits required him to spin magic with his craft. It was devastating to realize this was how his mother felt after completing an enchanted plaid.

"She made it sound as if the spirits want nothing to do with our children in their realm," Adaira was saying. "But I struggle to believe such a claim."

"Then we must ask ourselves what mortal children can do for them in the world beyond ours," Jack said. "Surely the spirits have uses for us, even if it is only to entertain them."

"Yes," Adaira said in a distant tone. "What do you think Ream meant about others being higher than them?"

Jack swallowed. He could taste a clot of blood, and he cleared his throat. "Who can guess? We should have known the spirits wouldn't speak plainly." As if they heard him, a wave broke hard on the rock and splashed him in the face. "Thank you for that," he muttered, irritated.

The bleeding was easing. So was the strain behind his eyes, but the pain lingered in his hands. He flexed his stiff fingers, full of worry.

Adaira herself was lost in thought. Eventually, she said, "I think she meant that the spirits of earth and air are above the water. I never realized that."

"Neither did I."

Adaira fell quiet. Her back was still pressed against his, and he felt her draw a deep breath.

"Jack? Could you play my mum's ballad to summon the spirits of the earth?"

He went rigid. "Your mum composed a ballad for earth?"

"Yes."

"And what of fire and wind?"

"She never composed music for them. At least, not to mine or my father's knowledge."

Jack was silent. He stared at the foaming water surrounding them, at the harp in his hands, at the bloodstain on his plaid. He didn't know how to tell Adaira what he was feeling—about his overwhelming sense of wonder, fear, intensity, and agony. To play for the spirits, to have been found worthy. To sense the power that hid in his hands and his voice. Even now, the lingering heat of magic still coursed through him.

It was a dangerous feeling. He wondered how quickly his vitality would wane.

It was also apparent that Alastair had failed to inform Adaira of the cost. Or perhaps Adaira simply didn't know. She didn't know her mother's health had been stolen, bit by bit, every time she played for the folk. Lorna's untimely death had come from an accident five years ago. A fall from a horse, not a

slow wasting sickness fueled by wielding magic. But her fate—
had she lived out her years singing for the spirits—now hung
like a constellation in the sky, and Jack could read it clearly.

To be the Bard of the East was an honor, but it came with
a terrible cost. And Jack didn't know if he was strong enough
to pay it.

"The folk have to know where the lasses are, which spirit is
offended and hiding them," Adaira said, speaking her thoughts
aloud. "They see nearly everything. The answers must rest with
them. And if the water spirits have had their mouths sealed
from speaking truth . . . we need to summon and speak to the
others. But what do you think?"

"I think that's our next step," Jack agreed. He didn't say out
loud what he and Adaira had both realized, although he knew
she was thinking it too. If the earth spirits couldn't help them,
he would have to compose a ballad for wind. He had no idea
what that would do to him. "I'll need time to study your mum's
music."

I'll need time to recover from this.

"Come to the castle later today," she said. "And I will give
it to you."

They sat in companionable silence for a while longer on
the rock, until the moon had started to set and the tides had
calmed.

Adaira eventually slipped into the water and swam around
the rock to look up at him. "Are you going to sit there all night,
bard?"

He tensed, hearing the mirth in her voice. "I don't think
it's wise to swim in the sea at night." He nearly added that this
was not just a mainland opinion, for the ocean was never safe.
But Jack suppressed those words, thinking Adaira would wield
anything mainland against him.

"So do you plan to sit there all night?" she asked.

"Until the tide goes down, yes," said Jack.

"Which is at *dawn*, you know."

He ignored her and the taunting invitation to join her in the water, holding his harp close. His gaze wandered up to the sky, seeking to read the time. But from the corner of his eye, he watched her as she continued to bob in the waves, waiting for him. And then she was gone, vanishing beneath the dark surface. Jack's full attention returned to where she had been wading.

He waited for her to resurface, watching the mesmerizing roll of the sea. But Adaira remained beneath the water, and Jack panicked.

"Adaira," he called to her, but the wind stole her name right from his mouth. *"Adaira!"*

There was no answer, no sign of her anywhere. Soon, his eyes ached from peeling the darkness and from the glimmer of waves. Half of him knew she was toying with him, but half of him was terrified a spirit had come to claim her and was holding her down beneath the surface.

He jumped into the water, one arm holding the instrument tight to his chest, the other searching frantically for her. His hand cut through the cold whirl of the tide. He knew as soon as their fingers entwined that she had been waiting for him, lurking like a patient predator. She had known he would come after her, and as he broke the surface with her, he was relieved and angry and a tiny bit amused.

He said nothing at first. The water dripped from his hair, and he glared when she smiled, when she laughed. His traitorous heart skipped at the sound.

"Go on," he said. "Take delight in my surrender."

"You should be *thanking* me. I just saved you from a long night perched on a rock." She slipped her fingers from his and splashed him in the face as she swam away.

Jack reached to snag her ankle, but Adaira evaded him. He couldn't catch her. She swam just ahead of him, leading him to the coastal path. After a moment, she turned to glide backwards, beholding his face.

"You've grown slow in the water, Jack."

He said nothing, because the music for the spirits had drained him. Let her blame his weak swimming on the mainland.

He followed her to where the path cut up through the rocks. Adaira pulled herself from the sea, elegant despite her drenched clothes. Jack remained in the water, waiting for her to turn and look at him.

He extended his hand; he didn't know if he was strong enough to climb out without her assistance. "Are you going to help me up?"

Adaira unwound her matted braid and laughed again. "Do you think I was born yesterday?"

She gave him a terrible idea. He almost smiled.

"Then will you at least take my harp? It's going to warp now, after all this time in the water." He held up his instrument, and Adaira studied it. Jack concealed his glee as she reached forward to take hold of his harp.

As soon as her fingers closed over the frame, he pulled. Adaira let out a shriek as she tumbled into the sea, just over his head. He couldn't resist it; a broad grin spread across his face as Adaira spluttered to the surface.

"You will soon pay for that," she said, wiping the water from her eyes. "Old *menace*."

"I have no doubt," he replied in a droll tone. "What will it be, heiress? Tar and feathers? The stocks? My firstborn son?"

She stared at him a moment, pearls of water on her long lashes. The sea lapped at their shoulders, and Jack could feel her fingers brush his as they both waded in the roll of the waves.

"I can think of something far worse." But she smiled when she said it, and he had never seen such a smile on her face before. Or maybe he had once, long ago when they were children.

She was making him remember those old days. Days spent in the sea and the caves. Nights spent roaming the wild places, the thistle patches and the glens and the rocks on the coast. She was making him remember what it felt like to belong on the isle. To belong to the east.

She wanted him to stay and play for their clan, and Jack was beginning to think that maybe he should seize that opportunity, even if it stole his health, song by song.

Just for a year. A full passing of seasons. Long enough to see her rise as laird.

He drew a tendril of golden algae from her hair and begrudgingly acknowledged it then.

He disliked her a little less than he had yesterday.

And that could only bring him trouble.

CHAPTER 9

Sidra dreamt she walked the shores of Cadence. In the beginning, Maisie was at her side, and then the little lass turned into a fish and leapt into the sea and Sidra was alone, standing on blood-soaked sand. She was worried about Maisie until she saw Donella in the distance. It surprised her at first. Torin's first wife had never appeared in her dreams, but Sidra waved as Donella Tamerlaine strode to her, dressed in armor and draped in the brown and red plaid of the guard.

"Donella? Why are you here?" Sidra asked, and her heart betrayed her. It began to hammer as she wondered if Donella had returned to take Torin and Maisie back.

"Sidra? Sidra, wake up," Donella said urgently. The sand crushed beneath her boots and she reached for Sidra's arm, to shake her. "This is a dream. Awaken."

Donella had never touched her before. The ghost's hand felt like ice on her arm, and Sidra gasped and woke.

Her pulse was thick in her throat.

Gradually, Sidra's awareness sharpened. The cottage was

dark with night and quiet save for the howl of the wind. She was lying in bed, and Maisie was snoring, curled up close beside her. She was exhausted after a long, strange day.

But her arm . . . it ached. Sidra rubbed it, noticing that Donella's ghost was in the room with her, hovering at the bedside, transparent like a stream of moonlight.

"Donella?"

"Make haste, Sidra," the ghost spoke. Her voice was not nearly as strong as it had been in the dream. In reality, it was delicate, like a fading note of music. "He's coming for her."

"Who?" Sidra rasped.

"Rise and go to Torin's oaken chest. At the very bottom, you will find a small dirk," Donella said, motioning for Sidra to hurry. "I had this blade forged for Maisie before I died. Take it in your hand and run with her to Graeme's croft. Hurry, hurry. He's coming, Sidra."

Donella surrendered to the moonlight on the floor, and Sidra wondered if she was still dreaming. But she did as the ghost had instructed. She slid from the bed and rushed into the next chamber, kneeling before Torin's oaken chest. Her fingers were slow from sleep, but she searched through his clothes and the juniper boughs until she found the dirk Donella had spoken of, snug in a leather sheath and hiding at the very bottom.

One of Una's creations.

Sidra took the hilt in her hand and hurried back into her bedroom, bare feet slapping on the floor. The wind had fallen quiet; its absence made her skin prickle as she gathered Maisie into her arms. There was no time to slip on stockings or boots or to wrap her and Maisie in a cloak. Sidra could hear the lock of the front door turning as she carried Maisie out the back.

"Sidra?" Maisie mumbled, rubbing her eyes. "Where are we going?"

"We are going to visit Grandda," Sidra whispered as she

carried the lass through the yard, trying to be as quiet as possible.

"But why?" Maisie asked loudly.

"Shh. Hold tight to me." She found the path to Graeme's cottage in the moonlight. It wound up the knoll, knee deep in heather, and Sidra began to run, even though her legs were trembling. She pressed Maisie's objections to her chest, sparing a frantic glance over her shoulder.

Something stood in her yard. It was a shadow, tall and built like a man. It tilted its head; she could feel it looking at her.

Terror turned Sidra's blood to ice as the shadow began to pursue her, impossibly swift. She struggled to breathe, to rush up the hill carrying a child in her arms. But she knew she wouldn't be able to outrun the darkness.

"Maisie? Listen to me. I want you to run straight to Grandda's door and knock as hard as you can on it. Wait for him to answer. I'll be right behind you." Sidra's chest smoldered as she set Maisie on the ground. "Remember how we like to play chase? I'm it, so you must run as fast as you can and don't look back. Go now!"

For once in her life, Maisie didn't object. The girl took off running up the hill, and Sidra stood and held her ground. She unsheathed the dirk and turned to meet the spirit.

It slowed when it realized Sidra was waiting with a flash of steel in her hand.

"Who are you? What do you want?" Her voice wavered.

The shadow came to a halt, a few paces away. She realized it was wearing a hood. Its cloak snapped in the sudden gust. "The captain's daughter. Give her to me and I won't harm you."

The voice was pitched deep and smooth. Her eyes strained in the darkness, eager to catch a glimpse of its face.

"You'll have to kill me first."

There was a low flicker of laughter. But Sidra wasn't afraid.

She stood resolute on the path, barefoot, wearing nothing but her chemise, a small dagger in her hand. The moment the shadow lunged to take her to the ground, Sidra hissed and stabbed.

It anticipated her movements, blocking with its forearm, solid as flesh.

Before Sidra could respond, the shadow backhanded her. The pain was sharp; her neck snapped, and she struggled to remain upright.

She stumbled but regained her balance just in time to see it was heading up the trail, pursuing Maisie. Sidra chased it, her ears ringing. She lunged and aimed, stabbing the shadow in the back.

She heard the cloak rip. She felt the blade puncture skin. She watched the world unspool as the spirit spun, looming over her.

"You *bitch*," it hissed.

She was raising her hand to strike again, the dirk catching the stars when she felt the kick to her chest. The shadow's boot struck her on the sternum so hard that she couldn't breathe. She collapsed and rolled in the heather. Her hands were numb as they dropped the dirk, scrambling for purchase.

She eventually came to a stop, gasping for breath. The pain was bright; she saw spots, eating the edges of her vision.

She had to get up. She had to find Maisie.

Sidra wheezed and tried to rise. She didn't know how much time had passed, because it felt as if everything had stopped around her. The wind, the moon's descent. Her own heart.

The shadow arrived, standing over her. She heard a whimper and her gaze snapped up. Maisie was in its arms, struggling.

"*Maisie*," Sidra rasped.

She held out her hand, willing to give anything. But she

never had the chance to speak. She felt a blow to the side of her head.

She folded into the darkness.

When Sidra woke facedown in the heather, she thought she was dreaming. The sun was just about to rise; it was bitterly cold, but the eastern horizon was swelling with light. A bird was trilling nearby, as if urging her to open her eyes. To get up.

She slowly pushed herself up to her knees. Her chest ached. There was blood dried on the front of her chemise, and she stared at it, her mind reeling as she tried to remember.

And then it hit her. The realization struck her harder than the spirit's boot to her chest.

"Maisie!" she screamed, her voice hoarse. *"Maisie!"*

She stumbled to her feet. The world spun for a moment— melting stars and a vermilion sunrise and the flap of a bird's wings.

"Maisie!" She began to tear through the heather. Her hands were so cold she could hardly feel them. "Maisie, answer me! Where are you? *Maisie!*"

Where had the spirit taken her?

She swallowed a sob as she frantically searched.

"Sidra? *Sidra!*"

She heard Graeme shouting for her in the distance. She winced as her chest throbbed, and she glanced up to dimly see Torin's father appear at the crest of the hill.

Overcome, she couldn't speak. Graeme hadn't left his house or his yard in all the years that Sidra had known him, and the emotion caught in her throat as he began to run down the hill.

"Sidra!" Graeme saw her. "Sidra, is that you? Are you all right, lass?"

"Da, I . . ." She didn't know what to say. Her blood was still pounding when Graeme finally reached her. She must have appeared far worse than she realized, because Graeme's face tensed. His eyes went wide as he looked at her.

"Daughter," he whispered. "What happened?"

"A spirit took Maisie," she said, struggling to keep her hysteria at bay.

His mouth went slack. "A *spirit* did this to you?"

"A spirit came for her, and I fought it, and it took her . . . we have to keep searching. She might still be here . . ." Sidra returned to the heather, even though every movement, every breath was like a knife in her chest.

"Maisie!" she shouted, over and over, seeking a trail, a spirit door, a scrap of clothing. Anything that would guide her.

Graeme firmly took her arm, drawing her close. "Sidra? Where are you wounded? We need to tend to you first, lass."

Sidra paused. She didn't realize how badly she was trembling or how cold she was until she felt his warmth and his strength. She frowned, struggling to understand why Graeme was staring at her with such stricken eyes until she glanced down, remembering the blood that stained her chemise. It had dried to a dark hue, crinkling the wool, but it was red as the blood in her veins.

"I'm not wounded," she whispered. "This . . . this isn't my blood. I struck the spirit with a dirk, and it bled."

Sidra met Graeme's gaze. She thought of the story she had read to Maisie, the night before. A story about Orenna having to prick her finger in order to bloom. How her blood ran thick and gold.

"The spirits . . ." Sidra began, but her voice faded.

Graeme read her thoughts, granting her a somber nod. "Don't bleed as mortals do."

Sidra stared at the bloodstains again. She felt as if the world had just cracked beneath her feet.

It wasn't a spirit stealing the girls.

It was a man.

"Sidra," Graeme rasped, still holding her arm, "we need to call for Torin."

Sidra's heart plummeted. The mere thought of telling Torin what had transpired . . . she felt like weeping. *This* was what he had married her for. *This* was woven into her vows to him. She had promised to raise, love, and protect his daughter.

She had failed him and failed Maisie. She had even failed Donella.

Sidra wavered for a moment, but the truth was beginning to eclipse the numbness of her thoughts. It hadn't been a spirit who had taken Maisie, but a man, moving with impossible speed and stealth. She didn't fully understand it, but she felt how precious time was.

"All right," Sidra whispered. "I'll call to him."

Graeme was quiet, waiting. His hand fell away from her as she took a step deeper into the heather.

The sun had risen. A mist was creeping over the land. A bird continued to sing in the shadows.

Sidra fell to her knees.

Her voice broke as she spoke his name into the southern wind.

"Torin."

PART TWO

A Song
for Earth

~~~~~~~~~~~~~~~~~~~~~~~~~~~~~~~~~~

A daira stood in her bedchamber before the window, watching the sun rise. Her hair was still damp from the sea, and her fingers were pruned from treading the waves with Jack. She wore nothing but a robe, and she shivered beneath its softness, remembering the way the spirits had stared at her, as if they were hungry.

She turned away from her reflection in the glass and walked to where her bath waited by the hearth, disrobing along the way. She stepped into the water, which was lukewarm, but sometimes the cold didn't bother her.

Sometimes she craved the icy embrace of winter.

She watched the ripples form around her as she settled, leaning against the copper tub. She thought about what the folk had said to her, and she remembered the way Jack's voice had melded with the music her mother had written years ago. Her chest ached, and she didn't know if it was from grief at hearing Lorna's music reborn or if it was frustration. Adaira had believed the spirits of the sea could help her find the girls. She had hoped to bring an end to this madness and the misery of vanished children.

But the truth was that she was nowhere closer to solving the mystery. In fact, her mind was only more scrambled now.

She covered her face with her hands and pressed her fingertips into her closed eyes, exhausted.

It is her, the folk of the tides had said. Even now, their voices echoed through her hollowness.

No, Adaira should have said to them. *No, I am nothing like my mum.*

Beware of blood in the water, mortal woman.

She let her hands drift away and opened her eyes, gazing at the water that embraced her. She thought of Jack again, of how he had come after her despite his own fear of the night sea. He had looked so angry breaking the surface with her—for some odd reason he had reminded Adaira of a cat that had been dunked in a rain barrel. But he had also looked content the longer he beheld her, as if he had finally remembered who he was. That he was isle born. And Adaira had done the most ridiculous thing. She had laughed, and it had felt like birds taking flight within her.

She stared at her wavering reflection in the bath and wondered what it would take to provoke a stoic man such as Jack Tamerlaine to laugh with her.

"Enough," she whispered to herself, reaching for the sponge and a bar of soap. She began to scrub her skin, but it did nothing to the memories she wanted to keep at bay.

The last time she had swum in isle waters had been with Callan Craig, years ago. She had been eighteen, searching for something to fill her loneliness. That keen, endless loneliness was magnified by her mother's recent passing, and Adaira found a remedy for those feelings in Callan.

She had been smitten with him and spent many stolen

hours with him sparring on castle grounds, riding the hills, tangled in bedsheets. Adaira winced when she thought about how naïve she had been, how eager and trusting. After their relationship ended, she hoped that time would dull the heartache, but it flared every now and then, like old bones in wintertime.

She cast off those painful memories and plunged beneath the water, holding her breath. The world was quiet here, and yet she could still hear Jack's music and voice as he sang. She wanted to sit and listen to him play for hours. She wanted to see the hall restored, the clan brought together by music.

She wanted Jack to be the one to do it.

It was strange how much time away had changed him. Adaira had first noticed two things about him: how deep and rich his voice was now, and how beautiful his hands were. But his grumpy disposition was the same. As were his many frowns.

She had hated him as a lass. But she was coming to learn that it was hard to hate what made her feel the most alive.

She rose from the water and dressed, then made her way to the bureau where her brush and mirror waited. A letter caught her eye. Its corner was tucked beneath a jar of moon thistles, and the parchment was crinkled, as though it had been carelessly handled.

It was also marked by the western seal.

Moray Breccan had written to her again. She almost hesitated to open it.

On the day Adaira had forged a letter to Jack, she had also sent a letter to the heir of the Breccan clan, expressing her desire to discuss the possibility of a trade. Moray had quickly replied and, to Adaira's surprise, had been well spoken and enthusiastic about her idea.

It seemed that peace might be attainable after centuries of strife, and Adaira was hopeful. She was tired of the raids, tired of the fear that laced the cold days in the east. She dreamt of a different isle, and if the Breccans wouldn't initiate it, she would.

Her father had been furious.

She could still remember how Alastair had railed at her, claiming it was foolish to open their storehouses for the Breccans. To begin a relationship with the clan that wanted nothing more than to harm them.

"I know you have raised me to never trust the western clan," she had replied. "For us to be self-sufficient. The history of raids alone is enough to make me despise the Breccans. But I confess that the hatred has worn me down—it has made me feel old and brittle, as if I have lived a thousand years—and I want to find another way. Have you never dreamt of peace, Da? Have you ever envisioned an isle that is united again?"

"Of course I have dreamt of it."

"Then is this not the first step toward such an ideal?"

Alastair had fallen silent. He refused to meet her gaze when he replied, "They have nothing we need, Adi. A trade, as much as you want to believe it will stave off winter raids, will not end them. The Breccans are a bloodthirsty lot."

She didn't agree. But he had grown so feeble over the past two years that Adaira had let the argument fade, worried it would overtax him.

Torin had responded in a similar manner, but Adaira understood the ground he stood on. How would this trade work with the clan line? Where should it take place? One foul move from either clan would shatter the trust, and some innocent person would most likely wind up dead.

Adaira reached for the letter. Since the disappearing girls had become the focus of her days and energy, she had almost forgotten about the trade and Moray's previous response: an invitation to her to visit the west. She held the letter close to her face, breathing in the wrinkled parchment. It carried the fragrance of rain and juniper and something else. Something that she couldn't name, something that stirred her apprehension.

She broke the wax seal and opened the letter. She read it by dawn's light.

Dear Adaira,

I hope all is well with you and your clan. It has been four days since I last heard from you, and my parents and I are eagerly awaiting your response to my invitation to visit the west. I wonder if my letter failed to reach your hands. If so, let me repeat what I said before:

As the next generation, you and I have been afforded the chance to change the fate of our clans. You write to us of peace, which I had not thought possible, given our history. But you have granted me hope with the offer of a trade, and I want to extend an invitation to you and you alone to visit the west. Come and see our lands, our ways. Come and meet our people. Afterward, I will follow you east, likewise alone and unarmed to show the measure of my trust.

Furthermore, I ask to meet you on the clan line in five days' time. I will bring the best my clan has to offer to trade with you. You may likewise bring the best your clan has to give, and we can begin a new season for the isle.

Meet me at noontide on the northern coast, where the sea cave marks the boundary between east and west. I will remain on my side of the clan line, as you should remain on yours. It will take some imagination to pass the goods back and forth, but I do have a plan. Alert your guards that you must come alone with your gift, so they must remain distant enough to be out of sight. I assure you that mine will do the same, and that I come unarmed to meet you.

Let us be an example to our clans that peace is attainable,
but that it must be built entirely on trust.
I will be awaiting your response,

Moray Breccan
HEIR OF THE WEST

She read it a second time. Then a third, just to be certain she understood the gravity of it. Adaira's hands shook as she folded Moray's letter and departed from her bedchamber.

Was it wise for her to go alone to the west? Was it hypo-critical of her to feel a pit in her stomach every time Moray mentioned trust?

She needed council.

She wanted to speak with Sidra first.

Sidra paced Graeme's common room, around piles of parch-ment and books. They were waiting for Torin to arrive. Every minute felt like an hour, and Sidra's heart continued to beat in her throat.

Her thoughts were consumed by Maisie. Where was she? Had she been harmed? *Who had taken her?*

"Sidra?" Graeme said gently. "Do you want to change? I have some spare garments in that oaken chest in the corner."

"No, I'm fine, Da," she said, distracted by her inner turmoil.

"I just thought . . ." Graeme paused, reaching for a decanter of whiskey. His hands shook as he poured two glasses. "It's go-ing to upset my son to see blood on your clothes."

Sidra halted and glanced down at her chemise. It looked like she had been stabbed.

"Of course," she whispered, realizing that the last thing she wanted was for Torin to see her like this. She walked through the maze of Graeme's possessions to the trunk in the corner and knelt. Her fingers were cold as they raced over the wooden carvings, hefting the lid open.

She knew what rested within.

Torin's mother had been gone for almost twenty-one years. Emma Tamerlaine had departed unexpectedly in the night when Torin was only six years old, leaving her son and her husband behind. She had been a mainlander; the isle was unfamiliar, frightening, and far away from her family. In the end, life here had been too difficult for her, and Emma had returned to the mainland without a backward glance.

Yet Graeme still had her raiment, as if she might return one day.

Sorrowfully, Sidra searched through the dresses. She eventually settled on a chemise, hoping Torin wouldn't realize who it once belonged to. But why should he? He rarely saw Sidra's own undergarments.

She held it up. The chemise was long and narrow, betraying how tall and svelte Torin's mother had been. Sidra knew it would never fit her curves, and she was considering her options when she heard the front door blow open. The entire cottage shook in response. A breeze whispered through the chamber, overturning papers.

Sidra knew it was Torin, and she froze on her knees, Emma's chemise gripped in her hands. Her view of the threshold was blocked by a dressing panel, but she could hear him clearly as he spoke.

"Where's Maisie?" Torin panted, as if he had run across the hills. "Is everything well? I stopped by the house on my way and neither she nor Sidra were there."

"Torin . . ." Graeme said.

Sidra shut her eyes. The house fell silent, and she wished that she could awaken. That this was only some terrible nightmare, and she wasn't about to shatter Torin's life.

"Sid?" he called.

She dropped his mother's garment and stiffly rose. She looked at the floor as she stepped around the panel, at last coming into Torin's line of sight.

It was the silence that made her glance upward.

His face was unnaturally pale. His eyes were glazed, betraying his shock. His lips parted, but he didn't speak. A gasp escaped him, and Sidra thought it sounded like he had just been stabbed, deep in the side.

Torin strode to her. He stepped through Graeme's clutter, kicking books and trinkets out of the way. All too soon, that distance between them was gone, and Torin framed her face in his hands. She could smell the coast on his fingers—the sand and seawater. She could feel the bite of his many calluses and yet he held her so gently, as if she might break.

"What happened?" he demanded. "Who did this to you?"

Sidra swallowed. It felt like a rock was in her throat. It hurt to breathe, and her eyes burned with tears.

"Torin," she whispered.

He knew it then. She felt how he stiffened, and his eyes began to frantically search the room.

"Where's Maisie?" he asked.

Sidra drew a deep breath. Her sternum ached; her words crumbled.

"Where is Maisie, Sidra?" Torin asked again, his gaze returning to hers.

She had never seen him appear so afraid. His blue eyes were dilated, bloodshot.

"I'm sorry, Torin," she said. "I'm so sorry."

His hands fell away from her. He took a step back, stumbling over a pair of boots. He heaved a breath and raked his fingers through his hair. Another sound slipped from him, soft yet guttural. Eventually, he glanced at Sidra, his face composed.

"I need you to tell me everything that happened last night," he said. "If I'm going to find Maisie . . . you need to tell me *every* detail, Sidra."

She was jarred by how reserved he now appeared, but she knew this was his training, to keep his emotions in check. He was speaking to her as the captain, not as her partner.

Sidra began to recount what had happened, save for Donella's warning, thankful that she was able to speak without weeping.

He listened, his eyes fixed on her. Every few breaths, he would study her blood-smeared chest, the snarls of her matted hair, and Sidra would feel how cold she was.

"The spirit spoke?" Torin interrupted when she reached that part.

Sidra hesitated. She glanced across the room at Graeme, whom she had all but forgotten about. Her father-in-law stood by the door, still holding the two glasses of whiskey. He nodded to her, quietly encouraging her to tell Torin. . . .

"It wasn't a spirit," Sidra said.

His brow furrowed. "What do you mean?"

She explained about spirit blood.

"Are you certain, Sidra?" Torin asked. "This isn't your blood?"

"I gave him a flesh wound in the back," she said flatly. "This is not my blood, nor is it a spirit's."

"Then if it was a man . . ." Torin exhaled through his teeth. "Describe him to me. How tall was he? What did his voice sound like?"

Sidra struggled to put her memory, which felt distorted by night and terror, into something that Torin could identify.

He listened, bent toward her words, but she could sense his frustration. "You didn't recognize his voice, but he asked for my daughter in particular?"

"Yes, Torin."

"So he knows me. He must be a clansman, someone I've

brushed shoulders with, or trained in the guard. Someone who knows the lay of the east." Torin pressed a knuckle to his lips and shut his eyes. He still looked far too pale, as if the blood had drained from him.

"Torin," Sidra whispered, reaching for his hand. She knew what he was feeling. That horrible wave of distress, to know it was a man stealing the lasses. To ask oneself, *Why would a man kidnap little girls?*

His eyes opened. He held Sidra's gaze for a beat, but there was no hope, no reassurance in him. There was only anguish, and she felt responsible for it. She should have fought harder. She should have run faster. She should have screamed for Graeme.

Her hand fell back to her side, but Torin reached for her fingers, drawing her across the room and out the front door.

"If you wounded him, he could not have gotten far. Show me the exact place where it happened," he said.

Sidra tripped as she matched his pace. She was still bare-foot, and the brightness of the sun was a shock to her. She squinted, then realized that several of Torin's guards were present, waiting by the road. They instantly moved forward when they saw her bloodied clothes.

"It was here, Torin," she said, stopping halfway down the hill. The heather around her was crushed, a testament to her struggle. "I stabbed him. And he . . ." She bit off the rest, but Torin's eyes were keen.

"What did he do next, Sidra?"

She resisted the urge to embrace herself and shivered. "He kicked me. In the chest. I rolled to there and lost the dirk on the way down."

Torin followed the trail, kneeling in the place where Sidra had sprawled. He was pensive, studying the ground. His fingers found a few drops of blood in the heather, and it gave Sidra hope. Torin would be able to find the culprit. When he rose, she could see the color had returned to his face. His eyes were blazing, his steps full of purpose as he came to her.

"I want you to stay with my da for the rest of the day," he said. "Please don't leave his croft. Do you hear me, Sid?"

Sidra frowned. "No. I planned to help you search, Torin."

"I would prefer if you stay with Graeme."

"But I *want* to search. I don't want to be locked away in a house, waiting on news."

"Listen to me, Sidra," Torin said, taking hold of her shoulders. "You were brutally attacked last night and injured. You need to rest."

"I'm fine—"

"I won't be able to focus on the search if I'm worried about you!" His words were sharp, cutting through her resolve. "Please, just do as I ask, this one time."

Sidra took a step away. His hands slipped from her shoulders, and he sighed. But he didn't stop her when she turned and ascended the hill, and she didn't look back.

She passed through the gate into the yard. Graeme was standing in the doorway, still holding the two glasses of whiskey.

He took one look at Sidra's face and said, "I'll make us some oatcakes."

She watched him step inside, grateful that he was granting her a moment alone. She took a step deeper into the yard and realized the glamour wasn't fading, as it always did when she approached Graeme's place.

The garden remained in utter disarray. Weeds grew in thick clots. Vines snaked across the pathway and up the cottage. Gossamer hung in golden webs. It shocked her. She had always seen through the glamour in the past. All the love and care she had given to this ground . . . it was like it had never happened.

The devastation she had been burying rose. Sidra's tears began to fall as she knelt amid the wildness.

My faith is gone, she thought, sensing that was the reason why the yard was so changed, why she saw the glamour.

She watched the sunrise gild the weeds.

She began to viciously uproot it all.

CHAPTER 11

J ack was sleeping when the pounding on the front door shook the cottage. He startled and sat up in bed, blinking against the sunlight. His head still ached from spinning music into magic for the water, and he winced as heavy footsteps shook his mother's house.

His first thought was that a raid was unfolding, and he stumbled to his feet, tangled in the blanket. The room spun until he reached out to lean on the wall, belatedly realizing that it was the middle of the day. The Breccans never came in the light, and he could hear his mother calmly speaking just beyond the door.

"He's in bed," she was saying. "What can I help you with, captain?"

"I need to see him, Mirin."

Jack was still leaning against the wall when Torin opened the door.

"Asleep at this hour?" the captain said brusquely, but Jack

could tell something wasn't right. Torin began to search his room, beneath the bed and in his oaken chest.

"I was until you called," Jack said. "Is something wrong?"

Torin turned to him with an impatient flip of his hand. "Lift up your tunic."

"What?"

"I need to search your back."

Jack gaped at him but consented, pulling up his garment. He felt Torin's cold hand skate across his shoulder blades before tugging Jack's tunic back down. The captain was gone before Jack could muster another word.

Mirin and Frae were standing by the loom, concern etched on their faces as Jack emerged. A few of the guards were finishing a search of the cottage, and they left in a whirlwind.

"What was that about?" Jack wondered.

Mirin glanced at him, wide eyed. "I don't have the slightest idea, Jack."

He frowned and returned to his room, opening the shutters. He caught a glimpse of Torin, striding across the yard to examine the byre and then the storehouse.

Jack reached for his plaid, buckling it at his shoulder. He tethered his boots to his knees and nearly collided with Frae in the common room.

"Jack, can I come with you?" she asked.

"I think it's best you stay with Mum for now," he said gently. He didn't want her to worry, but he could see the fear creeping across her face.

"Where do you think you're going?" Mirin demanded. "You're ill!"

He didn't know how she knew that, aside from the fact that he had overslept and looked pale. Or perhaps she sensed it in him—how music had drained a portion of his health.

Jack briefly met her gaze as he stood on the threshold. "I'm seeing if I can assist Torin. I'll be back in time for supper."

He shut the door before Mirin could protest, jumping over the garden wall to intercept the captain.

Jack took one look at Torin's face and knew it was bad.

"Another lass?" he asked.

Torin couldn't hide his grief. The sunshine washed over him, unforgivably bright. He refused to make eye contact and said, "Maisie."

Jack drew a sharp inhale. "I'm sorry, Torin."

Torin continued his brisk walk. "I don't need sympathy, I need answers."

"Then let me help," Jack said, rushing to keep stride with the captain. He remembered Maisie sitting next to him at breakfast, mere days ago. How curious and charming she had been, giving him a gap-toothed smile. It made Jack feel sick to know she was missing. "Tell me what to do."

Torin stopped abruptly on the road. His guards were in the distance, moving on to the next croft.

The wind soughed as Jack waited. He expected Torin to send him back to the house—Jack had never been strong enough or good enough to be one of the East Guard—but then the captain looked at him and nodded.

"Very well," he said. "Come with me."

Jack soon gathered all the pieces of what had happened the previous night. It galled him, to think that while he had been sitting on the coast and singing for the water, a man had walked across the hills, assaulted Sidra, and kidnapped Maisie.

Torin's orders were urgent. He told his guards to search the hills, the glens, the mountains, the caves, the coast, the city streets, and the byres and storehouses of crofts. To study the knoll between his land and his father's property for a blood trail and broken grass from boots that had fled, to look for a man with a wound in his back.

No one would be spared, Jack had discovered.

Torin challenged his guards to question even their own fathers, their brothers, their husbands, and friends. To doubt their kin, down to every branch and root of their family tree. To doubt those they loved most, for sometimes love was like dust in the eyes, a hindrance when it came to seeing truth.

The culprit could be any one of them in the east, and the air felt grim and heavy with disbelief as the news spread—another lass was missing, and the spirits were not to blame.

Jack had searched five crofts and the span of eleven different men's backs when Adaira appeared, riding a mud-splattered horse. Her countenance was rosy from the wind, her hair braided into a crown. She was dressed in a simple gray dress with a red plaid knotted across her body. She dismounted before the mare had even come to a halt, and Jack watched from where he stood in a yard as she went to her cousin.

She knew about Maisie then. Jack could see it on her face as she spoke to Torin. The panic, the fear, the desperation. The cousins spoke for a moment, low and urgent. Adaira's eyes suddenly flickered beyond Torin to find Jack in the shadows. Her gaze remained on him, the tension easing in her expression.

It still shocked Jack when she called him over. He felt like he was intruding on a private moment, especially when Torin raked his hand through his tangled hair.

"Jack," Adaira greeted him. "I think we should tell Torin what we've been doing."

Jack's brow arched. "Indeed?" It was not a light decision to reveal a secret she claimed had been held by bard and laird alone, but Jack saw how necessary it was to bring Torin into their confidence.

"What is it?" Torin barked. "What have the two of you been up to?"

Adaira turned to the wind. It was blowing from the south. "We need a private place to speak. There's a cave not far from here. Both of you, come with me." She reached out to snag the reins of her mare and began to walk into the hills.

Jack trailed her. He could hear Torin give his guards commands to move to the next croft before he followed Jack with a heavy tread.

Adaira led them to a steep hill, its exposed side showing layers of rock. About halfway up was a cave, indiscernible unless one squinted. Jack stopped abruptly, staring up at the cave's small, shadowed entrance.

He remembered this place. It had been one of his favorite caves as a boy, given how dangerous it was to climb into its mouth.

"Adaira," he began to warn her, but she was already climbing, nimble and confident, even with her long dress and shawl. Jack watched, but his stomach churned when he imagined her slipping and falling.

Within moments, she had made it to the perch of the cave, and she paused to look down at them.

"Are you coming, Torin? My old menace?"

Jack frowned up at her. "I think we are a little old for such antics. Surely there's another place more accommodating for this talk?"

She made no reply, but he watched her vanish into the cave. Jack glanced at Torin, who was regarding him with a strange gleam in his eyes.

"After you, bard," the captain said.

Jack had no choice. Here they were, grown adults, and they were clambering up to a cave like they were ten years old again. He swore under his breath as he approached the rocky wall.

All of this was ridiculous, he thought as he began to climb. He slipped, caught himself, uttered another curse, and then slowly ascended, following the path Adaira had taken.

He eventually made it to the cave, trembling from the height. Jack chose not to look down and eased into the cool shadows of the hollow space. It was dim, but he could faintly see Adaira sitting on the stone floor. He crawled to sit across from her, leaning back against the jagged wall, their boots touching.

The captain soon appeared, slipping into the cave in spite of his great stature.

As Jack waited for Adaira to speak first, he listened to water dripping, deep in the heart of the cave, and realized they were truly sheltered from the wind's curiosity. Adaira was wise to take such precautions.

"I delayed in sharing this with you, Torin," she began, "for two reasons. The first: I didn't know if Jack would return to the mainland when I summoned him. The second: I didn't know if what my father said was actually true. It seemed fanciful, and I wanted to see its proof before I gave you any hope."

Torin scowled. "What are you speaking about, Adi?"

Adaira drew a deep breath. She looked at Jack, as if she needed reassurance from him. He gave her a faint nod.

She told her cousin the same story she had once told Jack, then told him about Jack singing up the spirits of the sea the night before, and what they had said.

Torin exhaled. His eyes seemed to burn in the dim light. "You called the folk to you?"

Adaira nodded. "Yes. Jack did. And we plan to do it again with the earth."

Jack was staring at his lap, picking dirt from his nails until he felt Torin's gaze.

"I want to be there when it happens," Torin said.

"I'm sorry, cousin, but that won't be possible," Adaira replied. "It must be Jack and me, and us alone. I don't think the spirits will manifest if they are being watched by anyone else."

"Then I have questions I'd like for you to ask the earth," Torin countered. "One—we know now it's not the spirits stealing the lasses but a man. Who is this man? What is his name? Where does he reside? Is he working alone or does he have help? Second—where is he hiding the lasses, if they are still alive? And if they are dead . . ." Torin closed his eyes. "Then where are their bodies?"

Adaira and Jack were silent, listening to Torin rattle off queries. But when Jack shared a glance with her, he knew they were both thinking the same thing. The spirits of the sea hadn't been forthcoming with their responses. What if the earth was no more helpful? Would Jack and Adaira be able to ask all of these questions?

"We'll try our best to get the answers for you," Adaira said.

"There is one more thing I'd like you to ask them," Torin continued. "At the place where Catriona vanished, I found two red flowers lying in the grass. Shorn but unwilted, because they were enchanted. Strange, as I've never seen them grow in the east before. Sidra likewise didn't recognize them, but I have a strong inkling they are being used by the culprit to either entice the girls or to pass unnoticed by us."

Adaira frowned. "Where are these flowers at the moment?"

"With Sidra. She can give one to you, to show the spirits," Torin said, turning his attention next to Jack. "How soon can you play?"

Jack hesitated. He wasn't sure. He still felt weak from the night before, and he hadn't had a chance to prepare.

"It will take me a few days," he said, wishing he could give Torin the response he wanted. "I'm afraid I need time to study the music."

"You haven't looked at it yet?"

"No, he hasn't had a chance to," Adaira said. "My intention was to bring the music to him this morning, but I heard the news about Maisie and came directly to you, Torin. Now I'm about to take him home and give it to him."

Torin nodded. "All right. Thank you, Jack."

The captain departed, leaving Jack and Adaira behind in the cave.

A faint groan escaped her. The sound prompted Jack to study her face. Adaira had dropped her mask of confident, capable laird who was going to solve this mystery. In the wake of Torin's departure, she appeared uncertain and anxious. She was weary and sad, and when her gaze met Jack's, he didn't look away.

"Can you come with me now?" she asked.

"Yes," he answered, ignoring the ache that lingered in his hands.

He let her climb down first, so he could watch the path she took and mimic it. He shuddered to be back on solid ground until he realized Adaira had already mounted her horse and was waiting.

"Should I meet you there?" he said, giving the mare a wide berth.

Adaira smiled. "No. It'll be much faster if you ride with me."

Jack hesitated. The horse tossed her head and pawed the ground, sensing his reluctance.

"I don't mind walking," he insisted.

"When's the last time you rode a horse, Jack?"

"Close to eleven years now."

"Then it's a good time to get back in the saddle." Adaira slipped her foot from the stirrup, offering it to him. "Come on, my old menace."

This was bound to be a disaster, and Jack groaned as he slid his boot into the stirrup, hauling himself up. He sat, very uncomfortably, behind her. He didn't know where he should put his hands, where his feet should go. Adaira's back was aligned with his chest, and he leaned away so the wind could still blow between them.

"Are you settled?" she asked.

"As I'll ever be," he replied drolly.

Adaira clucked to the horse. The mare began to walk, and Jack felt how stiff his body was. He was trying to relax, to let the horse's gait melt through him, when Adaira clucked again. The horse lurched into a trot. Jack grimaced. Every thought was about to be knocked loose from his head.

"This is too fast," he said, scrambling to grip the edges of the saddle.

"Hold on, Jack."

"What?"

She clucked a third time, and the horse broke into a canter. Jack could feel the taunt of the ground as his balance teetered. He was about to tumble off and had no choice but to grasp her waist and sidle closer to her, so that no space remained between their bodies. He felt her palm cover his knuckles, warm with reassurance. She eased his hands forward to her navel, so that his arms embraced her, his fingers linked over the stays of her dress.

By the time they reached the castle courtyard, Jack was certain a few years had been shaved from his life and there were tangles in his hair that no comb would be able to tame. The mare came to a halt before the stable doors and nickered, announcing their arrival. Only then did Jack loosen his death grip on Adaira.

She dismounted first, a graceful slide to the cobblestones. She turned and held out her hand to him, wordlessly offering her assistance.

Jack scowled but accepted, surprised by how steady and

strong she was, even as he was unbalanced. Awkwardly, he eased himself to the ground. He winced as he straightened.

"You'll be sore tomorrow," Adaira warned.

"Excellent," he replied, thinking he couldn't afford to let one more thing ail him.

He relinquished her hand and fell into stride beside her, now that he knew where she was taking him. They passed through the garden in companionable silence and ascended to the music chamber, a place Jack was coming to love. He brushed the dust from his clothes as Adaira called for tea.

"Are you feeling well, Jack?" she asked, looking him over as she walked to her desk.

He paused, wondering if she was at last noticing the effects of last night. "I'm fine," he said. "Although I could wait another eleven years before riding a horse again."

She smiled, sorting through a stack of books. "I don't think I can allow that to happen."

"No, heiress?"

She didn't reply, nor did she need to. Jack saw the determined gleam in her eyes as she brought a book to him. It was only a matter of time before she would have him astride another horse.

"Here. The music is tucked within the leaves," Adaira said, extending the slender volume toward him. "I know you might feel pressured to rush because of Torin, but if you need several days to study the music, then take them, Jack. I would prefer that we be prepared when we approach the spirits."

"I think I can be ready in two days, at the soonest," he replied, accepting the book. He admired its illuminated cover before opening it to find the loose parchment, hidden in the pages. He could not deny that a part of him was eager to learn this next ballad of Lorna's. Anticipation shivered through him.

Jack had what he needed. He should go now. But he found that his feet were rooted to the floor, reluctant to leave so soon. His eyes lifted to meet Adaira's steady gaze.

"I know you have many things to do," she said. "But you should at least stay for tea. Let me feed you. Are you hungry?"

He hadn't eaten that morning. He was famished, and he nodded. It was strange to think back to how this day had begun with Torin searching his room. It was strange to think how it was coming to an end, spending the last, golden hours of afternoon with Adaira in her study.

A servant brought in a tray of tea, scones, small mince pies, wedges of cheese, and oatcakes with cream and berries. Jack joined Adaira at the table, watching as she poured them each a cup of tea. He accepted it and filled his plate, his mind racing.

He was sharing a private meal with her. He could ask her anything, and the silence between them felt tender, as if Adaira would honestly answer whatever he felt brave enough to voice.

His thoughts brimmed with possibilities.

He wanted to ask her if she had any news of the Breccans and the trade she wanted to establish. He wanted to ask what she had been doing the past decade while he had been gone. If she had thought of him from time to time. He wanted to ask why she was unwed, because it continued to shock him that she walked alone when there was a horde of eligible partners in the east. Unless, that is, she desired to be alone. Which was fine, but he couldn't help but wonder. He wanted to know if she was the one who desired him to stay a full year as bard, or if she was merely speaking for the good of the clan.

He wanted to know her, and that realization felt like a sting in his side.

The longer he stayed here on the isle—the longer he slept beneath the fire of the stars and listened to the sighs of the wind and ate the food and drank the water—the more muddled his fancies became, until he couldn't see the original path he had carved for himself. The safe path, the one that gave him purpose and place on the mainland.

He took a sip of tea, dismayed.

A piece of him still craved that dependable life, the one in which everything could be predicted. He would become a professor. He would grow old, gray, and even more crotchety than he already was. He would teach younger generations the secrets of instruments and how to write music, watching his students transform their sullenness and hesitancy into confidence and prowess.

That was the life he had envisioned for himself. It was a life with little risk. A life in which every day felt the same and his music was subdued. A life of partaking only of comfortable things and of sleeping alone at night, because it would be impossible to find a lover who would endure all his irascibility and the oddness of his isle blood, year after year.

Did he want such a fate?

"You're unnaturally quiet, Jack," Adaira remarked, lifting the teacup to her lips. There was a speck of cream at the corner of her mouth, and he was staring at it. "In the past, that meant you were plotting mischief."

Jack blinked. He would ask her the safest of his questions—ironically, the one pertaining to their raid-loving enemies.

"Have the Breccans agreed to your notion of trade, heiress?"

"They have," Adaira replied. "But they've made a request of me."

"And what is that?"

She finally licked the cream from her lips. "They want me to visit the west."

Jack thought she was jesting. He laughed, but it was a cold, bitter sound.

"I fail to see the humor in this," she said in a sharp tone.

"As do I, Adaira," he countered. "Perhaps I should sing you the ballad of Joan Tamerlaine and how she was doomed the moment she stepped foot in the west. How Fingal, her sulky husband, and his bloodthirsty clan drove her to a premature death."

"I know the story of my ancestor," Adaira replied through her teeth. "There's no need for you to sing it to me."

Jack quelled his sarcasm and drained his tea for courage. He wanted her to understand why her answer had upset him. He set a softer gaze upon her, only to find that she wasn't even looking at him. She was flushed, angry. She was pushing her plate aside, about to rise.

"Adaira," he said, gently.

She became still, her eyes flickering to his.

"So they've extended an invitation to you," he said. "Perhaps it *is* a wise thing to accept. You'd be the first Tamerlaine to behold the west in nearly two hundred years. Perhaps peace is indeed something attainable, and you are the one destined to bring the isle back together as one. But perhaps it's unwise, and the Breccans plan to harm you. You are the sole heiress. What would happen to the Tamerlaine clan if you perished?"

Adaira was silent.

Jack studied her face. She was still so much of a riddle to him. He asked, "What does your father think? Have you spoken of it to him yet?"

"About the visit? No. But I imagine his advice would strangely align with yours."

"Can a bard not give sage advice then?"

Adaira almost smiled. "Perhaps you can be both to me? Bard *and* adviser?"

"Does it pay twice as much, heiress?"

She was quick and drawled, "Does that mean you are choosing to accept the role of Bard of the East?"

"I am in the midst of deliberations with myself," he said. "But that's not what we're discussing at the moment. I just presented you with the possibility that the Breccans are devising to harm you, Adaira."

She released a deep breath. "I don't think the Breccans plan to harm me."

"How do you know that?"

"Because I'm offering them something they can't refuse. They *need* our winter stores. They *need* our resources when the ice comes. Why would they harm me when I am the first Tamerlaine to give that to them?"

"And yet they simply *take* what they want when winter comes," Jack argued. "They don't need you to grant them access."

"But perhaps they are weary of it," Adaira replied. "Perhaps they dream of a different life, one where the isle is united again and the two halves are restored." She stood and walked to the window. Jack could see her reflection, shining in the glass. "In five days' time, I am to meet Moray Breccan on the northern coast for a trade-by-trial. It's a test, both to see what the west has to offer us and to measure their trustworthiness before I visit them."

Jack listened to her every word. He had yet to take his gaze from her, and he didn't know why his heart was thrumming in that moment, as if he had run from one side of the isle to the other. He wanted to scoff at the fanciful notion of peace, but this was the second time he had been encouraged to think of the isle as one again, its two halves mended.

He could have said many things to Adaira in that moment, and yet the question that slipped from his lips as a growl was, "Who is Moray Breccan?"

"The Heir of the West."

Brilliant, Jack thought. Although why should he be surprised that the heir would want to meet her?

"So you will support me if I choose to visit?" she asked.

"It depends," Jack said.

"On what, old menace?"

"On who you take with you."

Adaira fell silent again. Jack was swiftly learning he didn't like these silences of hers.

"Who are you taking, Adaira?" he asked again. "Torin and a retinue of guards?"

"No one," she said.

"I'm sorry?"

She turned to face Jack once more. Her eyes were inscrutable as she looked at him. "They have asked me to come alone, as a measure of my trust in—"

"To hell with that!" Jack cried. The dishes on the table rattled as he stood. "Adaira, you shouldn't even *consider* visiting them alone."

"I know it sounds unwise, Jack."

"It sounds foolish and deadly. You forget who they are."

"I haven't forgotten, and I'm not afraid of them!" she shouted, as if raising her voice was the only way to get Jack to close his mouth.

And he did.

He stood face-to-face with her and felt the tension in his bones.

She sighed again. Her weariness was returning, but her voice was calm when she said, "So you advise that if I go, I shouldn't go alone. I suppose that means I need a husband before I visit the west. Two become one under matrimony, don't they?"

Jack remained silent. He was flooded by a strange emotion, one that made him feel like he was withering. It was jealousy, and he had rarely felt it on the mainland.

He briefly wondered if he was falling ill; he shouldn't have swum in the ocean at night, when a chill could set in. But as soon as he remembered the moment when they had broken the surface and Adaira had laughed, Jack knew he would choose to do it again, and again, even if time permitted him to redo the past. That he would follow her into the sea. And perhaps that was true only because Adaira held his allegiance and respect as his laird, but perhaps it was due to something else. Something that stirred his soul like breath on embers, rousing old fire.

Gods, he thought with a sharp intake. He needed to smother this feeling now, before it unfurled and grew wings.

Or perhaps he should let it fly.

If he became her husband, he would forfeit his life on the mainland. He would have no choice but to give up his plans to become a professor in order to remain with her, living out his days on the isle. The imagining made him feel cold at first, and his pride flared—all those years studying and working would be *wasted*—until he met her gaze.

No, not wasted, he realized. Because he would be Bard of the East, and this music turret would become his, and he would play songs for children like Frae and for adults like Mirin. By day he would belong to the clan, singing beneath the sun. But by night, when the stars burned, he would lie down beside Adaira, and he would wholly be hers, as she would be his.

Adaira continued to intently watch him, measuring his expression.

He swallowed, wondering if she saw the same vision he did. One where the two of them were united, bound, laying claim to the other. But then reality returned, rushing between them like a cold tide.

Surely not . . . Jack mused, and a warring medley of dread and desire rose within him. Surely, she would never want him in such a way, even as he felt static in the air between them.

Surely, he would be daft to agree to it. But then Adaira smiled, and he imagined that maybe he would. Maybe he would agree to it, but only out of duty. *If* she asked him, that is.

"Don't let me keep you from your study, bard," she said.

She was dismissing him.

Flustered, Jack strode to the table, retrieving the book. *You're being ridiculous,* he told himself. Assuming Adaira would ask him to wed her. She probably wouldn't even consider him for a partner.

Jack didn't grant her a bow, or a farewell. He was too angry for niceties, and he departed the room swiftly, the door slamming in his wake.

He didn't realize Alastair was in the inner garden until he was nearly upon him. The laird stood on the stone pathway by the roses, as if waiting for Jack to emerge from the music turret.

"My laird," Jack said, stopping abruptly.

Alastair granted him a wan smile. "Jack." His bloodshot eyes dropped to the book in Jack's hands. "I see you have Lorna's music."

Jack hesitated, suddenly feeling awkward. "Y-yes, I . . . Adaira gave it to me."

Alastair began to walk in a slow, feeble gait. "Come, Jack. I'd like to have a few words with you."

Jack's stomach twisted as he followed the laird into the castle library. The doors shut behind them, enclosing them in the vast chamber whose air smelled of leather and old parchment. Jack watched as Alastair approached two chairs by the hearth, where flames burned despite the summer heat.

"Have a seat, Jack," the laird said. "I won't take much of your time."

Jack obeyed, carefully setting Lorna's composition across his knees. He opened his mouth to speak but then thought better of it. Waiting, he watched as the laird proceeded to pour them each a dram of whiskey. Alastair's hands quivered as he brought a glass to Jack.

"Sidra says I can have one knuckle's worth a day," said Alastair, amused. His face appeared even gaunter, as if he had shed more weight since Jack had first seen him, only days prior. "I try to save it for a special hour."

"I'm honored, laird," Jack said.

Alastair carefully lowered himself into his chair, and the men drank the whiskey. Jack's mind sharpened; he didn't know if Alastair was displeased or relieved to see Lorna's music in his possession, and he was pondering what to say when the laird broke the silence.

"The sea has been calm today. I take it that you played 'The Song of the Tides' last night?"

"Yes, laird."

Alastair leaned back in the chair, a hint of a wistful smile on his face. "I remember those moments well. Those days and nights when I would stand close to Lorna, listening to her play for the folk. She would sing to them twice a year—once for the sea and once for the earth, to keep the spirits' favor on us in the east." He fell silent; Jack could see the memories take hold as the laird's dark eyes turned to a distant, inward place. But then he blinked, and the reminiscent glaze was gone. Alastair's gaze was keen as it returned to Jack. "I wanted to send word for you sooner, not long after Lorna perished. But Adaira told me to wait. I think she had full faith that you would return on your own."

Jack shifted his weight, his palms beginning to perspire. He didn't know what to say; he didn't know how he felt, envisioning Adaira with such hope.

Alastair's voice lowered as he asked, "Did my daughter see the effects that playing had on you?"

"No, laird."

"You were able to hide the pain and the blood from her?"

Jack nodded. "Should I have—?"

"She doesn't know of the cost," Alastair gently interrupted. "I never told her, and Lorna kept the side effects of wielding such magic a secret."

"You say Lorna only played twice a year for the spirits?" Jack tentatively asked.

"Indeed. She would play for the sea in autumn, and the earth in spring. It was part of her role as Bard of the East, although the clan never knew of it." He didn't mention Lorna playing for the fire or the wind, and Jack assumed that she had a reason not to. "It's why I believed the spirits were at fault for snatching the lasses. So much time has passed since a bard sang for them, and I thought they were angry at us."

Jack glanced down at the book on his lap, where Lorna's notes hid within the pages. He felt the creeping sensation of unworthiness, and he wished that he had been given the chance to see her again. To speak to her as one musician to another.

"Adaira doesn't know what playing for the folk will do to you, Jack," the laird said, breaking Jack's reveries. "But she will soon discover it, if you choose to become Bard of the East. It is a position of great honor, but this decision is one you should not make lightly."

"I will consider all that you have shared with me, laird," Jack replied. "And I thank you for telling me, for trusting me with Lorna's music."

"She would want it this way," Alastair said. "She would be pleased to know you're playing her songs. And she would want to see you compose your own."

Jack was humbled. All his life, he had convinced himself that no one had ever seen anything worthy in him. But Lorna had. Even in her death, she was granting him a rare opportunity.

"Now then," Alastair said, reaching for the whiskey decanter, "I've kept you long enough."

Jack rose and left the laird in the library with a second knuckle's worth of whiskey, having promised not to tell Sidra.

He emerged into the courtyard, where a breeze was blowing in from the sea, and came to a stop on the mossy flagstones to steady his heart. He didn't know how long he stood there, but he soon remembered the book in his hand. Curious, he opened it to skim Lorna's composition, "The Ballad for the Earth."

She had written page after page of music far more complex than the ballad for the tides. Jack noticed her instruction at the bottom of the very last page. A warning that gave him pause.

Play with the utmost caution.

CHAPTER 12

S idra didn't want to deceive Graeme, but neither could she remain in his house another minute. At midday, she convinced him to let her return home to change her clothes and gather herbs and materials so she could at least work while she waited for Torin to bring news.

She avoided the hill, choosing to walk by road to her front door.

Covered dishes were piled on the cottage's stoop. Pies, loaves of bannocks, creamy parritch, stews, cakes, pickled vegetables and fruits. Sidra stared at the jumbled assortment a full three breaths before she realized they were for *her*, because Maisie was missing.

The food only made it more visceral, and she wiped tears from her face as she struggled to carry everything inside to the kitchen. At Graeme's, she had sipped whiskey and eaten one oatcake, all that her stomach would permit. Everything within her was wound tight, and she wished Torin would understand that she needed to walk the hills. To sit and wait was agony. She needed to search for Maisie.

By the time she had all the food inside and had shut the front door, it was midday. Sidra stared into the silent chamber. At the patches of light on the floor. At the dust motes that spun in the air.

It was quiet without Maisie. It felt as if the croft had lost its heart, and Sidra sat at the kitchen table, overcome.

She rested her face in her hands, reliving the events, wondering what she could have done differently. She remembered Donella's warning. The ghost had seen the perpetrator's path. She had known he was coming for Maisie.

Sidra lifted her head and whispered, "Donella? Can you meet with me?"

She waited.

The ghost rarely visited twice a season, and she never materialized upon command. But Sidra believed Donella might find a way, given what had happened to her daughter.

Sidra's hope faltered as the silence stretched on. She heard someone knock on her door. She didn't answer it as she waited patiently for the ghost.

But Donella never came.

Soon, Graeme would call for her, and Sidra sighed. She began to gather her herbs, and that was when she saw them. The two red flowers. Orenna blossoms.

She took one in her hands and studied its small, fierce petals. The legend claimed that to eat one was to gain a spirit's secrets.

Without hesitation, Sidra placed a flower in her mouth and swallowed.

She felt nothing at first. The flower tasted like frosted grass and a hint of remorse. But then a sigh tugged on her mouth. Once, twice. As if she were breathing in a cold enchantment.

Sidra rose. She flexed her hands, her fingertips tingling. She blinked and saw a world lined with faint traces of gold. At first, she thought she was hallucinating, until she walked out the back door and beheld her garden.

She could see the life of the plants. The faint glow of their essence. She could see the lines running deep in the soil—roots that fed into a catacomb of intricate passages. Overhead, she could see the streaks in the clouds. The routes the wind blew.

She stood in the splendor, soaking it in.

My eyes are open, she thought. *I'm seeing both realms.*

She was straddling the mortal world and the domain of the spirits and could see how they overlapped. Sidra began to walk. Her bare feet met the ground with a whisper. She could feel the depth of the earth every time she stepped. She was weightless, as if nothing could hold her down.

She turned and looked behind. Her feet had left no tracks in the soil or the grass.

This is how he did it, her mind raced. *This is how he leaves no trace. He eats a flower and steals our girls.*

Sidra's breath caught. She returned to the hill, even though it made her shudder. Perspiration glistened on her skin as she studied the crushed heather. She could see how a spirit had wept when she fell and tumbled, its tears beading gold in the grass. She searched the area again now that her eyes were sharper, and she could see where Torin and his guards had marked the beginnings of a blood trail. It looked like the kidnapper had carried Maisie to the south, but Sidra wasn't certain.

After a few steps, the blood dried and there was no trace of where he had gone.

She followed the stakes the guard had set to mark a potential path, hoping she didn't run into Torin. She had washed the dirt from her hands and tended to her bruises earlier that morning.

She had even found a looser chemise of Emma's that fit her and had wrapped herself in one of Graeme's woolen cloaks to ward off chills, but she knew she still looked half dressed and wild.

Sidra didn't care.

She realized as she walked the hills that her steps had quickened. She could move thrice as fast as normal, and she almost laughed as she felt the magic rush through her. She could also sense how close other people were. There were four guards to her right, two kilometers away. There was a croft to her left, five kilometers away. She could feel the distance in her bones, and it enabled her to travel, undisturbed by others.

All too soon, she came upon the end of the marked path. She decided to continue walking to the southwest, following threads of gold in the air and in the grass. They brought her to a copse of birch trees. Sidra paused, confused when the golden essence flared violet on one of the trunks. She could sense the maiden in the birch tree; Sidra faintly heard her voice as she lamented. The spirit had been wounded.

Sidra reached out her fingers to trace the bark.

"Don't touch her," a voice thundered in the ground. The words raced up Sidra's legs, and she snatched her hand away before she could comfort the birch maiden.

She took a step away, but she could feel the sorrow in this place. The trees were in anguish, and she didn't know why.

Sidra pressed onward.

"Can you take me to my daughter?" she asked, but her voice fell unanswered, even as she sensed the spirits' wary attention. "Can you show me where she is?"

Her thirst suddenly became intense. She could hardly think of anything else, and she closed her eyes, seeking the closest water spirit. She sensed the cold, quiet presence of a loch, just over the next hill. Sidra hurried to find it—a narrow but deep body of water, nearly hidden in a secluded valley.

She hadn't been here before, and she heard her grand-mother's voice, echoing in her memory.

Never drink from strange lochs.

But Sidra was so thirsty. Her mouth and her soul were both parched, and she knelt at the bank and filled her hands with clear, icy water. She took her first sip—it was sweet, as if spun with honey. She took another draw before she paused, notic-ing the swirl of gold within the water. Like threads of flaxen hair. Disquieted, she lowered her hands. Her eyes drifted to the deeper side of the pool, where something was bubbling.

It was Maisie.

Maisie was in the water, held just beneath the surface.

Sidra cried out and lunged into the loch. She tore Graeme's cloak away from her collar and dived, pulling her body through the water in frantic strokes.

She was almost to Maisie, but then Sidra saw that her daugh-ter was farther below the surface than she had realized. Sidra cursed, returning to the surface to gasp fresh air. She plunged again, following those golden tendrils down, deep into the dark waters of the pond.

But every time Sidra stretched out her hand to grasp Maisie, she discovered the lass was just beyond her reach.

Maisie drifted farther and farther below, as if she were teth-ered to something in the heart of the loch. Sidra continued to chase her. Her open eyes burned as she reached for her daugh-ter again and again, to no avail.

She could feel her lungs begin to smolder. She was almost out of air.

Sidra glanced upward; the surface was far away. She hesi-tated, her black hair tangling like silk across her face.

From the corner of her eye, she saw movement. She wasn't alone in the water, and Sidra glanced sideways to see the wa-ter spirit approach. A woman with translucent skin, dark blue fins, and oversized, cat slit eyes. Sharp, pointed teeth and long, blond hair, its tendrils illumined in the dark water.

Sidra's fear and indignation morphed into a blazing fire.

This is a trick. She's fooling me.

She closed her eyes and began to kick to the surface. Sidra could feel the threads of the spirit pull against her, inviting her to stay. To sink into a place where the world shed its old skin. To be reborn in the weight of the loch.

Sidra desperately swam upwards, where she could feel the waters grow warm again. Her legs and hands felt heavy, but she opened her eyes and followed a bold wisp of gold now, as if another spirit was urging her to rise. Bubbles slipped from her lips as she struggled to keep her mouth shut. To resist taking a breath of water.

I'm not going to make it. . . .

She thought of Torin. His face appeared to her, stark and broken at a graveside, as if she had shattered the last of him.

Sidra found the surface with a gasp.

She trembled as she swam to the bank. She crawled upon the mossy rocks, spluttering and coughing. She lay down for a moment, until her heart was steady again. A spirit had tricked her, played her for a fool. Sidra covered her face and sobbed. She had been holding the tears in for hours, and she let them flow.

When her tears had dried, she noticed the time of day.

She had dived into the loch when the sun was at its zenith in the sky. It had now set behind the hills, leaving only a vestige of light on the horizon. The stars were winking overhead, and Sidra pushed herself to stand on shaky legs.

How much time had she lost? How many days had passed?

The panic coursed through her as she began to hurry home. She noticed that the effect of the Orenna flower had faded, zapping her energy. She could no longer see the spirit realm, and her head began to viciously ache.

The earth spirits must have felt compassion for her, although Sidra was reluctant to trust them. But five hills became one. The kilometers compressed, and the rocks receded, granting her a swift path to the croft.

She decided she should go directly to Graeme's. She knew her father-in-law would be worried over her lengthy absence, but then she noticed the firelight illuminating her house from within.

Sidra paused, wondering who was home. Following the light, she entered through the back door.

Torin sat at the table, waiting for Sidra to come home.

He had been waiting for a full hour now. Weary and heartsick from a long day of searching, he had gone to Graeme's at dusk, his arms aching to hold Sidra.

She wasn't there.

His father rambled anxiously, claiming she had gone home to fetch her herbs at noontide and had never returned. Adaira had even called that afternoon to visit with her, but Sidra had been absent and Graeme could only surmise that she had been summoned to help a patient.

Torin had swallowed his panic and rushed down the hill, only to find a cold, dark cottage full of untouched food.

He didn't know where she had gone, but he imagined she was searching for Maisie. He had seen the determination in her eyes when they had parted ways earlier, how his sharp orders had upset her. Torin was so exhausted now that he decided he should simply wait on her to return. Surely, the night would drive her back home. And he was so tired of searching.

He lit a candle.

He stared at her herbs, scattered on the table, an utter mystery to him.

He stared at Maisie's toys, tucked away in a basket by the hearth. He closed his eyes, unable to bear the sight of them.

The kittens were crying at the back door. Torin ground his teeth and poured a dish of milk, setting it on the stoop for the cats.

He paced the chamber but eventually sat again. He hadn't slept in two days. He could hardly see straight, and he knew he had run himself ragged that afternoon.

My daughter is missing.

It still didn't feel true. This happened to others, not to him.

You thought the same when Donella died, didn't you?

Torin felt numb, and he wondered when it would truly hit him. He wondered what more he could do. He had searched house after house, croft after croft, all the castle chambers. He had glanced over more backs than he'd have liked to, searching for a wounded man, and yet he had failed to find the answer he sought.

He thought of Jack. The secret Adaira had shared with him earlier.

The bard was Torin's last hope.

He was thinking of how long it had been since he had heard music when the back door creaked open. Torin stiffened, his eyes flickering to the threshold.

Sidra stepped into the house.

The first thing Torin noticed was that she was barefoot and completely drenched. He could discern every line and curve of her body through the damp chemise. The second thing he noticed was the strange expression on her face, as if she had just woken up and had no idea what had happened while she slumbered.

Seeing him sitting at the table, she closed the door and approached, but stopped a few paces away from him. Her long hair dripped water onto the floor.

"Where were you?" he asked. He sounded angry, but only because he was deeply afraid.

Sidra opened her mouth. Nothing but breath emerged. She was trembling; the sight made Torin ache. He could also see the bruises beginning to bloom on her chest, from where she had been kicked.

His hands curled into fists beneath the table.

"Sidra."

"I was looking for Maisie," she said, her gaze dropping to her feet.

He stared at her, wondering what she was withholding from him.

Since the moment he had met her, he had always been able to read Sidra's face. She was an openhearted woman, honest and genuine and fearless. He remembered the night when he had first held her, skin to skin. When she had invited him to share her bed at last, months after they had wed. The wonder, the pleasure that had been in her eyes when she looked at him.

He regarded her now, standing like a stranger in their house, and he couldn't read her face. He didn't know what she was feeling, what she was thinking. It felt like a wall had risen between them.

She lifted her eyes to his, as if she also felt the distance. Her voice was reserved when she asked, "Why are you here, Torin?"

"I came to be with you tonight, Sidra."

She blinked, surprised. It made him realize how few nights they had spent together. And even then, Maisie had often slept between them in the bed.

"Oh," Sidra said. "You . . . you didn't have to do that."

He studied her, his pulse throbbing in his temples. Did she want him to leave? "I can go, if you would rather that."

"No," she answered. "Stay, Torin. We shouldn't be alone to-night. And I have something I need to tell you."

Why did his stomach drop? He braced himself and motioned to the countless dishes, scattered across the kitchen. "We both need to eat. But you should change into some dry clothes first."

She nodded. While she went to the bedroom, Torin perused the offerings. He eventually brought a bannock, a cauldron of cold stew, and a bottle of wine to the table, careful not to disturb Sidra's herbs.

She returned a few moments later, dressed in a floor-length chemise. Torin noted that she had laced the collar tight, to conceal the bruises on her chest as if they didn't exist, and he felt a lance of pain in his stomach. He didn't want her to feel as if she had to hide things from him.

She looked at the stew he had chosen.

"Should I heat it?" she asked.

Torin should have thought of that. He wordlessly stoked a fire in the hearth, and Sidra set the cauldron over the iron hook. While they waited for the food to warm, he glanced at her.

"You have something to tell me?" he prompted.

"Yes," Sidra said, rubbing her arms with a shiver. "I know what the Orenna flower does."

He frowned as she brought the red flower to him. The very one he had once carried to her.

Slowly, she told him everything. The legend she had read in the tattered book. How she had planned to come home today to fetch her herbs and thought otherwise when she saw the crimson flower. How the petals had tasted, and how they had opened her eyes to the spirit realm.

Torin's shock gave way to anger. "You should have spoken to me first, Sid. Before you ate this. What if it was poison?"

Sidra was quiet. There was something far worse lurking in her eyes. "I think it saved me, Torin."

He listened as she continued about the reflection in the loch. Torin went cold with dread. He imagined Sidra swimming down into the darkness, only to return after a hundred years had passed. He would be long dead, his bones in a grave. He would have never known what had befallen her. He would have lost his daughter and his wife in the span of a day, and it would have obliterated him.

"At first, I didn't realize it was a trick," Sidra whispered. "But then I remembered how my eyes were open, and I could see all the threads . . . the spirit that wanted to claim me, and the one that wanted me to rise. If not for Orenna, I think I would have kept swimming the deep." She paused, her gaze on the fire. The stew was bubbling now, but neither of them made to remove it. "I'm sorry, Torin. I didn't mean to make you or Graeme worry. I just needed to do something to find Maisie. And I didn't realize so much time had passed. I dove into the loch at midday and returned at dusk, but only because I thought Maisie was in the water. It looked *just* like her."

Torin reached out to caress Sidra's hair. "Don't go back there, Sidra. Don't ever return to that loch."

She met his stare. She was remorseful and sad, but there was also a hint of defiance in her, and he knew he couldn't command her. Not even to spare his heart.

Sidra turned away to lift the cauldron from the fire, giving him no chance to speak further. She carried the pot to the table and served two bowls.

Torin sat across from her. He tried to eat, but the food was like ash in his mouth. He broke the bannock and offered her a piece, but even Sidra struggled to eat. She pushed the stew around with her spoon.

His stomach felt full of stones by the time they decided to rest.

Sidra banked the fire and crawled into bed, lying on her

side. Torin took his time removing his boots and dirty clothes, then eased onto the mattress beside her. He blew out the candle and stared up into the darkness. Sidra's back was angled to him; he felt the distance between them like a chasm.

He didn't know how to cross this divide, how to comfort her when his own soul was in anguish. His mind wandered the same tracks it had taken all day. He kept envisioning Maisie, terrified and hurt. Why couldn't he find her?

Torin went taut as the tension in his body intensified. He couldn't draw breath. His panic was a winged creature, beating within his rib cage. It wanted to consume him, but he focused on what was tangible around him—the soft mattress, the scent of lavender on the pillow, the rise and fall of Sidra's breaths.

She sniffed, like she was weeping and trying to hide it from him.

Torin's thoughts returned to her. He wanted to touch her but didn't know if she wanted the same. He chose to remain still, fettered by uncertainty, his face marked with pain as he listened to her tears finally ebb.

He remembered the first time he had met Sidra, four years ago.

He had been riding through the Vale of Stonehaven, a rarity, as it was one of the more peaceful places of the isle, inhabited by shepherds and their wandering flocks. He hadn't patrolled the valley since his first year as a guard, but for some reason he had taken the eastern road on his way home from a shift.

He was thinking about Maisie. She was eight months old, and Graeme was caring for her by day. But the arrangement couldn't go on forever. Torin knew he could do better by his daughter. That he should do better.

His stallion spooked at a shadow, a play of wind in the oak branches above him. Torin was tossed from the saddle and promptly found himself facedown in the dirt, his left shoulder throbbing. He couldn't even recall the last time he had been thrown by his horse.

Mortified, he rose and brushed the dirt from his clothes, hoping no one but the spirits had seen him fall. His shoulder was dislocated. He knew it was, and he gritted his teeth as one of the younger guards came trotting up the road behind him.

"Do you need help fetching your horse, Torin?"

"No."

Torin's stallion had wandered off toward one of the shepherd's houses. He motioned the guard to go on his way as he strode to reclaim his horse.

"Ah, that's convenient," the guard called after him.

"What is?" Torin ground out.

"Well, Senga Campbell and her granddaughter live there."

Senga Campbell was the castle healer. She personally attended to the laird and his family and was renowned for her skill. Despite that, Torin hadn't known she had a granddaughter, and he failed to make sense of what the guard was saying.

"Very well. She has a granddaughter." Torin threw up his hands and then winced.

"Her granddaughter is a healer as well, you know. I'm sure she'd be happy to reset your shoulder for you." The guard cantered off down the road with his amusement, and Torin swore as he finally chased his horse down in the Campbells' yard.

Their house was quiet. It seemed that no one was home, and Torin paused when he noticed their garden. He had never seen a more organized and beautiful kail yard.

He tethered his horse to the gate and walked to the front door, frightening a cat from the stoop. He knocked and waited, listening as someone moved within the house.

It was Sidra who answered the door.

She was dressed in simple homespun. A smudge of dirt

was on her cheek. Her long black hair was loose and spilled over her shoulders. A stray flower was caught within the tangles. All of his thoughts unexpectedly scattered at the sight of her, and he said nothing.

"Who is at the door, Sidra?" an older woman's voice—Senga's—rasped from within.

"I don't know who he is," Sidra said, to Torin's great shock. Nearly everyone knew who he was. He was the laird's nephew, and an esteemed member of the East Guard . . . "He is a man, and his horse just ate all the carrots in my garden."

Torin flushed. "Forgive me. But I seem to have dislocated my shoulder."

"You *seem* to have?" Sidra echoed, and her eyes drifted to it. "Ah, yes. You have. Come in. My nan can help you."

"Is that Torin Tamerlaine?" Senga asked, recognizing his voice as he followed Sidra into the cottage. The revered healer sat at the table, grinding herbs with her pestle and mortar. But she hadn't been the one to reset his shoulder. It had been Sidra.

Torin keenly felt the touch of her hands through his sleeve as she brought his shoulder back into its socket. It caught him by surprise; he had been numb for so long now. He had been merely existing for the past eight months. And yet he noticed Sidra's hands like they were sunlight, burning away the last of his fog.

"This is very unusual," he said as Sidra knotted a sling about his arm. "Me being tossed from my horse, that is. I can't remember the last time it happened. It rarely happens, you know. Or perhaps you wouldn't know, since this is our first time meeting." He was stammering, as if the words were thistledown in his mouth.

Sidra only smiled.

Her grandmother was listening to them, even though they

sat on the other side of the chamber, beside the slow burning embers of the hearth. Senga had ceased crushing her herbs, and the house fell quiet. There was only the sound of birdsong, drifting in through the cracked shutters, and a calico cat purring on a folded plaid.

"Why have I never seen you before?" Torin whispered to Sidra.

She met his gaze. Her eyes were the color of wildflower honey. She had freckles on her cheeks, across the bridge of her nose. One was at the corner of her lips.

He felt as though he should know her. As though he would remember if he had seen her before. Her grandmother frequently visited the city, caring for his uncle and cousin. Shouldn't Senga's apprentice be with her?

"I confess," Sidra began in a husky voice, "that I have seen you before, Torin Tamerlaine. Years ago, when Lady Lorna still lived and played for the clan on feast nights in the castle hall. But I believe you and I belonged to different circles at the time, didn't we?"

He didn't know what to say, because she was right. He wondered what else he had missed and overlooked in the past. "And what of now? Do you still come to the city these days, Sidra Campbell?"

She glanced away to fiddle with a bowl of herbs, as if she wanted a distraction. But she said, "My nan cares for the laird and his daughter in the city. I remain here in the vale, to care for the shepherds and the crofters."

"And for stupid men like me, I suppose."

Sidra's smile deepened, awakening a dimple in her left cheek. "Aye. And for men like you." She seemed to remember her grandmother's presence, because she said, "Here, let me walk you to the door."

Torin followed and asked how much he owed her.

"You don't owe me anything," Sidra replied, leaning against the doorframe. "But perhaps a basket of carrots."

The next day Torin sent *two* baskets of carrots to Sidra's door. To atone for the ones his horse had eaten and to express his gratitude to her.

That was how the isle brought them together.

Sidra stirred in the bed.

Torin listened as she turned on her back. He felt the warmth of her body as they touched. She stiffened in response.

"Torin?" she whispered, uncertain.

"Yes, it's me."

She was quiet, but her posture relaxed against him. He believed she had fallen back asleep until she whispered, "I'm ready."

"Ready for what, Sid?"

"For you to bring me a guard dog."

CHAPTER 13

Jack spent the next day studying Lorna's music for the earth. He gathered pieces of nature, holding them in his hands, breathing their fragrance, studying their intricacy along-side her music. She had written a stanza for the grass, for the wildflowers, for the stones, for the trees, for the bracken. There were many different elements to this ballad, and Jack wanted to perfect them all, thinking that so long as he respected the earth and strove to honor it, there would be no need for him to be worried when he played.

But there was one problem.

His hands still ached, down to his fingertips.

"Jack?" Mirin knocked on the bedroom door. "May I enter?"

He hesitated, wondering if he should hide the strange harvest on his desk. In the end, he let it be, although he turned over Lorna's music. "Yes. Come in, Mum."

Mirin stepped inside, holding a bowl. She approached his

desk, and while she noticed the stray pieces of nature scattered before him, she said nothing until she set the soup down.

"You need to eat."

Jack eyed the nettle soup. "I'm not hungry, Mum."

"I know you're not," said Mirin. "But you still need to eat."

"I'll eat later."

"You should eat now," she insisted. "It'll help you recover faster."

Jack glanced up at her, sharply. But when he saw the worry lining Mirin's expression, he let his protest fade.

"You thought I wouldn't notice?" she said. "Oh, Jack."

"It's nothing to fret about, Mum."

"As I'm sure you'd like for me to say to you," she countered. "Prove me wrong and take a few sips."

He sighed but relented, lifting the edge of the bowl to his lips. He drank until his stomach began to churn, and he set it aside.

"What's ailing you the most?" Mirin persisted.

"My hands," he said, curling his fingers inwards. Every knuckle emitted a vibrant ache, and he wasn't sure how long he would be able to play his harp.

"Have you seen Sidra about it?"

"No."

"You should visit her. She'll be able to provide you with tonics that will help ease your symptoms."

"I don't want something that will dull my senses," he said.

"They won't," Mirin replied. "Sidra knows what to mix to avoid such things."

She slipped out of the room, leaving behind the bowl of nettle soup. Jack stared at it, then flexed his hands again. After considering Mirin's suggestion for a few more minutes, he knew she was right.

Jack had never been one to ask for help, but if he was to play this long ballad, he needed it.

He rose from his desk, packed up his harp, and walked to Sidra's house.

Sidra wanted to lose herself in work. When she was in the company of her herbs, she didn't think about Maisie being lost, frightened, or dead. When she held her pestle and mortar, Sidra didn't think about being assaulted on the hill that had previously held nothing but good memories for her. When she brought ingredients together, she didn't think of the new strain on her marriage to Torin, because the one thing they had built it on had vanished.

No, she thought only of nettles and bogbean, spoonwort and coltsfoot, elderflower and primrose.

When it was dark, she feared being alone in this cottage. But in the light? She wanted to be on familiar ground, working. She wanted to make something good with her hands, or else she felt utterly useless.

She wanted to be here, in case Maisie found her way home.

Torin and the East Guard had all been tirelessly working—searching homes for the kidnapper and the lasses, searching graveyards for the flowers—and Sidra had concocted a new tonic for them. One that would keep them sharp and alert, even on little sleep. She was almost done with a new batch when a tentative knock sounded on her door.

Sidra paused. She wasn't expecting anyone, and she almost reached for her paring knife, her heart quickening.

"Sidra?" a voice called.

She recognized it. Jack Tamerlaine, the bard. One of the last people she ever expected to call upon her.

Sidra quickly answered the door. Jack stood in her yard,

squinting against the sunlight. He had brought his harp, which surprised her.

"I hope I'm not bothering you," he began, hesitant.

"No, not at all," Sidra replied. Her voice was hoarse from weeping, from a long night with little sleep. "How can I help you, Jack?"

"I wanted to see if you could make a tonic for me."

She nodded, motioning him to step inside. She shut the door and returned to her table. He was gazing down at all of her herbs, as if she had caught a rainbow and laid it over the wood.

"I want to say how sorry I am," he said, glancing at her. "About Maisie."

Sidra nodded. Her throat was suddenly too narrow to speak.

"And I wanted to tell you that I'm doing everything that I can to help find her," Jack said. It seemed like he wanted to say more but refrained. He flexed one of his hands; the motion caught Sidra's attention.

"Your hands ail you?" she asked.

"Yes. They ache when I play certain songs."

"Is that all of your symptoms?"

"No, there are others."

She listened as he described them. Sidra had assisted with enough magic-imposed illnesses to know Jack was suffering from one. Most magic wielders suffered from headaches, chills, loss of appetite, and fevers. Others developed hacking coughs, insomnia, pain in their extremities, even nosebleeds. It seemed Jack was experiencing several symptoms, which meant he had cast a powerful magic. And while she didn't have the details of its inspiration, she knew the magic had to come from his craft. From his music.

She wondered if he had come home just for the missing lasses or if he'd inadvertently become caught up in the mystery after he arrived. There seemed little that a bard could do to help find the clan's girls, even as talented as Jack likely was, but Sidra knew there was unspoken power in music. She remembered being a young girl, sitting in the hall on full moon feast nights. She remembered inhaling Lorna Tamerlaine's songs as if they were air.

An unexpected peace settled over Sidra as she worked to make Jack two different remedies: a salve to spread on his hands when they ached, and a tonic for him to drink to ease his headaches. There was nothing she could do for the nosebleeds, save instruct him on how to apply pressure to ease the bleeding when it happened.

"That's fine, Sidra," he said. "It's my hands I'm most concerned about."

He sat in a chair and watched her work. She was lost in her thoughts when he asked, "Have many of your patients died prematurely from wielding magic?"

Sidra paused, glancing across the table at him. "Yes. Although there are many factors at play."

"Such as what?"

"How often the magic is wielded," Sidra began, crushing a medley of herbs and ingredients together. "How long the magic is cast. And the depth of the magic. A weaver, for instance, casts deep magic standing at the loom, and it takes a good while to weave an enchanted plaid. But someone like a fisherman, making an enchanted net, can work faster and not have to worry about details as much. The magical cost, then, is not as demanding for a fisherman as it is for a weaver."

Jack was silent. Sidra looked at him and saw how pale he was. She should have used a different example, because she read his mind: he was worrying about Mirin.

"Your mother is very wise and cautious," Sidra added. "She takes time between enchanted commissions, and she is very faithful about drinking her tonics."

"Yes. But the cost has already stolen some of her best years, hasn't it?" he countered.

Sidra finished making the salve. She picked up the bowl and approached Jack, hating to see the sadness in his eyes.

"I may know the secrets of herbs," she said. "But I'm not a seer. I can't foretell what is to come, but I do know that the people who wield magic are made of a different mettle than most. They are passionate about what they do; their craft is as much a part of them as breathing. To deny it would be like losing a piece of themselves. And while there is a cost and a direct consequence to spinning enchantments, none of them see it as a burden but as a gift."

Jack was silent, scowling. But he was listening to her.

"So yes, the magic might steal years from you," she said. "Yes, it will make you ill and you will have to learn how to care for yourself in a new way. But I don't think you'll choose to give up your craft either, will you, Jack?"

"No," he said.

"Then hold out your hands."

He obliged, with his harp balanced carefully on his lap. Sidra spread the salve over the backs of his hands, over every knuckle and vein.

"It might take a moment to feel its effects," she said, transferring the rest of the salve into a jar he could take with him.

Jack closed his eyes. After a minute, he flexed his hands again and grinned. "Yes, this has been a tremendous help. Thank you, Sidra."

She brought him his tonic and the salve. Jack tucked both jars in his pocket before asking, "How much do I owe you?"

Sidra returned to the table. "You owe me nothing."

"I was worried you might say that," Jack said wryly. He began to remove his harp from its skin. "I would like to play for you, while you work. If you will let me."

Sidra was stunned. She stared as he propped the harp against his left shoulder. It had been so long since she had enjoyed music.

She smiled. "I would love that."

"Do you have any requests?" Jack asked as he tuned the harp.

"I do, in fact. Lorna used to play a ballad on feast nights. I believe it was called 'The Last Moon of Autumn.'"

"I know the very one," Jack replied.

He began to strum. His notes filled the chamber, driving away the sadness and the shadows. Sidra closed her eyes, amazed at how the song could take her back in time to a bittersweet moment. She was sixteen, her hair in two long braids, anchored by red ribbons. She was sitting in the castle hall with her grandmother, listening to Lorna play her harp. This very song.

A slight breeze touched her face.

Sidra opened her eyes and saw the front door was agape. Adaira stood on the threshold, frozen by Jack's music as it continued to trickle through the cottage. Sidra studied her friend closely; she had never seen this expression on Adaira's face before, as if all the longings within her had gathered into one place.

Jack was wholly unaware he had a new audience member until he reached the end. His music faded in the air and he glanced up, his eyes finding Adaira. The silence felt tense, as if the two of them wanted to speak but couldn't.

Sidra broke the spell.

"That was beautiful," she said. "Thank you, Jack."

He nodded and began to put his harp away. "I appreciate your help, Sidra."

"My door is always open to you." She watched as he rose and approached the threshold. Adaira angled her body so he could slip past her, and they still said nothing to each other, even as the air crackled.

Now that Jack was gone, Adaira entered the house, shutting the door. Sidra knew she had come to be with her, to keep her company, and to help create the guards' tonics.

Adaira glanced over the table and rolled up her sleeves. "Tell me what to do, Sid."

Sometimes this was what Sidra loved best about Adaira. Her willingness to get dirty, to learn new things. How direct she was.

She was the younger sister Sidra never had but always yearned for.

"Crush this stack of herbs for me," Sidra said, edging the pestle and mortar toward her.

Adaira began to work, crushing with intensity. Sidra understood it, that nagging feeling: *I need to do something. I need to do something that has meaning.*

"What did you help him with?" Adaira eventually asked.

"Who do you speak of, Adi?"

"Jack, of course. Why was he here?"

Sidra reached for an empty bottle. She began to pour the tonic within it. "You know I can't say why."

Adaira pressed her lips together. She was tempted to draw it out of Sidra, and as the future laird, perhaps she could. But Sidra held her patients' secrets like her own, and Adaira knew it.

The women fell silent, working together in tandem. Adaira was corking the bottles when she finally spoke again, her tone heavy.

"I need your advice, Sid." She hesitated. "I don't want to burden you with this. Not when you're going through so much yourself. But time is not on my side."

"Tell me what's on your mind, Adi," Sidra said gently.

She listened as Adaira spoke about the confidential trade, the letters she had been writing to Moray Breccan. The invitation to visit the west, and the first trade exchange, both of which were to be done alone.

"Sometimes I worry that I'm choosing the wrong path," Adaira said with a sigh. "That my inexperience is going to doom us. That I'm foolish to yearn for peace."

"It's not a foolish dream," Sidra was swift to respond. "And you are right to seek a new way of life for our clan, Adaira. For too long we've been raised on fear and hatred, and it's time for things to change. I think many of the Tamerlaines inwardly feel the same and would follow you anywhere, even if that means a few difficult years of rethinking who we are and what this isle beneath our feet should become."

Adaira met Sidra's gaze. "I'm relieved you agree, Sid. But I still have a problem with the trade."

"Tell me."

"The Breccans need our resources, but what do we need from them? Their enchanted plaids and swords that they use to attack us with? Do I dare ask for such things, knowing it's counterproductive for this notion of peace I'm working to establish between us?"

Sidra was quiet, but her mind was racing.

"This is what my father and Torin persist in asking me," Adaira continued. "The Breccans have nothing we need. This trade will favor them at our expense, and it may not even halt their raiding ways. Torin predicts this will happen—the trade will be good for a season, and we'll give our stores to them. But come winter, the Breccans will decide to raid. Such an action would tip us into war."

"There's a chance Torin is right," Sidra said. "It's a possibility we must prepare for, as much as I wish to reassure you peace would be easy and bloodless to obtain." Her gaze swept the table, absently passing over her herbs. Her eyes caught on the last Orenna flower, which she was storing in a glass vial. A chill coursed through her, and she rubbed her chest. Her bruises were aching today as her body began to heal. "But what if the Breccans have something we need?"

Adaira frowned. "What do you mean, Sid?"

Sidra reached for the vial. She held the Orenna flower up to the light and realized her hand was trembling. She hadn't dared to think along these lines yet because Torin was determined to find her assaulter in the east, having felt no one crossing the clan line. But neither had he found a graveyard, peppered with small crimson blooms.

"Has Torin told you about this flower?"

"Briefly," Adaira said. "He believes it may be aiding the kidnapper."

Sidra nodded. "This flower is called Orenna, and it only grows on a small patch of dry, heartsick land. Somewhere on the isle, in a graveyard. We have yet to find such a place in the east."

Adaira studied the flower. Her eyes widened. "You think . . ."

"This flower may be growing in the west," Sidra concluded. "I haven't said as much to Torin yet because I'm hopeful he will find the graveyard here. But if the Orenna flower *is* growing on Breccan soil, not only could we use it for ourselves, but it would mean that the west is somehow involved with our missing lasses."

Adaira released a deep breath. "Torin hasn't felt anyone crossing the clan line, though."

"No, he hasn't, which does lend credence to the perpetrator being one of our own," Sidra said. "But maybe there is a trade happening that we don't know of. Perhaps the culprit is secretly receiving flowers from the west."

Adaira bit her lip. Sidra could sense how conflicted she was, and yet her eyes were bright. Feverish. Now that Adaira had entertained Sidra's thoughts, she couldn't unsee them.

"What is the best way for me to receive this information?" Adaira asked.

Sidra set the glass vial in her palm. "I think you go to meet Moray Breccan on the clan line in three days' time, as he has requested. Generously bring him the best of the Tamerlaine oats, barley, honey, and wine. Whatever he offers you in return, accept with gratitude, but then ask him about this flower. Say you would like to trade for its blooms. If he says he doesn't recognize it, then he might be speaking truth or he might be lying. If he does recognize the flower, then we know the west is involved, even if it's something as simple as passing flowers over the clan line. Either way, you have a chance to discover it for yourself by participating in the trade, and I think you have the right to take someone with you."

Adaira was silent, regarding the flower.

Sidra glanced down at her hands, where her golden wedding band gleamed on her finger. She and Torin had had no qualms about exchanging a blood vow at their wedding. They spoke the ancient words and cut their palms. Their hands were bound together, wound to wound. *Bone of my bone, flesh of my flesh, blood of my blood.* It was a vow not easily broken, although Sidra was beginning to wonder how long it would last without Maisie.

"The Breccans may deny you a guard," Sidra said, watching Adaira. "Or your father. Or even a handmaiden. But they can't deny you a husband."

Adaira flushed, as if her mind had already gravitated toward such thoughts. She had been in no rush to marry in the past, which Sidra thought wise. But it was time for the future Laird of the East to take a partner. If she was going to forge a difficult and potentially bloody peace, she needed someone to carry her through it. To walk at her side. To confide in. To comfort her on long, lonely nights.

Sidra didn't have to ask who Adaira was considering.

She already knew.

Adaira gave herself the rest of the day to think about it. A day she spent roaming the hills, searching for a sign. A day that produced no answers from Torin and the guard, despite their interviews and observations. When Adaira realized she wasn't going to waver and that time was against her, she decided to move forward with her plans.

She waited until the moon rose, thinking she would be braver at night, and dressed simply in a dark dress and cloak. She rode to Mirin's croft, following the stars.

She dismounted at the road and left her horse hobbled by a tree. Quietly walking through the yard, she located Jack's bedroom window. He was still awake, as she hoped he would be. The candlelight seeped through his shutters, and she walked to them, a moth drawn to the fire.

Even so determined, she hesitated when she reached her destination. She stood at the window and debated with herself.

I can't believe I'm doing this, she thought and finally knocked.

She was tempted to turn and run when she heard him cautiously unlatch his shutters. They swung open, at last revealing Jack. His scowl melted into disbelief when he saw it was her.

"Adaira?"

"I need to have a word with you, Jack."

He glanced about his room before returning his gaze to her, standing in the moonlight. *"Now?"*

"Aye. It can't wait."

"Well, come in then. But be quiet. I don't want you to wake my mum." He extended his hand to her, and Adaira accepted it, shocked by how warm his fingers were as they entwined with her cold ones.

She lifted her hem and let Jack haul her up through the window. Her boots clunked on the top of his desk, which was strewn with all manner of oddities. Twigs, rocks, clumps of moss, braids of grass, wilted wildflowers. Adaira stepped down to the floor, still holding his hand, and she turned to gaze at the strange collection.

"What is all of this?" she asked.

"Preparation," he replied. "I should be ready to play for the earth by tomorrow afternoon."

"Good." Adaira felt his fingers unwind from hers. He flexed his hand, and she wondered if he disliked touching her. Or maybe there was another reason he disengaged his hand. She watched as he walked to his bed, where Lorna's music was scattered. He gathered up the loose sheets and attempted to straighten the wrinkled blanket, to offer her a place to sit.

"I prefer to stand," she said when he turned to her. "But you should sit."

Jack's brows lowered with suspicion. "Why?"

"Trust me."

To her surprise, he did. He sat on the edge of his bed and carefully set her mother's composition beside his pillow. "Now then. Are you going to tell me why you've come to my room like a thief in the night?"

She smiled but delayed answering him while she meandered around his chamber, studying it. Jack was quiet, suffering through her examination of his things. She expected him to protest or rush her along—he was such an impatient man—but he was silent, and when she at last came to a stop before him, his eyes, inscrutable and deliciously dark, were fixed on hers. Almost as if he knew why she had come.

She shivered.

Her heart quickened as she knelt on one knee before him, a position she would take for no other man save her father.

Jack watched her intently. She didn't know how exactly she had expected him to react—whether he would laugh, curse, frown, or scorn her. He did none of those things. As his eyes remained on her, she knew he realized the magnitude of her bending a knee to him.

Her hair flowed down her shoulders like a shield, and yet her courage wavered. *He will never agree to this,* she thought, but it was too late now. He must know her intentions, and she was too proud to alter her course.

"John Tamerlaine," she began to say.

"*Jack.*"

Adaira blinked, astounded he had just interrupted her proposal. "Your given and legal name is John."

"But I answer only to Jack."

"Very well then," Adaira said through her teeth, and she could feel the color rising in her face. "*Jack* Tamerlaine. Handfast yourself to me. Give me your vow and be my husband for a year and a day, and thereafter should we both desire it."

Jack was silent, as if he expected her to say more. Adaira keenly felt the pain in her knee as she held her position. The prickling dread of waiting for his answer. When his silence dragged on, she let out a huff of air.

"What do you say, Jack? Give me an answer, so I may rise."

He dragged his hand through his hair, leaving it more tousled than it had been before. His expression was solemn, conflicted, as he continued to regard her. "Why, Adaira? Why are you asking me? Is it because you need someone to go with you into the west?"

"Yes," she said. She didn't tell him the whole of it. She didn't tell him that she was lonely, that she was overwhelmed some days with all the responsibilities that were set before her. That she sometimes wanted to be held and listened to and touched, that she wanted to be with someone who challenged her, sharpened her, made her laugh. Someone she could trust.

She looked at Jack and she saw that person. She didn't love him, but maybe in time she would. If they decided to remain as one.

"You know what I am," he said in a flat voice.

"A bard?"

"A bastard. I have no father, no proud lineage, no lands. I have nothing to offer you, Adaira."

"There is much you can offer me," she countered, heady from the mere thought of his music. Spirits below, he had no idea the power he wielded. "And those things you mention don't matter to me."

"But they matter to *me*," Jack said, with a fist over his heart. He leaned closer to her, so that their breaths mingled. "People will be appalled when they realize you want to marry me. That you chose me. Out of all the men in the east, I am the most unworthy."

"Let them," Adaira said. "Let them be appalled, let them talk. Let them say whatever they want. It will soon fade, I promise you. And when it fades . . . it will be you and me and the truth. And that is all that matters in the end."

She studied his face—the faint lines in his brow made from a stern countenance, the press of his lips, the brown hair dangling over his left eye—and realized he was still unconvinced. He was debating if he wanted to accept her or not, and Adaira didn't know what she would do if he refused her. She didn't *need* him; she could rule the east on her own. Likewise, she could ask another man to marry and accompany her into the west. But in some deep, hidden place she had found that she *wanted* her husband to be him.

She had thought it wiser and more enticing for both of them

to offer him a handfast—a marriage by trial, which would last just over a year. If they came to hate one another again, they could part ways and be no longer bound by oath when the agreement ended. Or they could remain wed and take a blood vow, if they desired it.

"All of this," he said. "Marrying your 'old menace,' choosing to bind yourself to me—someone *far* beneath you. All of this trouble only to visit and establish trade with our enemies? Why wouldn't you choose a partner who could be your shield? A member of the guard, perhaps?"

He's being ridiculously logical, Adaira thought. She wondered how to reply to him. She wanted to tell him that she could see through him—he was holding to logic in order to keep his emotions at bay. But then she saw the glint of doubt in him. She saw the hurt in his eyes. He was hiding a wound. He had never felt claimed; he had never felt as if he belonged here. She vividly remembered him saying those words to her.

"You're right," she said. "I could choose a member of the guard to bind myself to. I could choose anyone in the east who is eligible. Yet there's a problem with such a choice, Jack."

He was quiet. She could sense the battle raging within him, to remain aloof and uninterested, or to ask her to explain.

"What problem do you speak of, Adaira?" he eventually said.

"None of them are the one that I want," she breathed.

She hadn't been this vulnerable with someone in a long time. It was terrifying, and she could feel the heat in her skin, the flush creeping over her. Because Jack was silent.

"I know you have a life on the mainland waiting for you," she rushed to add. "I know that our handfast would keep you away longer than you wanted. But the clan needs you. You can take up the mantle as Bard of the East, and even if we choose to end our marriage after a year and a day . . . you would remain bard here, should you desire it."

Jack was like stone.

Adaira must have miscalculated. He must still detest her and the clan.

When she made to rise, he stretched out his hand, as if to touch her, but then he hesitated, just before his fingers could caress her hair. "Wait, Adaira. *Wait.*"

She paused, thinking her knee would be completely out of socket by the end of this tumultuous night. But she watched the hint of a smile overcome his face, and she was stunned by the beauty of it. The promise that gleamed within him, a man who rarely smiled.

"I honestly don't even know what to say, Adaira."

"You say yes or no, Jack."

He covered his mouth with his hand, hiding his mirth, and stared at her with his ocean-dark eyes. But he rose, and he took hold of her fingers, bringing her with him, up to her tingling feet.

"Then my answer is yes," he whispered. "I'll marry you by handfast."

Relief rushed through her. She nearly sagged, and then felt how near he stood to her, so close she could feel the warmth of his body.

"Good. Oh, that reminds me, bard," she said and took a graceful step back, their hands still fastened. "I have a condition."

"Gods," Jack groaned. "You couldn't tell me your condition *before* you asked me to wed you?"

"No, but you won't mind." Her eyes flickered to the bed behind him, and the words nearly caught in her throat like a bone. "Once we're married, we keep to our separate beds. At least for now." When she met his gaze again, she couldn't discern if he was disappointed or relieved. His face was as composed as music, a language she couldn't read.

"Agreed," he said and squeezed her hands before releasing them. "And now I have something to say to you."

Adaira waited, her heart beating far too swiftly for her liking. Jack was staring at her, as if he were about to divulge dire information.

"Well?" she prodded, bracing herself for the worst. "What is it?"

"Quite impatient, aren't we?"

Adaira frowned, but she saw the amusement shining in his eyes. "You have made me wait quite a bit tonight, old menace."

"Only for a minute or two," he replied. "For which you will now have me for an entire year and a day, so I think it was worth the wait."

"Time will tell, won't it?" she quipped.

Jack snorted and crossed his arms, but she sensed he was enjoying their banter. "Perhaps I should tell you my news tomorrow then."

"But tomorrow already has enough trouble planned," Adaira said, biting her lip to resist begging him.

He grinned. She had never beheld such joy in him, and she almost reached out to trace his face.

"Then let me tell you now, heiress. I would be honored to play for the clan as Bard of the East."

She swallowed, struggling to hide her elation. But a smile broke across her lips; she could feel tears pricking the corners of her eyes.

"That's good news, Jack. Perhaps we can have a ceremony for you, and we can—"

"No ceremony," he gently interrupted. "When I become your husband, I also become the clan's bard. Don't you agree that is best?"

Adaira nodded, rubbing her collarbone. "Yes, you're right. This will help temper the clan's expectations as well, since you might only play for a year and a day. I know there is a chance of you deciding to leave if our handfast breaks, and . . . yes, the clan should know that."

Jack was silent for a beat. But his eyes held hers, and he whispered, "I think it's fair enough to say that I won't be returning to the mainland, Adaira."

She breathed in his words and held them deep within her, uncertain how to respond. "Are you certain, Jack? You might change your mind a few months from now."

"I'm certain. If I wanted to go back, I would have by now."

"The clan . . . the clan will be very happy to hear this."

"Yes," he said. "When is the handfast?"

"It needs to be soon."

"How soon?"

She hesitated before answering, "Two days?"

"Is that a question or a statement, Adaira?"

"I have to meet Moray Breccan at the clan line in three days for the trade of goods," she said. "I would like for you to be there with me, as my husband."

Jack stared at her, his lips parting. She knew this was happening fast. She could sense how he was reeling, and she worried that she had asked too much of him in one night.

"So we'll play for the earth tomorrow," he said, listing their tasks on his fingers. "The next day we'll marry. And the day after that we'll go to our deaths at the clan line for a trade?"

"We're not going to die," Adaira said. "But yes, that's the plan, if I'm not asking too much of you."

"It's not too much," said Jack. "Although I must confess . . . you have my thoughts spinning."

"Then I should go," she whispered. "Let you get some rest."

A small voice told her to prepare herself. That come morning Jack would have changed his mind and she would be deposited back where she started.

She had been let down before, broken by silver-tongued promises, and she wanted to protect herself from it. She wanted to slip back into her old armor, even as Jack's eyes traced her.

"I'll come to you tomorrow, just after noontide," he said. "There's something I must attend to in the morning, but after that I'll be ready to play."

"Yes, of course. Thank you, Jack."

He moved to clear off the center of his desk, so she could easily step on it this time without disturbing his fragments of nature. Jack offered his hand again, and she took it, her fingers like ice as she climbed onto the desk and slipped out the window, cloak flapping in her wake. Her ankles jarred when she hit the grass, and she stood for a moment, uncertain if she should bid her betrothed farewell.

She turned to see him leaning on his desk, staring at her as if he was trying to convince himself that this wasn't a dream. The firelight limned his face, burned in his eyes like stars.

No, Adaira thought as she drew up her hood, her face shadowed and hidden from him. No further words were necessary.

Adaira wrote her response that night, not long after she returned from visiting Jack. She sat at her desk in her bedroom and listened to the fire as it crackled in her hearth, listened to the wind as it tapped on the glass. She took out a sheet of parchment, selected a fresh quill, and opened her pot of ink.

> *Dear Moray,*
> *I have received your letter, and I agree to meet you at the clan line in three days' time at noontide on the northern coast. I will bring the best my clan has to offer you, and I am eager to see what the west will offer in return. As you stated before, let this exchange between us be the first step toward peace, and a new season for our isle.*

You asked me to come alone for the trade, and while I will meet you unarmed and without my guard, my husband will be present. We can then discuss my imminent visit to the west. We look forward to meeting you face-to-face.

Adaira Tamerlaine
HEIRESS OF THE EAST

She sealed it with her clan crest and watched the wax harden. It was midnight when she rose and carried the letter to the aviary, where she chose the sleekest raven to deliver her message.

She watched as it flew west, into the darkest hour of night.

CHAPTER 14

Frae stood beside Mirin, watching her weave on the loom. It was an ordinary plaid, one that didn't hold a secret because Frae wasn't to learn that skill until she came of age. And yet Frae's eyes felt crossed amongst all the threads. No matter how she tried, she didn't see what her mother did. She couldn't see the possibilities, how to make a pattern come to life, but she dutifully watched Mirin work.

The chamber brimmed with the clack of the shuttle, the musty fragrance of wool being woven—sounds and scents that were familiar but made Frae daydream. She stifled a yawn as her thoughts wandered.

When a knock sounded at the door, Frae's heart lifted, grateful for the interruption, and she went to answer it.

Torin stood on the threshold.

Frae gaped at the captain for a moment, wondering why he had come. She thought maybe he was back to search the house again, but then she noticed a black-and-white collie panting at his side.

"Good afternoon, Fraedah," Torin said. "Is your mum home?"

Frae shyly nodded and opened the door further.

Torin commanded the dog to sit and wait on the stoop before entering with muddy boots. Frae shut the door, uncertain whether to leave or stay.

"Captain," Mirin greeted him, turning away from the loom. "How may I help you?"

"I've come to commission you, Mirin," he replied.

"Another plaid, in the vein of your others?" Mirin asked, nodding to Frae, who hurried to boil some water for tea.

"No, not for me," Torin said. "It's for Sidra."

Frae listened to Torin describe the shawl he wanted Mirin to weave as she quietly filled the pot and carried it to the hearth. She had taught herself how to move without sound, how to move like a shadow. Her game of stealth ended only when she had to set the kettle on the iron hook and stir the logs, renewing the flames.

The talk began to drift from the plaid to what had transpired a few nights ago. Her mum hadn't wanted Frae to know all that had happened, but she had gathered bits and pieces of information, puzzling it all together to realize that Maisie had vanished and Sidra had been attacked. Sidra, who Frae thought was one of the most beautiful people on the isle.

The news had strengthened Frae's fears. It felt like her heart was bruised.

"How is Sidra today?" Mirin was asking.

"She's recovering," Torin answered. Frae thought his voice sounded different from normal. Like he was short of breath. "I'm still searching."

"No trace?"

He shook his head.

The tea prepared, Frae glanced at her mother, who was intently watching the captain.

"About this plaid, Mirin," he continued with an awkward wave of his hand. "I would like for it to be strong as steel. Something to guard her when I'm away."

He wanted it to be enchanted.

Mirin glanced at Frae, and Frae recognized it as *the* sign. The one that meant Frae was to go outside but to stay within the safety of the yard. She quickly filled two cups of tea and set them down on the table between Mirin and the captain, despite the fact neither of them had sat.

"Thank you, lass," Torin said with a sad smile. It made Frae feel like she was important, and she wished more than anything she could remain in the room and hear the secret Torin wanted Mirin to weave into the plaid.

"I'll go gather the eggs, Mum," Frae said and meekly departed, latching the front door behind her.

When she turned to the yard, she saw the dog, waiting on Torin to return. She tentatively stroked its fur before walking around the garden toward the coop.

Jack was in the byre yard, on his hands and knees. Frae ran to join him, her heart lifting. He had been working on the byre most of the morning, resetting stones and reframing the windows, thatching fresh straw for the roof. Frae was grateful for these repairs, because she worried about their three cows not having enough shelter when it rained and snowed. When the wind blew harshly from the north.

"Jack!" she greeted him, clambering over the stone wall.

He glanced up at her. His hair was tangled, his face sunburned. He looked so different now, Frae thought. The first night she had met him, she had thought he looked sad and pale, as if a breeze could sigh through him. Now his skin was darkening from the sun, his eyes were brighter, and his presence was strong, as if nothing could bend him.

"Did Mum send you to me, little sister?" he asked with a grin.

That was what she liked most about him. Almost as much as his music. Frae loved his smile, because it made her own rise, every time.

"Yes. Can I help?"

"Please do."

She knelt beside him and watched as he worked.

"I feel like you have always been here with us," she said. "It's hard to remember what it was like before you came home."

She hoped he never left.

"I'm glad to hear it, Frae. Here, why don't you help me bundle the straw?"

Together, they measured out golden heaps, which Jack would carry up the ladder to the roof, where he thatched the straw with sticks.

"I was so nervous," Frae blurted.

"What were you nervous about, sister?"

She wiped the dust from her hands and squinted up at him. "That you wouldn't like me."

Jack blinked. He looked stunned, as if she had just smacked him. Perhaps she shouldn't have said that, and Frae glanced down at her fingers, twirling a thread of straw. He reached over to affectionately tap her chin up.

"Impossible. You're the sister I always wanted."

Frae grinned. She was about to say something else when the back door of the cottage slammed, startling them both. Mirin never slammed doors. Their mother appeared in the yard, blazing a trail through the garden toward them.

"Uh-oh," Frae whispered, shooting to her feet.

Jack steadied her with a gentle hand on her shoulder.

"*John Tamerlaine!*" Mirin shouted and slammed the yard

gate next, so roughly that it bounced back open, creaking in protest. She was almost to the byre, and Jack slowly stood.

"Are you in trouble?" Frae asked him, anxiously twiddling the end of her braid.

"I think so," Jack replied.

Mirin came to a halt before them, but her glare was for Jack alone.

"When were you going to tell me, hmm?" she cried. "*After* you wed her?"

Frae's mouth fell open, and she turned to stare up at her brother.

Jack held Mirin's flinty stare, but he squeezed Frae's shoulder, as if silently begging her to remain at his side. Frae stepped closer to him.

"Of course not, Mum. She only just asked me."

"When is it? When is the wedding?"

"It's not a wedding. It's a handfast—"

Mirin tossed up her hands, her frustration palpable. "It'll be a wedding, son. You're marrying the heiress."

Frae gasped, her eyes round as saucers. She clapped her hand over her lips when Mirin and Jack both glanced at her.

Her brother was marrying *Adaira*.

Frae loved Adaira. She wanted to grow up to become Adaira. And now the heiress was going to be her sister.

Her heart began to pound with excitement. She could hardly keep still, and she felt like dancing.

"Marriage isn't a game, Jack," Mirin continued in a voice Frae rarely heard. A sharp, pointed cadence.

Jack shifted his weight. Frae could sense his anger. "I know what marriage is, and I don't step into it lightly, Mum."

"Do you love her?"

Jack was silent.

Frae laced her fingers together and gazed up at him, waiting to hear him say that he did.

"I care for her," he eventually said. "She has asked this of me, and I'm doing it because she wants it, and it's for the good of the clan."

Mirin's eyes thawed at last—Frae knew the worst of her temper was gone now. Her mother laid a hand over her throat, as if to calm her pulse. "What about your university, Jack?"

Frae winced, waiting for his reply. Would he take Adaira away with him?

"I'm done with teaching." The words slipped out of him in a growl. "I don't want to go back."

Frae almost jumped, a cheer rising in her throat. But she held it in, gazing up at her brother. Did that mean he was staying forever?

"And what do you plan to do here?" Mirin asked. "Other than be Adaira's partner?"

"She has asked me to become Bard of the East."

This time Frae couldn't hold in her excitement. She squealed and threw her arms around him. Sometimes Jack still felt stiff when she embraced him. But not that day. He hugged her back.

"This is a great honor she's giving you," Mirin said. "When is the wedding then?"

Jack hesitated before speaking in a very low voice. So deep Frae almost didn't catch his reply. "Tomorrow."

"*Tomorrow?*" Mirin shouted.

"Adaira's decision. Not mine."

"And what are you going to wear?"

"Clothes, I suppose."

Mirin swatted him, but she was hiding a smile, and the tension faded between them. "You've taken a few years off my life, Jack. Just . . . *look* at you. How did you convince her to ask you?"

He sighed. Frae studied him. She saw the dirt staining his nails, the splinters that had worked their way beneath his skin, the hay that hung in his hair like threads of gold.

He looked like he finally belonged here with them.

"Adaira asked me, and I said yes. Simple as that."

Mirin appeared unconvinced, but Frae knew better. She saw the light in her brother. She knew why Adaira had chosen him.

"I suppose I need to prepare your wedding garments then," Mirin said, hands on her hips as she studied him. "As quick as I can."

"Nothing enchanted, Mum," he warned her. "I will *only* wear ordinary clothes."

"And your hair needs trimming." She wasn't listening to him, and Jack stepped away when Mirin tried to pull the straw from his hair.

"My hair is fine." He began to stride to the back door, as if he wanted to escape.

Frae couldn't help but follow him, like a shadow. She followed him all the way to his bedroom, where he began to pack his harp.

She wondered where he was going, and then it struck her. Of course, he was going to see Adaira! He was so lucky; he could see her whenever he wanted now.

"Oh Jack!" Frae said, dancing on the balls of her feet. "It's like a dream come true."

He only smiled at her, reaching for a small stack of parchment. He tucked the paper into his harp case, and she sensed how anxious he was. Why was he nervous?

And then another realization hit her, like a fist to her stomach.

"*Oh no,*" Frae gasped.

Jack paused, glancing at her. "What's the matter, Frae?"

"Oh no," she said again, her joy disintegrating. She dragged her fingertips down her face. "If you marry Adaira . . . then you won't live here anymore."

Jack knelt before her. His harp was tucked beneath his arm, and his eyes were gentle as he looked at her.

"I'm honestly not sure what to expect in the next few days, sister," he said. "But I will never be far from you. That I can promise."

Frae nodded. He tapped her chin, provoking another smile from her.

The back door creaked, and Jack grimaced.

"Now I must fly," he whispered as he stood. "Before Mum catches me."

"You shouldn't run from Mum, Jack," Frae scolded. She watched, wide eyed, as her brother proceeded to climb on his desk. *"Jack!"*

He held his finger over his lips and winked at her. One moment he was there, crouched on his desk. The next he was gone, vanishing out the window.

"Frae?" Mirin said, pushing open the bedroom door. "Frae, where did your brother go?"

Frae was still staring at the window, amazed. "I think he went to see Adaira."

Mirin heaved a sigh. "A wedding. *Tomorrow.* Spirits below, what is Jack thinking?"

The excitement began to rise again. It tingled at Frae's fingertips, making her want to dance.

She was thrilled and astonished. And suddenly overwhelmed.

Frae turned, buried her face in Mirin's side, and wept.

The news spread like wildfire.

Jack stepped through pools of gossip as he walked the thoroughfare of Sloane. He felt every stare like a pinprick. He didn't falter, nor did he make eye contact, and he let the whispers drip off him like rain.

Why, the clan wondered. *Why would Adaira choose him?*

Why, indeed, Jack mused wryly as he was ushered into the hall to wait for Adaira. He sat at one of the dusty tables, thrumming his fingers on the wood, lost in contemplation.

He was still in shock that she had asked him to marry her, and that he had told her yes. He was beginning to realize more and more that he couldn't return to the mainland. Not when his mother was ill and he had a little sister and Adaira wanted him and the isle had embraced him despite all his years away. Not when he had played for the spirits of the sea.

He had changed, and he looked at his hands, now dirty from repairing the byre. He would have *never* attempted to rethatch a roof, or shovel manure, or reset stone walls in his academic life. His hands were his livelihood as a harpist—as vain as it sounded, he couldn't afford to break a nail—and yet he was pleased to know they had also made repairs on the byre. His hands could offer more to others than he had once thought or even wanted to give.

"Have you come to tell me you've changed your mind, bard?"

Adaira's voice was like a hook, reeling in his attention. Jack stood and turned to behold her standing in the aisle. Her hair was tamed into a braided crown that day. A moon thistle was tucked behind her ear like a rose, and there were faint smudges beneath her eyes. It was apparent she hadn't slept much either, Jack thought, admiring the crimson embroidery on her dress.

"My mind is unchanged, although I did wonder if I dreamt of you last night," he said, meeting her gaze. He was caught off guard by the defensive light that flickered within her, like moonlight on a steel blade. She had expected him to change his mind and disappoint her. Jack let the affront rise in him for a moment, then felt it fizzle away. This must be a wound within her; someone had once given her a promise and then broken it. Jack added, "I'll not go back on my word, Adaira."

She mellowed and stepped closer to him, noticing his harp. "You're prepared?"

Jack nodded, although he felt a pinch of worry. He had Sidra's tonic and salve packed away in his harp case, but he didn't know what to expect. He was both eager and hesitant to play for the spirits again, and he followed Adaira into the sunshine of the courtyard. She led him to the stables, to his great distress.

"Can't we walk?" he asked.

"This will be faster," Adaira said, mounting a dapple mare. "And besides, it will keep people from pestering us on the streets."

She made a good point. Jack still hesitated.

"I chose the gentlest of steeds for you to ride today," she said, indicating the bay gelding that waited beside her horse.

Jack gave Adaira a flat look but pulled himself up into the saddle.

They rode together to the Earie Stone, the heart of Eastern Cadence, where the hills began to rise into mountains.

Adaira and Jack left their horses safely hobbled by a creek and ascended the hill, where the stone sat jagged and proud on the summit, a ring of alder trees surrounding it like dancing maidens.

"It feels like yesterday, doesn't it, my old menace," Adaira said wistfully as she walked beneath the boughs.

Jack knew what she spoke of. He felt it too, the way time seemed to cease on this sacred ground. It was eleven years ago that he and Adaira had fought over the thistle patch, not far from here.

He stood beneath one of the trees, a reverent distance from the stone, and watched as Adaira continued to walk around the perimeter.

"I'm sorry, you know," she said, meeting his gaze. "I don't think I ever apologized for shoving my thistles into your face and then abandoning you to your fate."

"They were never your thistles to begin with," Jack teased. "You stole them from my secret patch. And you still do, I see." He nodded at the moon thistle tucked into her braid, and Adaira came to a stop an arm's length away from him.

"Shall we split the patch equally now? Would that make you happy, bard?"

Jack was silent for a beat, and then he said, "No. I don't want half of anything. Only all of it."

Adaira held his gaze. She drew a deep breath, as if she wanted to say something to him. Perhaps to acknowledge the electricity that was brewing between them. Jack hoped that she would speak it first. Every time he saw her, he felt it a little more. Felt the tension like a harp string within him, strung from rib to rib.

"Are you ready to play?" she asked.

He heaved a sigh, hiding his disappointment. But this was why he was here. To sing for the earth, not to name his feelings for Adaira.

Jack deliberated about where to sit—facing the stone or facing one of the trees. In the end, he opted to sit on the grass with his face to the stone, his harp arranged on his lap. Adaira only sat after he had settled, a few yards away from him.

As he began to strum on his harp, he filled his mind with images of earth. Old crumbling stones and tangled grasses, wildflowers and weeds and saplings that put down deep roots, growing into mighty trees. The color of dirt, the scent of it. How it felt clutched in the hollow of one's palm. The voice of branches, swaying in the breeze, and the slope of the earth as it rose and fell, faithful and steady.

Jack closed his eyes and began to sing. He didn't want to

see the spirits manifest, but he heard the grass hissing near his knees, and he heard the tree boughs groaning above him, and he heard the scratch of stone, as if two were being rubbed together. When he heard Adaira's soft gasp, Jack opened his eyes.

The spirits were forming themselves, gathering around him to listen. He played and sang and watched as the trees became maidens with long arms and hair made of leaves. The grass and pennywort knotted themselves into what looked to be mortal lads, small and green. The stones found their faces like old men waking from a long dream. The wildflowers broke their stems and gathered into the shape of a woman with long dark hair and eyes the color of honeysuckle, her skin purple as the heather that bloomed on the hills. Yellow gorse crowned her, and she waited beside the Earie Stone, whose face was still forming, craggy and ancient.

As Jack played Lorna's ballad he felt as if he was slowly sinking into the earth. His limbs were becoming heavy, and he drooped like a flower wilting beneath a fierce sun. It was like the sensation of falling asleep. He swore he saw daisies blooming from his fingertips, and every time he plucked his strings the petals broke away but regrew just as swiftly. And his ankles . . . he couldn't move them, the tree roots had begun to take hold of him. His hair was turning into grass, green and long and tangled, and as the song ended he struggled to remember who he was, that he was mortal, a man. Someone was coming to him, bright as a fallen star, and he felt her hands on his face, blissfully cold.

"Please," the woman said, but not to him. She beseeched the wildflower spirit with her long dark hair and crown of vibrant gorse. "Please, this man belongs to me. You cannot claim him."

"Why, mortal woman," one of the pennywort lads said from the ground, his words raspy as summer hay falling to a scythe.

"Why did you sit so far away from him? We thought he sang to be taken by us."

Jack snapped out of the haze. Adaira was kneeling beside him, her hand shifting to his arm. He was stricken to see that he truly had been turning into the earth—grass, flowers, and roots. His harp clattered from his tingling hands; he struggled to breathe as he watched his body return to him.

"He is mine, and he played to bring you forth by my command," Adaira said calmly. "I long to speak to you, spirits of the earth. If I may have your permission, Lady Whin of the Wildflowers."

Whin regarded Adaira for a long moment. She shifted her honeysuckle eyes to the Earie Stone, an old face who also was watching Adaira.

"It is her," Whin said, her voice light and airy.

"No, it cannot be," the Earie Stone countered. His words were hard to discern, crunching like gravel.

"It is," Whin persisted. "I have waited a long time for this moment." She turned her attention back to the mortals, and Jack felt Adaira shiver.

"I'm Adaira Tamerlaine," Adaira said, and her voice was strong in spite of her fear. "My bard has summoned you so I may ask for your help."

"What help, mortal lady?" one of the alder maidens asked.

"Four lasses have gone missing in the east," Adaira began. "We are desperate to find them, to reunite them with their families. I have questions that I would like to ask you."

"We can only answer so much, Adaira of the Tamerlaines," Whin said. "But ask, and if we may speak, we will."

"Can you tell me where the lasses are?" Adaira said.

Whin shook her head. "No, but we can say they are all together in one place."

Adaira's breath caught. "They're alive, then?"

"Yes. They live and they are hale."

Jack felt the relief trickle through him. He hadn't realized how afraid he had been to learn the girls were dead until that moment.

"The man who has been kidnapping them," Adaira rushed to continue. "Who is he, and is he working alone?"

Whin glanced back to the Earie Stone. Wildflowers fluttered with her every movement. Jack watched the blossoms drift from her arms, her hair. He sensed the spirits were about to retreat; his performance had not been strong enough to hold them long in their manifest forms.

"We cannot say who he is, but he is not working alone," Whin replied.

Adaira yearned to ask more. To make demands. Jack could see it in the clenching of her jaw and the curl of her fingers.

"Can you tell me where Orenna grows?"

A shadow of agony passed over Whin's face. She opened her mouth, but wildflowers tumbled from her lips. At her feet, the pennywort lads began to unravel, and the alder maidens began to groan back into trees.

"*Please,*" Adaira cried, ragged. She removed her hand from Jack and knelt before the Earie Stone and Whin. "Please help me. Please guide me. Where can I find the lasses?"

"Oh mortal woman," said Whin, sorrowful. Her flowers began to wilt as she faded. "I cannot tell you. My mouth is barred from speaking truth to you. You will have to find the answers elsewhere."

"Where? In the wind?" Adaira asked, but she was never answered.

The folk of the earth transformed into trees, stones, grass, and wildflowers. A clump of heather was the only evidence the spirits had manifested, a lingering trace of Lady Whin.

Jack felt sore and bruised as he continued to sit and stare

at the Earie Stone. All he could think of was Lady Whin's statement. A statement that was nearly identical to what the water spirits had uttered . . .

It is her.

His gaze slid to Adaira, on her hands and knees, discouraged and breathing like she was about to weep.

"Adaira," he rasped. "Adaira, it'll be all right. The earth told us more than we could have hoped for. The lasses are alive and well. It's only a matter of time before we find them."

She gradually regained her composure. She pushed herself up and drew a deep breath.

"You're right," she said, gazing up at the tree branches. "I'm just so *tired*, Jack."

"Then let me take you home," he said, brushing grass from his tunic. He made a note of his hands; they felt fine, as did his head. Perhaps he wouldn't suffer from the magic this time. He decided to leave the tonic bottle in his harp case.

Adaira looked at him. "I'm sorry, I shouldn't have said such a thing. We're all tired these days."

"Don't apologize," he said. "You can always speak your mind to me."

She looked at him, unguarded. Her father was dying, her lasses were missing. He could see her weariness mingled with her waning hope. He could see how much she wanted to be strong for the clan, strong for Torin and Sidra. And yet she was just one woman, and Jack wondered how she held everything together on her own.

He eased himself up to his feet. He felt drained, and a bit peculiar, but then he had nearly turned into the earth itself.

Play with caution, Lorna had said.

He understood now, and he offered his hand to Adaira, drawing her upright.

"We should get back to Torin," she said. "He'll be eager to know what we learned."

"Yes," Jack said. "We should hurry."

They approached their horses in silence, and as Jack mounted, he realized that he was marrying Adaira the following day and he had no idea what to expect.

"What's the plan for tomorrow?" he asked, gathering the reins.

"I don't have a plan," she replied, nudging her horse into a walk. "I'm making this up as I go."

Jack snorted, his gelding plodding after hers. He was about to make a smart remark when he felt the pain bloom behind his eyes, a sudden brightness that stole his breath. He couldn't see for a moment; there was nothing more than the agonizing sheen of lightning coursing through him, and he scrambled for his harp case. His hands were beginning to ache, as if he had set them in snow for hours.

Adaira was saying something. She was blithely unaware of his condition, riding ahead of him.

He felt a sharp pain in his nose; it began to bleed, and he knew he needed Adaira's help.

"Adaira," he whispered.

The world spun. He thought he was floating until he crashed to the ground, his shoulder smarting in pain. He could feel the grass, tickling his face. He could smell the loam of the isle. He could hear the sough of the wind.

"Jack? *Jack!*"

Adaira was shaking him. Her voice seemed far away, as if kilometers stretched between them.

"Tonic," he struggled to say, blinking against the light. "Harp case."

He listened as she searched for it. An excruciating minute

passed before her fingers wove into his hair, tilting his head up as she placed the bottle to his lips.

The tonic went down like honey, sweet and thick.

Jack swallowed once, twice. He was shaking, but the pain began to fade. He blinked, and Adaira's face came into focus, hovering over him.

"Do you need more?" she asked.

"Just . . . wait," he said.

The pain dulled behind his eyes, but his headache lingered. His hands were still in misery. He wouldn't have been surprised if he glanced down and found that claws had grown, breaking the skin beneath his nails.

He told Adaira about the salve, also in his case. She found it and rubbed the tingling ointment over his hands, into his palms and knuckles. It put him into a trance, to feel her touch him like that. A groan slipped from his lips.

He didn't know how much time passed until he felt restored, but when he could at last behold Adaira clearly, he saw she was furious.

"You foolish, irresponsible, *infuriating* bard," she said. "You should have told me!"

Jack sighed, leaning against her. He could feel the warmth of her, seeping into him, and he eased his head to her lap.

"Adaira . . . let's not fight about it."

"I'm trying to make sense of your reasoning. To withhold something this vital from me."

Jack didn't know how to answer her. Was it his pride? His fear that she might forbid him from playing? The realization that he was a hypocrite? The desire to find the lasses, no matter the cost he had to pay?

Adaira's silence prompted him to glance up at her. Her face was furrowed in pain, and he knew she was thinking back to her mother. He watched as she made the connection in her mind.

"All those years my mum played for the spirits in secret," she began softly. "I never realized how much it cost her, but I should have."

"She and your father kept those dealings private, Adaira. There was no way you could have known."

"But there were strange moments when she would fall ill," Adaira continued. "I remember she was always sick in spring and autumn, burning with fevers, her hands full of aches. She would be in bed for *days* and would always tell me it was just 'the change of weather' and she 'would be better soon.'"

Jack listened, and it felt like a bone had cracked in his chest. He hated to see her sadness, the way the truth was hurting her. But before he could draw breath and speak, Adaira turned her eyes to his, softly touching his hair.

"I never should have asked this of you," she whispered. "This music . . . it's not worth your health, Jack."

He nearly lost his train of thought beneath her caress.

"If not me, then who?" he managed to counter. "You know as well as your father does that the east needs a bard. The spirits only require a song twice a year. I can easily do that, Adaira."

She fell silent, her hand still in his hair. Jack watched her, but she was far away from him in that moment, lost to her thoughts.

"I'm sorry," he said. "I should have told you, but I didn't want it to interfere with finding the lasses."

Adaira sighed. "Your health is important to me. Surely, you can understand that."

"I thought I could handle this," he said. "On my own."

A flicker of emotion passed over Adaira's face. She understood the need to hide pain and perceived weakness from others.

"Is it just when you play for the spirits?" she asked.

"Yes. I'm fine when I play for the clan."

Adaira made no response, but she was watching the breeze pass through the trees again. Jack sensed her thoughts: they needed to call the spirits of the wind. They had no choice in the matter, as the earth hadn't been as forthright as they had hoped, and Jack knew Adaira would put the clan above his health. This was no surprise to him; he understood this reasoning and had expected no less when he had agreed to become Bard of the East.

Yet Lorna had never played for the wind. They were the highest of the folk, the most powerful. Jack had a terrible inkling they not only knew where the girls were being held but had also sealed the mouths of the other spirits. Jack would have to compose his own ballad for them, and he shivered, wondering what it would do to him. If the earth had nearly swallowed him whole, how would the wind react to his music?

"If this trade with the Breccans is successful," Adaira said, "if we can forge peace for the isle . . . then perhaps we will finally see a day when there is no cost to spin magic. When you can sing for the spirits without pain, and Mirin can weave without suffering, and Una can make blades without anguish."

Days ago, Jack would have scoffed at such a notion. But he was changing, and he felt it like a tide rising within him.

What have you done to me? he wondered as his gaze traced Adaira.

"Where should we get married?" she asked, tugging on his hair. "I suppose we should settle this now, since it's happening tomorrow."

The abrupt change of topic nearly made Jack laugh.

"The hall?" he suggested.

"Hmm. I think it should be outdoors," Adaira replied. "And besides, I want it to be small. Intimate. I want only our closest family there. I don't want an audience, and if we bind ourselves in the hall, the entire clan will want to watch."

Jack shuddered. Yes, that would be horrifying.

They both fell silent, thinking. But then Adaira smiled, and his heart quickened.

"Actually," she said. "I know *exactly* where we should take our vows, old menace."

CHAPTER 15

Jack waited for Adaira at the thistle patch. The sky was overcast and dour, and a brisk wind was blowing from the east. It was fitting weather for the two of them to bind themselves as one, he thought as he raked his fingers through his hair. There was only a faint trace of pain in his hands thanks to Sidra's medicine, but his head was aching and he hadn't slept the night before. He wasn't sure if his restlessness was penance for playing for the spirits or due to the fact that he was getting married.

In the distance, thunder rumbled as a storm billowed closer, and Jack resisted the urge to pace. Torin was waiting beside him, as were Mirin and Laird Alastair, who was so weak that a chair had been brought for him to sit in while the vows took place.

As the minutes continued to drag by Jack wondered if Adaira was planning to stand him up. He gave in to the temptation and walked around the thistles, the blooms white as fallen snow. This place hadn't changed; it was the same as it had been that night eleven years ago when he had clashed with her.

"Jack," Mirin said, reaching out to straighten his plaid. He had yanked it crooked, the golden brooch threatening to slip off his shoulder.

He let her fuss over him, knowing she was also nervous and had spent hours on his wedding garments. She had dressed him in the finest of wool—a cream-colored tunic that was soft as a cloud against his skin, and a red plaid that had never been worn before. Torin had additionally gifted him with a leather jerkin, studded with silver and etched with vines, and Alastair had bestowed the golden brooch, set with rubies. A Tamerlaine heirloom, and one that was most likely worth a fortune.

Jack tried to shake away his feelings of unworthiness, but they lingered, long enough to make him doubt himself and what he was doing. Until he remembered what Adaira had spoken to him nights ago, on her knees.

None of them are the one that I want.

She would never know what those words had done to him.

His eyes searched the hills. The land rolled like a song, dappled with purple heather and gorse. The light was beginning to cool with dusk, and Adaira had yet to appear.

He should have insisted they marry in the hall. A safe, predictable place where the spirits couldn't trick them. He envisioned the bracken, the rocks, and the grass manifested in physical forms, coming between her and him. What if they led Adaira astray and Jack was left here, standing in a thistle patch until midnight?

"Take a breath, Jack," Torin said. "She'll be along."

Jack swallowed a retort. He turned his face into the wind and closed his eyes, the air sweet with the fragrance of rain. A gust blew over him, lifting the hair from his brow as if fingers had brushed it away.

Faintly, he heard Frae calling his name.

Jack opened his eyes.

He saw Adaira walking through the grass to meet him, Sidra and Frae on either side, holding her hands. He watched her approach in a red dress, her hair loose and crowned with flowers, and he was struck almost senseless by the sight of her. Jack couldn't breathe, nor could he fathom the truth that she was coming to *him*. Or perhaps he could. Because the truth was . . . she wasn't looking at him.

Her eyes were cast down to the heather as she ascended the hill, stoic as if she were walking to her death.

Jack didn't take his eyes from her, waiting. *Look at me, Adaira.*

She was five steps away, her face pale until their gazes locked. Gradually, the color returned to her cheeks, like roses blooming in starlight. She stood, beautiful and proud in the gray-washed light; she seemed not of this earth, and Jack was like a shadow next to her. Serenity spread through him the longer he regarded her. Peace, like a gentle poison, quelled the anxious blood within him. He extended his hand to her, a quiet offering. He didn't quite believe this was happening, not until Sidra and Frae relinquished her, and Adaira claimed his waiting hand with her own.

Her fingers were shockingly cold. A brush of winter, defying the sultry air and the heat of his skin.

She glanced up at the churning clouds above them, and Jack felt how she trembled. It eased his own shaking, and he tightened his hold on her, hoping it would steady them both. *If we must drown, let us do so entwined.*

Adaira's gaze returned to him, as if she had heard his musings, and there her eyes remained, for she saw him at last. Her old menace. A slender smile danced on her lips, and he was relieved, recognizing that mirth within her. Despite the weight of the past few days, he could still coax it from her without a single word.

He acknowledged it then. She had just accomplished the sweetest revenge. Here he was, about to bind himself to her. To give his vow with a willing heart. And he marveled at her.

Torin was saying something. Jack didn't hear a word as Adaira brushed her thumb over his knuckles.

"Shall I go first?" she whispered, and Jack nodded, doubting his voice.

Mirin brought forward a long strip of plaid, surrendering it to Torin. Jack felt his and Adaira's family gather close around them in a loose circle as if they were embracing the two of them.

Torin began to wrap their hands with the strip of plaid, knotting it once as Adaira spoke her vow.

"I, Adaira Tamerlaine, hereby take you, Jack, to be my husband. I will comfort you in sadness; I will lift your head and be your strength when you are weak. I will sing with you when you are joyful. I will abide beside you and honor you for a year and a day, and thereafter should the spirits bless us."

Jack's thoughts whirled. Mirin had helped him memorize these vows last night, and yet his mind went utterly blank. Adaira's grip on him eased as the silence rang. The mere envisioning of her walking away broke the dam that had welled within him. The words rushed forward like a song he had learned, long ago.

"I, Jack Tamerlaine, hereby take you, Adaira, to be my wife. I will comfort you in sadness; I will lift your head and be your strength when you are weak. I will sing with you when you are joyful. I will abide beside you and honor you for a year and a day, and thereafter should the spirits bless us."

Torin made another knot around their hands, this time to represent Jack's vow. After that, Alastair provided a golden coin. It had been broken in half, and each piece strung onto a chain. The laird bestowed one half of the coin on Adaira; the gold flickered as the chain settled against her collarbones. He next draped the other chain over Jack's head.

Adaira hadn't wanted rings to symbolize their vows. Perhaps because she knew Jack was particular about his hands. But the truth was that Jack hadn't cared for either one—ring or half coin—until he listened to the chain settle and felt his piece of the coin rest close to his heart. He was glad to have something tangible to portray his promise to her.

"I hereby pronounce you bound as one," Torin declared, and a cheer rose from Frae. "Would you like to seal your vows with a kiss?"

Jack felt Adaira's hand stiffen in his. He watched her eyes narrow as she slightly angled back, a graceful warning. They hadn't discussed this, but it was evident that it was the last thing she wanted.

Jack hesitated only a moment before he lifted their bound hands and kissed Adaira's knuckles through the plaid.

It was over and done with. It had scarcely taken five minutes, and Jack felt weak in the knees when he thought about how much his life had just changed.

His mother was kissing Adaira's cheeks, and Sidra was squeezing his arm, and he didn't know what came next. They weren't sharing a bed; they weren't partaking in a wedding feast. *I don't want a celebration,* Adaira had said to him the day before. *The days are too heavy, too somber for such things.*

"Shall we return to the hall?" Alastair asked, rising from his chair with Torin's assistance.

"I . . ." Adaira began, but then frowned. "Da, I said I didn't want a feast."

"Adaira," the laird said, his voice a gentle rasp. "You are my only daughter and the heiress. Did you think you could escape a handfasting without a little celebration?"

Adaira glanced at Sidra and Torin. "The days are too dark for such things."

"The days may be dark," Sidra said. "But that doesn't mean you shouldn't feel joy. We *want* to celebrate with you."

"And perhaps your bard will play a song for us, Adi?" Torin added, brow arched as he met Jack's gaze.

Jack wasn't prepared to play for the clan. But everyone was suddenly looking at him, and he realized that he had secretly been waiting for such a moment.

"Yes, of course," he said, anxiously touching his plaid.

"Then let us go, before the rain comes," Torin said.

Their small party began the walk back to the castle.

Jack was surprised by the congregation that had gathered in the courtyard. At the sight of his hand bound to Adaira's, cheers rose.

He didn't stop; he led Adaira to the hall, forging a path in the crowd. He was only aware of her—how cold her hand was in his. How close she walked at his side, her crimson dress fluttering with each step. The sigh that escaped her.

Flowers rained down, soft and fragrant, catching like snow in their windswept hair.

The moment Jack and Adaira stepped into the hall as husband and wife for their celebration feast, the storm finally broke.

He took his place beside her at the laird's table on the dais. Their hands were still bound by two stubborn knots—his left hand and her right—and Jack studied their fingers, entwined and hanging between their chairs.

"Eager to untie us, bard?" Adaira asked, and he glanced up to see she was watching him, a tilt of a smile on her lips.

"Should I be?"

"No, not yet. We're supposed to be bound until I take you to bed, but I'll have to break with tradition and untether you long before then." Adaira indicated the dais, where Jack saw Lorna's grand harp, waiting to be played.

That was their last moment of peace. The clan began to flood the hall as the storm raged beyond the walls. Conversations and laughter rose, loud as the thunder that rattled the windows. It was warm and muggy and damp and boisterous and joyful, and Jack felt overwhelmed by how suddenly his life had become woven tightly with so many others.

Dinner was delivered from the kitchens. Platters of salmon, fresh oysters, scallops, and smoked mussels were laid out on the table alongside venison with rowan jelly and slow-roasted lamb with preserved lemons. Bride's pies were carried out next— small mince pies made of calves' feet and mutton, apples, cinnamon, currants, and brandy. There were bowls of colcannon, a dish made of cabbage, carrots, potatoes with brown sauce butter, fritters, barley bannocks, and oatcakes. And then the desserts arrived—almond flory and pudding, sponge cakes and creams, honey cakes, shortbread, and meringue with berries.

Jack had never seen so much food. His stomach still felt knotted from the vows, but as soon as Adaira began to fill her plate, he followed her lead. He promptly discovered there was no time to eat. Everyone wanted a moment to speak to Adaira and her new groom, and Jack had no choice but to endure it and let his food grow cold.

One at a time, the people stepped up to the dais to bow to them. Some were genuinely thrilled and delighted; some tried but couldn't hide their puzzlement. Some regarded Jack like he was a mainlander. He endured it all and spoke little, leaving the conversation to Adaira.

There was a lull, and Jack finally had the chance to stuff his mouth with a few scallops. He suddenly felt Adaira's grip tighten on his hand, slightly, as if she didn't mean to alert him but couldn't help it. He glanced up to see a young man ascending the dais. He was handsome, his complexion ruddy from wind and sun. His hair was blond, cascading in soft waves, and his eyes were the startling green of summer grass. And those eyes were for Adaira and Adaira alone.

He bowed deeply to her, his hand over his heart. Jack instantly noticed the dirt that stained his fingernails, even though his knuckles were raw, as if he had scrubbed them for hours, trying to wash the grime away. When he lifted his head, he stared across the table at Adaira, and his gaze was hungry, full of longing for her.

A cold, unexpected pang went through Jack.

"Adaira," the young man said, and her name was like a song, a promise. It was the sound of one who had shared many moments with her. One who knew her intimately.

Adaira stiffened. Her voice was hollow, emotionless. "Callan."

Callan swallowed. He was nervous, standing before her. But he smiled, and Jack's dread only deepened. "It's been a long while since we spoke."

Adaira said nothing. Her face was guarded. But her hold on Jack tightened.

Jack cleared his throat. "I don't believe we've met."

Callan spared him a glance. "Forgive me, but our paths never crossed before you left for the mainland. I'm Callan Craig." His eyes wandered back to Adaira.

"And what do you do on the isle?" Jack persisted, tracing Adaira's fingers with his own, hidden like a secret between them.

"I dig trenches and harvest peat."

Backbreaking work that no one on the isle wanted to do. The sort of labor given to men who had committed crimes and fallen out of grace.

An awkward silence welled between the three of them. Jack couldn't think of anything else to say or ask; he could only wonder what Callan Craig had done to doom himself to the marsh. Jack could even smell it on him—the pungent odor that no amount of water and soap could wash away.

"How are your wife and daughter?" Adaira finally asked. She was polite, just as she had sounded to every other person she had spoken to that night. But there was more to her words. A reminder, a warning.

Callan stared at her, a spark of remorse in his eyes. "They are well, heiress. My wife sends you her felicitations and hopes you will have a very happy marriage."

"Give her my gratitude then."

Callan bowed again and descended the dais. As soon as his back was turned, Adaira reached for her sparkling glass of summer wine and drained it. Jack said nothing, but he watched her from the corner of his eye.

"Are you all right?" he whispered.

Adaira fumbled for the amber wine bottle that sat between them on the table. She poured herself another glass and held it to her nose, breathing in its ambrosia.

"I'm quite well," she said, her gaze fixed absently on the crowd.

Jack also looked over the hall and saw that Callan Craig had situated himself at a nearby trestle table, where he could continue to regard Adaira, unhindered.

Jack felt his lip curl, but he hid it behind a long drought of wine. He set the empty glass down with a clunk before he tugged on Adaira's hand, inviting her to look at him.

"Untie me," he said.

She stared at him, as if hesitant to let him go now that he'd made his earnest request. But she conceded and stood, pulling

Jack up after her. The mere motion of her rising hushed the exuberant conversations, and every eye was drawn to her.

"My good people of the east," she began with a smile. "I'm breaking with tradition this evening and cutting my groom loose long before bed, so that he may reward us all with a little celebration music." She turned to Jack and unknotted the plaid that bound them, an intimate gesture that provoked whispers in the crowd.

The clan's attention shifted to him as he walked to where Lorna's harp waited on the dais. He sat on the stool and let out a long breath, the weight of expectation nearly cracking his confidence. But he could see Mirin and Frae sitting in the crowd nearby. Laird Alastair, Torin, and Sidra. Una and Ailsa and their son and daughter. This was home to him—these people with their enchanted plaids and dirks, with their laughter and weeping and stories and fears and dreams. They were his clan, and he belonged among them, even though he had returned as a stranger.

Jack positioned his hands on the strings and began to play a joyful song. His notes reverberated in the hall, full of life and merriment, but it did nothing to ease the storm that stirred within him. He was acutely annoyed by Callan Craig, who continued to shamelessly stare at Adaira. But then Jack dared to glance at her too, and found that she was sitting in her chair watching Jack as if he were the only one in the hall.

The firelight and shadows danced on her collarbones; her half of the golden coin gleamed like a fallen star at her breast. Her hair cascaded around her in soft waves, the crown of wildflowers a contrast to her fair coloring.

He was struck by her sharp beauty and missed a note with his left hand but recovered quickly; he didn't think anyone had noticed. Save for Adaira. She grinned as if she heard his misstep, and he knew he should look away from her before the music came unraveled in his hands.

He glanced back to the strings and remembered his purpose—he was playing for the clan, not for her.

And so he did.

Frae had been overcome with all sorts of feelings the entire day. Ever since she had joined Sidra to walk Adaira to the thistles, witnessing her brother marrying the heiress. She was terrified it was a dream, that she would wake up and discover that all of it—even Jack's return home—had been her imagination.

But nothing prepared her for the moment when he played for the clan.

She sat on the bench beside Mirin, so eager that she bounced on the balls of her feet. The moment his music touched the air the hall seemed to wake. Frae noticed the tapestry colors becoming vibrant again, and the carvings in the timber beams seeming to stir with sentience. The fire burned higher in the glazed hearth and in the torch sconces, and the shadows danced low and gentle.

The isle was stirring, coming to life. Frae was transfixed by its awakening, and she could almost swear that she felt a rumble beneath her feet, as if the stones were basking in the sound of Jack's music.

His song ended all too soon. When he was begged to play another, he did. He played three songs in all, and to the last one he gave his voice as well as his notes.

Frae was overcome with pride. A roar of applause filled the hall when Jack reached the end. Frae jumped to her feet and clapped; she could feel the fervor in her teeth, and she wanted to tell everyone, "That's my brother! That's my brother!" Especially when Jack rose and bowed to the clan and everyone in the hall stood to honor him. Frae noticed Mirin had tears in her eyes again, as she had the first time she heard Jack's music. She wiped them away before they could fall.

It was the happiest Frae had felt in weeks.

She had been so afraid when her friends began to go missing. Girls she went to school with. Girls she sometimes passed in the city or on the road. She wanted them to be well. She wanted them to be found.

Listening to Jack's music . . . Frae's hope was restored.

She didn't quite understand how, but her brother's music was going to save them.

Adaira was weary of the revelry. The feast began to dwindle; the fire began to burn low. She had wanted no celebration, no dancing, no games, no toasts at her handfasting. She was still surprised that her father had managed to arrange a feast without her knowing.

But perhaps her father and Torin had planned it together, if only to have Jack play for the clan. Because Adaira had felt it— the shift in hearts. The clan feeling the balm of Jack's music, the peace and light suffusing the gathering.

She still felt his music echoing in her bones hours later.

She glanced sidelong at him, noticing his eyes were bloodshot.

"Shall we retire?" she asked and held out her hand.

He nodded and entwined his fingers with hers, as if he had been waiting for it.

"Torin and Sidra and a few other couples are going to follow us to my bedchamber," Adaira explained in a low tone as they stepped down from the dais. "It's tradition, you know. They're supposed to stand outside the door until you and I consummate the marriage, but I've already told Sidra not to linger once we're inside my chamber. All this is to say . . . don't let their presence alarm you."

Jack had no chance to reply to her. The crowd cheered to see them walk the aisle of the hall, whooping and throwing a few lingering, wilted blooms upon them. Adaira walked through it with a smile, but she was relieved to leave the hall behind. Sidra and Torin followed them, as well as Una and Ailsa and several other married couples.

She hurried to guide Jack up the stairs. They were almost to her quarters, and she would at last be able to breathe. Ailsa, who was like an aunt to Adaira, teased her for the rush.

Adaira glanced over her shoulder, boldly saying, "I have waited long enough, I think."

Jack coughed; he was certainly embarrassed. Adaira didn't dare look at him.

The couples laughed, save for Torin.

At last, the entourage reached her bedroom door.

Adaira opened it and all but yanked her new husband over the threshold behind her. She thanked the couples for their escort and shut the door. It was only her and Jack now. No more prying gazes, no more skeptical eyes. No more conversations and questions and scrutiny.

She slumped against the wood and sighed, meeting Jack's gaze. Her flower crown sat crooked on her head, and her bones felt heavy as iron. She waited until she heard Sidra usher the group of witnesses away from her door before unwinding her fingers from Jack's. Then she walked deeper into her room, massaging the heel of her hand. Jack awkwardly remained where he was.

"You are welcome here, Jack," said Adaira, stopping by the hearth. A fire was burning, casting a rosy, inviting hue over the chamber.

From the corner of her eye, she watched Jack examine her quarters, much as she had done the night she came to his bedroom, just before she had proposed to him.

He meandered past her large bed, its canopy tasseled back to reveal a glimpse of the quilts and pillows. Wildflowers were strewn across Adaira's blanket, as was a gauzy, transparent robe that her chambermaids must have laid out for her. Jack certainly took note of the robe but smoothly shifted his focus to the tapestry that hung nearby, and then the painted wooden panels that graced her walls. Paintings of forests and vines and harts and phases of the moon. Some of the artistry was ancient and chipped—older than the castle—but those panels happened to be Adaira's favorites, and she had refused to let her father replace them.

From there, Jack noticed the bookshelves, crowded with volumes, and the windows, which were cracked to welcome in the night. The storm had left a trace of sweetness in the air. He admired the stars that burned in clusters beyond the glass, and the distant gleam of the ocean.

Adaira wondered what he was thinking as he at last found his way to her by the fire, and she marveled at how the sight of him walking to her made her heart quicken. She wasn't taking him to bed, and she didn't know when she would want to, but she sensed it might come sooner than she had once believed.

She busied herself pouring two glasses of red wine, flavored with fruit. She gave one to Jack and said, "That wasn't so terrible, was it?"

He took the cup from her and didn't smile, but his voice was husky with mirth. "I had a moment of trepidation."

"Oh?"

"I thought you were going to stand me up," Jack confessed.

"You think *I* would ask to marry *you* and then fail to appear?" Adaira asked, amused.

He met her gaze, his eyes incandescent with firelight. "It felt like I waited an eternity for you."

She fell quiet, his words coaxing a flush across her skin. When he continued to hold her stare, she clinked her glass to his as a distraction. "To you and me and this year and a day that belongs to us."

They drank to each other. Adaira felt her weariness burn away, and she imagined it was Jack's fault, for being so attentive and for standing in her room, as if awaiting orders from her.

Her stomach growled, so loudly she knew Jack heard it.

"I didn't eat enough," she said, sheepish.

"I myself am famished," he said.

Adaira set her wine down to shut the windows and summon dinner.

It didn't take long before the servants brought up two trays of food left over from the wedding feast. The meal was set on the round table before the hearth. Jack joined Adaira, and they sat in their rumpled wedding clothes before a dancing fire and finally ate their fill.

It was a quiet meal, but there was nothing strained about it. Adaira realized she and Jack could have moments together in silence that were just as comfortable as the ones filled with conversation. Or even arguments.

"I have a request," Jack finally said, pushing his plate aside.

"Yes, Jack?"

He hesitated, staring into his wine, and she braced herself. She didn't know why she was expecting him to let her down, to fail her in some way, but his hesitation kept her on her guard.

"I know we're not sharing a bed," he began, glancing at her. "And I wondered if you would grant me permission to spend the nights at my mum's, so I may watch over her and Frae. Just until we solve the mystery of the missing lasses and justice is served. I am yours by day, but come night . . . I would like to stay with them."

His request caught Adaira by surprise. She softened when

she saw the worry lining his face. "Yes, of course. Do you want to go to them tonight?"

"No," Jack said with a slight laugh. "I'm fairly certain my mum would skin me alive if I turned up to sleep in my old bed on my wedding night. She would no doubt think me a terrible lover to you, and then word would spread, and . . . no."

Adaira smiled. "Ah, I see. Then would you like for me to send a guard to stay with them tonight?"

"I've thought about it, but no. Because if you grant such a thing for my sister, then you would need to grant it to every lass in the east. I don't want any special favors because I'm bound to you."

"I understand your reasoning," Adaira said, "but if you change your mind, let me know. And you don't need my permission to go stay at your mum's."

"Don't I?" he countered, looking at her. "You're my wife and my laird."

"So I am," she whispered. "How did this come to be?"

He smiled, as if he felt the same awe. "I haven't the slightest inkling, Adaira."

They fell silent again.

"There is something else I would like to ask you," Jack said, breaking the quiet.

She knew what it was. She had been waiting for it, and she could hear it in his voice, a tremor of uncertainty.

Adaira exhaled a long breath, her gaze straying to the fire. "Ask me, and I will answer you, Jack."

"Who is he?"

He being Callan Craig.

Adaira rubbed her brow, only to remember she still wore her flower crown. She drew it away from her head and set it on the table.

"You don't have to tell me if you don't want to," Jack said.

"He was my first love," she began. "I was eighteen and lonely. I was still struggling with my mother's death, and Callan was there. I fell for him, quickly, recklessly. I was naïve and believed every promise he gave me. He was all I wanted, and I thought I was enough for him, that he loved me as I loved him. I soon realized I didn't know him as well as I thought. He was dishonest and sought to use me to get into the guard. And when that didn't work, he tried to bribe his way there, which Torin and my father settled by sending him to work in the marsh. At first, I was tempted to defend him, until I learned I was not the only one he spoke promises to. But alas, hearts are made to be broken, aren't they, bard?"

"If they must break," Jack said, "then they break and remake themselves into stronger vessels."

"Spoken as one who has likewise had his heart broken," Adaira countered.

Now Jack was the one to glance away from her, into the mesmerizing safety of the fire. Adaira thought he wouldn't speak, even as she longed to know the events of his past. But then he opened his mouth and began to breathe words.

"She was a fellow student at the university, in the same year as me. We had a few classes together. I noticed her long before she noticed me. And then one day she heard me play the harp, and she began to speak to me, more and more. My feelings ran deeper than hers. She loved my music more than she loved me, and at first I couldn't understand what I was doing wrong. But then I realized . . . she had *always* loved music. It was something that would forever challenge her, something that would never fade or age or betray her. It sadly wasn't the same for me, though. I struggled to earn music's favor—it was forced upon me in the beginning—and even when I had attained a portion of it, I never felt worthy of its beauty.

"But I'm rambling. The moral of this long-winded tale is

that I realized music would always be more important to her, so I tried to turn myself into stone. To not feel anything. But now I realize that it is better to live, to feel and have a clean break than be half-dead and cold, cracked from resentment."

"I'll drink to that," Adaira whispered and lifted her cup.

Jack clinked his glass against hers, and they both drank. It felt like a garment had slipped away between them, as if to utter and confess was the first step to healing, to putting broken pieces back together.

She could see more of him now—the mist-laden years when he had dwelled on the mainland and she had roamed the isle.

They sat for a while longer in companionable silence, and when the fire began to die, Adaira rose.

"I've kept you up far too late," she said, brushing the wrinkles from her wedding dress. "The trade is tomorrow, and I should let you rest. Come, I'll show you to your room."

Jack made for the door, but Adaira cleared her throat, catching his attention.

"You and I have a secret door that connects our chambers," she said with a crafty grin, lifting a latch in one of the wooden panels on the other side of her room. Jack's eyes widened as he watched the secret door creak open, leading into a shadowy corridor.

Adaira stepped into the secret passage, ducking beneath a curtain of gossamer.

Jack followed her. The short corridor led to a door that fed into his chamber. Adaira opened it and let him take the first step into his new room. It was similar to hers: wide and spacious with painted panels and bookshelves, a hearth that had almost extinguished into embers, and a bed with a grand tapestry for a headboard.

"Does this suit you?" Adaira asked.

"More than enough," Jack said, glancing at her. "Thank you."

She nodded and began to draw the door closed. "Then sleep well tonight, Jack." She shut the panel before he could respond, but she stood there for a moment and drank the shadows of the passage, thinking how strange life was. How different her days were bound to be now, with him on the other side of this secret corridor.

Jack stood in his new room.

He stared at the bed—it was far too grand for him—and walked to the desk, where parchment was stacked. His harp rested on the floor nearby. He studied the bookshelves and the painted panels on the walls before he wandered to the hearth, where he threw another log on the fire. He succumbed to the nearby leather chair and felt a restless pang of longing.

It had been quite some time since he had composed music.

On the mainland, his compositions had gravitated to sorrow and laments. To doomed ballads. But he wondered what his notes would sound like here, on the isle. How they would form now that he was home.

He was exhausted, and yet he felt keenly aware of his surroundings. The bed looked inviting, but Jack knew he wouldn't be able to sleep.

He rose and returned to the desk. He sat and chose a quill, then opened a glass well brimming with walnut ink.

He reflected on the day. How sweet the eastern wind had tasted, how it had touched Adaira's hair as she stood before him when they spoke their vows.

He envisioned wings, gliding over the hills, beating against the stars. Stealing words and carrying them across the heather. Chasing rain and dancing with smoke.

Slowly, he remembered years he had once longed to bury.

Jack began to write a song for the spirits of the wind.

CHAPTER 16

I t was sweltering by noontide. A hazy, sun-drenched day for the first trade to take place between east and west. Jack stood beside Adaira in an old fisherman's hut, with a crate of the Tamerlaines' best grains, honey, milk, and wine at their feet. The goods had been gathered in secret and were ready to be carried down to the northern coast, where they would meet Moray Breccan. Their only obstacle was Torin, who hovered between them and the hut's door.

"This is foolish, Adi," he said, glaring at her. "You should let me come with you."

"We've already discussed this, Torin," Adaira said in a clipped tone. She was exhausted. Jack knew they had both stolen only a few hours of sleep last night, in their separate beds. "I'm to approach unarmed and without my guard, as is Jack."

"Aye, so Moray Breccan can sink an arrow into you," Torin said. "And I won't be there to stop it, or even see it happen."

Adaira was quiet, but her eyes were on her cousin. "What

are you afraid of, Torin? Give this fear a name, so I can put your mind at ease."

That brought Torin upright. He stared at her, jaw clenched and eyes glinting in the light.

In that tense moment, Jack saw through the captain as if he were made of glass. Torin never wanted to appear weak or incapable; Jack imagined this must be a Tamerlaine trait. Pride and the need to appear invincible must have been passed down in their blood, generation after generation.

"If they kill you," Torin said in a low voice. "I will burn the west to the ground. I won't spare a single Breccan life."

"You would kill innocent women and children, Torin?" Adaira countered. She didn't give him a chance to reply before she continued. "You're afraid of losing me. I understand your fear because I have also felt its many shades. But while I may be your imminent laird, I am not yours to lose. I belong to the clan as a whole, and my choice to participate in the trade today is for the good of all the Tamerlaines."

Torin sighed. "Adi . . ."

"I'm also going to find an answer we are desperate to know," she said, touching her bodice, where the last Orenna flower had been tucked away in a vial.

Torin's scowl only deepened. He knew what she inferred. "Did Sidra put you up to this?"

"Sidra has given me advice I desperately needed," Adaira said. "Knowing where this flower grows is going to help us solve this mystery. It could help us find Maisie."

Torin was silent, and Jack took that moment to study him. The captain's clothes looked looser, as if he had lost weight. His skin was sallow, and a few silver threads gleamed in his blond hair. Jack wondered if Torin had slept or eaten a proper meal since his daughter had been kidnapped. It seemed like he would slowly wither away without answers, and the thought made Jack feel laden with sorrow.

Torin drew a sharp breath and said, "If a Breccan was crossing the clan line, I'd know instantly. Sidra mentioned to me that she thinks the west is involved, and yet I don't see how they could be."

"They might be involved in a trade with one of our own," Adaira said. "Not crossing themselves but sending the flowers over to the east."

"I still don't see how this is possible," Torin countered.

"This is why you must let me go to meet Moray," she replied. "To discover how we're going to send this crate of goods over to the west without crossing the clan line."

Torin made no reply, but he wanted to protest. Jack could see the captain's frustration building, but Adaira added in a soft voice, "You and your guards have been searching endlessly, Torin. Let me help by doing this."

Torin, at last, nodded and stepped back, clearing the way to the hut's door.

Adaira turned to Jack. "Help me carry the crate."

Jack took one side, Adaira the other, and together they slipped from the hut and began the careful trek down the rocks. Torin and a few of his trusted guards remained behind, ensuring that no one approached or caught a glimpse of Jack and Adaira. This trade-by-trial was still steeped in secret, and only a select few had been given knowledge of it.

Jack didn't know what to expect. He tried to appear optimistic for Adaira's sake, even as he felt more inclined to agree with Torin. The one thing he could be assured of was that the cave they were visiting was a forbidden place, and it would soon fill with water as the tide rose.

They finally reached the shore. A western wind blew, hot

with curiosity as birds cawed and swooped down to the water. The waves surged and retreated, leaving pieces of conch shells and tendrils of algae in their wake. The sand was soft, crushed beneath Jack's boots as he walked with Adaira, the crate bumping against his leg. The clan line loomed in the distance, a chain of stones on the beach smudged with the heat of the air.

It made Jack think of his return to the isle. How he had washed up on the Breccans' southern coast. There had been no one in the west to greet or threaten him, even for the short amount of time he had inadvertently trespassed. And yet he knew the Breccans had their own watch. Sometimes it felt as if keeping secrets on this isle was impossible, as if the best place for them might be in the woven pattern of a plaid, as Mirin knew best.

All too soon, Jack and Adaira reached the boundary. The edge of the east. They followed the rocks to the cave, its mouth invisible until Jack squinted. Into the shadows he went, Adaira following. They were the first to arrive, and the water was already knee deep. Jack shivered as it soaked through his boots. His eyes swept their surroundings; he took the crate and set it on a rock to keep it dry.

It was dim in the cave, the air cold and prickled with brine. It was a small, round space, and only a few threads of sunlight streamed in from cracks overhead.

Jack didn't like it here. The place felt dangerous, eager to drown them if they weren't vigilant about the tide. Ream's words came to mind, as clear as if she stood in the foam of the cave, speaking to them again. *Beware of blood in the water.* Had the folk of the tide seen a glimpse of the future? Had they anticipated that this meeting would take place here and sought to give a warning to Adaira?

Jack shifted his weight, uneasy.

The wait for Moray's arrival felt unbearable. Trying to ease his worries, Jack studied Adaira. He had scarcely given himself a moment to look at her that day, it had begun so madly with covertly preparing for the trade. But his eyes traced her now.

She wore a green dress and her enchanted plaid shawl. Her hair was braided with silver chains and tiny hearts of gemstones. The half coin shone at her neck, its glimmer matching his own, hidden beneath his plaid.

Jack almost said to her that he was glad she had asked him— *chosen* him—to stand with her in this moment as her partner. A moment that could unfold in a hundred different ways. A beginning or an end, and yet she had wanted it to be him.

She felt his gaze and glanced at him. She frowned. "Is something wrong, bard?"

He shook his head, but his hand found hers, weaving their fingers together. He returned his attention to the other side of the cave.

A few minutes passed. Soon Jack could hear pebbles shifting and the scrape of boots on the rocks. There was a strange echo, and Jack braced himself as Moray Breccan stepped into the western side of the cave.

He was tall and lean with dark blond hair and striking, angular features. A blue plaid was draped from his shoulder. On his forearms, woad tattoos danced in interlocked patterns. An old scar shone on his cheek, cutting through his braided beard. He carried a burlap sack and a narrow boat made from a hollowed tree trunk.

In some ways, Moray Breccan was exactly as Jack had envisioned him. A warrior, with stories on his pale skin. But in other ways, his appearance was surprising. He was dressed similarly to Jack—tunic and plaid and belt, with soft boots tethered up to his knees. If not for the proud display of blue and the tattoos, he might have passed as one of their own. And then came his smile. A grin spread across his face the moment he beheld Adaira, even as the tide whirled between them.

Jack didn't know if the smile was friendly or predatory. He tightened his grip on her hand.

"Heiress," Moray said. His voice was rough at the edges, resonating in the cave. It reminded Jack of splintered wood. "At last we meet face-to-face."

"Heir of the West," Adaira greeted him. "Thank you for coming. This is my husband, Jack."

The Breccan's eyes shifted, meeting Jack's stare. "A pleasure," Moray said, but his gaze returned swiftly to Adaira. She was the one he was interested in, and Jack felt his stomach knot.

"Is it not odd to you, heiress," Moray said, "that you and I have breathed the same wind and walked the same isle, swum in the same tides and slept beneath the same stars, and yet we have been raised as enemies?"

Adaira was quiet, but Jack could feel her draw a deep breath. "Our isle was divided long ago by the decision of one of my ancestors, as well as one of yours. I have hope that Cadence can be restored, and I believe this trade is the first step to seeing the balance return. We have brought the best of the east as a sign of our goodwill. This is only a prelude to what we can offer your clan should peace be upheld."

"And we are grateful for your benevolence, Adaira," said Moray, and he sounded genuine. "Likewise, we have something to give to you, in hopes that it will be a worthy enough exchange."

"Then let us make the trade," Adaira said, but she hesitated. She couldn't cross the line lurking beneath the water, and neither could Moray. Or, Jack supposed, they physically *could*, but doing so would sound alarms to both sets of guards. To Torin, pacing on the hill, eager for a reason to arrive, and to Moray's guards, who Jack surmised were also not far from the coast.

"I've thought long about how we could safely partake in this first exchange without stepping foot off our lands," Moray said. "Hence, this cave and this boat. I will put my goods in the boat and pass it over to you. After you take my offering, grant me yours, and I will pull the boat back to my side."

Jack remained quiet as he stood beside Adaira, and they watched as Moray prepared his boat. He tied a rope to the stern and set his burlap bag in the hull. He let the rope go slack in his blue printed hands, and the boat began to float toward them. It sailed over the clan line, from western waters into eastern ones. Jack grasped the boat to hold it steady while Adaira opened the sack.

She withdrew a large blanket, woven from the finest of dyed wool. It was a vibrant purple, even in the dusky light, with traces of gold in the pattern. Jack had an inkling it was enchanted; did all the Breccans sleep beneath charmed weavings?

"The blanket will keep you warm in the winter and cool in the summer," Moray explained. "It will also protect you from any harm that might befall you in the night."

"It's beautiful," Adaira said. "Thank you."

Next, she found a bottle, sloshing with amber liquid. She held it up to a stream of sun, and Moray said, "It's called gra. A fermented drink that is revered in the west. We consume it only in the presence of those we trust."

Adaira nodded, appreciating the message, and reached for the last object in the sack. Jack watched, his brow creasing as she withdrew a piece of an antler.

"I couldn't bring you a dirk," Moray explained. "Because we had agreed to come unarmed for this first meeting. But you're holding a hilt in your hand, Adaira. Tell me what enchanted blade you long for, and I will have it forged for you."

Adaira was quiet, studying the piece of antler. There were countless charms she could ask for. Jack had heard of blades being enchanted with terror, confusion, weariness. There were tales of swords stealing joyful memories from the mortals they cut. Most enchanted weapons held terrible things, emotions and feelings that one would only desire to bestow upon an enemy.

Jack sensed this was a test. Moray wanted to arm her, which felt strange until Jack realized this was his way of measuring Adaira's true determination to seek peace. It was tempting to ask for the Breccan's steel. To ask the Breccans to forge them weapons that the Tamerlaines could in turn use against them.

Adaira returned the antler to the sack. She looked across the water at Moray and said, "Forge me a blade with an enchantment of your choosing. I'll trust your judgment."

Moray nodded, his expression neutral. Jack couldn't read the slant of his thoughts, but it seemed Adaira had answered correctly.

"Will you bring our crate to me, Jack?" Adaira whispered to him.

Jack nodded, gathering the blanket and the bottle of gra. The tide was rising; the water was beginning to reach their waists and he felt a tremor of fear as he half-walked, half-waded to their crate. He set Moray's offerings on the rock and took the box in his hands, bringing it to Adaira's side.

She felt the rising tide as well and quickly loaded their resources into the boat. A sack of oats. A sack of barley. A jug of milk. A jar of honey with the comb. A bottle of blood red wine. A taste of the east.

"All right," Adaira said, and Moray began to pull the boat back to him.

He touched each of the offerings, and when he glanced across the water again, a smile had warmed his face.

"Thank you, Adaira. This is generous of you and your clan," he said. "Now I would like to ask when you can visit the west. Both my mother and my father are keen to meet you and learn more of the trade you dream of."

No further preamble. This was the heart of the matter. Jack was tense, waiting for Adaira to speak. He still didn't think the visit was a good idea. Even if he was with her, there was only so much he could do to protect her. He wasn't Torin. He wasn't a guard. He was a musician who was siphoning away his vitality to sing for spirits.

"It might be another month or so," Adaira replied. "I'm unable to give you a determined date at this time."

She wanted to settle the mystery of the missing girls first, Jack knew. She wouldn't even consider leaving the east until the lasses were returned to their families.

"Very well," Moray said. "We can wait, although I do believe we need to establish a place for trade to happen, and the best way to do so will be through a visit. I don't think we can continue to pass goods back and forth in this cave."

"No," Adaira agreed. "I do want to see the west and your people. But perhaps you could visit us first?"

Yes, Jack thought. Let the Breccans take the initial risk.

Moray's smile stretched wide. "I'm afraid that isn't possible, for a number of reasons. The first is that my clan would never allow it, given how many Breccans have been killed on Tamerlaine soil by your captain and his guards. But if my people see you come to us first, Adaira, it would diminish that fear."

"I fail to see the rationale in that," Jack said tersely. "Your people have been killed in the east because we have had to defend ourselves from your violence."

Moray cast a languid glance at him. "Is that so? Perhaps

you should ask your captain then. Ask him how many innocent Breccans he's killed over the years."

Jack's blood turned cold. His hands felt like ice when he recalled his first night on Cadence. Sitting in a sea cave with Torin.

You meet every stray who crosses the clan line with instant death?

"Then I will come to you first," Adaira said, seeking to smooth out the tension that was gathering between them. "I'll write when the time is acceptable for the visit. But in the meantime, I do have one more request of you, Moray."

"Speak it, heiress."

She held up the vial with the Orenna blossom. "I've been seeking this flower in the east, and I wonder if you recognize it. Perhaps it flourishes in the west? If so, this flower is something that I would like to trade with you for."

Moray squinted as he studied it. "It's hard to see clearly from here"—Jack almost rolled his eyes—"but I don't recognize it. Despite that, I'll ask others in the clan, to see if they know of it. What's the flower called, by chance?"

"Orenna," Adaira said. "It has four petals and is crimson in color, veined with gold. An enchanted flower, as it continues to live long after it has been cut. I appreciate any advice or knowledge you could give about it."

"I'll do what I can, heiress," Moray said. "Now, I should depart, but I'll await word from you?"

Adaira nodded.

The trade had finally ended. They had survived it unscathed, and Jack took a stiff step away. It felt wrong to turn his back on Moray, but Adaira did, gathering the blanket and the bottle of strange western alcohol.

Jack held out the crate, and she placed the items within. Moray was still in the cave fiddling with his boat when they departed out the eastern side. They walked away, past their footsteps still pressed in the sand, although the tide was threatening to wash them away.

The wind had died, and the air was strangely calm.

"Do you think he was lying, Jack?" she asked in a low voice. "About the flower?"

Jack shifted the crate to his other hip. "I'm not sure. He wasn't what I expected."

"Yes. I'm not sure what I think about him yet," Adaira agreed. "But if we've proven anything today . . . it *is* possible to move products over the clan line without alerting Torin. It feels fanciful to even think this, but one of our own might be secretly obtaining the flower from the west, delivering them in the tides. Just as we did today."

The thought was disturbing.

When they had almost reached the rock path, Jack drawled, "So. They want to give us blankets we don't need and get us drunk. An excellent trade, if I may say so myself."

Adaira only laughed. It was surprise and joy, mingled into one.

Jack discovered he loved the sound of it.

Sidra stood in her yard, staring at the vegetables, herbs, and flowers. She hadn't watered them or harvested their fruit. Weeds were beginning to snake across the soil.

She should kneel. She should work, put her hands in the loam.

But she didn't have the heart to.

Sidra went inside, past Yirr curled up on the stoop, keeping watch. She stood at the table, staring at her pestle and mortar. Her dried herbs, stems, leaves, and flowers. A language she had grown up speaking, and yet it now felt scrambled and dissonant.

The house was so quiet. She wanted to drown in such silence. Gazing into space, Sidra didn't know how long she had been standing there when the door creaked open.

Yirr hadn't barked to alert her that someone had entered the yard.

Sidra's heart leapt into her throat as she turned, afraid until she saw it was Torin. His face was ruddy, whether from sunburn or anger, she wasn't sure yet. He smelled of summer wind and grass, and she realized he was holding a handful of tonic bottles. The ones she had made for his guard to decrease their need for sleep and to sharpen their focus on the search.

"I'm sorry, Torin," she said reflexively. She was sorry for the anguished gleam in his eyes, for how his body was losing its strength, hour by hour. She was sorry to see how exhausted he was, and how he was grinding himself down to pieces.

"What are you sorry about?" he countered briskly, as if he were sick of her apologies. "Could you make another batch of these for my guards?"

She didn't want to make anything with her hands. But she nodded and accepted the bottles from him, setting them on the table. "I'll bring a new batch by the barracks later."

"I'll wait for them now," he said.

He wanted to watch her work. He had never cared for such things before, and Sidra felt anxious as she began to gather fresh herbs.

"You should sit," she said. "This will take a while."

She hoped he would change his mind and leave. There was always someone else who needed him more. Another task more pressing than her.

Torin drew out a chair and sat.

He was quiet for a full five minutes as Sidra set a pot to boil over the fire and began to mix her herbs.

"If a Breccan was wounded and knocked on your door," Torin began, "would you heal them?"

Sidra glanced up. She wasn't sure what answer he wanted to hear from her. And then she realized it wasn't what Torin was asking for. He yearned to know her truths, even if they were sharp and difficult for him to fathom.

"Yes," she said.

"If a Breccan wounded me and then knocked on your door with pains of their own, would you heal them?"

"Yes," she whispered.

"Then you should prepare yourself for it," he said. "Prepare your salves for our enemies. To heal their wounds, as well as the ones they'll give to us in return. It's imminent."

"What are you speaking of, Torin?"

"The trade that you advised my cousin to go forward with? It happened today, and according to Adaira, it was a success. She now wants to establish a permanent trade with the Breccans, as if one good encounter can wash away all the terror and raids they've bestowed upon us for decades."

"And this is a terrible thing? That your cousin dreams of peace?"

Torin leaned forward in the chair. "I don't think the Breccans truly want peace. I think they want to drain our resources to weaken us before they overtake the east."

Sidra swallowed. "Did they recognize the Orenna?"

Torin's eyes darkened. "No. Which means we are no closer to solving this mystery than we were a day ago. I wish you would trust me to do my job, Sidra."

She was angry now. Her blood was simmering. He had not only accused her of giving Adaira ill advice but dropped an innuendo that she was meddling in affairs that didn't concern her.

"What is this really about, Torin?" she asked, slamming her pestle down on the table. "Tell me honestly."

She had never been one to raise her voice. They had never argued like this. And while she seemed to burn, he withdrew into ice.

"Everything I've built with my hands is about to come undone," he said in a low, hoarse voice. "I've been charged to protect the east, to give up my own life for it if necessary. It's how I was raised. It's why I have this scar on my hand. I've given *all* of myself to this endeavor. I've surrendered so much of my time, so much of my devotion, that I often feel as if I can give you and Maisie nothing more than scraps of me, when you both deserve so much more."

His words caught her by surprise. Her fury waned, leaving ash in its wake.

"The truth is . . . my hands are stained, Sidra. I've craved violence, and I've drunk willingly from its cup. I've beaten the men who trespass over the clan line, beaten them until they cower and yield. And those who don't? I've ended their lives without a moment of hesitation. I've slit their throats and pierced their hearts. I've stolen their voices and dropped their bodies into the sea, as if the water could wash away my deeds."

Sidra was silent as she listened, but her heart was pounding.

"So when you speak of peace," he said, "when Adaira speaks of peace, I'm unable to see it. It's a sentiment that is unattainable in my mind, given all the things I've done to the Breccans in order to keep the east *safe*. And if the trade does happen the way my cousin hopes, I will have to encounter people marked by my actions. Do you think they'll be glad to see me, Sid? Do you think they'll want to trade with the man who killed their son or beat their brother?"

Torin was staring at his hands, as if he could see the blood on them. Sidra watched him with a knot in her throat. She thought he might be struggling to express his guilt, and while the healer within her wanted to smooth his brow and give him words to ease his pain, she sensed this was a festering wound in him that needed to be opened.

"I know you've killed men, Torin," she said, drawing his eyes to hers. "I've seen the blood that stains your plaid, the blood beneath your nails. I've seen the haunted gleam in your eye, even though it is fleeting. I know that you are the captain of the guard, that you must protect us from the west, and that sometimes that requires you to kill. But there is more to you than violence. And I don't want to see you become a man who kills without reason. A man who lets revenge turn his heart into a cold, bitter vessel."

Now she was the one to take him by surprise. For a moment, he merely gazed up at her. "How would you stop it then? A heart turning to stone?"

"There is another way to protect our clan. A way that veers away from vengeance and enmity. But you must strive to find it, and you must lead the others by example." She paused, turning her own palms upwards. "Our hands can steal, or they can give. They can harm, or they can comfort. They can wound and kill, or they can heal and save. Which will you choose for your hands, Torin?"

He answered, through his teeth, "This is the way it has always been done. The way I have been taught."

"And sometimes we must look inward and change ourselves," she said. "If you have killed men without cause, if you have struck them out of vengeance just because they live on a different side of the isle, then you must search within and ask yourself *why* you have done these things, and what is the cost for them, and how you can make reparations for them. The trade would be a good place to start."

Torin stood. He paced the room, breathing heavily. Sidra thought he might flee, but he stopped and looked at her again.

"And if I don't agree with your thoughts? If I can't change to become what you hope for? Is losing you one of the costs for my sins?"

"I have been with you all this time," she said, a soft answer that eased his rigid posture. "The good as well as the bad. Once, we were acquaintances sharing a vow. But you have become more to me than mere words spoken on a midsummer night. And I have never been one to love conditionally."

"And yet you ask me to change?" he asked, fist over his heart.

Sidra wondered if he had even heard what she had just said to him. She had never spoken such words aloud before—that she had come to love him in a deep, quiet way. Completely, with all of his scars and mistakes and glory.

She realized she and Torin stood on two different mountains, with a deep valley between them. They saw the world from opposing sides, and she didn't know if they would be able to find a middle ground. Their differences could be enough to break their vows, despite her feelings for him.

"You haven't heard the things I've heard," he said, as if he also sensed the divide. "You haven't gone hungry after a raid, or watched your storehouse go lean, losing all of your winter provisions. You haven't had to draw a sword and fight them, Sidra."

"I haven't," Sidra agreed. "But I've had to heal wounds caused by the raids. I've given to those who have suffered losses, and I have been with them through their pain. And so I must say this, Torin . . . what has brought on these feelings within you? It doesn't sound as if *I* am asking you to change, but that your own blood and bones are aching for it."

His face went pale. He stared at her with a clenched jaw, and she sensed the divide between them grow.

"Bring the tonics to the barracks when they're ready," he said in a cold voice.

Sidra watched as he turned and departed. He was running from the things she had said to him, and she stood for a moment longer before sinking into a chair.

She had never felt more defeated.

~~~~~~~~~~~~~~~~~~~~~~~~~~~~~~~~

CHAPTER 17

Frae was dreaming of chocolate cake and snow when she heard the hooves in the garden. A horse was stomping through the vegetables, its noble neck arched, its nostrils flaring with breath like clouds. At first, Frae thought the horse was part of her dream—she had always longed for one, despite Mirin insisting the chickens and the three cows were more than enough animals for them—until she startled awake.

She opened her eyes to the darkness and listened. She could hear Mirin's soft, deep breaths beside her, but there . . . just beyond the bolted shutters, to her left. A horse whickered.

She sat forward, the blanket tumbling away from her shoulders. Without a sound, she stood and walked all the way to the bedroom door. She unlatched it very quietly and slipped into the common chamber, where the hearth embers still glowed and Mirin's loom sat in the corner like a dark, slumbering beast. She made to go to Jack's door but then paused, thinking she had better check and make sure a horse was truly in the yard before she woke her brother.

Frae crept to the back door. There was a small iron grill with a sliding panel built in the upper wood—a peeping window—which was a little too high for Frae's line of vision, but if she raised up on her toes, she would be able to see out of it. She held her breath, her hands suddenly clammy as she worked to unlock the narrow panel, sliding it back until she could taste fresh air and see the constellations glittering like crystals in the sky.

She raised up on the balls of her feet and peered through the narrow opening.

She saw the horse instantly. It stood only a stone's throw away, grazing in the garden. It was huge and beautiful, tacked with saddle and bridle, the silver buckles winking in the starlight.

Then it must have a rider, she thought, her eyes sweeping the garden.

He could have been a statue standing in the herbs, etched in moonlight. He stood facing the house, staring in Frae's direction.

She dropped down, heart beating wildly in her chest, but then realized he probably couldn't see her, not through the dark shadows that draped the backside of the cottage.

She dared to peep again.

She couldn't fully make out the features of his face, but she saw the woad tattoos that marked his forearms and the backs of his hands. She saw the plaid that was draped across his chest and knew it would be blue in color. A sword was sheathed at his belt.

Frae panicked and slid the panel. It shut with a click, a quiet sound but in that midnight moment it was horribly loud to her and she cowered, slowly backing away from the door.

What was the first rule? The first was to be silent. *Don't make a noise if they come.*

She darted to Jack's room, throwing his door open.

"Jack!" she cried, but her voice had withered. It came out nothing more than a rasp and Frae hurried to his bedside. "Jack, wake up!"

"Mm?" He rolled over. "Where should we sing?"

Frae blinked, realized he was sleep-talking. She shook his shoulder, adamant.

"Jack!"

He sat forward, reached out to trace her face in the dark. His voice was thick but lucid as he said her name. "Frae?"

"There's a Breccan in our backyard," she whispered.

Her brother nearly knocked her over as he lurched out of bed. He strode into the common room, Frae right behind him, twisting her hands together as Jack stood at the back door and opened the sliding panel.

She waited, holding her breath. The moonlight doused Jack's face in silver as he studied the yard. It felt like an eternity had passed before he looked at Frae and whispered, "I don't see anyone. Where was he?"

"He was right there standing in the herbs! He was looking at the house. His horse was eating our vegetables." She hurried to his side and peered through the grate.

Jack spoke truth. The Breccan and his horse were gone.

Both relieved and disappointed, Frae slumped against the door, wondering if she had imagined it.

"Was there just one of them, Frae?"

She let out a quivering breath. "I . . . yes. I think so."

"Where does Mum keep the sword?"

"In her bedroom, in the oaken chest."

"Will you get it for me?"

Frae nodded and retreated back to the bedroom, feeling her way to the chest in the corner. Mirin still slumbered, and Frae sorted through the weapons gathered within the chest—

a quiver of arrows, a bow made of yew wood, and the broadsword in its leather scabbard. Though it was dusty and dull from disuse, Frae secretly hoped Mirin would give the blade to her one day.

When Frae returned to the common room, sword in hand, she saw that Jack had opened the back door and was standing on the threshold, staring boldly into the yard.

"What are you doing?" she hissed at him. "The second rule is to stay inside, lock the doors, and wait for the East Guard to come!"

"Thank you, sister," Jack said, taking the sword from her. "I'm going to look through the yard, just to make sure no one is here. Go wake Mum and stay with her, do you hear me, Frae?"

His voice was stern, and Frae nodded, wide eyed.

She listened as Jack unsheathed the sword; she could see the blade drink the moonlight, and the moment her brother stepped into the yard, she panicked again.

"Jack! Please stay inside," she begged, even though she felt a strong urge to follow him.

Jack only spun on his heel in the dirt, lifting a forefinger to his lips.

The first rule. Don't make a sound.

Frae swallowed the knot in her throat and watched as Jack silently stepped through the garden, searching. She strained her eyes in the dark as she watched him, anxious until she heard Mirin's soothing voice speak behind her.

"It'll be all right, Frae."

She jumped and turned to see her mother directly behind her, her eyes wide as she, too, watched Jack move through the garden.

"I saw a horse and a man in the yard," Frae whispered, and Mirin's gaze flickered down to hers. "He was a Breccan."

"Just now?"

"A few moments ago, Mum."

Mirin stepped closer and laid her hands on Frae's shoulders, and it made Frae feel safer. They both continued to watch Jack walk the perimeter of the yard and Frae finally noticed it—the gate was sitting open, groaning in the sudden gust of wind. That was one of her final chores of the day—to ensure all of the gates were closed.

"The gate!" she cried just as Jack approached it. "Mum, the gate's open!"

"I see it too, Frae."

"Jack will close it, won't he?" Frae said, but then to her horror, her brother stepped *through* it, and she realized he was about to walk down the hill, out of sight. "Jack! *Jack!* Come back!"

She was screaming and didn't even know that she was until Mirin knelt and framed Frae's face in her cold hands.

"We must be quiet, Frae. Remember the rules? Jack will be fine. All of us will be fine. We are safe here, but you must be quiet."

Frae nodded, but her breaths were rapid again, and she felt light-headed.

"Come, let's make a cup of tea and rouse the fire while we wait for your brother." Mirin shut the back door, but she didn't lock it, and Frae felt torn as she followed her mother to the hearth.

Mirin threw a log on the coals and stirred a tired flame to life. Frae struggled to put the tea leaves in the strainer and carry the kettle to the hearth. The water was just beginning to boil when Jack returned, bounding in through the back door, his hair tangled, his face flushed. There was a wild, angry gleam in his eyes.

"Jack?" Mirin prompted.

"I counted ten of them," he said, grabbing his boots. He stood on one foot and struggled to knot the tethers up to his knees. "They're riding along the valley floor by the river, follow-ing the tree line to the north. To the Elliotts' croft, I believe."

"Are they going to come here, Jack?" Frae asked, tremulous.

"No, Frae. They've passed us by. We're safe."

But there had been that one Breccan and his horse, Frae thought with a perplexed frown. What had he been doing? She was certain she hadn't imagined him.

"And where are you going, Jack?" Mirin asked in a mea-sured tone. As if she felt nothing—no fear, no relief, no worry.

Jack finished knotting his boot tethers. He met Mirin's gaze from the other side of the room. "I'm going to the Elliotts'."

"That's six kilometers from here, son."

"Well, I'll not sit here and do nothing. I'll run there. Per-haps the land will aid me tonight." He glanced down to the sword in his hand. "Do you have another sword, Mum?"

"No. A bow and a quiver."

"May I use them?"

Mirin was silent, but then she looked at Frae. "Go and get the bow and quiver for your brother, Frae."

Frae scampered into the bedroom for the second time that night, her fingers like ice as she found the weapons. When she returned, she saw her mother had knotted a plaid across Jack's chest, to guard his heart and his lungs. It was enchanted. Mirin had woven it for him years ago, and he didn't look thrilled to be wearing it until Mirin took a firm hold of his chin—Frae knew that meant she was very angry—and stared at Jack, say-ing, "You wear the plaid and go, or you don't and stay here with us, Jack. Which will it be?"

He decided to wear the plaid, as Frae knew he would. She didn't understand why he hated the enchantment so much, and she brought him the quiver and the bow, her heart ham-mering fiercely in her chest.

Jack smiled at her, as if it was a peaceful night. It calmed her as he buckled the quiver to his shoulder. He set the sword in her hands. "I'll return soon."

And then he was gone. Frae stood by the fire, numb at first until her fear returned, swelling like a wasp sting. The hilt of the sword was warm and heavy in her grip. She stared at it as if she had never seen a sword before.

"Remember the third rule, Frae?" Mirin said as she poured them a cup of tea.

Frae remembered. The rules brought her back to life, and she walked into her bedchamber yet again and found her own plaid, folded on the bench.

Frae returned to the fire and stood before her mother as Mirin wrapped the plaid around her thin body, knotting it firmly at Frae's shoulder.

"There," said Mirin. "That's how the guards wear their plaids too."

Frae tried to smile, but her eyes burned with tears. She wished Jack had stayed in the house.

She propped the weapon on the tea table and curled up beside her mother on the divan, determined to stay awake, listening to every sound—the howl of the wind, the occasional rattle of the shutters, the creaks of the cottage, the pop of the fire. Sounds that made her stiffen, until she set her head on Mirin's lap and her mother caressed her hair, humming a happy song. A song Frae had not heard in a long time.

She drifted to sleep, but the stranger with his blue tattoos and his great horse followed her into her dreams.

Torin was standing on the hill between his croft and his father's, desperate for an answer as to where his daughter had been taken. He always began in the place where Sidra had stabbed the culprit, following her descent down the hill until anger burned in his marrow. Sidra had lain here, unconscious for only the spirits knew how long. Whoever this man was, Torin was going to find and kill him. As he crouched in the crushed heather, he thought about how he would slowly end this person's life. The sky above him teemed with stars and a waxing moon, and he let out a frustrated sigh when suddenly his left hand began to ache, as if he had plunged it into ice water. The throbbing quickly intensified, stealing his breath.

Torin waited for the pain to either subside or expand, counting the pulses. Five trespassers. He closed his eyes, seeing the place where the Breccans had crossed. The Elliotts' croft.

He wanted to be surprised that the Breccans were raiding in summer, the day after the successful trade. But Torin could only chide himself.

He should have expected this.

He turned and ran back to the cottage, which was dark. Sidra was staying with Graeme at night, to Torin's immense relief. He didn't want her to be alone, and he couldn't afford to sleep. Only a span of an hour here and there when his exhaustion was debilitating. But he had learned how to push his body, to find an unexpected thread of strength even when he felt like he had reached the end of himself.

He tapped into that source as he approached his stallion in the byre. Torin tacked and mounted him, then set off at a gallop along the western road, his teeth cutting the wind. When the road curved back to the east, Torin departed from it and rode across the hills, heading directly for the Elliotts'.

The raid might be over by the time he reached the farm, he thought with irritation. He hadn't doubled the watchmen at the clan line yet; traditionally, he waited to do so until after the autumnal equinox, when the weather began to turn cold. This attack was very unexpected, and Torin felt scattered and unprepared. His eyes watered as the wind bit his face and clawed his hair.

A new season of peace, Adaira had said with such hope that Torin had wanted to believe her.

But now all he could envision was how foolish he had been to let her put herself in a vulnerable situation, meeting with the Breccan on the northern shore. To let her give up their food and drink. To expose their knowledge of the Orenna flower.

His cousin's voice came again, a whisper in his mind. *What are you afraid of, Torin? Give this fear a name, so I can put your mind at ease.*

A sound slipped from him. His stomach had ached for days now, ever since he had opened his father's door and beheld Sidra, battered and devastated. When he had realized Maisie had been taken.

I'm afraid of losing everything I love. The east, his purpose. The people woven into his life.

He had been too proud to say it to Adaira, but he confessed it now as he flew across the hills. He didn't want to think about the ones he had lost, but they rose like specters. His mother, whom he vaguely remembered, whose voice had been gentle but sad. He had been so young when she abandoned him. Donella, once a vibrant soul, had faded in his mind over the years. He had been so defiant when she died. Maisie, his own flesh and blood that he had failed to protect and was currently failing to find. Sidra, who was bound to him by a blood vow. She had arrived home drenched from the cursed loch, her eyes searching and lost.

You have become more to me than mere words spoken on a midsummer night.

He had retraced that revelation of hers endless times in the past few hours. So much that he felt the groove of it in his thoughts. He had been startled by her confession—he thought her so far above him. He'd never expected to earn her love, and he didn't know how to show her how deeply he felt for her.

But Torin didn't have time to think about this.

He was almost to the Elliotts' when a moving shadow caught his attention. It was on the path ahead of him, pressing west. He realized it was a man, running, and Torin unsheathed his sword, urging his stead to quicken his pace.

The runner heard his approach and whirled with an arrow nocked on his bow. Torin was preparing to strike when the man lowered his weapon, then tucked and rolled to avoid being trampled by the horse.

Torin turned the stallion about, nearly unseating himself in his haste, and his gaze swept the moonlit grass. The man with the bow was easy to find, a thin shadow rising from the ground, brushing dirt from his clothes.

"That's the *second* time you've almost killed me, Torin."

Jack's unmistakable, peevish voice.

"Dammit, Jack!" Torin could have strangled him. "What are you doing?"

"I'm going to assist the Elliotts."

"How did you know they were being raided?"

"I saw ten Breccans ride by my mum's croft. Heading this way."

Torin frowned, his thoughts reeling. "Ten? I sensed only five crossing the clan line."

Jack approached the horse. Torin could barely discern his face in the celestial light, but he was frowning as well. "I clearly counted ten of them."

Something was off, Torin thought with a huff of air. Perhaps he had been too distracted when he was searching the trail on the hill, when the pain in his hand had flared.

"Are you going to give me a ride?" Jack drawled.

"You should go home, Jack."

The bard released a scathing laugh. "Not tonight, captain. You need my help, and I'm eager to spill some blood."

Torin couldn't refute it, and they were wasting time. He gave Jack a hand and hauled him up behind the saddle. Torin didn't wait to ensure the bard was holding on before he nudged his stallion onward again.

He and Jack saw the rosy hue on the horizon at the same moment. It speared Torin with dread, filling him with cold silence, but Jack muttered, "My gods, what is that?"

Torin didn't answer, saving his voice. They crested the hill to see that the Elliott cottage, storehouse, and byre were burning. The flames had just been set, the smoke rising in great white billows. This was new, Torin thought, assessing the valley. The Breccan raids had always followed the same pattern in the past: they crossed the clan line, they raided, stole food and livestock and anything else of worth, and they retreated. Quick bursts of violence. They never killed, although they sometimes wounded, and they never set fire to buildings.

"Why?" Jack snarled. "Why is the west sabotaging itself when Adaira wants to trade?"

"Because they will never change," Torin replied tersely.

The watchmen were already present. Torin could see them on their horses, chasing the last of the Breccans away while the Elliott family ran across the yard, salvaging what little they could from their burning home and yard.

There were more than five Breccans riding with their torches, hurling them onto the thatched roofs. Torin was astounded when he counted eleven blue plaids in the limited view that he had on the hill.

He directed his horse down to the valley, where the heat of the fire met him like a hot summer day. The flames were growing at an alarming rate, perilously fed by the hay and the wind. Torin dismounted, sword in hand, and ordered Jack to stay on the horse, where he had the best chance of remaining unharmed. The last thing he wanted was for Adaira's new husband to get himself killed.

Torin didn't glance behind to see what the bard did, although he did notice an arrow streak by, harmlessly hitting the cottage.

Satisfied that they had plundered what they wanted and set fire to everything, the Breccans retreated into the woods, melting into the darkness like cowards.

Torin coughed as he rounded the burning house. The air was thick, the smoke stinging his eyes. He gave half of his guard orders to begin hauling water from the nearby stream, to put the fire out. He motioned his remaining guard, the watchmen, to pursue the Breccans into the Aithwood, all the way to the clan line.

"Take prisoners if you can!" he shouted. He craved answers.

The trees of the forest grew thick, the air sweet and dark. Torin ran on foot, weaving around the trunks and kicking through patches of bracken. The clan line was close; he could feel it, humming in the earth.

Suddenly, he realized he was alone. None of his watchmen were with him.

He came to a stop, his eyes cutting through the night. It was quiet, but his breaths were ragged, his pulse thundering in his ears.

The Breccan seemed to come from the shadows, his boots making no sound on the loam. Torin saw him a moment too late, raising his sword to deflect a blow. The Breccan's steel sliced his forearm. The pain was bright and merciless.

Torin fell to his knees, gasping. He felt the coldness seep into him—the sting of an enchanted blade. He parried another cut with his sword, driving the Breccan back. But then he was stung again in his shoulder, just beneath the protective drape of his plaid.

This pain was cool too, but sent a flare to Torin's mind.

Run, escape, hide, run.

The orders permeated him. He staggered up to his feet, abandoned his sword, and ran, the fear rotten within him. Behind him someone spoke, an amused and cruel voice—"A fine captain you are"—and it only fueled Torin's irrational desire to run, escape, *hide.*

He lost track of his direction, weaving deep into the woods. The forest eventually ended, spilling him out into a stark landscape. He could hear the roar of the coast nearby. The fog was rolling in from the ocean, cold and thick and hungry.

Torin ran into its embrace.

Jack sprinted through the Elliotts' yard with a bucket of water. He had been useless with the bow and arrows, but this was something he could do. He dumped the water onto the house, which continued to roil with flames. Back and forth he ran, following a line of guards. From the stream to the yard, from the yard back to the stream, his skin grimy with sweat and flecked with ash.

The cottage continued to burn.

Jack panted, hurling another bucket of water onto the fire. He heard someone wailing and turned to see Grace Elliott on her knees, rocking. Her husband Hendry was beside her, trying to comfort her. Their two sons were quiet with shock, the flames reflected in their eyes.

For a moment, Jack was terrified someone else was in the house, and he approached the family.

"Did all of you make it out?" he asked.

"Yes," Hendry said. "All of us but . . . Eliza. She's missing, though. Hasn't been home in almost three weeks now."

Jack nodded. His mouth was dry and his eyes stung.

The Elliotts had salvaged an old cow, but they had lost everything else. Jack stumbled away, his eyes peeling the darkness. His vision was blighted from the fire, but he could faintly see the Aithwood. He wondered where Torin and the rest of the watchmen were and fought the uneasiness he felt, deciding he would keep running to the stream until ordered otherwise.

The command came minutes later, when the wind began to howl from the north. The fire billowed and the charred remains of the house began to crackle.

"Move back!" one of the guards shouted.

Jack scrambled to help the Elliotts escape the yard as the cottage collapsed in a burst of sparks and a wash of blistering heat. There was nothing more he could do; he remained beside the family in the grass and continued to look around, searching for Torin, particularly when a few of the watchmen rode in from the woods.

No Breccans had been caught or taken prisoner.

All of them had escaped.

Torin failed to appear, even as the stars began to vanish. The eastern sky was laced with gold when a few of the guards approached the family.

"We're still waiting to hear from the captain, but we feel it's best to escort you to the castle," one of them said. "The laird and heiress will want you looked after until we can rebuild. Come, mount our horses and we will take you to Sloane."

Grace Elliott nodded in defeat, clutching her shawl at her collar. She looked so weary, her eyes rimmed in red as she moved to the closest horse. She was about to slip her foot into the stirrup when she froze.

"Do you hear that?" she said, whirling to where her cottage smoldered in a heap.

"It's just the wind, my love," Hendry Elliott said. He sounded desperate to get her away from the fire and the clan line. "Let's get you up on the horse now."

"No, it's Eliza," Grace insisted, pushing away from her husband. "Eliza! *Eliza!*"

The hair rose on Jack's arms as he watched Grace Elliott stride through the grass, screaming for her missing daughter.

Hendry trailed her, tearing his hands through his hair. "Grace, *please*. Stop this."

"Don't you hear her, Hendry? She's calling for us!"

Jack listened. He took a step closer to the ruins. "Wait!" he said. "I hear it too."

Their party fell painfully silent. The wind was gusting, and the fire was still crackling, but there was a small voice, calling in the distance.

Shouts rose. The watchmen had now heard it, or perhaps had seen something.

Grace and Hendry broke into a frantic run to their demolished home. Jack was behind them, the Elliott brothers and the guards in his wake. They darted through the ruins, emerging on the other side of the yard, facing the dark, looming southern sky.

Through the languid dance of smoke, Jack could discern a little girl hurrying down a hill. She was coming from the very trail he and Torin had taken to reach the Elliotts' croft. The direction of Mirin's lands. Her brown hair was braided with ribbons, her dress was clean and immaculate, and yet her face was crumpled with emotion as she saw her parents.

"Eliza!" Grace shouted, sweeping the girl into her arms.

Hendry and the two brothers gathered around her, until

Jack could no longer see the lass. But he felt the weeping, the joy, the wonder as the family was reunited.

Slowly, he sank to his knees, overcome with the bewildering realization.

A missing girl had been found.

Eliza Elliott had come home on the heels of a raid.

PART THREE

A Song
for Wind

CHAPTER 18

Sidra was in a dreamless sleep when she felt Graeme's hand on her shoulder.

"Sidra, lass. Adaira is here for you."

She roused in an instant, blinking as she sat upright. Graeme had given her his bed in the corner, while he had been sleeping on a pallet before the fire. Carefully, Sidra walked around the cluttered table to find Adaira standing on the threshold.

Instantly, Sidra knew something was wrong. Adaira's face was pale and lined with worry.

"What's happened?" Sidra asked in a wavering voice.

"I need your help at the castle today," Adaira said. "Get dressed and meet me in the yard. Bring your herbs."

Sidra nodded, rushing to don her clothes behind the wooden dressing panel. She drew on the same skirt and bodice she had worn the day before, and she noticed her hands were trembling as she knotted her boots.

"Here, lass," Graeme said on her way out, handing her an oatcake wrapped in cloth as well as her basket of healing supplies. "If you stay at the castle tonight, send word and let me know."

"I will, Da," Sidra agreed, thanking him for the breakfast as she walked out the door.

Adaira and two of her guards were waiting on the road, mounted on horses. Sidra approached Adaira and hauled herself up into the saddle behind her. It was awkward with her basket, but Sidra held it close to her side, her other arm wrapping around Adaira's slender waist.

"What's happened?" she asked again. Her first thought was that Adaira's father was about to die, and Sidra sought to prepare herself for that moment.

"I'll tell you when we reach Sloane," Adaira replied, urging her horse onward.

The ride to the city felt unbearably long. Sidra's mind was laden with worry when they reached the courtyard. Adaira helped her down to the cobblestones, and she helplessly looked for Torin. There was no sign of him as Sidra followed Adaira into the hall and down winding corridors, eventually coming to a small private chamber where they could talk.

Sidra stood in a slant of morning light, watching as Adaira poured them each a knuckle of whiskey.

"What's this about, Adi?" she asked, warily accepting the glass.

"Drink," Adaira replied. "You're going to need it."

Sidra didn't often partake of whiskey, but she tossed back the burning liquid. Her sight felt sharper, her hearing keener as she swallowed. She winced and set her gaze on Adaira, expectant.

Adaira held her stare, her blue eyes bloodshot. "Eliza Elliott was found early this morning."

Sidra startled. It felt like the ground quaked beneath her feet as she whispered, "Where?"

She listened as Adaira told her of the raid, the burning croft, and Eliza's miraculous return. She paced the small chamber, overwhelmed and full of questions that wanted to burst out of her.

"I think the lasses are in the west, Sidra," Adaira finally concluded. "I think the Breccans have somehow figured out a way to cross the clan line without Torin's knowledge, and they have been stealing our girls, one by one."

Sidra halted. The thought of Maisie being held in the west turned her blood to ice. But it made sense, as if the last piece of a puzzle had snapped into place. "It's why we can't find the lasses here in the east, isn't it? They've been with the Breccans the entire time."

Adaira nodded. "And I think the Breccans are harnessing the power of the Orenna flower to accomplish this. Perhaps the flower grants them the ability to cross over undetected."

Sidra rubbed the ache in her brow. "You still have the flower I gave you?"

"Yes, although I am afraid to consume it and test this theory, as it is the only one we have and my presumption could be false."

"What does Torin think?"

Adaira hesitated a beat. "I'm not sure yet. But he *did* mention something odd to Jack during the raid. Torin felt only five Breccans crossing the clan line, but Jack counted twice as many, riding past the valley by Mirin's croft. It's apparent that they have some secret way of crossing over now. Five of them drew the watchmen, the guard, and Torin to the Elliotts', while the rest of them clandestinely crossed farther down the territory boundary and dropped Eliza off."

Sidra felt a strange tug in her chest to think that the enchantment in Torin's scar might have been fooling him.

"The raid last night was a power play, but I also believe it was a diversion," Adaira continued. "The Breccans used it to send one of the lasses back home to us."

"Why would they reveal their hand?" Sidra asked. "Why not stay silent and continue to steal our girls? Why are they taking our children to begin with?"

Adaira sighed, as if she had been haunted by these very thoughts all morning. "I'm not sure, but I think it's a clear sign that the Breccans don't want peace. They want me to strike back and incite a war. I have no choice but to prepare for it now, although I must be very careful. I don't have irrefutable proof they have the lasses, even though Eliza's appearance after the raid is remarkable. I need to procure proof another way, and then I think we will need to get the girls safely home before any sort of open conflict happens."

"Yes," Sidra whispered. The safety of the girls was of the utmost importance. She didn't dare to hope—it felt far too fragile these days—but she wanted to embrace the comfort of Maisie returning home soon. The vision nearly brought Sidra to her knees, and she blinked it away before her emotions could overtake her. "What do you need me to do, Adi?"

"I need you to first examine Eliza," Adaira replied. "She returned home with ribbons in her hair and not a speck of dirt on her clothes. By all appearances, it seems as if she's been well looked after, but I need you to confirm she hasn't been abused or mistreated. She's also unable to answer any questions about who took her or where she's been the past few weeks, which would be a tremendous help to us if she eventually felt safe enough to talk about it. But I want her needs to come first, and I hope you can help me realize what they are."

Sidra was silent. She rarely had to examine a child for abuse, although it occasionally did happen. It always made her feel sick, and she had to reach out and support herself on the wall.

"Sid?" Adaira whispered, coming to her.

Sidra released a deep breath. She closed her eyes and centered herself, and when she met Adaira's concerned gaze again, she nodded. "I will do this for you. Take me to Eliza."

"I don't know what to do, Jack," Adaira confessed. She was pacing her chambers, waiting while Sidra examined Eliza. It seemed like everything she had been planning, everything she had been working toward, was crumbling in her hands.

"Come and eat something, Adaira," Jack replied. He was sitting by the hearth, where he had called up a tea tray for them. "You can't maintain your strength if you don't feed yourself."

She knew Jack was right, but her stomach was wound in a knot, wondering what Eliza had been through. Wondering where the other lasses were.

She tried to take a bite of a scone but set it back down and resumed her restless pacing. "If they harmed this child . . . the Breccans will wish they had never been born. I will teach them not to steal lasses. I will burn the west into ashes. I will raze it to the ground."

Jack rose and stood before her. She knew she sounded like Torin. Her cousin who was missing. The captain of the guard, whose reluctance to trust the Breccans had been well founded all along. It only made her temper flare brighter until she felt Jack's cold hands frame her face.

"We still need proof it's them. But there are two things we can do at the moment, Adaira," he said in a calm voice. "The first? You should write to Moray Breccan. Don't say a word about Eliza, but give him an ultimatum. Tell him that you will grant him one day to return what his clan has stolen from us, or else the future of the trade and your visit is forfeit. Make no declarations of war yet. The second? I'm composing a ballad for the spirits of the wind. I believe I can have it completed very soon, if I spend most of my hours devoted to it."

Adaira studied him. Her heart was pounding in excitement as well as fear as she listened to his suggestions. "I don't want you to play for the wind, Jack."

He frowned, his hands falling away from her. "Why not? They are the most powerful of the spirits. They have sealed the mouths of the earth and the water. They have no doubt seen where the west is holding the girls. If I summon them, they could give us the confirmation we need to find and bring the lasses home."

Adaira sighed. "I don't want you to play because it drains your health."

"And yet *this* is why you called me home, Adaira," he said gently. "We are so close to solving this mystery. Please use me and my gift to find the answers you need."

She felt torn, though she knew he was right.

A knock sounded on the door. Adaira was relieved to see it was Sidra, returning from the examination.

"How is Eliza?" she asked.

"From what I can tell," Sidra began, "she suffered no physical trauma. She was gently looked after, well fed, and rested during her time away. But her inability to speak about what happened tells me that she is afraid, and that someone threatened her to stay silent."

"What can we do for her to make her feel safe again?" Adaira asked.

"Keeping her with her family for now," Sidra replied. "Ensuring life feels normal and secure for her, despite the fact they are residing in the castle and her home has been burned to the ground."

"I'll see to this," Adaira replied. "Thank you."

Sidra nodded and turned to go. Jack glanced at Adaira; she could read his eyes, the way they gleamed in warning.

"Sid, wait," Adaira said.

Sidra paused at the threshold.

"I need to tell you about Torin."

"Yes, where is he?" Sidra asked. "I was hoping to speak with him this morning."

When Adaira hesitated, Jack spoke.

"We're not certain where he is. He pursued the Breccans into the Aithwood during the raid."

Sidra's face blanched. "Do you think he was wounded? Or taken prisoner?"

"One of the watchmen claims to have seen him running from the forest on foot," Adaira said. "But a fog was descending, which has made it very difficult to locate him. We believe he's injured, and I have the guard combing the northern hills. I'll let you know as soon as we find him."

"You should have told me he was missing the moment you saw me," Sidra said. Adaira had never heard her speak with such ire in her voice, and it made her shame rise.

She had waited to tell Sidra because she needed the healer to give her whole focus to examining Eliza Elliott. But perhaps Adaira had erred. She felt as if she were making mistake after mistake, and she watched as Sidra left without another word, her throat narrow. Things were falling apart, and Adaira didn't know how to hold everything together.

When Jack retreated to his chamber, to work on the ballad Adaira didn't want him to sing, she finally sat at her desk and pulled out a sheet of parchment and a freshly cut quill.

She didn't know if Moray had ordered the raid. There was the slight possibility that he had not, that perhaps a group of Breccans who opposed the trade agreement were responsible. But now that Adaira suspected the west had been stealing their girls, her heart was smoldering. She felt as if peace had been a naïve illusion.

Why would the west want our lasses?

She had no answer, other than briefly imagining that life beyond the clan line was far worse than she knew. Perhaps the Breccans' daughters were dying. And yet why would they return Eliza?

Adaira dipped her quill into her inkwell. She wrote Moray an ultimatum.

Torin lay in a patch of moon thistle, half aware of where he was, of what he was doing. He blinked and tried to move, only to have his left arm respond with excruciating pain. Grimacing, he glanced down to look at his wounds.

There were two shallow cuts on his arm, oozing foul-smelling blood.

A small voice forged from years of training commanded him to get up. *Get up and walk and get these wounds cleaned before they fester any worse.* And yet he didn't want to; he battled an overwhelming urge to remain hidden and safe. Nothing would come near a thistle patch. Nothing save for Adaira and damselflies and bees. He found a little humor in the sad thought.

So he lay there, among the thistles, blanketed by the morning fog.

It wasn't long before he heard his name, carried on the wind.

"Captain Tamerlaine!"

He heard the call over and over, like a herd of cows. Torin pulled himself along the ground, deeper into the thistles, oblivious to the needles because more than anything, he didn't want his guard to find him like this. Like a coward who had run, who couldn't even rise to his feet and clean his wounds and recover his sword, which he had dropped like a novice.

He lay there and prayed they would all go away. He pressed his face into the ground and gritted his teeth against the pain in his arm and tried to calm his mind, but he wondered how long the enchantment would fetter him. A day? Several days?

He needed to get up. *Get up!*

And then he saw her. She walked past the thistle patch, her dark hair catching his eye in the fog.

Sidra.

At once, he began to crawl to her, through the thistles. She hadn't seen him. She was walking away, but her black hair was his marker in the mist—she was his refuge—and Torin dragged himself free from the thistles and up to his feet.

He swayed for a moment. The world spun and the fog was deceptive. He lost sight of her and felt the sting of his wounds again, the panic and the fear that had made him run. But that fear was nothing compared to what he felt when he parted his lips to call her name.

Sidra!

It rang in his mind, but no sound emerged from his mouth. Only a roaring silence.

He tried again, but his voice was lost. He couldn't speak, and he realized what the first enchanted blade had done when it nicked his forearm.

He stumbled over a pile of loose stones. The sound of the falling rocks brought Sidra back around, and Torin watched as she reemerged from the fog. He watched her eyes widen the moment she saw him, ragged and desperate.

"Torin," she breathed and stretched out her hand.

He couldn't hold himself up. He leaned into her, a woman who didn't reach his shoulder in height, and yet she steadied him.

And even as he pressed his face into her hair and wept, he could make no sound.

CHAPTER 19

S idra listened to the rain as she stood at the kitchen table, grinding an endless pile of herbs. She had been crushing them for what felt like hours now, until her hands were numb, until every mixture she could create had been made and spread over Torin's wounds. The one on his shoulder was healing swiftly—the shallow wound stung by fear. But the cut on his forearm, the one that had stolen his voice . . . Sidra couldn't staunch its slow but steady ooze. And enchanted wounds, while miserable to suffer through, were known to heal twice as fast as mortal wounds with the proper care.

What was she missing? *Other than my faith,* she thought with exasperation, setting down her pestle. She stared at the array of dried herbs she had spread over her table, the fresh bundles that hung from the timber beams. The honey pot and the bowl of butter and the small jar of oil. She was missing something that would heal his wound and return his voice, and she didn't know what it was.

Weary, she created a new salve to try and carried the bowl

into the bedroom. Torin was asleep, his mouth slightly ajar, his long legs nearly dangling off the foot of the bed. He was shirtless, his chest rising and falling with deep measured breaths, but she knew he would awaken soon. She had drawn eight moon thistle needles from his hands and face; he would be prey to nightmares, despite the stout sleeping tonic she had given him hours ago.

He looked so vulnerable, so young, she thought, gazing at him. Sidra wondered if they would have been friends years ago if their paths had ever crossed, but then she thought no, probably not.

Quietly, she sat beside him on the bed and peeled back the damp linen that covered his wounds, then coated them with her new salve. Feeling the cold trace of magic in his skin, she took out her frustration on the fresh bolt of linen, which she tore into strips. She finished redressing the wounds and watched as the lower cut quickly bled through its bandage. It wasn't healing but growing worse. And she felt her first tremor of fear.

What am I missing?

It was then that Sidra fully acknowledged the truth. She didn't know if she would be able to heal Torin. Her faith was still some strange, broken mirror in her chest, the pieces sharp and jagged, reflecting years of her life out of order.

She covered her face with her hands, her breath hitching. She could smell the countless herbs on her palms, secrets that she had always known how to wield, and she let the truth wash over her until it felt like she was drowning in her own skin.

I don't know how to heal him.

The rain continued to fall, and Sidra remained at Torin's side. Eventually she lowered her hands and reached for the wooden figurine of Lady Whin of the Wildflowers. Maisie had left it at the bedside days ago, and Sidra had yet to touch it. But she claimed it now, tracing the spirit's long hair, the flowers that bloomed from her fingers, the extraordinary details of her lovely face.

How easy it would be if faith was something tangible like a figurine, something she could hold in her hands, seeing all of the details and how they made the whole. And yet, didn't the earth prove its faithfulness to her, year after year? Even in winter, when it fell dormant? Sidra always knew the flowers and the grass and the fruit would return come spring.

Even with those memories, she had no prayers to whisper. There seemed to be nothing but emptiness and exhaustion in her, and Sidra set the figurine back down, closing her eyes *just for a moment.*

She was dozing, sitting upright on the bed, when the dog let out a shrill bark.

Sidra stood, her mixing bowl clattering to the floor. Torin continued to sleep, oblivious to the alert. The dog Yirr had remained in the front yard since Torin had brought him to Sidra.

She listened as he barked again. Warning sounds.

She suddenly wished she hadn't sent Torin's guards away. A group of them had hovered in the common room and the yard, anxious as Sidra had cared for their captain. She had seen the fear and humiliation in Torin's face. He wanted all of his guard gone. He didn't want them to behold him like this.

So Sidra had ordered them back to Sloane, and now she wished she had let at least one of them remain.

Yirr continued to bark, and Sidra stepped into the common room. It was late afternoon, and the light was failing. But she saw the gleam of her paring knife on the table, and she took it in her hand before approaching the door.

She stood for a rigid moment, breathing against the wood, listening as Yirr endlessly barked. The door wasn't locked, and she dared to open it by a sliver, gazing out into the rain-smeared yard. There was Yirr, his black-and-white coat a clear marker in the storm. He was planted on the stone path that led to the threshold, barking at two slim figures who stood just within the gate.

Sidra's fear abated the moment she recognized Mirin and Frae.

"Hush, Yirr," she said, opening the door wider. "Mirin? Come inside, out of the rain."

The dog consented to sit, letting the visitors approach, although Mirin still appeared wary. She removed the hood of her drenched cloak, Frae close at her side, as they stepped into the common room.

"It's good to see you both," Sidra said, setting her knife aside. She smiled tenderly at Frae. "How can I help you?"

"I wanted to first ask how Torin is," Mirin said, her eyes darting to the bedroom. "I heard the news he was wounded."

"He's healing and resting," Sidra replied. "He was struck by two different blades."

"Enchanted?"

Sidra nodded, hoping her fear wasn't evident.

"Then it's a good thing he has you, Sidra," Mirin said kindly. "I know you can heal him swiftly."

Sidra could have melted to the floor in that moment, feeling the suffocating weight of her defeat. But she was thankfully afforded a distraction. Mirin held out a folded plaid, a beautiful green shawl the shades of moss, bracken, and juniper. The colors of the earth, like all the growing plants in her neglected garden.

"For you," Mirin said, sensing Sidra's admiration and confusion.

"It's beautiful, but I didn't commission this," said Sidra.

She reached out and let her fingertips trace the softness of the wool. The moment she touched it, she knew the plaid was enchanted.

"Torin did," the weaver said. "He came to me days ago, asking if I could make a shawl for you. And as you well know, it can take me a while to create an enchanted plaid, but I wanted to get this one ready for you as soon as I could."

"Oh." Sidra didn't know why that surprised her, but the revelation warmed her spirit like a flame. "I . . . thank you, Mirin. It's lovely." She accepted the plaid, holding it close to her chest. The realization that Mirin had expedited this order humbled Sidra, and she said, "Let me provide you with a tonic, to help you recover."

The weaver nodded, and Sidra rushed to fetch a bottle of Mirin's favored brew.

"Frae has something for you as well," Mirin said after accepting Sidra's tonic. She gently nudged her daughter forward.

Sidra crouched so she could be level with Frae's gaze. The lass was regarding her shyly until she extended a covered dish.

"I made a pie for you and the captain," Frae said. "I hope you both like it."

"I *love* pie!" Sidra said. "And so does Torin. I bet he will eat the whole thing when he wakes from his nap."

Frae beamed, and Sidra stood to set the pie and the plaid down on the table. She wanted to give something to Frae in return, and she chose a stem of dried primrose.

"For you," Sidra said, tucking the flower into Frae's hair.

Protect her. The prayer rose naturally, surprising Sidra. She wondered if the spirits would hear her plea, and she inwardly added, *Watch over this little one.*

Frae grinned and blushed. It made Sidra remember a time when she was Frae's age. How many days she had spent in the pastures as she watched over the flock, weaving wildflowers into crowns.

"Before we go," Mirin said, breaking Sidra's reveries, "is there anything more we can do for you?"

"The plaid and the pie are plenty," Sidra said, honestly. "But thank you for asking."

She watched the weaver and her daughter depart, the sun breaking through the clouds. Sidra decided to leave the front door open to welcome the rain-washed air into the cottage.

She wrapped the shawl around her shoulders. It was an odd size, a bit too large for a typical shawl, but it made her feel safe. She reached for a spoon and sat at the table, eating Frae's pie. The tart berries melted on her tongue, summoning memories of long summers with her grandmother, foraging amongst the hills and woods.

Sidra closed her eyes, the remembrances bittersweet. Knowing she could get lost in those old days, she brought herself back to the present. To the table strewn with materials that had turned powerless in her hands.

And she thought, *How do I find my faith?*

Torin knew he was dreaming, because he was looking at the men he had killed.

He saw the mortal wounds he had given them. They bled and bled, their throats sliced open and chests gaping, exposing splintered bones and sputtering hearts, and the men beseeched him with requests. Feed their wives, their children, their lovers, because the northern wind would soon come with ice and darkness and hunger in his breath.

"They are not mine to feed!" Torin replied, angry. He was tired of the guilt he felt. "You should have stayed in the west. You should have known better than to raid the innocents of the east. We have wives and bairns and lovers to feed and protect here, as you do on your lands."

"Why did you kill us?" one of them asked.

"You take a life," another said, "then you must take care of the ones your violence marks."

Torin was exasperated. It was frustrating, speaking to dead men, and it was grim, having to look their ghosts in the eye, even if it was in the boundary of a dream. He shouldn't care about what they were saying to him, for he had done his job, he had completed his task. They had raided, they had stolen, they had trespassed with ill intent. He had defended his clan, as he had been raised to do. Why should he feel guilt over this?

Then the dream shifted, but the six ghosts remained with him, as if they were fastened to his life. He was standing in a meadow, and the world was blurry until he saw Sidra walking toward him in her vermilion wedding gown, wildflowers in her sable hair. His breath caught; he was about to marry her, and he realized the ghosts could see her. They crowded around Torin.

"Brave of you, to tell her of your guilt," one remarked. "To tell her of *us*."

"And yet how foolish you are," another hissed, "to believe her when she says she loves you, even with such blood on your hands."

"Don't you know that her eyes will soon be open to see us?" a last one stated. "When she weaves her life with yours, we will haunt her as we haunt you."

Torin shut his eyes, but when he opened them, Sidra was still approaching him, and he saw that he had blood on his hands. Blood that was not his and blood that he couldn't wipe off. Sidra was reaching for him, a tentative smile on her face.

Torin jolted awake.

He didn't know where he was at first. He was gazing up at a shadowed ceiling, and the bed beneath him was too soft to be the cot he slept on at the barracks. But then he smelled the fragrance of herbs, which meant he was home.

He didn't even try to speak. A talon was hooked in his throat, holding his voice captive. The sting in his shoulder was still vibrant, feeding his irrational fears.

Torin raised his head from the pillow and caught a glimpse of Sidra, working at the table. He could hear her grinding herbs, and he relaxed until he remembered his dream.

Slowly, he rose from the bed. His body felt weak and the world spun for a moment; he waited until his eyes had focused before he walked barefoot into the kitchen.

Sidra felt his presence. She turned, wide eyed, and he thought she was about to scold him for being out of bed. He just wanted to be near her. Then he realized she was wearing the plaid he'd commissioned. She had it wrapped around her shoulders like a shawl, but Torin had requested a longer length, and its edges were getting in Sidra's way.

"You should be in bed," she said, her eyes racing over him.

Torin reached out and took hold of the plaid, gently tugging it from her shoulders. Sidra let it fall away, although her brow was furrowed in confusion.

"Mirin brought it. I'm sorry, I thought it was for me."

Torin hated every time she said *sorry*. Sidra took responsibility for too many things, and he worried it would break her one day. He opened his mouth to speak before remembering his voice was gone, and he realized he would have to express this another way. A way without words.

He needed something to hold the plaid together.

He shuffled into the spare room, where his oaken chest sat against the wall. He searched through his raiment before finding a spare brooch, a golden ring of bracken with a long pin.

When he returned to the kitchen, clammy and light-headed, he noticed Sidra had stopped working. Her face was flushed, her eyes staring vacantly at the table.

She looked lost, and then surprised when Torin took her arm, turning her body to face him.

"You should be in *bed*!" she scolded again, but she sounded like she was about to cry.

Torin began to fold the plaid, in the same way he liked to fold his own. He brought it behind her, then across her chest before cinching it in place at her right shoulder.

Yes, he thought. It was perfect on her.

He stepped back to regard Mirin's handiwork. Sidra glanced down at it, and she still appeared confused until Torin laid his palm over her chest, where the plaid now granted her protection. He could feel the enchantment within the pattern, holding firm, like steel. He touched the place she had been kicked, where her bruises were slow to heal, as if her heart had shattered beneath her skin and bones.

She understood now.

She gasped and glanced up at him. Again, he wished that he could speak to her. Their last conversation still rattled in his mind, and he didn't like the distance that had come between them.

Let my secret guard your heart, he thought.

"Thank you," Sidra whispered, as if she had heard him.

It renewed his hope, and he sat at the table before his knees gave out. His gaze snagged on a pie whose center had been eaten away in a perfect circle, the spoon still in the dish. He pointed to the gaping hole, brow arched.

Sidra smiled. "The middle is the best part."

No, the crust is. He shook his head, reaching for the spoon to eat the crisp places she had left behind.

He was halfway done when there came a bark, followed by

a knock on the open door. Torin turned to see Adaira, and his heart lifted.

"Sit, Yirr," Sidra said to the dog, and he obeyed, hushing.

Adaira carefully passed the collie and approached Torin, a slight smile on her haggard face.

"Look at you, sitting at the table and eating pie," she teased. "One would never think you'd been wounded last night."

She sounded lighthearted, but Torin knew how worried she truly was. He didn't want to give her any reason to doubt his capability as captain. He drew out the chair next to him, and Adaira sat, her eyes going instantly to the demolished pie.

"You could have saved me a piece," she said.

Torin pushed the dish toward her, and Adaira took a few bites, closing her eyes as if she had been hungry for days. When she was done, she set down the spoon and studied Torin closely.

"How are you, Torin?"

He lifted his hand to Sidra, asking her to speak for him.

"The wound on his shoulder is healing swiftly," she replied. "But the one on his forearm is proving to be far more stubborn than I'd like. I'm hoping if he continues to rest today, he will feel much better by tomorrow."

Adaira's gaze dropped to his bound forearm, where blood had stained the linen. "Good. The first thing I want to say to you is that I'm giving you time off to rest and heal. In the meantime, I've taken command of the guard and have sent the auxiliary force to the clan line, to assist the watchmen. If the Breccans try to cross again, we'll catch them, so don't worry about respond-ing if your scar flares. Do you hear me, cousin?"

Torin reluctantly nodded.

"The second thing I need to discuss with you is more com-plex," Adaira said. "Is it possible for you to communicate by writing?"

Torin glanced at Sidra. She swiftly went to the cupboard to find a sheet of parchment, an inkwell, and a quill.

"I wrote to Moray Breccan this morning," Adaira began. "I gave him an ultimatum, to return what his clan stole from the Elliotts, or else face an end to the trade agreement. And I received a response, but it wasn't from who I was expecting."

She withdrew a letter from the inner pocket of her cloak and set it in Torin's hands.

He unfolded the paper and read, the words swimming on the page. His eyesight was watery, and it took him a second to focus and make sense of the elegant scrawl:

Dear Adaira,

My sincerest apologies about the raid that unfolded on your lands last night. I was utterly unaware of it, but that is no excuse on my part. I will see to it that the goods and livestock that were stolen are returned, and I will promptly execute justice on those who were involved.

We are hopeful to continue the trade you have offered us, although it is apparent members of my clan have yet to fully understand the gravity of your invitation. I will strive to amend such mindsets.

If you can meet me tomorrow at midday, I will bring the stolen goods to the clan line, at the northern signpost. Please advise the captain of your guard that I will need to briefly step over the boundary into your territory in order to return the resources. If you approve, please reply to me, and I will make preparations.

Respectfully yours,

Innes Breccan
Laird of the West

Torin reached for the parchment Sidra had set down before him. His mind was reeling, and he began to write. *This
is strange, Adi. The Laird of the West never cared to atone for the
raids in the past. I don't trust her.* But as soon as the nib lifted,
his handwriting became twisted and illegible.

He stared at the inky mess, despairing until Adaira touched
his arm.

"It's all right, cousin. I can imagine you don't approve of
this meeting."

Torin shook his head. *But only because the Breccans are acting strangely. They agree to peace, give us the best they have to offer,
raid us, and then scramble to appease us again.* If the west was
playing a game, it was one that Torin didn't understand, but it
filled him with a sense of foreboding.

"I think, despite how strange this offer is, that it's crucial
that I meet with Innes tomorrow," said Adaira. "I not only want
to recover what was stolen from the Elliotts, but there are a few
things that I need to put to rest. Jack is going with me, and I
will—"

Torin began to wildly gesture to himself.

"Yes, I'm taking a few guards," Adaira added.

"No," Sidra said, watching Torin's movements. "He wants
to go with you."

"But you're wounded, Torin."

He didn't care. He laid his fist over his heart. *All I ask is to
stand beside you. To be present.*

Adaira stared at him. She looked exhausted, as if she hadn't
been sleeping at night. There was a hint of sorrow in her eyes,
and it worried Torin. He hadn't seen her like this since her
mother had died.

"Very well," she said at last. "You may come with me, so
long as you're continuing to improve tomorrow."

He nodded. He thought that was the end of Adaira's visit, but she turned her eyes to Sidra, hesitant.

"Have you told him, Sid?"

Torin glanced between the two women. Sidra grimaced. "No, I wanted to wait until he felt better."

Torin scowled. Adaira sighed and met his gaze again. "It's about Eliza Elliott. We found her."

He listened in cold shock as Adaira told him everything.

Jack sat at his childhood desk, composing a ballad for the wind by candlelight. With each passing night, he slept more and more uneasily, and he wished he could persuade his mother to take Frae and lodge in the castle until the days felt safer.

It always came back to the loom. Mirin couldn't afford to leave it, even for a matter of days. Her weaving was her livelihood, and if she let fear of the Breccans rule her, then she'd never get anything done.

He paused, closing his eyes to rest them. His hand was cramping from writing for hours, and his head throbbed with a dull ache. He needed sleep, but he wanted the music more.

When Mirin rapped on his door, he frowned, turning in the chair. "Come in."

His mother appeared, a dirk balanced on her palm.

"I'm sorry to interrupt you, Jack, but there's something I've been meaning to give to you."

He rose to meet her in the center of the chamber, surprised when she extended the blade to him. He recognized it as the enchanted weapon she wore at her belt.

"Your dirk?"

"It was never mine, Jack. This blade has always been yours, a gift to you from your father. He made me vow to give it to you when you came of age, but you were away on the mainland at the time, and so I give it to you now, as a wedding gift."

He stared at her, then at the dirk. He thought about all of the moments he had seen it fastened to her side, how she had been carrying it for years. It was a simple weapon with the faint radiance of an enchantment.

Jack hesitated before taking the hilt, unsheathing the slender blade. He caught his reflection in the steel, and curiosity built within him.

"This blade is enchanted," he stated. "What with?"

Mirin tilted her head. "I don't know. Your father never told me, and I have never properly used it."

His father. This was the first time Mirin had spoken that word in so many breaths, and Jack didn't know what to make of it. Was it her way of inviting him to ask the questions he had been burying for years?

Jack slid the blade back into its scabbard. "Mum . . ." He lost his courage. He struggled to speak the words, and he glanced at Mirin. "Did my father . . . did he hurt you? Is that why you sent me away to the mainland? So you wouldn't have to be reminded of him when you looked at me?"

Mirin reached across the distance and took his hand. Her affection was a shock to him at first. "No, Jack. You and Frae were both made in love." She paused, and Jack could hear her breaths, rasping as her cough flared. "I loved your father, as he did me."

Loved. She cast the word in the past, and Jack wouldn't press her for more answers. Not as he once would have done before, bitter and impatient and angry. He gently squeezed her fingers, and Mirin smiled at him, a sad but honest smile, before her hand slipped away from his.

"You're busy working, I see," she said in a lighter tone, indicating the ink stains on his fingers.

"Yes. A new ballad."

"I can't wait to hear it then," Mirin said, stepping away. "Don't let me keep you any longer from your music."

Jack wanted to say that she wasn't keeping him from any-thing. That he would like for her to stay and talk with him a while longer. To make up for all the years lost to them.

But he also sensed the worry in his mother. She was anx-ious, although she was too proud to admit it.

She slipped from the room, latching the door behind her. Jack stood frozen, studying the dirk.

He knew that he would never ask his mother again about the name of his father, but there was now another way for him to learn the truth.

It was resting in his hands, a blade created from steel and enchantment.

CHAPTER 20

S idra woke to an empty bed. She lingered in the blankets
for a moment, letting her eyes adjust to the dawn. She slid
her hand to Torin's side of the mattress and found it cold,
as if he had been gone for a while.

Her heart was heavy as she rose. She was surprised to find
a fire burning in the hearth, a cauldron of parritch cooking,
and the tea kettle simmering. But there was no sign of Torin
in the cottage, and Sidra frowned as she peeked out the front
shutters. The yard was empty, save for the plants, dancing to
the morning breeze.

She went to the back door and cracked it open.

He was there, kneeling in the garden. Sidra watched for
a moment, startled as she realized Torin held a kitten in one
hand while he weeded with the other. He was uprooting all
the wild things she had let grow in her herbs and vegetables,
setting them aside in a pile. She glanced down when she felt
something claw at her stocking. The other cats had gathered on
the stoop, where he had set out a bowl of milk for them.

She didn't know what to think, but she was smiling when she looked at Torin again.

He hadn't heard the door open, and he steadily continued to work, eventually setting the kitten down so he could gather up all the weeds. He stood and walked to the edge of the garden, where he tossed the weeds over the stone wall. Sidra was amused by that—she always took the weeds to a pile down the hill—and stepped out to greet him.

Torin saw her as he returned. The corner of his mouth tugged upward, as if he were embarrassed to be caught gardening.

"You're up early," Sidra remarked, hoping to hear his voice.

He only lifted his dirt-steaked hand, and she noticed the wound on his forearm was still weeping. Her mood instantly fell, and she beckoned him inside.

Torin washed his hands before sitting at the table, enduring her ministrations. She saw that the wound on his shoulder had closed up overnight, leaving behind a cold, gleaming scar. The cut of fear. But the wound that had stolen his voice and words still festered, and Sidra swallowed as she applied a new salve and rebandaged it.

"Perhaps I should find another healer to tend to you," she said, gathering the soiled linens.

Torin was quick to stop her, grasping her chemise. He shook his head, adamant. His faith in her was absolute, as if it had never crossed his mind that she might be unable to restore his voice. To distract her from her statement, he rose and served the parritch.

Sidra sat when he motioned her to, and she let him fill her bowl with clumpy oats.

"I didn't realize you knew how to cook parritch," she said.

Torin made a motion with his hand, as if to say, *What islander doesn't know how to make parritch?*

The oats smelled a bit burned, but Sidra added some cream and berries and was able to force a few spoonfuls down before Torin tasted his own cooking. His face puckered, but he scraped the bowl clean, wasting nothing.

His appetite was back. He was doing chores around the house, which he had never done before. Sidra knew he was trying to prove to her that he was better, so she would permit him to escort Adaira at noontide.

Together, they washed the bowls and the cauldron, where burnt oats were now welded to the bottom. They both dressed for the day, and Sidra asked Torin to drape and pin the plaid over her again. She read through her grandmother's old healing account while Torin returned to the yard, determined to free the garden of weeds. He left the back door open so he could behold Sidra from time to time as he moved down the rows.

She watched him, thinking how much he had changed over the past few days.

She closed her eyes when the ache within her turned vibrant, as if she had stepped into the point of a sword.

She had given her vow to him four years ago. She had chosen to weave her future with Torin's, because she knew life would be good with him. She would have a little companion in Maisie. She would have her own croft at last; her father and brother would no longer hover over her. She would have a cottage to conduct her profession of healing, a kail yard to grow all the things she loved. And it felt like her own place, because Torin was rarely there, which Sidra liked in the beginning.

But he would come if she needed him. All she had to do was stand in her garden and speak his name into the wind, and he would come when the whisper on the breeze found him. When he recognized her voice within it, whether the wind blew from the north, the south, the east, or the west. Sometimes it took hours for him to arrive, but he always faithfully answered her.

She remembered one particular instance. A spring evening when she had summoned him, how he had appeared only moments after she breathed his name. He had arrived with dusk-tangled hair and worried eyes, thinking something was wrong. There had been nothing amiss, only the two of them standing in a quiet cottage with elderflower wine on the table and a chemise with loose draws at Sidra's collarbones, ready to fall.

Even then, it had not been love but something like hunger. Sidra had never hoped for the impassioned love that bards sang of, the sort that warmed blood like fire. She had always trusted Torin, even knowing who and what he was, but she had never expected him to love her as he once had loved Donella.

He and Donella had been of one mind. He and Sidra were stark opposites; he killed while she healed.

Sidra opened her eyes. They were brimming with tears, and she blinked them away, trying to set her focus on her grandmother's words. She read one salve recipe of Senga's, and then notes about how to cure a cough before she closed the book.

How can I heal him when I haven't healed myself?

She needed to tell Torin how she was feeling. She needed to be honest with him, to share the most vulnerable parts of herself. But Sidra realized she was afraid.

She was afraid to be so open with him, uncertain how he would respond. Would he want to break their vows? Would he want to let her go? Would he want to continue life with her, just the two of them?

The thought of drifting away from him created such agony within her that she had no choice but to admit that she had indeed been pierced by a blade, one that made a heart wound she didn't know how to mend.

There was a glimmer on the other side of the table. Donella materialized with her diaphanous beauty, and Sidra stiffened. The ghost had never visited her while Torin was on the grounds, and Sidra didn't know what to think of it now. If he happened to glance into the house, would he catch a glimpse of her?

"Donella," Sidra greeted her, speaking in a low tone so her words wouldn't drift beyond the door.

"He is afraid, Sidra," Donella said, and her voice was faint, as if she were about to fully fade. As if her wandering soul had found its peace at last.

"What does he fear?" Sidra thought she knew the answer, but she decided to ask it, knowing Donella had insight she didn't.

"He is afraid of losing you, first in heart, then in body. And if you follow me to the grave, he will not be far behind you. His soul has found its counterpart in yours, and he belongs with you, even after Death's sting."

Sidra flushed, her blood coursing through her. She let a moment pass before she whispered, "I don't know if he wants to stay with me. I can't . . . I can't even heal him when he needs me the most."

"You must heal yourself first, Sidra," Donella said.

Sidra, wide eyed, stared at the ghost. Without another word, Donella evanesced with a sigh.

She decided she couldn't bear to dwell on those parting words. Sidra made a second breakfast, which Torin was thankful for. They ate in the sunlight on the back stoop, watching the kittens scurry across the garden path.

"I'll find a home for them soon," Sidra said, ignoring the welt in her throat.

Torin touched her knee. *No, they're fine,* she read in his hand, in his eyes.

She nodded, and they remained there a while longer, quiet and warmed by the sun.

When Adaira came for Torin, Sidra stood in the front yard with Yirr, watching them depart. Their entourage soon melted into the hills, pressing north, and Sidra stood like a statue until the afternoon brought an unexpected squall.

The rain dampened her dress, brought her to her senses.

She turned to go inside, but the house felt too empty without Maisie and Torin. She didn't want to wait inside its shell; she wanted to disregard the overwhelming voice in her mind. One that was whispering for her to look inward, to acknowledge her many pieces.

To heal herself.

I'll go to Graeme's, she thought, shutting the door and beginning to walk the hill between their crofts, Yirr trotting dutifully behind her. Graeme would be able to distract her with his stories of the mainland.

But she stopped in the heather, her heart pounding.

This was the place where her faith had first cracked. The ground where she had been attacked and had come to know firsthand the sinister ways of the world. And she heard a beloved voice in her mind, as if it were carried on the wind. Her grandmother said, *Go to the place where your faith began.*

Sidra stood in the storm until the rain hid her tears, and yet she didn't go to Graeme's, which would have been the easiest path. She yearned for her grandmother, and she turned and walked south with Yirr, into the mist of the valley.

Adaira waited on the abandoned northern road that led into the west. The old signpost was weathered and gray but still stood, even after centuries of being forgotten. Waist-high weeds had grown up through the packed dirt, marking the clan line with thorny stems and yellow blooms.

The Aithwood surrounded them, granting Adaira only a slender view of the Breccans' land. From where she stood, it looked the same as the east, a thick gathering of pines, junipers, oaks, and rowans, with a rug of bracken on the forest floor. She wondered what it would feel like to step foot on her enemy's territory. If they would truly welcome her, or if Moray had been playing her for a fool.

She still had yet to hear from him, but she could only surmise that his mother had learned of the raid and read his post, coming across Adaira's ultimatum.

It was odd, how obliging the Laird of the West was being. Innes had never been so before now. She had always permitted the raids to continue in their cycle of violence and thievery.

But what would you do if your clan was starving in winter? Adaira asked herself, her eyes fixed on the overgrown curve of western road. *What would you do if your people were bloodthirsty, their children skin and bones when the ice arrived?*

Adaira wasn't sure, but she wouldn't be stealing lasses from the clan who was feeding them.

She didn't know what Torin would advise, but Jack had been adamant that Adaira withhold the information about the missing girls.

"If Innes knows about it," he had said to her that morning, "then she is complicit and she isn't an ally to us in this matter, no matter how gracious she appears today. It would be better for us to gain our confirmation another way, and to take our lasses back by surprise."

Such as a raid.

Adaira almost laughed, envisioning Tamerlaines secretly crossing into the west, to take back what belonged to them. But it was a heady imagining, and it had haunted her sleep at night.

She felt that Jack's advice was sound, and while she wanted to make an emotional decision about the girls, she knew she had to be patient and be wise. Above all, she didn't want the lasses harmed or moved to a different location.

She had to maintain the appearance of ignorance.

Adaira continued to wait. They had arrived early. Jack and Torin stood close behind her on the road, and ten other guards were stationed, deep into the woods but within sight. She didn't anticipate a skirmish, but neither had she thought a raid would happen in summer.

Sweat traced down the curve of her back. It was warm in the forest, and the wind was quiet that day.

At last, Adaira could hear the Breccans approach. Clomps of hooves and the rattle of a wagon disturbed the peace of the woods, and she flexed her hands.

A breath later, she took her first glimpse of Innes Breccan.

The Laird of the West rode a great horse, and she was dressed as a warrior—in knee-high boots, a tunic, a leather jerkin, and a swath of blue plaid. She was older, but the strength gathered around her, as if she were a storm. The silver shone in her long blond hair, contrasting with the golden circlet on her brow. Her face was narrow, difficult to look away from, and woad tattoos danced up her throat and along the backs of her hands and fingers. Her eyes were keen as she brought her horse to a halt, just before the clan line. She met Adaira's stare, and there her gaze rested for a heavy moment, as if she were measuring her opponent.

Adaira stood in her leather armor and crimson plaid, her face carefully guarded. But her bones were buzzing with tension. She was beholding her enemy, the nemesis of her clan. She was seeing her face-to-face, with only a few handbreadths between them.

Perhaps she comes to kill me, Adaira thought, even though Innes was unarmed. The leather scabbard hung empty from her belt. *Perhaps this will be the beginning of the war.*

Behind Innes, a wagon came to a halt. She had brought only three guards with her, although perhaps there were more, waiting in the woods. She dismounted and moved to stand before Adaira.

"Heiress," she said, her voice deep and smoky as a forge.

"Laird," Adaira responded.

"I have recovered most of everything that was taken," Innes replied. "However, the livestock has been lost. I can offer only gold coins in reparation."

Adaira was quiet, wondering if the Elliotts' cows and sheep had already been slaughtered. It inspired a shiver in her spine, but she nodded.

"The coins will suffice for now."

"May I cross over to your side?" Innes asked, and her gaze shifted to Torin. She must have recognized him as the Captain of the East Guard, since he was standing armed and directly behind Adaira.

"You alone have permission," Adaira replied.

Innes nodded and walked to the wagon. She took a crate, loaded with sacks of grain, and walked it over the clan line. She set it down at Adaira's feet before returning to fetch another crate. One by one, the laird brought three crates total, brimming with the Elliotts' winter stores. After that, she stood face-to-face with Adaira and extended a purse of coins.

"This should be enough, I hope?" she asked.

Adaira accepted the payment and looked inside the purse. It brimmed with gold, and she nodded, thinking this was overpayment for the missing cows and sheep.

It was odd, how generous Innes was being. Adaira didn't know what to make of her, whether she was genuine or only engaged in a diversion, with another betrayal soon to follow.

As if reading her thoughts, Innes said, "I hope this ill decision of my clan's can be forgiven, and that the trade you suggested can be continued between us."

"I've been speaking to Moray about the trade," Adaira said, making a point to glance around at the guards Innes had brought. "I was hoping to see him today."

"My son is currently disciplining the men who raided your lands," Innes replied, and her voice turned a shade cooler. "Or else he would have accompanied me today."

Adaira felt uneasy. This meeting could still go awry. She said, "We also desire to move forward with the trade, and there is a specific item that we would like to receive from your clan."

"Name it, heiress," Innes said. "And I will bring it myself to the next exchange."

Adaira held up the glass vial. The Orenna flower had yet to wilt, and the golden sheen on its petals glistened in the light. She watched Innes's face closely, and the laird's brow rose.

"Your clan desires the Orenna flower?" she asked.

"It grows in the west?" Adaira countered.

"It does," Innes replied. "Although it is quite useless to us, as the spirits are weak."

"The same can't be said of the spirits in the east," Adaira said. "If you can provide us with a basket of flowers, then I can bring resources your clan needs to prepare for winter."

"Very well," Innes said. "I will harvest these flowers for you. Give me three days to prepare, and we can meet again for the trade, in a place of your choosing."

"Agreed," Adaira said.

She watched as Innes returned to her side of the clan line. She mounted her horse and gave Adaira a nod in farewell before she trotted away, the guards following her with the empty wagon.

Adaira released a shaky breath. She turned only when she felt it was safe to, and even then, Torin immediately guarded her back. Jack, who had been a quiet support, fell into stride beside her. She waited to speak until they had emerged from the woods and returned to their horses, hobbled beneath an elm tree.

"I have at least one thread of proof now," Adaira said.

Jack frowned. "Which one?"

She met his gaze and held up the Orenna again. "Moray Breccan has lied to me."

Jack parted ways with Adaira in Sloane, making a stop at Una's forge. His dirk was sheathed at his side, and his heart was pounding as he waited to speak with her. Una was bustling about her work with sharp focus, and she had several apprentices working with her, one her own daughter, who pumped the bellows and hurried to bring her mother tools.

"Forgive me for interrupting your work," Jack said when Una had a spare moment to speak with him. "Is everything well?"

She only arched her brow, the silver in her black hair catching the afternoon light. "Of course it is, Jack. What have you brought me today?"

He set the dirk in her waiting hands. "I would like to know who commissioned you to make this blade. Do you remember his name? It was most likely a long time ago."

"I remember all my clients and all of my blades," Una said, continuing to scrutinize the dirk. "And I fear I can't tell you the name you seek, Jack."

"Why is that?"

Una leveled her dark eyes at him. "Because I didn't make this blade."

He frowned. "Are you certain?"

She laughed, but he could tell she was annoyed by his question. "Do you remember each piece of music you compose? Recognize each instrument you have ever held and played?"

Jack felt his face warm. "Forgive me, Una. I meant no offense."

"None is taken, Jack." She handed the dirk back to him.

"I merely thought . . ."

She waited, and he sighed.

"You are the most skilled blacksmith in the east," he contin-ued. "And whoever had this blade forged . . . I believe he would want only the finest hands to create it."

"It's fine work, I won't deny it," she said, her gaze lingering on the dirk. "But it's not mine."

"Is there a way to discover what enchantment it holds?"

"There's a way, yes. And it's not by looking at it."

He knew what she was implying. He slid the dirk back into its sheath.

"As I thought. Thank you for your help, Una."

Una watched as he began to drift into the street. "Be care-ful, Jack."

He lifted his hand to her, acknowledging her admonition. But his thoughts were troubled. If this blade had been forged in the east, Una would have known it.

He retreated to his castle chambers for the remainder of the afternoon. He didn't pass Adaira in the corridors, and he imag-ined she was with her father.

When Jack removed his plaid, he noticed that a thread in the wool had started to unravel. He stared at it for a disbeliev-ing moment, tracing the pattern with his fingertip. Part of the enchantment was gone, and he could see that the green fabric had lost its luster. He swallowed hard as he sat at his desk. Whatever secret his mother had woven into this plaid was com-ing to light.

Jack attempted to distract himself by working on his com-position. The ballad for the wind was nearly complete, but he could focus on it only for so long. His mind was swimming with questions, and he eventually unsheathed the dirk once more, to study the slender blade in the fading sunlight.

He had never felt the sting of an enchanted weapon. And he never wanted to, especially after witnessing Torin's most recent wounds. But if his father had this blade made for him . . . Jack needed to know what enchantment it possessed. His hands trembled as he stood up from his desk and walked to the fire that burned in his hearth, deliberating.

A small cut, he decided, remembering how swiftly these sorts of wounds healed. A shallow slice on the forearm.

Jack drew in a breath as he traced a cut, just above his wrist. The dirk was sharp; it gleamed as it bit his skin, and his blood welled in the mark, bright as summer wine.

He waited to see which enchantment would greet him, his blood dripping onto the hearth stone between his boots. He waited, and yet nothing happened. He didn't feel compelled to flee, he wasn't afraid, he didn't lose his voice. He didn't feel despair, nor did he feel anything taken from him, like memories or peace or confidence.

Jack stared at the cut and his blood, full of wonder and irritation.

That was when a knock sounded on the hidden door.

"Jack?" Adaira's voice melted through the wood. "Jack, may I enter?"

He froze, torn between telling her no and telling her yes. He hid his hands and dirk behind his back. "Come in."

Adaira opened the door and stepped into his chamber. She had changed since their meeting with Innes. Her hair was loose, untamed waves drifting past her shoulders, and she wore a simple black gown. She noticed his stiff posture, his hesitation. How his hands were clasped out of sight.

She drew closer to him. "Are you hiding something from me?"

And that was when he discovered the enchantment of his father's dirk. Jack wanted to respond one way, to give her an evasive reply. But he was compelled to speak truth, and it spilled from his mouth.

"Yes. An enchanted blade."

If Adaira was surprised by his stilted reply, she gave no evidence of it. She reached out to touch his arm, light but confident, and her fingers traced downwards, where the weapon was clenched in his fingers. She brought his stubborn hand forward and studied the dirk's gleam, the bloody edge of the steel.

"What have you done?" she whispered.

Once again, he was compelled to respond with the truth, and he ground out, "Like a fool, I cut myself to discover which enchantment it holds."

Adaira reached for his other hand and drew forth his bleeding forearm. "A truth blade then?" she mused. Her gaze united with his, and he saw the mirth gathering within her. "You know that while your blood runs from this blade, you are compelled to answer anything I ask you with brutal honesty."

"I know that all too well."

Jack was eaten up by dread as he waited for Adaira to begin asking him all manner of uncomfortable questions. But when the silence deepened, he remembered how she often surprised him. She was not one who conformed to his assumptions, but one who shattered them.

She took the hilt of the dirk from him and cut her palm. Her blood welled, and he wanted to scold her. But her voice emerged first, sharper than any blade he had ever felt.

"I want no secrets between us, Jack."

His gaze dropped as he studied their wounds. He thought about the blood vow that often took place at weddings, the deepest and strongest of bindings when palms were cut and laid against each other, blood mingling. He and Adaira hadn't taken that vow, and they wouldn't do so unless they decided to remain married after the term of the handfast.

And yet seeing Adaira's blood and her willingness to meet his vulnerability, wound for wound . . . the air began to change between them.

"I want to talk about the meeting with the west, Jack," she said, her voice breaking his introspection. "But before I do . . . let us speak as old friends who have been separated for many years and who realize they now have much ground to regain. Tell me something about you that I don't know, and I will do the same."

She walked to the chair that sat before the hearth, and Jack followed with two strips of cloth, one for her and one for him. She bound her hand as he wrapped his forearm, and afterward he drew up another chair to sit across from her. He realized he wanted to behold her fully, no matter what words sounded from his mouth.

He was quiet for a moment, uncertain. But then he began to speak, and it was like a door unlocking and opening just a sliver, but enough to allow the light to spill in.

"When I was younger," Jack said, "I wanted nothing more than to be worthy of the clan and to find my place. Growing up without a father only fueled those feelings, and I longed to be claimed by something, by someone. I could think of no better honor than to join the East Guard by proving myself to Torin."

"As I already know," said Adaira, but she smiled. "That is, perhaps, the most common ground between us. We once dreamt of the same thing."

"So we did," he agreed in a reminiscent tone. "But sometimes you discover your place and purpose is not as you once thought. When I was sent away to the mainland, I was full of bitterness and anger. I thought Mirin wanted nothing to do with me, and so after my homesickness eased, I began to settle in at the university and I swore that I would never step foot on Cadence again. Despite those claims, I still dreamt of home when I slept. I could see Cadence and her hills and mountains and the lochs. I could smell the herbs in the kail yard and hear the gossip riding the wind. I can't tell you when the dreams began to fade, when it was that I had fully convinced myself I didn't belong here. But I suppose it happened in my third year of schooling, when I had my first harp lesson. As soon as I passed my fingers over the strings, the storm and anger that had endlessly brewed in me dimmed, and I realized that I could indeed prove myself worthy of something."

"And so you have, bard," Adaira said.

He smiled. "Now tell me something about you that I don't know, wife."

"That might be more of a challenge," she said, settling deeper into the chair and crossing her legs. "I fear my life is often on display."

"But we are two old friends who have just been reunited," Jack reminded her. "A stormy expanse of water and an unforgiving stretch of kilometers have been between us for a decade."

"Then let me begin as you did," said Adaira. "My greatest aspiration was the same as yours. I wanted to join the guard and fight at Torin's side. He was like an older brother to me, and ever since I can remember, I have yearned for a sibling. I saw how the guard were like brothers and sisters, like one united family, and I wanted to be a part of that comradery.

"But my father swiftly cut that dream away. It was too dangerous for me to join the guard. Being their only living child and heiress . . . there were many things I couldn't do. My mum saw the anger in me and tried to ease it in the only way she knew how. She began to teach me how to play the harp. She thought I might find myself in the music, but while it calmed the storm in someone like you, Jack, it only deepened the resentment within me.

"I was young and full of spite, and I scorned the lessons she tried to give me. The music would not take to my hands, and all I could think of was the guard I was not able to join. It is the greatest regret of my life now. To think back on those years and how I wasted those moments with her. There are some days when I can hardly bear to look upon her harp, because I am seized by the desire to find a way to step back in time, to choose differently. If I could only speak to my younger self . . . oh, the things I would say to her. I never once imagined I would lose my mum so soon, and I long for those moments with her, for the music she once tried to give me.

"These things I share with you, Jack . . . they are like thorns in my mouth. I rarely speak of my regrets and my heartache. As a laird, I am not to dwell on such things. But I also know that to hold my tongue and remain silent is sometimes the greatest regret of all for our kind. So let me say this to you: a small part of me looks at you and sounds a warning. *He will leave after a year and a day. He will return to the mainland, where his heart yearns to be.*

"I tell myself I should remain guarded against you, even as we are fastened together. And yet another side of me believes that you and I could make something of this arrangement. That you and I are complements, that we are made to clash and sharpen each other like iron. That you and I will stay bound together by that which is nameless and runs deeper than vows, until the very end, when the isle takes my bones into the ground and my name is nothing but memory carved into a headstone."

Jack stood. She had captivated him, and he needed a distraction before the truth spilled out of him. Before he confessed how his feelings for her were becoming entwined with everything—his dreams, aspirations, desires. He wanted to re-assure her, to answer her without words, but first he walked to his bureau, where a bottle of birk wine sat.

He poured them each a sparkling glass. Her fingers were cold as they brushed his, accepting his offering. She didn't re-main seated but rose, so their eyes were nearly level, with little space between them. They drank to their wounds, their regrets, and their hopes, to the past, to how the choices each had made unknowingly brought them back together.

"My heart doesn't yearn for the mainland," he said at last. "I thought I told you, Adaira, that it's safe to say I won't be re-turning."

"And yet you've told me from the beginning that the main-land is your home," she countered.

Jack wanted to tell her that he had been withering away there, bit by bit. So infinitesimally that he hadn't realized how faded he was until he returned to Cadence and found that he could set down roots in a place, roots deep and entwined.

Instead, he whispered, "Yes, but I once thought home was simply a place. Four walls to hold you at night while you slept. But I was wrong. It's people. It's being with the ones that you love, and maybe even the ones that you hate." He couldn't help but smile, watching how his words raced across her skin, mak-ing her flush.

Adaira set aside her glass. Her eyes were keen when she looked at him and said, "Do you know that I once hated you?"

He laughed, and the sound spread through his chest, warm and rich as the wine. "I thought we were telling each other things we did *not* know."

"I was glad to see you leave that evening ten years ago," she confessed. "I stood on the hill at dusk and watched you board the boat. I watched until I could no longer see you, and I counted it a triumph, for my old menace would no longer haunt the isle. I had defeated and banished you, and you would no longer steal my thistles, or feed me pimpleberries, or yank the ribbons from my braids. You can imagine my shock when I saw you weeks ago. After all this time when I had convinced myself that you were my nemesis, that I was destined to hate you even ten years later . . . I felt a portion of gladness again, but it had nothing to do with your leaving."

Jack set his glass down and shifted closer to her. The wound in his arm was beginning to itch; it was healing swiftly, and soon this moment would be lost to them. He gently traced the golden light that danced on her cheek.

"Are you telling me that you were glad to see me, Adaira?"

"I was," she said, and her breath caught beneath his caress. "I was glad to feel something stir within me after years of being cold and empty. I just never imagined I would find it in you."

It was like she had stolen the very words from his mouth. And he wanted them back.

He brushed her lips with his own, a taunting kiss. She tasted like dark red fruit, like the summer berries that grew wild on the fells, and she took hold of his tunic and drew him closer until they were sharing the same sweetened breath. The air crackled as their raiment caught the static between them. Jack's mouth was gentle as he drank her sighs and memorized her mouth. But all too soon he felt an obliterating ache in his chest. Dazed, he realized that he was overwhelmed by Adaira, by the feelings she roused within him. He wondered how something as soft as a brushing of lips could resound with such agony in his body.

She must have felt it too. She broke the kiss and released her hold on him, stepping away. Her face was composed, her eyes calm. But her mouth was swollen from his, and she rolled her lips together as if tasting a lingering trace of him.

"Are you hungry?" she asked.

Jack merely stared at her, uncertain what sort of hunger she spoke of. Half a beat later, he was thankful for his silence, because Adaira said, "I think our next conversation will go down better with a plate of haggis."

He had forgotten all about her initial intention to discuss the meeting with Innes. He watched as she strode to the door and sent a request with one of the servants to bring dinner up to Jack's room. She approached his desk and took hold of it, inching it across the floor toward the hearth. She seemed to burn with endless energy, while he was utterly zapped and frozen, as if drunk from their kiss. But he joined her at last, helping her carry the table to the fire and their two chairs. His musical composition was still carefully piled on the polished oak. Adaira noticed it, and he saw that, while she couldn't read the notes, she studied them intently.

"Is this your ballad for the wind?" she inquired in a careful tone.

"It is."

"Nearly complete?"

"Not quite."

He was relieved that dinner arrived then. He didn't know if Adaira would forbid him to play the ballad. But his health was *fine*. He still suffered from bouts of headaches and throbbing fingers, but it would take many years for such symptoms to kill him.

Jack carefully cleared the table, and they sat across from each other with steaming plates of haggis and potatoes and wilted greens, bread and a crock of butter arranged between them. He didn't notice until he was pouring them each a fresh glass of wine that the wound in his arm had healed and the truth enchantment had fully waned in power, leaving behind nothing more than a cold, tender scab on his skin. And yet, when he looked at Adaira, he realized that the words and affection they had shared were not lost to either of them. The feelings hung like stars above them, waiting for another moment to align, and he felt the anticipation in his bones, humming like a harp string.

"What do you wish to discuss, Adaira?" he asked.

She gave him a half smile. "Eat first, Jack."

He heeded her but soon noticed she was struggling to eat, as if her mind was overcome with thoughts. She studied her palm, the cold scar now marking it, and drank her wine to the dregs.

"All right," she eventually said. "I have a plan to take our lasses back."

Jack set down his fork, watching her intently. He had a feeling he wasn't going to like it, but he was quiet, waiting for her to explain.

Adaira took him completely by surprise when she asked, "Could you finish the ballad for the wind tomorrow?"

His brow lowered. "Is this your way of asking me to play, Adaira?"

"Yes. But with one condition, Jack."

He groaned. "What is that?"

Adaira drew the glass vial with the Orenna and set it down before him. "You consume this flower before you play."

She had been saving this blossom for days now, uncertain when to use it. He studied it, seemingly innocent in the glass, and said, "What is your reasoning behind this?"

"I've talked to Sidra," Adaira said. "She has consumed one, and said it granted her the ability to see the spirit realm. It gave her unnatural strength, speed, and awareness. I think it will guard you from the worst of the magic's cost."

Jack sighed. "But what if it affects me otherwise? What if it interferes with my ability to play?"

"Then you won't play. We'll wait until its effects have passed, and you'll play in your own strength, with your tonics prepared," she answered. "Because you're right, Jack. The wind knows where the lasses are in the west. If they can provide us with the exact location, then we can execute a plan to save them."

"And you think we'll be able to do so after Innes Breccan provides us with enough flowers to eat and cross the clan line unnoticed?" Jack said.

Adaira nodded. "Yes."

His stomach clenched. He felt a pulse of dread, thinking how many things could go wrong. Imagining sneaking through the west like a shadow. Being caught and imprisoned or possibly killed.

"What if you're wrong, Adaira?" he asked. "What if the Orenna flower doesn't grant the power to cross over the clan line?"

"I think there's a strong possibility it does," she said. "How else would the Breccans be doing it? If the flower grants them heightened awareness and power between our realm and the spirits' realm, how could it not?"

"But if they knew of this earlier, why didn't they harness this flower before?" Jack argued. "Why not use it to their advantage when they raid? It seems they only began to use it weeks ago, with the sole purpose to steal lasses."

"And the most recent of raids," Adaira added. "You claim you saw more Breccans than Torin counted."

He sighed, leaning back in his chair. His sister had also seen a Breccan standing in their garden that night, and he worried Frae was next. She would be easy to snatch, so close to the clan line.

"Perhaps the Breccans didn't know of the Orenna flower until now," Adaira said. "Either way, whether it is or it isn't the secret to crossing, we're going to find the location of the lasses via the wind, and then we are going to steal into the west to take them back."

"Then we should prepare for war, Adaira," Jack said. "For whatever reason the Breccans are taking eastern lasses, they'll be angry when they discover we used the object of their trade to deceive them and sneak into the west."

"I don't think I can make peace with a clan that steals children," she said.

He nodded, but that icy feeling was creeping up his spine. What would war on the isle look like? Could the Tamerlaines prevail against a clan built of warriors? If they lost, what would become of Adaira?

Jack stared at her, lost in terrible thoughts.

The firelight and shadows danced over her, and her eyes glittered like two dark gemstones as she held his gaze. The sun was beginning to set; he had been oblivious to the fading light. Only an hour ago, he and Adaira had stood in a different world, with time crystallized around them. Now time rushed, caught up in an alarming current. He could feel it pull on him, the minutes slipping away one by one.

"If this is what you want," he said. "Then I am with you."

She stood and walked to his side. He felt her fingers in his hair, a faint caress.

"Thank you," she breathed. "I should leave you now. The sun is setting, and I know you need to return to Mirin's. But if you're ready to play tomorrow, come find me."

She retreated to her chamber before he could say another word. But she left the Orenna behind, and Jack tucked the vial away in his pocket as he began to pack up his music.

He hadn't given himself time to think deeply about what had happened today. He didn't have the chance until he was walking home to Mirin's.

He thought about the night of the raid, and he could hear Frae's voice saying to him in the dark, *There's a Breccan in our backyard.* Perhaps the man had come to steal his little sister away, but perhaps he had stood as a sentry over their home, to deflect a raid from descending upon them.

Jack saw his mother in his mind's eye, remaining on the lands she had earned despite the danger of the clan line that was so close to her croft. He recalled all the times he had asked for his father's name, and every time Mirin had been unwilling to share even the smallest of morsels about him.

Walking the hills, Jack unsheathed his dirk. The only tangible legacy he now possessed, for he had been given no name, no lands. He had been granted nothing but a lone blade enchanted with truth, as if Jack's father had anticipated all of the lies and secrets his son would be raised beneath.

Jack would have never believed it possible, not until Torin claimed that Breccans were passing over the clan line without notice, and Adaira claimed they were stealing the girls of the east. If they crossed secretly now, perhaps they had done so then, long ago when Jack's mother lived alone on the edge of the border.

He had always wondered if he had ever unknowingly seen his father in the city market, on the road, in the castle hall. Jack had always wondered, and those thoughts had fallen on fallow ground over the years, left to rot. But no longer.

He had always wondered why his father had never claimed him. He now knew why.

His father was a Breccan.

CHAPTER 21

~~~~~~

Torin rode back to the croft, eager to see Sidra. The meeting at the clan line had gone better than expected, and this was the most hopeful he had felt in a long time. If Innes Breccan continued to be agreeable and provided them with Orenna flowers, then they would be one step closer to finding Maisie and the other lasses. He could be days away from holding his daughter. Days away from carrying her home.

He just needed to be patient. Torin inhaled, slow and deep, to calm his heart.

He dismounted and left his horse by the gate. It had rained here while he had been away; the front yard glistened in the sunlight. He then noticed that Yirr wasn't guarding the front door, and Torin felt his first pang of unease. He stepped inside, opening his mouth to call for Sidra.

His voice was still dust in his throat. His wound still ached.

Torin swallowed and searched the rooms. Her basket of herbs and ointments was sitting on the shelf, so Torin knew she wasn't visiting her patients. Perhaps she had returned to the garden. He walked the rows, but Sidra was absent. He stood for a moment in the midst of the towering stalks, lush flowers, and vegetables ripe on the vine. She wasn't here, but Torin could feel a trace of her among the green living things of the earth, amongst the wildflowers.

He next rushed up the hill to his father's, but she wasn't with Graeme.

Torin returned to his yard, frowning. He realized that he had no inkling where she had gone, and that brought him to his knees beside the herbs. He thought again of the last time he had spoken to her. The things that had come from his mouth—sharp, angry, and prideful.

She had said that she loved him, even at his worst. And he hadn't responded. He had never told her how he felt, and now the chance had been stolen from him.

But in this forced silence, he had noticed the weeds over-coming the garden. He had noticed the sorrow in Sidra's eyes and the exhaustion in her posture. She was hurting, and he wanted to help her carry that pain, as she had carried his.

He looked at his hands, lined with dirt and grime, scarred from blades.

Which will you choose for your hands, Torin? she had once said to him, words that had offended him. But they had been living words—a phrase that wouldn't die no matter how he tried to snuff it. Words like seeds that had slowly been germinating in him, unfurling new growth.

He dwelt on his dreams. The ghosts of the men he had killed. He wanted to change.

He rose and fetched his horse. He didn't even know where he was going, and he rode aimlessly, listening to the wind and studying the ground beneath him. He remembered the first day he had met Sidra. How he had fallen from his horse.

Torin turned the stallion south and rode to the most peaceful place on the isle, where Sidra had been born. The Vale of Stonehaven.

Sidra first visited her grandmother's grave in the vale. She knelt and spoke to the grass, the soil, and the stone that held a trace of the woman who had raised her. She also stopped at her mother's grave, although Sidra held no remembrances of her. After she lingered in the valley's cemetery, she walked to the cottage where she had grown up.

This ground was marked by memories. She passed through them one by one. First the stream that led to a loch where Sidra had spent time with her taciturn father, catching fish from the rapids. Next came the orchard, where she had experienced her first kiss. The paddocks where she had guarded the sheep with her brother. And lastly, the kail yard, where she first discovered her faith in the earth spirits. Where she had spent hours beside her grandmother, with soil cupped in her hands. Where she had learned the secret of herbs and the might of a small seed. This ground had seen her grow from child to girl to woman, and she hoped it would feel like reuniting with an intimate friend.

The cottage looked the same as she remembered; her father and brother had diligently kept up with the work. The kail yard, though, was a disaster, unorganized and beset with weeds. The trees were heavy laden with fruit in the orchard, and the sheep still roamed the hills like tufts of clouds. But Sidra acknowledged, with an ache in her soul, that this place no longer felt like home.

Yirr whined beside her.

She glanced down at the dog and touched his head, but his eyes were on the sheep. She released him to run and herd. Alone, she passed through the gate and stood in the kail yard, surveying the mess. Slowly, she knelt.

The soil was damp. She could feel it seeping through her dress as she began to pull up the weeds, examining them.

A weed is just a plant out of place, her grandmother had once said to her. *Treat them kindly, even if they are a nuisance, for they can make a faithful ally amongst the spirits.*

Sidra smiled, cradling one of the weeds. It was beautiful, with small white blooms. She didn't know its name, and she tucked it away into her pocket to press and examine later.

She moved across the rows, harvesting the fruits that were ready, knocking away insects that were chewing the leaves. The dirt soon crowded her fingernails, and her skirt was muddy, but she was remembering.

She remembered all the times her brother Irving got lost on the hills as a boy. But Sidra never had, not with wildflowers in her hair and trust in her heart. She had always felt safe on the summits and in the vale. She remembered seasons of plenty, how this garden had overflowed with harvest. She had never gone hungry or wanted for food. She remembered the first time Senga had let her dress a wound on her own. How day by day, the injury had closed and healed itself beneath Sidra's attentive care. As if there were magic at her fingertips.

Her memories drew closer to the present, and she wanted to fight them. But the deeper she put her hands into the soil, the brighter her thoughts flared.

She remembered tasting the Orenna flower, and how her eyes had been open. She had gone to the hillside and beheld the crushed heather. She had seen how the spirits wept when she fell, and how, even when she had lain unconscious, they embraced her. She remembered the treacherous spirit of the loch, and the other, the blazing tendril of gold, urging her to rise. To break the surface.

"All this time when I felt alone," she whispered to the earth, "you were with me. And yet I couldn't see you, because my pain clouded my sight. I don't know what to do with this agony. I don't know how to carry this."

Give it to the soil, child. It was a phrase Senga had said countless times in the past.

Sidra rose, unsteady for a moment. The shed was still in the corner of the yard, its door draped in cobwebs. She stepped inside and found it exactly as it had been years ago before she left. Seeds were still hiding in a small sack; she took a handful and carried them back to the garden.

Sidra dug into the soil, angry. It was strong enough to bear her ire, and she raked her fingers through the loam. Digging trenches with her nails, she gave to the ground the words *You should have fought harder.*

"I fought as hard as I could, and I'm still strong," she said.

She dropped the seeds into the furrows and added more words: *You failed Torin and Maisie.* These words were harder to relinquish. She was still waiting on a promise that she didn't know would be fulfilled or not. She was waiting for Maisie to come home, and it might not happen. She was waiting to discover if Torin loved her in the way she loved him.

Her grief welling, Sidra stared at the seeds she had dropped, waiting for earth and rain and time to transform them.

"There is no failure in love," she said and covered the furrows. The soil was rich; it swallowed a portion of her grief. "And I have loved without measure."

In this, I am complete.

Sidra continued to kneel, staring at the spontaneous row she had planted. She was hardly aware that time had passed until she heard the back door of the cottage swing open with a bang. Her brother Irving bounded out, staring agape at the strange dog rounding up his sheep.

"The dog is mine," Sidra said, and her brother startled, finally noticing her kneeling in the garden.

"*Sidra?*" Irving asked, squinting at her.

She knew she looked a mess. Drenched from the rain and smudged with dirt, with her hair like unspooled darkness. It had been years since they had seen each other. "I was in the vale and thought I would visit you and Da."

"Da is kilometers away, in the earie paddock," Irving said, still scowling at Yirr. "He won't be back until dusk most likely."

"I see," said Sidra, rising. "Then I should probably go."

"Don't be silly," her brother said with an impish smile. "I could use your help snapping beans."

And that is how Sidra found herself sitting in the same chair at the same kitchen table, working with her hands, when Torin arrived. The same place and same time of day and same season—only the sun and her grandmother were missing. Or else Sidra could have fooled herself for a moment, believing time was a circle and this was the moment when Torin first knocked on the door with a displaced shoulder.

There was static in the air again, gathering in Sidra's fingertips. Just as it had that day long ago. As if she had rushed her hands over wool, over threads unseen. Something was about to change, and she didn't know what that *thing* was, but she felt it all the same in her bones.

Torin knocked on the door. His customary trio of raps, hard and urgent.

Irving huffed. He had snapped only half as many beans as Sidra had, and when he made to rise, she said, "I'll answer the door."

Her brother began to protest, but he must have seen that flicker of strange energy in Sidra, and he shut his mouth and lowered himself back down to the bench.

She delayed, though, until Torin knocked again, not as insistent this time.

She rose and answered the door.

Torin stared at her a long moment, a moment that needed no words. Behind her, Sidra heard the bench scraping the floor as Irving asked, "Is that Torin?"

"It is," she replied after a beat, realizing Torin was still voiceless. "Why have you come?" she asked him in a whisper.

Torin held out his hand to her, a quiet invitation.

She knew if she passed beyond this threshold with him, that unknown change would ignite in the air. For a moment she feared it, because she sensed the path ahead would be hard. It would be forged through tears and heartache and patience and vulnerability. She couldn't see the ending, but neither did she want to remain, stagnant and passive, in the place where she had begun.

She took his hand and passed over the threshold, closing the door behind her.

Yirr was panting in a mud puddle, content after his run with the sheep. He leapt up and followed Sidra and Torin through the long grass to the orchard. The air here smelled forbidden, sweet from rotten fruit, and Sidra at last came to a halt beneath the boughs, the wind stirring her hair.

"It wasn't my intention to worry you," she said. "I came to the vale to visit my grandmother's grave, and I wanted to see home for a spell. I would have returned long before dusk."

Torin held her gaze, and she could see a trace of apprehension in him. He wanted to speak; she sensed his frustration as he opened his mouth, only to sigh. But he noticed the dirt beneath her nails. The weed poking its flowery head from her skirt pocket.

He gently laid his palm over her chest, and she knew he wanted her to open herself to him.

She glanced down at the grass, hesitant.

"I don't know where to begin, Torin," she said. It was odd,

how she kept waiting for him to say something. She met his gaze, tears in her eyes. "I've always been devout. I'm sure you've realized that about me by now. Faith was woven deeply into my life, but it cracked when Maisie was taken. When the stranger beat me down into the heather, as if my life meant nothing."

Torin's hand moved to take her own. He was so warm, as if a fire were lit within him.

"Nearly every night when I tried to sleep," she continued, "I would tell myself, *You should have fought harder. You should have been stronger. You've failed Maisie and Torin. You've failed as a mother, as a wife, and now as a healer, and what is left for you?* I believed those words. They planted so much doubt and pain in me . . . I didn't know how to uproot them."

Torin drew a sharp breath. Sidra dared to study his face and saw his anguish. He looked the same as he had the morning when he'd first seen her, battered and blood-stained. Like a blade had been plunged into him.

"I know now those words are lies," she said, but her voice broke. "I also know there is nothing weak about grieving, or feeling sorrow, or being angry. But I always wanted to prove myself worthy of you, and losing Maisie has made me question everything about myself. Who I was, who I am. Who I want to become."

She began to weep, unashamed of her tears or how she trembled. It felt like a cleansing, and she wanted it to flow, unhindered.

Torin embraced her. He pressed his face into her hair, and she could feel his chest shudder as he cried with her. Together, they wept for the child they had lost.

Eventually, Sidra leaned back so she could look at his face, flushed and red eyed.

"I need to finish by saying this," she said, wiping her cheeks. "It's hard for me to admit, but I realize I've built my life upon something that can be taken from me, and I'm afraid. I long for Maisie to come home, and yet there is no promise that she will, and what does that leave for you and me? We see the world from different angles, and I wonder . . . I wonder if there is a place for us within it."

Torin's breaths quickened. He took her hand and held it to his breast, slipping her palm beneath the protective enchantment of his plaid, so she could feel the beat of his heart. She stood with him beneath the boughs, and she closed her eyes, feeling the rhythm of his life.

It began to rain. A soft whisper through the orchard.

Torin drew her hand away from his chest, but then he laced his fingers with hers, and she sensed his determination. He wanted to try this with her, just the two of them. If they needed to carve their own place together, then he would attempt it. He leaned his brow to hers, and they stood breathing the same air, the same thoughts.

He traced her jaw, the rain now shining like tears on her face.

Come home with me.

Sidra nodded.

The rain had intensified by the time Torin led her back to where his horse waited in her father's yard. The valley roads were swollen with mud, and Torin guided them carefully across the hills, Yirr trailing behind. The afternoon was melting into evening, and the sky was still churning with the storm when they returned to their croft. They were both soaked to the bone.

Sidra stepped into the common room. She would never get over how empty it was without Maisie; it always felt the worst the moment she returned home. She cleared her throat, searching for something to do. She wondered if she should spark the fire in the hearth, or if she should change her clothes first. Before she could decide, she felt Torin's steady gaze.

He was standing very still, his flaxen hair drenched across his brow. Sidra didn't understand why he was so attentive until she realized he was waiting for her command.

She walked to him, afraid of the desire she felt—how sharp it was within her—until she saw it mirrored in his own face.

Sidra's fingers drifted up to the brooch at his shoulder, unclasping it. His plaid cascaded beneath her hands, and she found the buckles on his jerkin next, unfastening them one by one. She removed his raiment—belt and weapons and tunic—all the way down to his muddy boots. And then he returned the motions, but it had been a while since he had undressed her. His eager hands tangled the laces of her bodice, and he let out a wisp of frustrated breath.

Sidra smiled, but her stomach was full of wings, as if this were their first time again.

It took her a moment to loosen the knot he'd made, and she hardly had time to lower her fingers before he pulled the dress and the chemise from her, leaving her clothes in a heap on the floor beside his.

Bared to each other, Torin traced her skin, as if he was memorizing her every line and curve. When she gasped, his mouth was there to catch it, settling against hers like a seal, and he tasted of rain and salt.

He carried her to the bed.

Together, they sank into the blankets. He kissed the curve of her throat, the valleys of her collarbones. His body was warm, comforting against hers. And for once, Torin took his time. She knew he had countless important things to do, but he chose her that night.

The light was fading. Sidra drank the scent of his skin—the traces of leather and wool, the loam of the isle, the sweat from endless work, and a slight touch of the wind—and it was familiar and beloved to her, as if she had found home in the most unexpected of places.

She drew him closer, deeper. The room was dark now, but she could faintly discern his face. The wonder in his eyes. Soon, they couldn't see at all, but they felt and they breathed and they moved as one. The eyes of their hearts were open, and they beheld each other vividly, even in the darkness.

She woke before him. She had dreamt of a strange path in the hills, one she felt compelled to find. Quietly, Sidra slipped from the bed and found clean clothes in her wardrobe. Torin had suffered another nightmare last night. She didn't know what he was seeing while he slept, but it worried her.

She found an empty basket and her foraging knife, donned her plaid and her boots, and emerged into the front yard.

It was dawn, and the light was a milky blue.

She left the croft for the hills, setting out on a muddy path, uncertain where she was going. But she dared to stray from the road into knee-deep heather as she looked for the path in her dreams. So entirely focused on looking for Torin's cure, she nearly missed the trail of gorse that bloomed before her, a slender thread of gold that made her stop, amazed. It reminded her of the pathways she had seen in the spirit realm, and she followed its winding route, careful not to crush the blooms beneath her feet.

It led her into a glen that she had never seen before, a shifting location in the hills. The gorse eventually meandered up the rocky wall to a patch of fire spurge. The weeds boasted short red stalks, their fiery blooms reminding Sidra of the anemones that flourished in the bay. She knew this plant was vengeful if picked, inflicting painful blisters on hands bold enough to harvest it.

She stood and stared up at the beautiful, monstrous weed, let out a deep breath, and began to climb with her basket and knife. But the gorse hissed and wilted at her approach, and she understood the price that was required—she would have to harvest and carry the fire spurge with her bare hands. She dropped the basket and blade, then continued her ascent.

Sidra didn't hesitate when she reached the spurge. The moment her hand closed around the first bloom, the pain swelled within her. She cried out, but she didn't release it. She tugged until the blossom broke free and the pain burned, bright and intense, as if she had set her hand on fire. Trembling, she took hold of another, unable to swallow her cries of agony as she harvested.

Her hands took the pain for Torin; her voice rose for his lost one.

And if she thought that she could measure the depth of her love for him before, she was mistaken.

It ran far deeper than she knew.

CHAPTER 22

When Jack arrived at the castle the following morning, harp in hand, Adaira knew he was ready to play. As she expected, they had a quick argument about the spirits.

"You think we can trust them?" Jack questioned. He sounded irritated, as if something was bothering him.

"We've trusted all the others," Adaira replied, studying his frown. He looked tired, and she wondered if he had been restless last night.

"Yes, Adaira. We nearly drowned the first time, and the second? I was one breath away from being immortalized as grass."

"None of the folk are safe," she said, feeling her anger rise. "There is always the danger of them harming or deceiving us, although what do you expect when you dance with something wild, Jack?"

He didn't reply, and Adaira's temper began to wane.

"Do you really want to play for the wind, old menace? If not . . . I understand."

He sagged, the fight leaving him. "Yes, of course I want to play for them."

Then what is wrong? she wanted to ask. The words were ready on her tongue when he spoke first.

"You're right. I'm just tired. Let's go while we still have plenty of daylight."

Adaira led Jack to the slopes of Tilting Thom, the highest peak on the isle. The way up was narrow and steep, but she could think of no better place for Jack to sing wholeheartedly for the wind, even with the hint of peril. He followed close behind her on the path, but she could hear his labored breaths and turned to see the fear marring his countenance, how he clung to the rock face with each step. She realized only then that he was afraid of heights.

"Is this a wise choice?" he asked, ragged. "The wind could blow us off the cliff."

"It could," she said. "But I have faith that it won't."

He scowled at her, his face alarmingly pale.

"Come," she beckoned, and reached for his hand. "You will soon understand why I have chosen this place."

Jack threaded his fingers with hers and let her lead him onward, but he added, "You do know, Adaira, that the air tastes different on a mountain, and it might affect my voice."

She hadn't thought of that, but she wouldn't admit it now. She took a deep breath—the air was sharp and thin and cold, tasting like woodsmoke and juniper and salt from the sea. She only smiled at him, guiding him farther up the path. She had been here many times before, often alone, sometimes with Torin when she was younger.

Halfway up Tilting Thom, they arrived at the perch—a wide ledge perfect for sitting and enjoying the view. Behind it was a small cave cut into the mountain's craggy face. The shadows gathered within it, and Jack's fingers slipped from hers as he came to a halt close to the cave's maw, as far away from the edge as he could manage.

But Adaira stood on the sun-warmed rock of the ledge and said to him, "Look, Jack. What do you see?"

He reluctantly joined her, standing close at her back. She felt his warmth as he shared the same view with her. Through low swaths of clouds, the isle spread before them with verdant patches of green and brown and dark pools of lochs, with silver threads of rivers and stone walls of paddocks, with clusters of cottages and woods and rocks. The sight of it never failed to humble Adaira, to stir her blood.

And then Jack realized why she wanted to summon the spirits here. "A glimpse of the west," he said.

They could both see it—a fleeting view of the western half of the isle. The clouds hung low and thick over it like a shield, but a few patches of green and brown were sneaking through the weak points of gray. Adaira felt her heart skip, apprehensive as she imagined Annabel, Catriona, and Maisie in those small breaks of sunlight.

"Let us summon the spirits with our faces to the west," she said. "Are you ready to play?"

He nodded, but she saw the doubt and worry in him. She knew he was more than worthy to play his own composition for the powers of the isle, and she hoped he would sing through those feelings of inadequacy. For Adaira had come to love the deep timber of his voice when he sang, the deftness of his hands when he played the strings.

"This is your moment, Jack," she said. "You are worthy of the music you sing, and the spirits know it and are eager to gather at your feet."

Jack nodded, and the doubt relinquished him. He found a safe place to sit with the cave at his back; the sun danced on his face and the wind tousled his hair as he unpacked his harp.

Adaira settled beside him. She watched as he found the glass vial in his harp case. His hands trembled, but he opened the cork.

"I hope this works," he mumbled. "Because I don't want to make this climb again."

"If it proves otherwise, I'll let you choose where to play next time," she promised.

He glanced at her, but her face was inscrutable. Jack had no idea that her heart was pounding as he swallowed the western flower.

He felt no different at first. But when Jack propped his harp against his left shoulder and began to strum, he felt the power in his hands. He could see his notes in the air like rings of gold, spreading wide around him.

The height no longer frightened him. He felt the depth of the mountain beneath him, aware of everything living within the summit—on its craggy slopes and deep in its heart, where caves ran crooked like veins. He could sense Adaira—her presence like a dancing flame beside him—and he turned to look at her.

She was watching him intently; he could see his music, illumined in her eyes.

"How do you feel, Jack?"

He almost laughed. "I've never felt better." His hands no longer ached. His fingers felt as if he could play for an endless era.

He gave himself another moment to adjust to how effortless it was to pluck the strings, watching the music caress the breeze. Eventually, he felt an overwhelming urge to meld his voice with the notes, and he began to play his ballad for the wind.

Jack sang his verses, his fingers strumming with confidence. He sang to the southern wind with its promise of harvest. He sang to the eastern wind with its promise of strength in battle. He sang to the western wind with its promise of healing. He sang to the northern wind with its promise of vindication.

The notes rose and fell, undulating like the hills far beneath him. But while the wind carried his music and his voice, the folk of the air didn't answer.

What if they refuse to come? Jack wondered, with a pulse of worry. From the corner of his eye, he watched as Adaira rose to her feet.

The wind seemed to be waiting for her to move. To stand and meet it. She stood planted on the rock as Jack continued to play, shielded by the Orenna's essence. Twice, he had played for the spirits and had nearly forgotten he was a man, that he was not a part of them. But this time he held firmly to himself as he watched the folk answer.

The southern wind manifested first. They arrived with a sigh and formed themselves from the gust, individualizing into men and women with hair like fire—red and amber with a trace of blue. Great feathered wings bloomed from their backs like those of a bird, and each beat of their pinions emitted a wash of warmth and longing. Jack could taste the nostalgia they offered; he drank it like a bittersweet wine, like the memories of a summer long ago.

The east wind was the next to arrive. They manifested in a flurry of leaves, their hair like molten gold. Their wings were fashioned like those of a bat, long and pronged and the shade of dusk. They carried the fragrance of rain in their wings.

The west wind spun themselves out of whispers, with hair the shade of midnight, long and jeweled with stars. Their wings were like those of a moth, patterned with moons, beating softly and evoking both beauty and dread as Jack beheld them. The air shimmered at their edges like a dream, as if they might melt at any moment, and their skin smelled of smoke and cloves as they hovered in place, unable to depart as Jack's music captivated them.

Half of the spirits watched him, entranced by his ballad. But half of them watched Adaira, their eyes wide and brimming with light.

"It's her," some of them whispered.

Jack missed a note. He quickly regained his place, pushing his concern aside. It felt like his nails were creating sparks on the brass strings.

He sang the verse for the northern wind again.

The sky darkened. Thunder rumbled in the distance as the north reluctantly answered Jack's summoning. The air plunged cold and bitter as the strongest of the winds manifested from wisps of clouds and stinging gales. It answered the music, fragmenting into men and women with flaxen hair, dressed in leather and links of silver webs. Their wings were translucent and veined, reminiscent of a dragonfly's, boasting every color found beneath the sun.

They came reluctantly, defiantly. Their eyes bore into him like needles.

Jack was alarmed by their reaction to him. Some of them hissed through their sharp teeth, while others cowered as if awaiting a death blow.

His ballad came to its end, and the absence of his voice and music sharpened the terror of the moment. Adaira continued to stand before an audience of manifested spirits, and Jack was stunned by the sight of them. To know that they had rushed alongside him as he walked the east. That he had felt their fingers in his hair, felt them kiss his mouth and steal words from his lips, carrying his voice in their hands.

And his music had just summoned them. His voice and song now held them captive, beholden to him.

He studied the horde. Some of the spirits looked amused, others shocked. Some were afraid, and some were angry.

Just as Adaira was taking a step forward to beseech the spirits, their gathering parted to make way for one of their own to come forward. Jack saw the threads of gold in the air; he felt the rock tremble beneath him. He watched as the south, the east, and the west drew in their wings, watched the spirits quiver and bow to the one who was coming to meet Adaira.

He was taller, greater than the others. His skin was pale, as if he had forged himself from the clouds, his wings were the shade of blood, veined with silver, and his hair was long, the color of the moon. His face was beautiful, terrifying to look upon, and his eyes smoldered. A lance was in his hand; its arrowhead flickered with tendrils of lightning. A chain of stars crowned him, and the longer he stood, held by Jack's music, the stormier the sky churned and the deeper the mountain quaked.

It was Bane, the king of the northern wind. A name that Jack had only heard whispered in children's stories, in old legends that flowed with fear and reverence. Bane brought storms, death, famine. He was a wind one wanted to evade. And yet Jack knew the answers they sought were held in his hands; he had been the one to seal the mouths of the other spirits, to keep the truth concealed from them.

Bane motioned for Adaira to approach him, and Jack's heart blazed with fear.

"Come, mortal woman. You have been clever, tricking this bard into summoning me. Come and speak to me, for I have long awaited this moment."

Adaira stopped a few steps away from him. Jack noticed

how close she was to the edge. If she fell, would the wind catch her? Or would it watch her break on the rocks far below?

Jack slowly lowered his harp, wrapping his fingers around the frame.

"My name is Adaira Tamerlaine," she said. "I am the Heiress of the East."

"I know who you are," Bane replied, his voice deep and cold as a valley loch. "Do not waste your words, Adaira. The bard's music will tether me only so long."

Adaira began to speak of the missing girls. As the words spilled out of her, Jack noticed the eastern and southern winds began to stir. They glanced at each other with amused faces. The western wind remained guarded, but their sorrow was nearly tangible as they watched her speak.

Quietly, Jack rose to his feet. He was struck by the thought that this was nothing more than a game driven by bored spirits, and he and Adaira were pawns who had just played into Bane's elaborate scheme.

"Are the Breccans to blame for the disappearances?" Adaira asked. She stood tall and proud, but her voice was brittle. "Have they been stealing the lasses?"

Bane smiled. "A bold question, but one that I will honor." He paused, as if he wanted Adaira to further grovel. When she didn't, his eyes narrowed as he said, "Yes, the Breccans are the ones who have been stealing the lasses."

It was the confirmation they needed. Jack didn't know how to feel. His emotions burned through him like fire and ice. Relief and dread, excitement and fear.

"Then I must ask you for the location of the lasses," Adaira said calmly. "You roam the east and the west. You wander the south and the north, and you see beyond that which I see. You watched as the Breccans stole the girls from my lands. Where can I find them?"

"What would you do if I told you where the lasses are, Adaira?" Bane asked. "Would you wage war? Would you seek retaliation?"

"I think you already know my plans."

The northern wind smiled at her. His teeth gleamed like a scythe. "Why do you care for these three lasses? They are not your flesh and blood."

"They are under my protection all the same," Adaira replied.

"And what if they would prefer to live in the west? What if they are happier with the Breccans?"

Adaira was astounded. Jack sensed that she didn't know how to reply, and her temper flared. "They will be happiest with their families at home, where they belong. And so I will ask you again, majesty. Where are the Breccans hiding the Tamerlaine lasses?"

"The mortal lasses are alive and have been well looked after," Bane replied. "But you did not have to go through the trouble of summoning me to locate them. One of your very own knows where to find the children you seek."

Jack took a step closer to Adaira, channeling the Orenna's power to avoid drawing the attention of the spirits. His pulse was pounding in his ears. He could feel the beat of a hundred wings upon his skin.

Adaira held out her hands. "Who?" she demanded. "Who among my clan has betrayed me?"

Bane leaned on his lance, exhaling his stormy breath upon her face. But then his lambent eyes found Jack.

Jack froze, pierced by the intensity of the northern wind. He could see the threads of gold surrounding Bane's body, all the many paths the spirit could take in the air. His unsung power. The other spirits were dull in comparison. "A dark-eyed weaver who lives on the edge of the east. She knows where the lasses are."

Jack felt the blood drain from his face.

"You seek to fool us?" Adaira countered, emotion in her voice. She didn't want to believe it, and Jack felt a pinch of relief that she would be bold enough to defend his mother. "What evidence can you give to support such a claim, when you yourself have seen fit to bind the mouths of the other spirits?"

"Can the spirits lie, mortal woman?" he countered. "That is why I bound the tongues of my subjects, to keep them from speaking the truth before its time had come."

Adaira was silent. She knew as well as Jack did that the folk couldn't lie. They could carry the gossip and lies that mortal mouths had already spoken, but they couldn't inspire their own in words. Even as they often played games of deceit.

Bane's full attention returned to her. The king reached out to touch Adaira's face, and she didn't resist it. She stood quiet and fixed, a glimmer of light in his great shadow.

"Do you want to come with me?" Bane asked, and his fingers tangled in her hair with a painful jerk. "I will carry you in my arms and take you to the lasses now, but only if your courage can be found."

Jack's horror deepened when he realized Adaira was considering his offer. He could see the edges of her beginning to fade, as if she were about to melt into wind, and his fury carved through his fear.

He closed the distance between them, harp cradled against his chest. He reached out and grasped her arm. Is this how she had felt when she had beheld him turning into the earth? A mix of panic, indignation, and bone-aching possession?

"*Adaira!*" Jack's voice rent the air.

He was relieved when Adaira glanced over her shoulder, meeting his stare. She took a step back when he tugged, and he realized the Orenna was granting him the strength to draw her away from Bane's icy hold.

The northern king looked at him again. The other spirits took flight in a rush of wings, dissolving into their natural state. Jack's heart drummed as he watched them flee. But their king remained, standing firm. Bane's cloying fingers fell away from Adaira's hair as his eyes continued to bore into Jack.

Jack's mortality shivered through him. He felt a vibration in his teeth. The wind from Bane's wings blew, holding the sting of an axe, seeking to divide him and Adaira. Her hair tangled across her face when she looked at him again, and he saw she was also frozen. Her teeth were bared, her eyes wide.

"I have let you play once, mortal bard, but do not test my mercy. Do not dare to play again," Bane said as he pointed his lance at Jack, the lightning dancing from it. Even then, Jack didn't let go of Adaira.

The northern king shot a bolt of white heat at Jack's harp. The light met his chest like the lash of a whip, hurling him up and away. He slammed into the mountain beside the cave's mouth and slumped to the ground. The pain echoed through his veins as he struggled to breathe, to see. He could hear his harp's last metallic note as it died, scorched and ruined.

"Jack!"

Adaira sounded far away, but he felt her hands touch him, desperate to rouse him.

"Adaira," he whispered in a broken voice. "Stay with me."

Speaking took the last of his strength. He remembered her cold fingers, lacing with his burning ones, holding him close.

Then he slipped away, deep into the darkness where not even the wind could reach.

CHAPTER 23

J ack woke to the sound of rain pattering on rock. He opened his eyes and slowly gained his bearings: he was lying on the hard floor of a cave, and the air was cold and dusky with the tang of lightning. Beyond the shelter, a storm raged. He shivered until he felt warmth radiate at his side.

"Jack."

He turned his face to behold Adaira lying next to him. His sight was blurred around the edges, and it took everything within him to find and raise his hand, to rub the throb in his temples.

"Where are we?" he asked. "Are we in the west?"

"The west? No, we're still in the cave on the mountain ledge of Tilting Thom. You've been passed out for hours."

He swallowed. It felt like a splinter was lodged in his throat.

"Hours?" He looked at her again. "Why didn't you leave me?"

"Don't you remember the last thing you said to me? You asked me to remain with you."

The memories gathered in his mind with an ache as he re-membered all that had passed earlier on the mountain. But in the darkness that had followed, there had been dreams. Vivid, stark dreams. He blinked and saw a lingering trace of them, as if Bane had pressed his thumbs against Jack's eyes, making the colors swarm.

"Do you feel strong enough to sit forward?" Adaira asked him gently, and when Jack floundered, she laced her fingers with his and eased him up.

He saw the mouth of the cave, streaked with rain. The hour was gray, bewitching. And there sat his harp at his feet, warped in the fading light.

"I'm so sorry, Jack," Adaira whispered, mournful.

He stared at the ruined instrument for a moment. It felt like a piece of him had died, broken and fallen away into obliv-ion, and he struggled to hide the wave of emotion that crested within him.

Adaira looked away. Her hair was unbraided and loose, beaded with mist. She hid half of her face behind its curtain. "What do you make of the wind's answer?"

Jack hesitated, recalling those piercing words. Bane had made a wild claim about Mirin, one that Jack would have scoffed at had he not recently realized his mother had once been in love with a Breccan.

He didn't think Mirin knew anything about where the lasses were being held, but she did know *something*. She had been hiding her knowledge for years, weaving those secrets into the plaids she dressed him and Frae in.

Jack glanced at Adaira. She was pale, her mouth pressed into a thin line. He worried the truth might change the tenta-tive bond they had formed, and his heart dropped. To reveal his suspicions about Mirin would be to reveal his suspicions about his father.

"The wind could be tricking us," he said. "But either way, I ask one thing of you, Adaira."

She met his gaze. "Anything, Jack."

"Let me speak to my mother first. Privately. If there's something she knows, she'll most likely be forthright if I'm the one asking."

Adaira paused. Jack could read the flash of her thoughts—she wanted to go directly to Mirin. She wanted the answers this afternoon. But Adaira nodded and whispered, "Yes, I'll agree to that."

They sat for a moment more in silence, until a burst of cold shocked them both. The storm swelled, and the rain drove deeper into the cave, stinging their faces like needles. A voice haunted the gust, a sound of misery. There was a gasp, like a final draw of breath. Somewhere on the isle, life was being extinguished, snuffed by the deadly brunt of northern wind. The hair rose on Jack's arms as he listened.

Adaira must have heard it as well. She stood and stared into the storm. "Do you feel strong enough to walk down the mountain? I worry that I've been away far too long."

He nodded, and she hauled him up to his feet. The world spun for a moment, and he caught his balance on the cave wall. He watched as Adaira knelt and slipped his harp back into its sheath, strapping it to her back. When she returned to his side and offered her arm, he accepted her assistance.

He leaned upon her shoulder, and they approached the cave mouth together. But Adaira paused before the sheet of rain and said, "Why did you ask me if we were in the west when you woke?"

He suddenly hated that he didn't know what she was thinking. If it raised suspicions about him now that Bane had tossed Mirin's name before them like a snare.

But the truth was . . . his body had been with Adaira in the east, but his mind had been roaming the west.

"Because I saw it," he said. "In my dreams."

The descent was slow and precarious, the rain refusing to relent and only beating harder upon them. Adaira kept Jack on her left, between her and the mountain wall, because she worried if he stumbled, she would be unable to keep him from plunging over the edge of the path. They had angered the northern wind, and now Bane was making them pay for it.

When Jack struggled to stay upright, easing to his knees with a groan, Adaira was beside him. She refused to yield him to the storm, to leave him behind so she could hurry.

"I am with you," she said, uncertain if Jack could hear her over the rattle of thunder and the howl of the wind. "I won't let you go." And he rose. She brought him back to his feet, and they continued onward until he slipped to his knees again, his strength ebbing.

There was a shot of silver in his brown hair now, gleaming at his left temple, as if he had aged years in a day. She didn't know if it was from the magic or from Bane, but it worried her. She didn't say that they would return to the ground in one piece, because she didn't know. Every moment felt long and arduous, and Adaira couldn't shake the chill that had overcome her in the cave. Her legs went weak when the path at last gave way to the grass and she stood on flat earth again.

She hurried with Jack to where they had left their horses, her heart like a hammer in her breast. She could scarcely draw breath, so heavy did the dread weigh upon her shoulders, and Bane didn't make it simple for her. He continued to rage, impeding her at every turn. With a curse, Adaira realized the horses were gone, spooked by the storm.

"Leave me here, Adaira," said Jack, sagging from exhaustion. "You will be much faster without me holding you back."

"No," she replied. "No, I'm not leaving you. Come, just a little farther."

She hauled him toward the road. They had just crested a hill when she saw shapes moving through the haze of the rain. Knowing it was the guard, Adaira came to a gradual halt in the mud, waiting for one of them to see her and Jack.

It was Torin who reached them first. Adaira sensed his ire as he drew his horse to a sliding halt. He dismounted in a rush and took hold of her arm, his grip firm as he gave her a slight shake.

Though his wound was finally healing, he still couldn't speak. But he didn't need to. Rain sluiced down his face as he stared at her. His hair was lank on his broad shoulders, like tangled threads of gold. Mud splattered his raiment.

She saw the fear shining in his eyes. She had told him where Jack was going to play for the wind, but she hadn't thought it would take hours, ending in a tremendous storm.

This day had gone completely awry. She felt like collapsing.

"Torin," Adaira said, and she hardly recognized the sound of her own voice. "Torin, my da . . ." She couldn't finish the words. She watched the shift of Torin's expression, how his fear burned away into sadness. She knew it then. She had felt it in the cave; she had heard it in the storm. The passing of life into death—the vengeance of the north wind—and yet she waited for her cousin to confirm it.

Torin drew her into his embrace, holding her tight against him.

Adaira closed her eyes, feeling his plaid brush her cheek.

Her father was dead.

Laird Alastair was laid to rest beside his wife and three children in the castle graveyard, in unrelenting rain and thunder.

The clan was devastated, and life seemed to come to a halt. But the storm hadn't ceased, and the roads had become streams. A few low paddocks had begun to flood.

Torin watched it all in silence.

He watched as his uncle was buried in the soggy earth. He watched Adaira stand in the graveyard, soaked from the storm with eyes that seemed dead. The clan gathered around her. Torin couldn't hear what was spoken, but he saw the Elliotts approach her, faces red from weeping. He saw Una and Ailsa embrace her. He saw Mirin hold her hand, and Frae wrap her arms around Adaira's waist.

Ever since he had lost his voice, Torin had begun to notice things that he would have missed before. Weeds in the garden, the difficulty of making parritch, how empty rooms felt without Sidra and Maisie. And now he lifted his eyes and watched the northern wind rake across the east. This storm was a display of power and a warning. Torin felt the fear of Bane in his bones and knew Jack's music must have challenged the northern king.

An hour later, Torin found his cousin sitting in the library, cradling a cup of tea, as if her hands couldn't shake their chill. The laird's signet ring shone on her forefinger. Her hair was still damp from the funeral, but she was dressed in dry clothes, and she sat in the chair Alastair had loved, facing the hearth as the fire crackled.

Torin shut the door and stared at Adaira. He knew she heard him enter, but she said nothing, her gaze captive to the flames.

He walked closer, sat in the chair next to hers, and listened as the storm seethed beyond the windows. Glancing down to his forearm, he saw that his silencing wound had almost healed, thanks to Sidra's tenacity with the fire spurge. She applied the salve three times a day, and every time he felt the heat of the plant seeping into his wound, closing it bit by bit.

Soon he would be able to speak again, and yet what words would suffice in this moment? Torin knew the heavy burdens Adaira carried. And while he once would have endeavored to take them from her, those thoughts had died over the years as he found his place with the guard. She was laird now, and the best he could do was carry the burdens alongside her.

He sat with her in that tender silence.

If his life had not been interrupted by the sting of an enchanted blade, he would have spoken. He probably would have become frustrated, wondering what Adaira and Jack had done to bring the storm. He would have peppered her with questions he felt entitled to have answers to. He would have said anything to fill the roar of such silence, but now he understood it better. The weight of each word he uttered, and how his words unfolded in the air. He was far more mindful of them now, understanding that most of them were worthless.

He was a man built from many regrets, and he didn't want to add to that number.

"Torin," Adaira said at last. "If I call upon you to ride with me into war . . . will you support my decision?"

He was silent a beat too long. She had expected him to agree instantly, and Adaira shivered in alarm as she glanced at him.

He was thinking of the ghosts in his dreams. Now that Torin had beheld the Breccans' faces and listened to their grief, he had begun to see the trade as a way to atone for his actions. He couldn't bring the lives back, but he could ensure the widows, the children, and the lovers were still looked after.

But he nodded, in spite of his conflicted feelings.

"Bane confirmed our suspicions. The Breccans have been stealing the girls," Adaira said. "They're alive and well looked after, but we still need to learn of their location."

Torin's hands curled into fists. He wanted to go *now*, to

cross the clan line and bring Maisie home, and he struggled to rein in his impulsivity.

Adaira must have sensed the impatience within him, because she said, "There are a few more things I need to do before we'll be ready to steal into the west and find the girls. In the meantime, I'm going to ask your second in command to very quietly tell Una to begin forging as many swords and axes as she can, Ailsa to prepare her finest horses, Ansel to begin fletching arrows and stringing as many yew bows as he is able, Sidra to prepare tonics and healing salves, and the guard and watchmen to train, to sharpen their swords, to wear their enchanted plaids like armor. We need to be prepared for conflict when we bring the lasses home."

Torin nodded again, agreeing with her. He would have to be patient; he would have to trust Adaira's judgment.

He sat with her a while longer, his mind whirling with images of Maisie and the thought of bringing his daughter home to war.

"What happened to your hands?" Jack said.

Sidra didn't pause as she prepared a tonic for him. For the past two days, the bard had looked the worst she had ever seen him, his skin pallid, his eyes bloodshot. His voice was hoarse, and his hands trembled when he raised them. He was sitting upright in his bed at the castle, watching her work.

She was worried about him and the strong magic he was casting. The cost was too heavy for him to bear so frequently, and she debated over how much she could fuss over him.

"I picked a spiteful weed," she explained. The splotches of red and the blisters on her palms had been slow to heal, but Torin's wound was nearly mended. She met Jack's gaze as she brought the healing brew to his lips. "Here, drink all of this. You pushed yourself too hard this time, Jack. You need to be mindful of the things I mentioned to you before: how long you wield magic and how intricate it is. You also need to give your body time to rest in between, as your mum does with her plaids."

Jack grimaced at her gentle scolding. "I know. I didn't have much choice, though, Sidra."

She wondered what he meant, but he didn't offer an explanation as he took a sip, wincing at the taste.

"I'm sorry," Sidra said, lowering the cup. "I know it's bitter."

"I've tasted far worse on the mainland," he replied, and Sidra was glad to hear a touch of wry humor in his voice.

"Do you miss it?" she asked.

Jack was pensive for a moment. She worried she had offended him until he said, "No. I did when I first returned to Cadence, but this place is home to me."

She smiled, wondering if he would stay wed to Adaira. She thought that he would. She was setting out a salve and tonic for him to take later when Jack took her by surprise.

"What do you know of Bane, Sidra?"

She paused, but her gaze flickered to the window, where the storm continued to howl for a third day beyond the glass. "The king of the northern wind? I'm afraid I don't know much about him, other than to prepare for the worst when he decides to blow."

Jack was silent. Sidra began to pack her basket but suddenly remembered a story her grandmother used to tell her often.

"One of my favorite legends is from the time preceding his reign, when the folk of fire reigned on the isle."

"Tell me," Jack said softly.

Sidra settled on her stool beside the bed. "Before the clan line was split between the east and the west and Bane rose to power in the north, Ash was a beloved leader amongst the fire spirits. He was generous and warm, full of light and goodness.

All of the spirits answered to him, even those of the wind, the water, and the earth. All save one, that is. Ream of the Sea had always detested him, for she was made from tides and he was made of sparks, and every time they met threatened a catastrophe.

"But then one day Ash found out that a member of his court had set an ancient grove aflame and the fire was devouring the trees and the earthen spirits within them. Desperate, Ash had no choice but to go to the shore, where Ream dwelt in the foam of the sea, and call her forth to help him. Ream, however, wouldn't do it without seeing Ash on his knees, willing to be doused first. He submitted without qualm, even though he knew what would come of it: he knelt before her and allowed her tide to wash over him. A great portion of his power turned to smoke and left him, but he continued to kneel despite the pain of the water.

"When Ream saw her enemy's resilience, her respect for him grew and she called upon her river attendants to rise up and flood the burning grove. She put out the wildfire, and Ash retreated back to his dwelling place in the sky. Once, he had governed the sun during the day, but now he was so weak that he had to choose the night, when his muted fire could burn among the constellations. His twin sister, Cinder, took over the rule of the sun and daylight. Meanwhile, Ream, who had always hated fire, began to see its beauty, how it burned so passionate and constant, even as it fell to embers. That is why the sea is often gentle at night, for the fire of the stars and the moon reflect upon the waves, and Ream remembers how her old enemy became her friend."

A smile had spread over Jack's face as he listened. Sidra saw that some color had returned to his countenance.

"I suppose that since Ash lost his power, Bane rose to replace him?" Jack mused.

"Yes," Sidra said. "Although I think it took a few more years before the northern wind became a threat. My nan said that for a while the spirits were all equal, and the balance of the isle reflected it."

"I wonder what that would feel like," he said.

Sidra had thought the same. How would Cadence feel if it was united and restored? Was it even possible?

She didn't know anymore, and her sorrow deepened.

She gave Jack orders to stay in bed and to avoid wielding magic until he had fully recovered. But her worry followed her down the corridor as she went to visit her next patient.

When she finished her rounds, it was late and she was exceedingly tired. Sidra stepped into the courtyard, relieved to see the storm had finally abated. The air was chilled and peaceful; few stars shone through wisps of clouds. The flagstones were slick from the rain, and Sidra prepared to walk home in the dark.

She was nearing the gates when she recognized Torin, standing with his horse. The lantern light trickled over his face as he watched her approach.

She nearly asked him what he was doing; it was so rare to see him standing idle. But then he reached for her basket and offered his knee to help her mount his gigantic horse.

Shocked, she realized he had been waiting to take her home.

CHAPTER 24

Torin dreamt of blood again.

He saw the first Breccan scout he had dispatched years ago. The killing stroke was still there, gaping at the man's neck, but he seemed to neither notice it nor feel his life dwindle away. Blood dripped down his blue plaid as he stared at Torin.

"Will you take care of them then?" said the Breccan, his voice perfectly intact despite his torn vocal chords.

"Who?" Torin asked, staring at the wound he had made.

"My wife, my daughters," the Breccan whispered, and suddenly they were around him. A woman with gray-blond hair, a gaunt face, and shoulders that curved inward, as if she were starving, and three young daughters with hair the shade of flax, copper, and honey. The women began to weep when they saw the blood and the wound. His wife clung to him, trying to close the gash with her hands.

"They'll be hungry this winter when the north wind blows

and the ice comes," the Breccan said, and his voice was hoarse, fading. "They'll starve if you don't feed them, Torin."

He turned into ash and blew through his wife's fingers. His daughters wept and cried for him.

"Da! *Da!*"

Their voices cut into Torin like three different blades. They needed a healer, and he searched for Sidra in the mist.

"Sidra?" he called, but there was no answer. He realized that these were wounds for him alone to heal, and he looked at his hands, overcome. He thought about what she had once said to him: *What will you choose for your hands?* His eyes crowded with tears.

"Sidra," he said, his heart beating a lament. "*Sidra*," he whispered, and as he woke the sound of her name broke the darkness and his silence.

He lay in the bed for a shocked moment, drenched through with sweat. It was just before dawn, the coldest and loneliest hour, one that Torin was far too familiar with.

He dared to say her name again, his voice rough-hewn from disuse.

"Sidra?"

She woke.

She sat up in the bed, and her breaths were heavy, as if she had also been captive to a terrible dream. "Torin?"

He slipped from the bed and stumbled into the common room, feeling her presence behind him. She rushed to spark a candle, and they stared at each other in the faint light.

Torin moved to sit at the table, trembling. He rubbed his hands over his face.

"I need to confess to you, Sid."

Her apprehension was evident as she whispered, "Should I make some tea first?"

"No. Come here, please."

She set down the candle, her eyes wide, wary of what he was going to tell her. She stood an arm's length away from him, her chemise slipping from her shoulder.

He couldn't bear the distance, and he reached for her. She took a step closer to stand between his knees. His hands settled on her waist.

"I've made many mistakes in my life," he began. "But I refuse to let this one get the best of me. I've never said this to you, and I didn't realize how much I desired to speak such truth to you, every sunrise and every sunset, until my voice was taken." He paused. He was parched, and he longed to drink her in. "I love you, Sidra. My love for you knows no bounds."

She was quiet. But she touched his hair, and he felt reassured by the gesture.

"I have told you of my struggles," he said. "I continue to relive the last time I spoke to you. I was angry about the trade and the notion of peace Adaira was striving for. I was angry because it made me feel guilty for all the things I've done. When you told me that you would heal a Breccan in need . . . the indignation within me rose and I couldn't see past it. All I could see was the terror of the raids I have fought off. All I could think of were the nights I have surrendered being with you in order to keep the east secure. All I could feel was the pain in my old wounds. Because of that, I couldn't see that you were right. You have the ability to behold our enemy as a person in need. You see what I cannot, Sidra. And I'm sorry. I'm sorry for what I said to you that day, and I'm sorry that I didn't listen when you spoke."

Sidra exhaled. "Torin . . ."

He was waiting for her to respond, feeling like his heart was unmoored. Gently, he eased her down to his lap. Her eyes were aligned with his, her breaths mingling with his own.

"In the past," she began, "I'd look at Maisie and think of

who she would become in five years, ten years, thirty years, fifty years. I'd think of what her life on the isle would be like. I'd think about the legacy I wanted to leave for her. Would she be full of fear? Of hatred? Or would she be full of what we've taught her? Would she be compassionate? Would she be swift to listen, to learn and change?"

"I want a life for Maisie that is better than my own," Torin agreed, as if their daughter were asleep in the next room. "I want to change. But my bones are old, my heart is selfish, my spirit is weary. I look at me and I look at you, and I see two different dreams. I am death. And you, Sidra . . ." He reached out to touch her face, softly, as if she might vanish beneath his fingers. "You are life."

She closed her eyes beneath his caress. When his hand eased away, she looked at him and whispered, "Does that mean we cannot exist as one?"

He had been waiting for her to ask this. He had yearned to answer her in the orchard, when she had made it evident that they were vastly contrasting souls.

"No," Torin said. "It means that without you, I am nothing."

He felt her shiver. His hands were on her hips, and he was tempted to draw her closer. But there was still more he needed to say.

"You said to me that you felt like you had failed me and Maisie." He paused, his throat suddenly narrow. "You have never failed me, or our daughter. I know life feels different now, but you are free to choose what you want. If you desire to go your own way, then I will see our vows broken and I will let you go. But if there is a place for me within your heart . . . will you stay?"

Sidra framed his face. Her eyes were like dew, and her voice as warm as a summer night, when she whispered, "Yes."

Torin took her hands and kissed the blisters on her palms. To see the agony she had taken for him made him ache, deep in his soul.

They came together just as dawn began to illuminate the windows. Torin held Sidra in the lavender light, his hands spread across the curve of her back. His fingers traced the eaves of her shoulders.

He couldn't describe what he felt for her, but it possessed the power to sunder his bones. To lay him open and vulnerable. There were still corners of himself that Torin was ashamed of. He was afraid to fully let her in, to let her see him at his worst, to let her touch the bloodstained palms in his dreams. But then he opened his eyes and beheld her, joined to him. To his present. To his pain and his past. Weaving her fate with his, willingly.

"Torin," she breathed. Her black hair spilled across her shoulders as she moved.

"*Sidra,*" he whispered.

No sound had ever been sweeter to him.

Jack was worried that if he didn't speak to Mirin that day, Adaira would. He woke up with a headache, but the worst of his pain had subsided. He washed the grime from his eyes and dressed. His plaid was wrinkled from the disaster on the summit. A hole had emerged in the wool, as if the secret tucked within the pattern was quickly rising to the surface, and the sight of it stirred Jack's apprehension. He draped the plaid across himself, choosing to display its disrepair. His mother would see it and know why he needed to speak with her.

He packed up his warped harp and carried it on his back. He didn't know what to do with the instrument, but he didn't want it lying around his chambers as a visible reminder of

Bane's power. He found comfort in feeling the harp's familiar weight; the instrument, though damaged, still felt like a shield, and he was now ready for whatever the day might bring.

Jack found Adaira in the library, sitting at her father's desk. Books and papers were spread before her, as was a collection of broken quills. Her father's signet ring flashed on her hand. Jack had noticed the first time she wore it, because Adaira rarely wore jewelry. Her hands were often bare, and only the half coin that connected her to him typically hung from her neck.

She looked as though she hadn't slept, and he paused, uncertain what to say. He had stayed in his castle chambers the past two nights, not only because Sidra had ordered him to do so, but also so that he could remain close to Adaira. He had sent a guard to remain with Mirin and Frae in his stead, unwilling to take any chances.

"You look better today," Adaira said, her eyes quickly looking him over. "Are you going to speak with Mirin?"

Jack nodded. He could see her desire to bring the girls home simmering in her mind. She had delayed the trade with Innes because of her father's death, but the exchange was supposed to happen on the morrow. They might have the Orenna and know the location of the girls by the next evening.

Everything was coming together at last, and yet Jack had never felt such heavy misgivings.

"I'll send for you when I'm finished," he said.

"Good. Thank you," Adaira said, before returning her attention to the papers.

Jack watched her for a beat longer. She had scarcely spoken to him since her father died. He had wanted to play a lament in the hall after the burial, to comfort her and the clan, but found he was too light-headed to do it. He had wanted to go to Adaira in her chambers at night, to be with her in her grief, but discovered he was too anxious to approach without her invitation.

And so he had done nothing but lie in his bed, forcing down Sidra's tonics in hopes that they would restore him.

Realizing that Adaira was preoccupied with her task, Jack turned and departed. He went to the stables, requested the gentlest horse available, and then rode a slow, plodding gelding to his mother's land.

Mirin greeted him at the door, as if she had known he was coming.

"We don't need a guard here at night, Jack," she said. "Although I appreciate the thought."

Jack dismounted and walked into the kail yard. He didn't want to have this conversation. This was his last true moment of ignorance. After this hour had shed its minutes, he would know the truth about his blood and what his mother had done, and it would change him.

"I need to have a serious conversation with you, Mum," he said.

A frown crossed Mirin's brow when she noticed the disrepair of his plaid, the garment she had fortified with a secret only she knew. Her gaze shifted to his face next, and she seemed to finally see him, how battle-weary he appeared. She saw the silver that now graced his hair, as if he had been touched by death's finger.

"Jack!" Frae cried, slipping past their mother to embrace him in the yard. "I thought you'd never come home."

"I had things to do in Sloane, but I should be back for a little while. Here, let me ask you something, Frae." He crouched down to meet her gaze, noticing how much his knees hurt with the action. "I need to talk privately to Mum. Do you think you can stay in the yard for a little while?"

Frae's eyes widened. She sensed the tension, glancing from him to Mirin.

Their mother gave her a nod of permission, and Frae offered Jack a small smile.

"All right," she said, holding up her slingshot. "But afterward, can you practice with me?"

"Yes," he said. "I'll come find you when I'm done. Please don't leave the yard."

Frae skipped off toward the byre, where the cows were eating their hay. Jack straightened, waiting for Mirin to invite him in.

She did, but her face was pale.

It felt like he hadn't been home in ages. The first thing he did was begin to close all of the shutters.

"Leave one open so I can see Frae," Mirin said sharply.

Jack glanced at his mother. "This is not a conversation you want to ride the wind. Or for Frae to overhear."

Mirin gripped the front of her dress. "What is this about, Jack?"

He latched the final shutter, motioning for Mirin to sit on the divan. She did so, albeit reluctantly, and he took the chair across from her, setting the harp on the floor. He listened to the rasp of her inhalations. How they caught on the web of secrets she held.

He was staring at her when he asked, "Is there a chance my father has taken the Tamerlaine lasses?"

Mirin froze. But her eyes widened as they met Jack's. He saw the shock in her; she had never entertained this thought. "Your father? No, Jack." But her voice softened, as if she was beginning to see what he did. "No, that cannot . . . he would not . . ."

Jack's blood was coursing, fast and warm beneath his skin, but he kept his tone calm as he spoke. "You have held this secret for decades, Mum. I never understood why, and for years I resented you for your silence. But now I see. I understand why you wove and held it close to your heart. But the time has come to let it unravel. I need to find the missing lasses, and the answer lies within your past."

"But that would mean . . ." Mirin couldn't finish her phrase.

"That Annabel, Catriona, and Maisie have been kidnapped by a Breccan and taken into the west."

Mirin closed her eyes, as if his words had struck her. She remained silent, so Jack began to speak, as if he had uncovered an old ballad.

"Long ago, you came to love your greatest enemy. A man of the west. I don't know how he crossed the clan line unnoticed by the east, but he did, and you held the secret of him until I made that impossible. And so you led us all to believe I was the bastard of an unfaithful man in the east, and you wove the truth into a plaid because the threads would never betray or condemn you. Once I was sent away to the mainland, you must have seen him again, for Frae came into the world, and our two lives defied everything—east, west, and the hatred that thrives in between. You had no choice but to raise her as you raised me, as a Tamerlaine without a father."

Mirin looked at him. Her face was pallid, but her eyes were lucid and dark as new moons, and she held Jack's gaze. She laced her fingers together to hide their shaking.

"Do I speak truth, Mum?"

"Yes, Jack. Your father is a Breccan. But he wouldn't steal children from the east."

"And how do you know that?" Jack's temper flared. "Lasses are going missing, vanishing into the mist, taken by the west. Could my father be the force behind it all? Because he was robbed of his own children?"

"He would *never* steal a child," Mirin said again in a voice like iron. "Your father is a good man—the best I have ever known—and he has loved you and Frae from a distance, staying in his place so that you could have a whole life with me rather than a divided one."

"But he has crossed into Tamerlaine territory without notice," Jack countered. "He has broken the laws of the isle and has stood in this cottage with you, time and time again. He has trespassed and roamed the east, which means there is a break in the clan line, and the Breccans know of it and are using it as a weapon against us, taking lasses one by one. Stealing the daughters of innocent people."

Mirin shook her head, but her eyes gleamed with tears. "Your father wouldn't do this, Jack."

"When was the last time you saw him then, Mum? Last month? Last year? How long has it been since you spoke with him, and is he the same man you knew in the beginning? Is there a chance he has changed over time?" And Jack inwardly added, *Could years of denying himself, his lover, and his children drive him to madness and fury? Could years of being so close and yet so far from his family make him snap at last?*

A tear streaked down Mirin's cheek. She hastily wiped it away and said, "It's been nearly nine years since I saw him last. He came to visit a few days after Frae was born, to hold her for the first and last time. As he once held you when you were but a babe."

She paused to swallow more of her tears. Jack felt his heart go quiet, every fiber of him focused on Mirin's words.

"Neither of us wanted to fall for the other, to embrace the impossible. We were brought together by a strange necessity, and the love bloomed quiet but deep between us. When I realized I was carrying you . . . I was terrified. I didn't know how I could raise a child that was both east and west, and your father decided the two of us would steal away in the night. We would leave everything behind and start a new life on the mainland. But it's nearly impossible to depart the isle without someone, whether spirit or mortal, knowing.

"Our first attempt was thwarted by the wind. It stormed and made it impossible to leave the coast. We had a little boat in which your father planned to row us to the mainland, but the waves broke it on the rocks. A few weeks passed while your father worked to find another vessel, which he kept hidden in a cave. During that time we both had to learn the rhythm of the watchmen of the east and the west, because the patrol was always there, a hovering threat to us.

"And yet it wasn't the guard that nearly ruined our second attempt, but one of the neighbor's dogs, who must have picked up the scent of the west left by your father on the hills. I was too afraid to attempt a third departure—your father and I were bound to be discovered fleeing together—and so I determined that I would raise you alone in the east as a Tamerlaine and your father would keep his distance. So that is what we did, but once you left for the mainland school . . . my loneliness was keen."

Jack knew Frae came next, but in his mother's silence he realized that she had been the one who crossed the clan line. "You reunited with my father in the west," he said. He thought her foolish, impulsive, brave, and fierce. It had been a long time since a Tamerlaine had willingly walked in the west, but she had done it and hadn't been caught.

And it was Mirin, he realized, who knew the secret of crossing the clan line. She had used it herself.

"I did," she whispered. "Your father was not difficult to find. He is the Keeper of the Aithwood and lives in the heart of the forest on the western side, beside the river that flows into the east. The river connects the two of us like a silver thread, and I followed it to his cottage and found him there, quietly living out his life, as I did mine. Drinking hope and sorrow, both of us full of wonderings about the other and the life we might have shared had things been different between our two clans."

"How did you make the crossing into the west?" he asked. "How did my father make the crossing into the east? Is it one and the same way? Did you use the Orenna flowers?"

Mirin held Jack's gaze, and he saw the resistance within her, burning brighter than a flame. She didn't want to tell him; it went against every grain of her being to let this final secret loose.

"*Mum*," he pleaded. "Mum, please. If you want to help these lasses return home . . . I need to know how to make the crossing."

Mirin stood and walked away from him, but there was nowhere for her to retreat to.

Jack slowly rose to his feet.

"It's not the flower," Mirin finally said, turning to regard him once more. "It's the river. Your father discovered its secret by happenstance. One autumn night he was wounded and had an urgent need for assistance. He had lost quite a bit of blood and become disoriented. He was following the river and its current downstream, thinking it would lead him home. He was shocked when he realized that he stood in the east, and that no alarm had been raised. He believed it must be the river, shielding his presence. He followed it to my lands and dared to knock upon my door, asking for my help. We soon realized it was not just the river but blood within the water that made it possible for him to cross unnoticed to meet with me."

Jack remembered the night of the raid, how he had seen the

Breccans ride along the river valley, undetected. The words of Ream of the Sea rang in his ears.

Beware of blood in the water.

Frae brushed the cows in the byre until she could hear her mum and brother. She couldn't make out the words, but their voices were rising, as if they were arguing.

It made her anxious, and eventually she wandered to the backyard, her slingshot in hand.

The sun was at last shining, breaking through the clouds. The light gilded the valley and the river, and Frae watched how the water sparkled as it flowed into the east. She knew she wasn't supposed to leave the yard, but she wanted to practice before Jack joined her.

She slipped out the back gate and skipped down the hill to the riverbank. The currents were swollen from the rain, and she carefully drew stones from the water. Her target was still sitting in the grass, and Frae began to shoot. She missed the first two attempts but made a hit on her third.

"Yes!" she cried, bouncing on her toes.

She decided she would shoot three more times before returning to the yard and hurried to fetch her stones. Frae didn't notice the man standing on the riverbank behind her, not until it was too late.

She gasped and froze. The first thing she noticed was his blue plaid. He was a Breccan. The second thing she noticed was his drenched boots, as if he had been walking in the river, and his hand was bleeding.

"You shouldn't be here," she said, taking a step back, heart pounding.

"I know," he replied in a deep voice. "What's your name, lass?"

Her throat narrowed. She felt her knees quaking, and she glanced up the hill, where she could just see the roof of her home.

"What's your name?" the Breccan asked again.

Alarmed, Frae realized he was closer to her, although it seemed like he had only taken one step. She looked at his long, blond hair and wondered if this was the Breccan who had stood in the backyard before the raid. But then she realized this man was bigger, stronger than the one she had seen that night.

"F-Fraedah," she said, taking a step back.

"That's a lovely name," he said. "Would you like to visit the west, Fraedah?"

Frae was truly afraid now. Her hands felt cold, and her heart was hammering so hard she could scarcely breathe. She didn't know why this Breccan was here, but she wished he would leave, or Jack would arrive. . . .

"I don't think so," Frae said, and made to bolt up the hill.

The Breccan's speed was shocking. He caught her by the arm within seconds, then gently drew her to him.

"Now listen to me, Fraedah," he said. "If you come peacefully, you won't be hurt. But I can't guarantee that if you fight me. So be a smart lass and come along."

Frae gaped up at the stranger in horror, and then it hit her: nothing she could say would change his mind. He was going to take her to the west, whether she wanted to go or not, and her panic surged.

"Jack!" she screamed, fighting to slip away. *"Jack!"* She remembered her slingshot in her hand. The stone she held in the other.

Frae whirled and hurled the rock at the Breccan's face. It smashed into his nose, and he grunted, releasing her. She took that slender moment to run again, thinking she was fast, she could outrun him—

"Jack!" she cried as the Breccan caught her again.

He was no longer gentle. With one hand, he covered her mouth. With the other, he picked her up and began to carry her to the river.

The world felt upside down. Frae flailed, kicking and biting his palm, but the Breccan wouldn't release her. Her terror was sharper than a knife, cutting her up from within.

She could hear the water splashing as the Breccan carried her upstream. He slid a plaid over her eyes and a gag into her mouth.

She dropped Jack's slingshot in the river.

"Jack?" Mirin's voice broke his reveries. She touched his arm. "Jack, what are you going to do with what I've told you?"

She was afraid of what the clan would do to her. If the news came to light of her love for the enemy, it would destroy her life.

It would destroy him and Frae.

Jack swallowed, but it felt like his heart was in his throat when he whispered, "I'm not sure yet, Mum." He looked at Mirin, remembering Bane's words. "I can't tell you how I know this, but I was informed that you might know where the lasses are being held in the west."

Mirin startled. "What? I . . . I have no idea, Jack."

Jack decided some tea would help them both get through this conversation. He needed to do something with his hands, and he thought about how to frame his next questions as the kettle boiled. He was pouring two cups of tea when he heard a faint shout.

"Did you hear that?" he asked, setting the kettle down.

Mirin fell quiet. "No, what was it, Jack?"

He thought it might have been Frae, and a chill swept through him as he strode to the window, opening a shutter. He could see the cows in the byre, but his sister wasn't there.

Maybe she was in the backyard.

Jack began to head to the door when he heard it, clearer this time. Frae was screaming for him, and his blood went cold. He and Mirin both rushed to the garden, but there was no sign of Frae.

"Frae?" he shouted, stomping through the vegetables. *"Frae!"*

He was almost at the gate when movement in the valley caught his eye. Jack stopped, staring down at the river. Moray Breccan was carrying Frae upstream.

Mirin emitted a shrill cry. Jack's heart melted, first in shock, then in terrible fury. He felt like he was a breath away from combusting into flames as he darted through the gate, his eyes fixed on Frae as she fought, kicking and flailing.

Jack made it all of three steps before Moray saw him. The Breccan vanished upstream with impossible speed, into the shadows of the Aithwood, and Jack slid to a halt in the grass, stricken.

He was weak and frail. He had no chance of catching Moray before he crossed the clan line with Frae. Not if Moray had consumed one of the Orenna flowers.

I can't defeat him in my own strength, Jack thought, grief and terror tangling in him, and then it occurred to him like a blinding light.

He turned and rushed back into the garden, grasping Mirin's arm as she tried to dash past him.

"Find a strip of plaid," he ordered, dragging her into the house with him.

"What are you doing?" she cried, nearly clawing his face. "He has Frae! Let me go, Jack."

"*Listen* to me!" he shouted, and Mirin startled. She fell quiet, staring at him. "Take my plaid and tear it into strips, and then meet me on the hill. I'll catch him, but you have to trust me, Mum."

She nodded, taking his plaid when he shoved it into her hands. Its enchantment was completely gone now, and Jack strode across the room to pick up his harp.

Half of the strings had broken, but half were still intact, albeit darkened with soot. Jack tucked the instrument beneath his arm and returned to the backyard, running as fast as his feet and lungs would allow him. He went halfway down the hill and sat in the grass, his hands trembling as he tried to find a way to comfortably hold his twisted harp.

He didn't know if this would work. He didn't know what the music would sound like coming from a harp that was warped. He hadn't even thought about trying to play it again.

But he set his gaze on the river, where it slithered from the Aithwood. Where Frae had vanished into the shadows.

Jack couldn't afford to let his emotions escape. He had to quell his fear, his anger, his distress, burning deep within him, like salt in a wound.

He needed to steady himself.

He closed his eyes and became aware of the earth beneath him. The grass at his knees. The scent of the loam. He stretched that awareness out further, to the voice of the river, the deep roots of the forest.

His fingers found a place on the strings. He began to play, and the notes emerged strange and wild, as if they had come from embers. They were tinny and sharp, cutting through the air with a haunting sound, and Jack opened his eyes again to watch the river flow.

This music was spontaneous, passing through him like breath. He began to sing to the spirits of the forest, to the spirits of the river. To the grass and the loam and the wildflowers. To Orenna.

Bring them back to me.

Jack could hear a beat in his mind. He played to it, his notes coming faster, faster with his urgency, knowing Moray Breccan might already be in the west. Jack offered his faith to the spirits around him, weaving a command into the notes.

Bring them back to me.

He waited, his vision bent upon the distant sun-speckled rapids and arching branches. He gave his words to the essence of a red flower with gold-laced petals that grew on dry, heart-sick land. He sang to the power that had once invigorated him, when his eyes had been opened to see beyond his world.

Bring them back to me.

Jack could feel his strength ebbing. His hands were aching, his head throbbing. A trickle of blood emerged from his nose, coating his lips. He pushed himself to keep strumming, to keep singing, even though he feared he had nearly reached the end of himself and his abilities.

His nails were splitting, the quicks bright with blood. But he pressed on through the pain and was rewarded with a glimmer of movement.

Moray Breccan was returning, his face furrowed in confusion until he saw Jack singing on the hill. His bewilderment gave way to anger, but the power that had granted Moray the ability to move with speed and prowess was now dragging him to Jack.

Jack didn't care to look at Moray's face. He looked at Frae, who was still fighting to get free. She was blindfolded, but Jack could see the gleam of her teeth as she kicked and clawed.

He was moved by both pride and grief.

He continued to play, his voice a raspy offering. The notes were slowing, like the final aspirations before death, but Moray was still tethered to the music. Even as it faded, he was beholden to its creator.

The Breccan heir walked Frae up the hill. He was moving

more and more slowly the closer he came to Jack, as if he were wading through honey. When he at last came to a stop at Jack's feet, the magic held him completely still. Only then did Jack rise. Mirin was beside him—he realized she had been beside him the entire time—and he met Moray's defiant gaze with a cold, deadly stare of his own.

"Release my sister," he said.

Moray loosened his hold on Frae. She was weeping now, hearing Jack's voice.

"Come to me, Frae," he said, holding out his hand to her. Frae ripped off the blindfold and gag, leaping toward her brother. He could feel how she trembled, and he held her close to his side before Mirin embraced her.

Moray snickered, glancing over Jack. "You never said you were a bard."

"You never asked," Jack replied.

There were many things Jack needed to know. The questions were like a flood within him, and he wanted Moray Breccan to answer every single one.

That is, if Jack didn't murder him. The temptation was keen, pounding in his skull as Moray continued to stare at him, unrepentant.

The Breccan was opening his mouth, beginning to say Adaira's name.

Jack snapped. Reality began to overtake him, and he bared his teeth and swung the corner of his harp. It caught Moray in the side of his head.

Down he went into the grass, limp and pale. Blood began to pool in Moray's golden hair.

Jack stared at the Breccan for a moment, wondering if he had just killed the Heir of the West.

"Jack . . ." Mirin sounded hesitant.

"Bind his wrists, Mum," Jack said. His strength was waning. He could no longer stand and slowly sank to his knees. "We need to take him inside, tie him to a chair." His hands were tingling, going numb. Jack's harp tumbled to the ground. "Call for Adaira."

It was his last request before he was captured by exhaustion. Jack sprawled facedown in the grass next to Moray Breccan.

His enemy.

His laird by half.

CHAPTER 25

Sidra was walking along the western road on the way to visit a patient when she heard Mirin's voice on the wind. She was calling for Adaira, and she sounded desperate.

Concerned, Sidra quickened her pace, heading in the direction of Mirin's croft. She veered from the road and trusted the hills, Yirr in her shadow. The land shifted for her, folding kilometers and flattening craggy slopes, urging her forward through deer trails in the heather.

She was anxious when she reached Mirin's gate. By appearances, everything seemed well, and Sidra approached the front door.

"Mirin? Frae?" She knocked and waited. Sweat was beginning to seep through her dress when Sidra decided to open the door. "Hello?"

She ordered Yirr to wait for her in the yard and stepped inside the cottage. It was empty and dimly lit, all of the shutters latched save for one. The back door was cracked open, inviting a stream of morning light. Sidra set down her basket of herbs and slowly walked to it.

She stepped onto the rear stoop and was amazed to find Mirin and Frae attempting to drag a body through the garden. Sidra didn't know what shocked her more: the blue plaid on the man, how his hands were bound, or the blood on Mirin's dress as she struggled to haul him to the house.

Mirin has killed a Breccan, Sidra thought, mouth agape. *And she's trying to hide the body.*

"Mum!" Frae cried, pointing at Sidra.

Mirin whirled, tense until she recognized the healer. "Blessed spirits! Can you help us, Sidra?"

Sidra didn't hesitate. She stepped forward, the ground soft beneath her boots. "Yes. Where are we taking him?"

"Inside," Mirin panted. Her face was ruddy, and stray hairs were escaping her braid.

"Are you wounded, Mirin?" Sidra asked, glancing again at the blood on the weaver's skirts.

"No, it's his blood. Is he . . . is he dead, Sidra?"

Sidra knelt and quickly glanced over him. A head wound, which looked far worse than it was. One of his palms bore a shallow, intentional slice. She checked his pulse; it was slow but strong.

"He's alive," she said, moving to take hold of his ankles. "He'll most likely wake soon."

"Frae?" Mirin said, clearing her throat. "Will you run inside and clear a space in the common room? Set out one of the kitchen chairs. And close the shutter."

Frae nodded and dashed to obey.

A strange feeling began to creep over Sidra. She paused, staring at the Breccan's boot.

Is this him?

She didn't know where the query came from, but it made

her stomach clench. She was wearing the green plaid Torin had commissioned for her, and she felt safe beneath its enchantment. But her chest began to ache.

"Sidra?" Mirin gently asked, breaking her strange reverie.

Sidra hurried to lift the man's feet as Mirin heaved his upper body, and together they painstakingly carried him into the house and to the chair Frae had arranged. It took a bit of shuffling to get him seated upright—he was backbreakingly heavy—and Sidra was sore for breath by the time she and Mirin had removed his plaid and weapons.

"Will you bind his ankles to the chair?" Mirin asked, handing her two strips of plaid. "As tight as you can."

Sidra nodded. "What happened?"

"I . . ." Mirin paused, laying her hand on her forehead. "Jack is unwell. I had to leave him on the hill, and I need to keep the Breccan under watch until Adaira arrives. Do you mind going to Jack and seeing if there's anything you can do to heal him?"

"Yes," Sidra said, her heart racing. She grabbed her basket and returned to the back garden, following the path Mirin and Frae had made dragging the Breccan. She saw Jack lying in the grass, and her fears rose. Every horrible thought was blooming in her mind—a Breccan must have crossed and Jack had fought him and was now critically wounded—and Sidra prepared herself as she knelt in the grass and turned him over.

He had been lying on his harp. The instrument was crooked and burned, as if it had been held over a fire, and he groaned as he settled on his back.

"Adaira?" he croaked, opening his eyes a sliver.

Sidra touched his brow. "No, it's me. Sidra. Can you tell me what happened, Jack?" She prepared a cloth to wipe the dried blood from his face and fingers. His nails were broken and jagged at the edges. That's when she knew it hadn't been a fight but magic that had done this to him.

"The music's cost was more than I could pay," he said, wincing as she cleaned his nails. "It's the same as before. I'm just . . . exhausted."

"*Jack.*"

"Yes, I know," he said. "Don't scold me, Sidra."

Sidra held her tongue and worked quickly, full of questions. She made herself focus on the most pressing matter, which was healing Jack. But other thoughts were simmering.

"Can you give me something that will make me hale?" Jack said. He had opened his eyes fully now, watching Sidra prepare his tonic.

She paused, glancing at him.

"I need to appear strong for Adaira," he explained. "Give me your most potent tonic."

"If I do that, Jack, it might take you longer to heal," Sidra warned. "I can give you something that will make you lively, but it will wear off within hours and might make your other symptoms worse."

"I'll take that chance," he said. "Because the truth of the matter is, there's currently a Breccan in my mother's house, who may or may not be dead."

"He's alive."

"Well, that's a relief," Jack said, and Sidra was pleased to hear his dry humor had returned. "Or else I might have forfeited my life for killing the Heir of the West."

Sidra's hands froze. "He's the heir?"

"Yes," Jack groaned as he sat forward. "He came to steal Frae, and I thwarted him."

An icy finger traced Sidra's spine.

It's him.

The man she had just helped carry into Mirin's house was the one who had assaulted her on the hill to Graeme's. Who had stolen Maisie.

"Sidra?" Jack said, concerned.

She didn't know how long she had been sitting beside him, lost in an eddy of thought. Jack was frowning, watching her closely.

"Moray was the one who attacked you that night," he whispered.

She hesitated, but nodded.

"That *bastard*," Jack said.

Sidra focused on her herbs, preparing one of the brews she had created for the guard to keep them sharp and aware during long nights. "Here, Jack. This will help with your exhaustion and a few of your aches and pains."

He accepted the cup and drank.

They sat together in the grass, silent for a few moments. Sidra was trying to decide what to do—whether she wanted to speak to Moray or not, let alone look him in the face—and Jack was waiting for the tonic to take full effect. Then Sidra noticed that some color had returned to his countenance—although he was still remarkably pale—and his eyes looked brighter. She was gathering her supplies together when she heard footsteps approaching.

Sidra and Jack both turned to see Frae running to them.

"Jack!" she panted, slowing to a walk.

"What's happened, Frae?" Jack said, reaching for her. He wobbled for a spell, but only Sidra noticed.

Frae sighed, visibly relieved to see him better. She looked up at him before glancing at Sidra and said, "Mum sent me. The Breccan's awake."

Adaira should have known that on the day Torin regained his voice, all hell would break loose. She and her cousin were poring over maps and plans for the rescue crossing when Roban interrupted them with a message.

"I've heard your name on the wind, laird," the young guard said. "It sounded like Mirin's voice."

Adaira paused, leaning on her father's desk. Her heart dropped. If Mirin was summoning her instead of Jack, that meant something must have gone awry. It seemed like every passing day met such a fate, and Adaira wondered when life would feel calm and predictable again.

She and Torin rode to the weaver's croft with a small retinue of guards. She had no idea what to expect, but it wasn't to find Moray Breccan bound to a chair in the center of the room, gagged and blindfolded, with dried blood in his hair.

Adaira came to a halt over the threshold so abruptly that Torin stepped on her heels.

Her eyes quickly took inventory of her surroundings. She found Jack first. He was standing by the loom, behind Moray. Sidra was sitting on a stool at his side, as if the two of them wanted to remain out of sight. Mirin was by the hearth, Frae's long arms wrapped around her waist.

"A word, Jack?" Torin said.

Jack nodded, and Adaira followed the men into Jack's bedroom for a debriefing. Sidra joined them, and they closed the door, leaving the guards in the common room to watch Moray.

"What happened?" Adaira asked.

Jack began to recount the recent events, but his voice sounded odd, as if he couldn't catch his breath. Adaira noticed there was a slight tremor in his hands, and his nails were broken to the quick. He refrained from saying that he had played for the spirits, but Adaira knew that was exactly what he had done. He also seemed to be holding something back, breaking his sentences and leaving them incomplete.

"He was trying to kidnap Frae," Jack finally said, wavering like he was about to collapse.

Adaira reached out to steady him, and Sidra hurried to say, "You need to sit down, Jack."

"Here, over to the bed," Adaira said, and together they shuffled him to the bedside.

Jack groaned as he sat. Perspiration beaded his upper lip. "I'm fine. It's just stifling in here, isn't it?"

Sidra glanced at Torin. "Will you crack open the shutter? He needs fresh air."

Torin obeyed, and Adaira felt like she could also breathe a little deeper, now that cool air was trickling into the small chamber.

"Do you think he's the one who stole the other lasses?" Torin asked in a clipped tone.

Jack hesitated, looking at Sidra. Adaira knew it then. She knew Moray had fooled her, time and time again, and her face flushed.

Torin was the first to respond. He nearly ripped the bedroom door from its hinges as he stormed back into the common room. His rage was like lightning striking the ground, and Adaira had no choice but to chase after him. Her cousin made a beeline for Moray, and before Adaira could command him, Torin's fist was smashing into the Breccan's jaw.

Adaira halted.

"You stole my daughter," Torin said, looming over Moray. "You wounded my wife, and I will kill you for it."

He kicked Moray in the chest. The very place the Breccan had once booted Sidra. The blow rocked him, overturning the chair. Moray hit the ground with a grunt of pain, sliding across the floor until he and his chair hit the back of the divan.

"*Adaira*," Moray wheezed through the gag.

She didn't know how Moray knew she was present. He was still blindfolded, and she had made no indication that she was present. Chills swept through her as she watched Torin stalk him, preparing to land another blow.

At last, Adaira moved to interfere. She needed Moray Breccan conscious and whole and most of all able to *speak*.

Sidra beat her to it, moving to stand behind Moray, in Torin's line of sight. She reached out her hand to him and said, "Not like this, Torin."

Adaira watched as Torin's breaths heaved. Her cousin had never been one to back down in a fight, and she was amazed when he calmed himself, accepting Sidra's hand. He stepped over the Breccan, finding a place along the back wall to stand and watch, with Sidra tucked under his arm.

Rattled, Adaira took a moment to steady her voice. She turned to the guards and said, "Will two of you please set Moray Breccan and his chair upright?"

Her guards hurried to obey. Moray's breaths were labored, and blood was trickling from the corner of his mouth. It suddenly felt warm and cramped in the cottage as Adaira stepped closer to the western heir. Her heart was beating far too swiftly for her liking, but her face was composed and cold. The expression her father taught her to wear when it came to justice.

Adaira yanked the blindfold away from Moray's eyes. She watched the harsh lines in his brow ease as he stared up at her, as if he believed she would save him.

"Before I remove this gag from your mouth," she began, "I want you to know that we kill Breccans who trespass into the east with ill intent. You're here on my lands, uninvited and unexpected, and I can only presume you came either to betray me or cause pain to my clan. I'm going to ask you questions, and I expect you to answer everything with honesty. If you understand and agree to that, nod your head."

Moray's eyes smoldered, but he nodded.

Adaira pulled the gag from his mouth, and he coughed.

One of the guards brought her a chair, to sit before the Breccan, and she was about to take a seat when Jack stepped forward.

"Laird?" he said, and while his voice still sounded strained, he stepped toward her with confidence. "May I share a suggestion?"

"Go on," she said. But he didn't have to explain. Jack unsheathed the dirk at his belt. His truth blade. Adaira accepted his offering and returned to stand before Moray.

"Are you going to cut my throat before giving me the chance to speak?" Moray asked. "Because I have a story you will want to hear."

Adaira ignored his sarcasm and the curiosity she felt at his taunt. "While your blood runs from this blade, you will be compelled to answer everything I ask you in truth. I'm going to cut you now, because I don't trust you to speak honestly without it." She sliced his skin, just below his knee. Moray didn't react; the sting of blades was familiar to him.

Adaira finally sat, her eyes fixed on his. But she could see his blood running in thin ribbons down the hide and leather of his boot.

"Why are you in the east, Moray Breccan?" she asked.

He bared his teeth. He was trying to resist answering, but the enchantment was in his blood.

"To steal a lass," he replied.

Adaira was prepared for this answer, but his acknowledgment of his intent still hit her like a fist. She struggled to tamp down her rising gorge, to keep her mind sharp and uncluttered from emotion.

She asked, "Were you the one who stole the other Tamerlaine lasses?"

"I was."

"Where are the three lasses being held?"

"They're in the Keeper of the Aithwood's cottage."

Adaira noticed that Jack shifted. He was standing near his bedroom door, but he glanced at Mirin, who continued to stand with Frae before the hearth. The weaver looked pale as she stared at her son, and Adaira made a note to ask Mirin about this later.

"And where is that?" she continued.

"Upstream and past the clan line, deep in the heart of the woods."

Torin flinched. Adaira held up her hand, silently commanding him to stay where he was.

"Did you partake in the most recent raid to cover your move of returning Eliza Elliott to the east?" she asked.

"Indeed."

"Why return only one of the lasses?"

"Because I wanted to prove to you that I am merciful and I do nothing without thought," Moray answered. "I knew you would soon discover I was the one stealing them, and you would burn with anger toward me. I needed to prove to you that there was a reason for the snatchings, and that, most of all, the lasses were being treated gently in the west."

"Why steal them?" Adaira asked. "Why have you and your clan sunk so low as to take our daughters?"

A hint of a smile played over Moray's lips. "Grant me another cut, Adaira. Because what I'm about to tell you . . . I need you to know it's truth."

She sat there for a moment, solemn and full of worry. But he was right; the first cut was already mending. So she granted him another wound, deep enough this time to draw a grimace across his face.

"Now then," Adaira said. "Why?"

Moray seemed to settle in the chair, as if preparing for a long encounter. "On a stormy autumn night nearly twenty-three years ago," he began, "the Laird of the West and her consort welcomed their first child into the world. A lad with hair like corn silk and a voice like a bleating goat. And yet he was not alone. Another bairn followed on his heels. A very small lass. She was tiny compared to her twin, with hair white as moon thistle."

Moray paused.

Adaira swallowed and said, "Go on."

Her enemy smiled and continued.

"She seemed shocked to enter the world on such a night, and my parents held her in awe, willing her to cry, to nurse, to open her eyes. Even then she defied them, and when the druid entered the chamber to bless the new bairns three days after their birth, he would not bless the lass. 'She is sickly,' he said. 'There is a great chance your true daughter has been stolen by the spirits. Appoint a person you trust to set this lass in a place where the wind is gentle, where the earth is soft, where fire can strike in a moment, and where the water flows with a comforting song. A place where the old spirits gather, for they can return your true daughter, who is strong and destined for greatness in our clan.'

"My parents consulted with each other, and they both concluded there was one person they trusted to exchange their daughter—the Keeper of the Aithwood.

"The Keeper of the Aithwood was a good man, one who lived in solitude in the wood. He was a watchman and loyal to the clan, and he knew of a place where the folk of earth, air, fire, and water gathered. He took Cora, my sister, from my parents and carried her deep into the wood. He was given orders to lay her in a place where the spirits would find her and then to leave her there. If he was present, the spirits wouldn't manifest to switch the children. So the keeper found a blanket of moss near a river, in the heart of the forest where the wind blew through the boughs and fire could rise and burn at a moment's notice. And he left my sister there.

"For almost my entire life, I believed what the keeper told my parents about that day: he left my sister on the moss to be taken. But when he returned hours later, Cora was gone, and there was no bairn for him to carry back to my parents. For years my family and my clan believed what he told us: one of the folk of the wind took my sister into their kingdom and raised her there, knowing she would not survive the mortal realm. And we found painful peace in the thought, and we bowed to the wind, believing she was within it.

"But secrets refuse to stay buried on the isle. They have an uncanny way of rising, and they are vengeful.

"I had grown suspicious of the keeper over the years. His loyalty seemed to waver at times—he protested the raids and refused to let us ride through the Aithwood when we conducted them. I decided to watch him closely. It took a few years, but I finally caught him on the clan line, returning to the west. He had been walking the east without detection, and I wanted to know how he had accomplished such a feat.

"It took me months to wear him down. To break his stubbornness. In the end, he confessed and gave me his full allegiance in order to preserve his life. And the story he had once given about my sister's disappearance? It had been a lie.

"This is what truly happened:

"On the day he left Cora on the moss, he walked away from her, as he had been ordered to do. But where she had been silent before, her cries now echoed through the forest, and they drew him back to her. He stood a safe distance away, so as not to interfere with the folk, and watched as the day began to fade into evening. It was bitterly cold, and the spirits refused to come and claim her. Soon, her cries drew a wolf, and the keeper fought off the beast and was wounded. His arm bled, and he chose to pick up my sister and deliver her elsewhere. He had lost a good deal of blood and become disoriented, but he knew the river would lead him home.

"He stepped into the currents and followed the river, unaware that he was walking in the opposite direction of his home. He claims that he didn't realize the moment he crossed, owing to his distress, but soon the trees fell away, and he stood in an unfamiliar valley. He knew he was no longer in the west, but the East Guard had taken no note of his presence. A terrible inkling came to the keeper.

"Which Tamerlaine he first gave my sister up to, I don't know, for he would never say their name. But I believe they live near the clan line, and that is how the east committed the worst of crimes: they took a daughter of the west as their own.

"I've always wondered what the Tamerlaines who accepted her were thinking. Perhaps they didn't want my sister to grow up so close to the clan line, where the west and her true clan might call to her blood one day. Perhaps at first the Tamerlaines didn't fully know who my sister was—a child of their greatest enemy. The offspring of the western laird. The keeper wouldn't tell me, but when I asked him where Cora now lived in the east, he only smiled and said, 'The Breccan druid once said she was destined for greatness in the west, but he must have misread the stars.'

"I doubted him at first. I believed the keeper's claims were those of a man gone mad after a life of solitude in the woods. But I also was determined to find my sister. And what better way than to walk the east, listening to the gossip that rides your winds?

"I visited numerous times, entering through the secret of the river and empowered by the Orenna's essence. I learned the lay of your lands, and I listened to the wind. I soon learned of the heiress. The only living child of the laird. And the

Tamerlaines loved you. They called you Adaira, with hair the color of the moon and eyes the shade of the sea. And I knew it was you, Cora."

"Enough!" Torin's voice cut through the chamber. "Enough with this dribble. With your lies and your cunning, Breccan. Silence him, cousin."

Adaira sat like stone, watching Moray's blood continue to spill from his wound and pool on the floor at his feet. Her breaths felt shallow, and her heart was beating against her ribs. She raised her gaze back to his eyes and saw herself reflected in them.

"Why, then, did you steal the Tamerlaine daughters?" she asked.

"I wanted to tell you that day we met in the cave," Moray said. "When you first wrote to me of a trade, it gave me hope. It was a sign that you were ready to come home. And I wanted to tell you the truth, so you would understand why I longed for vengeance. Why I chose to strike at the Tamerlaines' hearts. But it was not my place to tell you.

"I took one of the Tamerlaine daughters, hoping to gain the attention of the eastern laird. For him to realize what was happening and tell you who you truly are. And when he did nothing, I took another. I determined to keep stealing lasses until someone in the east gave up the secret and spoke truth. I simply didn't think it would take so long, that the Tamerlaines would be so tenacious and stubborn. I didn't think the laird would pass away during my attempts, taking his secret to the grave as you rose in his place. I didn't think that I would have to be the one to speak your story, to behold your face when you heard it for the first time, Adaira. Laird of the East who was born in the west. But here we are."

Moray paused, his voice softening. "I've come to bring you home, Cora."

Adaira had told herself that she wouldn't feel anything, that she would take him prisoner after he reached the end of his tale. But she couldn't ignore the mark, like a bruise, that the story left on her. The story was also like a sword—she couldn't prevent it from cutting her heart in two. And the story was like a veil torn from her eyes—she couldn't help but see her past from a different angle, even if it was ugly, terrible, and absurd.

In the moment of quiet that followed, when Moray Breccan's story had ended and everyone in the chamber waited to see what she would do, Adaira remembered the spirits. *It is her,* they had said when they saw her on the shore and on the holy hill. *It is her.* They had known who she truly was. A girl of the west, raised by her enemies. Perhaps the folk had been watching her life, year after year, anticipating this moment.

"Will you come home with me, Cora?" Moray said again. "If you'll come home, the Tamerlaine lasses I took will be returned to their families. Just as you were cared for in the east, we have cared for the lasses in the west. Come, sister. A better life awaits you with the people you belong to. Let this exchange be made without bloodshed."

Torin approached the back of Moray's chair. He didn't wait for Adaira's command; he gagged the Breccan with a hard jerk, and Moray winced.

But the silence was worse than the noise. For now Adaira could feel the full weight of everyone looking at her. Mirin and Frae. Sidra and Torin. Her guards. Moray. *Jack.*

She didn't know what to do. She didn't know if she should acknowledge Moray's claims or sneer at them. Adaira rose.

"Torin, escort our prisoner to the dungeons of Sloane," she said.

She stood aside as Torin blindfolded Moray again and loosened the bindings that had kept him strapped in the chair. The guards surrounded and dragged him from Mirin's cottage to the yard, where the horses were waiting.

Adaira followed, preparing to ride with them. She didn't want to look at Torin, or Sidra, or Jack. She didn't want to see the doubt and the suspicion in their eyes, didn't want to know how this revelation of her blood would change their opinion of her.

"Adaira," Jack whispered. She felt him take a gentle hold of her arm, turning her toward him. "Where are you going?"

She stared at Jack's chest. She couldn't tell if he was wearing his half coin. In fact, she had never seen it around his neck, wondering if it merely hid beneath his tunic or if he chose not to don it.

It didn't matter.

She realized she would need to break their handfast. Jack had inadvertently bound himself to a Breccan. The truth was slowly eating through her, as if her past and her soul were a feast to ravage. Her mind reeled with the list of things she needed to do—*should* do—but her primary focus was getting Moray secure in the holding.

"I'm escorting the prisoner with Torin," she said in a flat tone.

"Then let me come with you," Jack said.

She didn't want him beside her. She wanted a moment alone, to weep and rage in privacy. To sink into the pain of realizing her entire life had been a lie.

"Stay here with your mum and sister," Adaira said, licking her lips. She felt parched. Cracked to her bones. "You should be with them after what happened this morning, and you need to rest. The worst of this is far from over."

She mounted her horse and gathered the reins. She looked at Torin, who was waiting for her nod, and then they began to ride east, with Moray Breccan in the center of their tight formation.

Adaira felt Jack's gaze. But she couldn't bear to look behind and meet it.

Jack watched her ride away. He was numb, and the tonic was beginning to lose its edge. A throb drummed at his temples; his thoughts were overflowing.

He didn't know what to do, but he knew he wanted to be with Adaira. He dragged his hands over his face, breathing into his palms as he considered chasing after her on foot.

"Jack."

He turned when Sidra's soft voice broke his thoughts. She was standing in the yard behind him, her dark brows slanted in concern. "I think your mum might be in a bit of shock. I set a kettle on the fire to boil and left a calming brew of tea, but I think you should sit with her until the worst passes."

He hadn't even been thinking about the impact of Moray's confession on his mother. His mind had been wholly consumed by Adaira.

"Yes, of course," he said, and hurried back inside.

The light was still dim, but he could see Mirin sitting on the floor before the hearth, as if her knees had become disjointed. Frae was fluttering around her, trying to get her up.

"Jack!" his sister cried. "Something's wrong with Mum!"

"It's all right, Frae," Jack said. He gently eased Mirin up and into a chair. He glanced at Sidra, uncertain.

The healer reached for Frae's hand and smiled. "Frae? Would you like to come to work with me today? I have two patients I need to see, not far from here. You can help me with the herbs, and then we can bring some food back for Jack and your mum."

The fear in Frae's face turned into awe. "Could I really, Sidra?"

"Yes, I would love to have you accompany me. That is, if your mum and brother agree?"

Jack looked at Mirin. Her face was pale, her eyes glazed. He didn't think she'd heard a word Sidra had said.

"Yes," he replied, forcing a smile. "I think that sounds nice, Frae. Fetch your plaid."

Frae darted into the bedroom. Jack sagged in relief.

"I don't know how to thank you," he said as Sidra set two more vials in his hands.

"There's no need to. These are for you. Take them when the pain returns," she said, glancing at Mirin. "Keep your mother warm and calm. The tea will help."

Frae bounded back into the chamber, shawl in hand. Jack knotted it at her collar before trailing the women to the door.

He had a moment of apprehension, letting Frae out of his sight. But he saw Sidra linking their fingers, her dog following them like a diligent guard.

"We'll be back in two hours," Sidra called to him.

He nodded. He waited until they had faded from sight before he shut the front door.

He exhaled against the wood. His exhaustion was rising, but there was no time to rest.

He believed Moray Breccan's story. He believed every word, but Jack knew there were pieces still missing. Pieces only his mother held.

The kettle was hissing.

Jack removed it from the fire, adding the herbs Sidra had given him for tea. He poured two cups and brought one to Mirin, ensuring that her hands could hold it before he tucked a blanket over her knees.

He sat down in the chair across from her, waiting until she took a few sips.

She seemed to return to life, remembering herself. The color gradually blossomed on her cheeks, and he sighed in relief.

"Can I ask you something, Mum?"

Mirin looked at him. Her shoulders were still stooped, as if she was in pain. But her voice was clear when she spoke. "Yes, Jack."

He drew in a shaky breath. He could smell the fragrance of the tea, the musty scent of the wool strung over her loom. He wondered how much this little cottage on the hill, built of stone and wood and thatch, had seen in its lifetime. He wondered what the walls would say if they could speak. What stories they guarded.

"On the night the Keeper of the Aithwood crossed the clan line with the Breccans' daughter in his arms . . . he came to you," Jack said. "My father brought Adaira to you."

Mirin, eyes shining with tears and decades of secrets, whispered, "*Yes.*"

CHAPTER 26

A crowd had gathered in Sloane.

The sight deepened Torin's worry as he and the guard approached, Moray still bound in the midst of them. The entire ride, Adaira had refused to meet Torin's gaze. He had glanced sidelong at her occasionally, tracing her profile. Her expression was like steel as they passed the city gates.

The moment the Breccan was seen in the streets, the people's anger ignited.

Torin drew his horse to a halt, watching as Una Carlow pushed through the crowd.

"Is it true, laird?" Una's voice cut through the air as she looked at Adaira. "Is it true you're a daughter of the west? That you're a Breccan by blood?"

Adaira seemed to blanch. At last, she glanced at Torin, and he was struck by a horrible realization.

He had opened the shutter in Jack's bedroom during the debriefing, but in his fury, he had forgotten to close it. Moray's story of Adaira's origins must have slipped out that small crack, riding the wind. This was not the way Torin envisioned the clan learning the truth, and when more questions were shot at Adaira—questions laced with wariness and devastation— Torin swiftly turned his horse around to face his cousin.

"Escort Moray on to the dungeons," he told the closest guard. "See to it that no harm comes to him."

It was a mess as the guards moved forward with Moray, forcing the crowd to part. Adaira remained frozen and mounted on her horse, listening as the din rose around her. Torin wove his way to her side, his stallion nearly trampling a few people in the process.

The Elliott boys had approached her now. Eliza's older brothers.

"You knew all along the Breccans were taking the lasses!" the younger Elliott boy shouted, veins pulsing in his temples. "You *knew* and were trading with our enemies in secret!"

"Of course she would!" the other brother snarled. "She was giving away our goods, rewarding them for snatching our sister."

"That's not true!" Adaira said, but her voice broke.

"You were fraternizing with our enemies!"

"Why would we believe you, when you've played us for fools and lied to us for years?"

"Whose side holds your allegiance?"

The comments and questions rose and spun like a whirlwind. Adaira tried to respond again, to calm the people's distress and anger, but their voices were overpowering hers.

Spirits below, Torin thought. The clan knew of the trade. Like a fool, Moray had remarked about that private meeting between him and Adaira, and now everyone knew only bits and pieces. Enough for the information to become twisted against Adaira, even as she had only striven for peace and the Tamerlaines' good.

"*Quiet!*" Torin shouted.

To his shock, the crowd heeded him. Their eyes shifted from Adaira to him, and he suddenly didn't know what to say as he felt the weight of their gaze on him.

"We have a culprit in custody for the kidnappings," Torin continued. "Which he committed on his own, without Adaira's knowledge or assistance."

"But what of the illegal trade she was partaking in?" an Elliott shouted. "What of justice for our sister? For the other girls still missing?"

"Justice will be served," Torin said. "But first, you must let me and your laird pass safely and quickly to the castle, where we can settle the matter and bring home the other lasses."

The crowd began to step back, clearing a path.

Adaira still seemed frozen, and Torin reached over to grab her reins, urging both of their horses forward. He didn't relax, not even when they reached the safety of the castle courtyard.

"Adi," he said, watching her dismount.

"I'm fine, Torin," she replied, but her face was pale. "Go see to Moray in the dungeons. And then meet me in the library. We have things we need to discuss."

He nodded, watching her stride into the castle.

His thoughts were roaring as he hurried down to the coldest, dampest cell. Moray was being thoroughly searched, and Torin watched by torchlight as his guards found a hidden dirk in the Breccan's boot. The blindfold and gag were removed, and Moray took his first look at his new surroundings. Stone, iron, and meager firelight.

His wrists and ankles were shackled to the wall.

"I want to speak to Adaira," he demanded as his cell was latched and bolted.

"She'll speak to you when she wants to," Torin said.

He appointed five guards to keep watch and then ascended to the brighter levels of the castle.

At last, Torin thought. They had found the girls' kidnapper. He knew Maisie's exact location. At last, he had imprisoned the guilty Breccan in the dungeons. And yet how heavy his heart was. This day had dawned with hope, with his voice restored and plans coming together. One confession had now altered everything.

There was no triumph within him as he found Adaira sitting at her father's desk, writing a letter.

Torin watched her intently for a moment, as if she had changed. He tried to find traces of his enemy in the features of her face, in the color of her hair, in the sprawl of her handwriting. But she was his cousin. She was the same Adaira he had grown up protecting and adoring. He didn't care what blood she hailed from; he loved her and he would fight for her.

"I'm writing Innes Breccan," she said, dipping her quill into the ink. "I want you to read this letter after I'm done, to approve it."

Torin shifted his weight. "Very well. But you don't need my approval, Adi."

The sound of her nickname made her pause. He waited, hoping she would breathe, that she would *look* at him and tell him what was cascading through her mind. But Adaira continued with her writing.

Soon, she was finished. She stood and brought the letter to him.

Dear Innes,
The Heir of the West has trespassed into the east with ill intent.
I had no choice but to bring your son to the fortress, where he
will be held until we can settle an important matter between

*our two clans. I would like to meet you tomorrow at sunrise
at the northern signpost. I cannot ask you to come alone or
unarmed, but all the same, I ask for this exchange between us
to be peaceful. I don't desire to see blood shed or lives lost, even
as this matter is one that is driven by the fires of emotion.*

*I believe we can reach a settlement that will appease both of
our clans, face-to-face. I will await you tomorrow at first light.*

Respectfully yours,

Adaira Tamerlaine
LAIRD OF THE EAST

Torin sighed. "What is the settlement?"

"I'm not sure yet," Adaira replied. "I need to see how angry
Innes is going to be upon discovering that her son and heir is
imprisoned and guilty of stealing children, or relieved upon
learning that her lost daughter is indeed very much alive and
well."

Torin studied her face. She was staring at her written words,
held in his hands. He whispered, "Look at me, Adi."

She did. And he saw the fear in her eyes, as if she was waiting for him to reject her.

"I don't care whose blood you belong to," he said. "You're a
Tamerlaine, and that's the end of it."

She nodded, but he could tell she was struggling to find
comfort in his statement. "Whatever comes tomorrow, I think
we need to prepare for conflict at the clan line."

"I'll send the auxiliary forces," Torin said, handing her the
letter. "And yes, of course I approve your letter."

Adaira folded and sealed it. She pressed her signet ring into
the wax, marking the Tamerlaine crest.

Torin's breath caught when he saw that Adaira was removing the ring from her hand, still warm from the wax. He felt

the blood drain from his face when she approached him, the golden ring cupped in her palm. She extended it out to him, waiting for him to accept.

"What are you doing?" he growled at her. "I don't want this."

"I cannot lead this clan in good faith," she said. "Not knowing who I truly am."

"You're a Tamerlaine, Adi. One wild story from the enemy doesn't change that."

"No, it doesn't," she agreed sadly. "But it has pierced the hearts of the clan, and I no longer have their trust. They will listen to you, Torin. You saw what happened outside. You are their protector. You are of their blood. After I meet with Innes and the settlement is made tomorrow, I will announce that you have replaced me as laird, and hopefully the east will be at peace again."

Torin glared at her. Her edges were blurring; he blinked away his tears before they could fall. What was this *settlement* she continued to speak of? Why did the notion of it terrify him?

"Please, Torin," she whispered. "Take the ring."

He knew she was right. And he hated it.

He hated that their lives were breaking apart, and he was powerless to stop it.

He hated that she was stepping down.

He hated that he now had to carry this weight.

But he did as she asked. He followed her last order; he slipped the ring onto his finger.

Adaira retreated to her room. She locked the door and melted to the rug, weeping until she felt hollow. She lay there, longing for her parents as she watched the sunlight move across the floor with the passing hours.

Eventually, a rap sounded on her door, and she forced herself to stand.

Answering the knock with a hitch of anxiousness, Adaira was surprised to see two guards stationed at her threshold. She wasn't sure if they were there by Torin's orders, to protect her, or had been appointed to keep an eye on her. To prevent her from leaving.

"A letter has arrived for you," one of them said, extending the parchment.

Adaira knew it was Innes's reply. She accepted the letter and shut the door, breaking the seal. The Laird of the West's response was surprisingly terse:

I agree to your terms, Adaira. I will see you at dawn.

—I.L.B.

Adaira threw the letter into the fire. She watched it turn to ash until her red shawl caught her eye, draped over the back of her reading chair. Lorna had given her this plaid years ago. Her mother had asked Mirin to weave one of her secrets into the pattern.

Adaira was weary of secrets. She was weary of lies. She hated how she had worn one around her shoulders for years.

She gathered her plaid in her hands. It was soft, well worn from years of guarding her against the wind when she roamed the hills. She pulled at it with all the fury and anguish within her. The enchantment was gone, and the plaid tore apart in her hands.

It was late afternoon when auxiliary forces arrived to keep watch over the river in Mirin's valley. Jack needed to speak with Adaira. He left his mother and Frae under the protection of the East Guard and walked the hills to Sloane, slowly, as his body still felt weak. He had filed down the worn edges of his nails, but there was still a tremor in his hands. He wondered how long it would be before he could play again.

This entire day had been strange, almost dreamlike. As if an entire season had bloomed and died in a matter of hours.

Eventide was on the cusp of surrendering to a dark night and the shadows had grown thick at Jack's feet by the time he walked into Sloane.

He didn't know what to expect, but he was surprised by the animosity in the city. He walked through gossip and whispers, and most of it was about Adaira, about who she was and what the clan wanted to do about her. Some thought she had known who she was all along and had willingly fooled them. Some were sympathetic to her plight. Some thought she had been fraternizing with the enemy, beneath the guise of a trade, and should face a trial. Others thought she should abdicate her lairdship by sundown, but not before she ensured the safe return of the three girls.

Disconcerted, Jack went straight to Adaira's quarters by way of the main corridor, only to discover that guards were stationed there. He didn't know if they were present to protect her or keep her locked within. So Jack slipped into his chamber and used the secret passage to approach Adaira's room.

He stood in the cobwebbed shadows, gently knocking on the panel.

"Adaira?"

There was silence. Jack's hand was seeking the latch in the darkness when he heard the panel pop open. A thread of light spilled over him as Adaira opened the door.

She was wearing nothing more than a thin robe, and her hair was loose and damp, spilling across her shoulders. Jack stiffened; he could smell the fragrance of lavender and honey on her skin, and he glanced beyond her, to where a copper tub sat in the corner of the room.

"Am I interrupting you?" he whispered, lamenting his poor timing.

"I just finished. Come in, Jack." Adaira shifted, welcoming him inside, and Jack stepped over the threshold.

As a moment of silence passed between them, Jack found himself unable to look away from her. There were many things he wanted to share with her tonight, yet the sight of her so undressed had surprised him. She stole his attention entirely as she walked to the fire. Her feet were bare, her face was flushed, and her wet hair had left diaphanous patches on the front of her robe. Adaira had yet to truly look at him, to speak to him. It was as though she was alone as she reached for the bottle of wine on a hearthside table and poured herself a glass.

She broke the silence before he could. "I suppose you want our handfast revoked. I'll see to it first thing tomorrow."

"And why would I want that?" Jack countered.

His sharp tone drew her eyes. She stared at him, at last noticing how nice he looked. He had come to her wearing his best. His wedding raiment. "You didn't know you were marrying a Breccan," she drawled.

"No," he said gently. "I didn't know."

She narrowed her eyes at him and drained her wine. "What *I* know is that the people are talking about me. And it isn't good talk. You should distance yourself from me immediately, Jack. This cannot end well."

Jack stepped forward to catch her hand. Her fingers were hot in his, as if she were burning from within. He noticed the signet ring was gone, and he was swarmed with unspeakable sadness, sensing she had willingly removed it. He raised his eyes to meet hers. She was rigid, guarded. As if she was waiting to hear him reject her.

"Let them," he said. "Let them talk. All that matters in this moment is you and me and what we know is true."

She was surprised. He watched her remember, the memory flickering across her face. She had once said similar words to him, on the night she had bent a knee and proposed.

"You're scaring me, Jack."

"Have I smiled too much then?"

That drew a slight grin from her. But it swiftly faded. "Your reaction to this revelation . . . you should revile me. You should call me your enemy. You shouldn't want to hold my hand."

He only laced his fingers with hers, tugging her closer to him. "Do you think it matters to me where you were born, Adaira?"

"It should."

"Would it matter to you if I had been born in the west?"

She sighed. "Maybe once, long ago, I would have cared. But I've changed in a way I hardly recognize. I don't know who I am anymore."

Jack traced her cheek, tilting her chin up so she would look at him. "There are pieces missing from Moray Breccan's story. Vital pieces that I want you to know."

She was silent, expectant. Waiting for him to speak.

"The Keeper of the Aithwood could have returned you to your blood parents that fateful night," Jack began. "But to do so would mean he had broken a law, because he was given an order not to bring you back. He feared his life would be forfeit, as would yours.

"He found the river and stepped into it, disoriented from bleeding as he was, with you in his arms. He was going to take you home with him, to think about what he should do. The tree boughs danced above him, and the water guided him downstream, and it would seem all the spirits, even the stars that burned distantly in the sky, were leading him to the east. When he made the crossing, he stood in a valley and looked upward and saw a cottage on a hill, the firelight seeping through the shutters. Little did he know that a weaver lived there alone, young and lonely and married to secrets, and that she often remained awake, deep into the night, weaving at her loom.

"He chose to knock on her door, and she welcomed him inside, despite the fact that he wore a blue plaid at his shoulder and woad tattoos on his skin. She swiftly realized he held a babe, and he asked for the weaver's help. Mirin assisted him, and she said the moment she cradled you, her heart leapt in joy. She could scarcely understand it, but she said it was like finding a piece of herself that had been missing. And the keeper thought, here is a good woman who will love this lass as her own and give her the tender care she needs to survive. He left you with my mum, and they both swore to hold this secret between them, and he believed he would never cross through the river again.

"But he returned not a day later, to check on you and the dark-eyed weaver. He had learned the secret flaw of the clan line, that if he gave his blood to the river and walked in the water, he could pass undetected. And so he visited frequently, as if there were a cord tying him to that cottage on the hill, pulling him to the east. He was concerned, for you were still very small, and my mum didn't know much about newborn babes. She had no choice but to bring Senga Campbell into the arrangement, and the healer did all she could to help you grow.

"Senga told Mirin that the Laird and Lady of the East longed for a bairn, but she feared that Lorna Tamerlaine would have complications in her imminent delivery. The healer asked Mirin if she would give you up to them. And while my mum never wanted to surrender you—she had kept you a secret for several weeks—she agreed.

"Soon, Lorna's labor began. It was long and difficult, and

the babe was stillborn. Senga said they all wept in the birthing chamber. They wept and mourned in that hour, and Senga
thought the grief would crush them. But then Mirin brought
in a bundle of blankets. You wailed until my mother set you in
Lorna's weary arms. You fell silent and content, and my mum
says that's when she knew that you were supposed to belong to
them. Those who were gathered in that chamber decided they
would hold this secret of your origins and let the clan believe
you were Alastair and Lorna's blood-born daughter.

"You belonged to them, in love and in vows. They didn't
care if your ancestry was of the west. You healed this clan and
gave them joy. You brought laughter and life into the once dismal corridors of the castle. You brought hope to the east.

"And my mum . . . she was at peace, even though she missed
you fiercely in the beginning. But little did she know that she
would have her own son only eight months later."

He paused, surprised by how his voice wavered. Adaira
raised her hand and laid it against the arch of his cheek, and he
knew she was beginning to see him as he saw her. The threads
that held them together.

"My father was the Keeper of the Aithwood. It was he who
brought you into the east, where he knew you would be safe
and loved," said Jack. It was liberating to speak those forbidden
words aloud. The weight slipped from his chest like a stone,
and he shivered to feel the space it left behind, waiting to be
filled. "From your life came mine. I would not exist if you had
been born in the east. I am but a verse inspired by your cho-
rus, and I will follow you until the end, when the isle takes my
bones and my name is nothing more than a remembrance on a
headstone, next to yours."

Adaira smiled, tears shining in her eyes. Jack waited for her
to break the silence that welled, a bright and heady moment

that could morph into anything. He waited, knowing they could claim this day as their own. Fully and unapologetically, with all of its blood, agony, and windswept secrets. The wounds and the scars and the uncertainty of the future.

"*Jack,*" she said at last, drawing him into her embrace.

Jack breathed her in, hiding his face in the soft, quicksilver waves of her hair.

Adaira invited him to remain with her that night. She sensed no expectations within Jack, only his contentment. Contentment to be in her company, shut away from the spinning world beyond the chamber, if only for a span of a few starlit hours.

She still marveled over his words, words that bound them closer than spoken vows had done.

She opened one of the windows, welcoming a warm summer night into the chamber. For a moment, she could fool herself. Gazing out over the darkened isle, she believed her father still lived, that he could be found in the library by the fire, her mother close beside him with her harp, plucking a waterfall of notes. For a moment, she was Adaira Tamerlaine and she had always belonged to the east.

But the imagining faded into ash when she realized she didn't want such a life anymore. She wanted the truth. She wanted to feel it brush against her skin, wanted to claim it with her hands. She wanted honesty, even if it felt like claws raking across her soul.

When she turned around, Jack was watching her. A sultry breeze slipped into the chamber, stirring Adaira's long, unbound hair.

"It feels strange," she whispered. "To not know which side I belong to."

"You belong to both," he replied. "You are the east as you are the west. You are mine as I am yours."

She walked to meet him in the heart of the room, where the shadows danced on the floor.

Jack eased the knot holding her robe. His deft hand slipped beneath it, touching her faintly at first, reverence in his eyes. His thumb left a trail of gooseflesh on her skin. And then he kissed her with an intensity that shook all holiness from her, sparking a passion she had been longing for, and she knew she had found her match in him as they edged toward the bed. They followed an urgent beat at first, one punctuated with gasps and shed garments and their names tangling together, as if time would expire on them. But then Jack drew slightly away so he could fully behold her on the bed beneath him, his hand fanning over her ribs. His half of the coin caught the light, hanging from a long chain about his neck.

"Whatever comes in the days ahead, I am with you," he said. "If you want to go to the mainland, I will take you there. If you want to remain in the east, so will I. And if you want to venture into the west, let me be at your side."

She could hardly find the breath to speak. She nodded, and Jack kissed her palm, the cold scar from his truth blade. He slowed their pace, as if he wanted to savor each moment of their joining. His gaze lingered on hers as he found a new rhythm between them, a song they could lose themselves within, and Adaira felt as if he were drawing music from her bones.

The candles burned down into wax remnants; the fire crackled into blue embers. Soon it was just the constellations, the moon, and a gentle wind blowing through the window. The wings of a western spirit. Adaira and Jack, wholly consumed and gleaming, fell asleep entwined in her sheets.

CHAPTER 27

Frae was dreaming of the river. She was standing in it, uncertain if she should follow the water downstream or go against the current to reach home. She saw Moray in the distance, walking toward her.

"Come with me, Fraedah," he said, and her heart beat with fear.

She turned to run, but the water made her slow, and she knew he was going to catch her.

"Frae," he growled.

She was afraid to look over her shoulder. His voice was changing, though. It sounded strange when he spoke again, and she realized the dream was breaking.

"Frae? *Frae*, wake up."

She startled, opening her eyes to find Mirin hovering above her. It was dark, and for a moment Frae was confused. But then she heard the noise beyond the shutters, beyond the walls of their home. The clash of swords, shouts, and grunts. Horses whinnying, the thump of hooves on the ground. Sounds of pain and fury.

"Mum?" Frae whispered, and terror spun a chill through her. *"Mum!"*

"Shh," Mirin said, stroking Frae's hair. "Remember the rules?" She took Frae's hand and drew her from the bed. Mirin had laid Frae's enchanted plaid on the bench, and the sword was already belted to her waist, as if she had been ready for this night.

Frae waited as her mother knotted the plaid over her chest, to protect her heart.

Without a word, Mirin led her into the common room, to the corner by the hearth, where the fire flickered. Frae sat first, and then her mother unsheathed the sword and settled in front of her like a shield. *This is nothing more than a dream,* Frae thought, leaning into Mirin's back. But over her mother's shoulder, she could dimly see the chamber, the shadows and the firelight that fought each other. The violent sounds grew louder, closer, and Frae began to cry.

"We are safe here, Frae," Mirin said, but her voice was hoarse, and there was fear buried within it. "Don't cry, my love. We are strong; we are brave. And this will be over soon."

Frae wanted to believe her. But her thoughts became a roar, and all she could think was, *This is just a dream. Wake up! Wake up . . .*

The back door blew open.

The Breccan warriors spilled into the house like a flood, their blue plaids the color of the sky just before dawn. Frae clung to Mirin and watched as they searched the house. They took note of Frae and her mother in the corner, the sword in Mirin's hands, but the Breccans didn't approach them.

Frae recognized Captain Torin stepping into the house,

blood streaming down his face. One of the Breccans held a dirk to his throat.

This was bad. This was very bad, Frae thought, and she whimpered and buried her face in Mirin's hair.

It suddenly grew quiet and still in the house, as if ice had formed. Frae lifted her head to see what had inspired this strange reverence.

A tall man stood in the chamber. He was dressed like the other Breccans, but there was something different about him. His face was softer, kinder. His hair was red like fire. Like copper. Like her own, Frae realized, and grabbed the end of her braid. His hands were bound behind him, and Frae wondered what he had done to become a prisoner of his own kind.

The man stared at Mirin, anguished.

Frae could hear her mother's breath catch. The sword clattered from her hands, and Frae tugged on Mirin's chemise, thinking she shouldn't have dropped it.

"Mum!" Frae whispered, tremulous.

But she sensed her mother was far away as she stared at the Breccan and the Breccan stared at her.

"Mirin," the man said. Her name was sweet in his voice, as if he had spoken it many times before, as a whisper, as a prayer. "*Mirin.*"

Frae was astounded. Her mother knew him?

Frae felt his gaze shift to her, and she couldn't fight the draw of his stare. He looked different in the firelight, but she recognized him with a gasp. He had stood in the yard weeks ago. It had been him she had seen, the man who had visited the garden with his horse, staring at the cottage by starlight.

He began to weep as he looked at Frae. Deep, broken sounds emerged from him. They made Frae's tears surge again, and she didn't know why it felt like someone had punched her.

"You've looked upon them both," a Breccan with a scar on

his face said to the red-haired man, "as per our agreement. And the legends will remember you not as a keeper, not as a man of valor and strength, but as a fool. They will call you traitor to your clan, Niall Breccan. Oath breaker." He motioned to the men gathered around him. "Now take him back and lock him in the keep."

Three Breccan warriors surrounded the weeping man. They drew him away, and before Frae could wipe the blurriness from her eyes, he was gone, dragged from the house.

Gone, as if he had never been.

Mirin flinched, as though she wanted to follow him. She began to lean forward, her hands reaching outward, her breaths turning fast and shallow. Frae's terror swarmed. She clung to her mother's arm, holding her back.

The Breccan with the scar on his face began to walk around the chamber. He studied Mirin's loom, running his grimy fingers over it. He studied the dried wildflower chain hanging from the hearth. His eyes then settled on Mirin and Frae, and he smiled. "This house will do just fine for the exchange. The winds work here as they do in the west, don't they? Tell the captain to summon Cora. Or should I call her Adaira for now?"

Torin was hauled up to his feet and dragged out the front door into the garden.

Frae hunched in her corner, holding tightly to Mirin as she cried. She was frightened until she thought of Adaira, and she wiped away her tears and her runny nose. She had heard the mean Breccan's story yesterday, when he had been bound to the chair. She had heard every word, even though she struggled to fully understand what it meant.

But there was one thing that Frae did know, and it settled over her like a warm plaid.

Adaira would come. Adaira would save them.

Torin stood in Mirin's garden, a blade shining at his throat.

"Summon her," the Breccan ordered.

Torin couldn't form a coherent thought. Blood continued to drip from his beard, and he felt dazed. They had arrived so swiftly by river. The Breccans had overcome him and his guards with hardly any effort. And even though he had been prepared for the worst—for the Breccans to descend in their customary way—Torin had been bested.

The defeat spread through him like a disease, softening him from the inside out. He could hardly stand upright.

"Summon her," the Breccan said again, shifting the dirk so Torin could feel its sting against his neck.

Torin gazed at the stars. When he felt the wind pass by, he spoke her name, and he put the last of his hope into the sound.

"Adaira."

Adaira stirred, uncertain what had woken her. Jack lay close, his breaths deep with dreams, his arm draped across her waist. She listened to the crackling silence and watched the curtains billow in the slight breeze. The night felt serene, and she languidly shifted, her legs sliding along Jack's.

Her eyes were closing when she heard it again. Torin's voice, calling for her.

Adaira stiffened.

She knew Torin was stationed at the river. If he was summoning her, then the Breccans must have come in the night, disregarding the agreement she had with Innes. Which meant they had arrived with vengeance.

"Jack," Adaira said, sitting up. His arm was heavy; his hand glided across her stomach. "Jack, wake up."

He groaned. "Adaira?"

"Torin's summoning me."

Jack went still, listening as the wind carried Torin's voice a third and final time.

"Is he on my mother's lands?" he asked.

"Yes," Adaira said. "We need to ride there immediately."

Jack launched himself from the bed, scrambling in the dark to find his trail of clothes on the floor. Adaira rushed to light a candle and opened her wardrobe. She decided to dress for potential battle and grabbed a woolen tunic, a leather jerkin studded with metal, and an enchanted plaid woven of brown and red. She had a moment of grief as she pinned the plaid at her shoulder. It might be the last time she wore these colors, and she swallowed the lump in her throat as she hastened to tether her boots up to her knees.

"Were there guards at my door when you arrived?" she asked, glancing across the room at Jack as he also finished dressing.

Jack met her gaze. "Yes."

"They might not let me leave."

"You're serious?" Jack sounded angry. "Even under Torin's orders?"

Adaira nodded, motioning for Jack to align himself with the wall, out of sight. He did so, and Adaira steeled herself as she unbolted and cracked open her door.

One of the guards turned to look at her.

"Will you stand aside and let me pass?" Adaira asked.

"We have orders to ensure you stay in your chamber until further notice," he said.

"Is this my cousin's order?"

The guard was silent, choosing not to answer her. Adaira knew Torin would never lock her in her room and offered the guard a watery smile. They had lost faith in her, and she tried to ease the pain of this revelation as she shut the door.

Jack had already opened the panel of the secret passage. She grabbed her cloak, knowing she needed to conceal her hair, and drew up the hood, following him into his quarters.

"I doubt they will let me request a horse from the stables," she said to Jack. "You'll have to do it. I can find a way out of the castle walls and meet you by Una's forge."

Jack hesitated. She could sense his reluctance in the dark, to be separated from her.

"All right," he said. "I'll find you there." He kissed her brow before they slipped out into the corridor.

They rushed through the winding, quiet hallways of the castle, going their separate ways when they reached the lower level. Jack headed to the stables, and Adaira turned to the southern wing of the castle. She stepped into the moonlit garden and moved soundlessly over the flagstone pathways. Passing the door that led to Lorna's turret, she found the hidden egress in the wall, covered in ivy.

She and Torin had found this secret passage when they were young and bored one summer. Or rather, Adaira had discovered it and eventually consented to show Torin when he realized she had been sneaking out of the fortress without notice from the guard. It led directly to the castle wall and another hidden door that would spill her out close to Una's forge.

Adaira followed it now, her hands reaching out in the dark. The corridor was narrow and cold, and the air smelled like damp earth and stones. She eventually reached the end. The door cracked open, and she entered a side street of Sloane.

She found Una's forge, darkened with sleep, and waited in the shadows for Jack.

He arrived moments later, astride her favorite horse. He shifted, making space for her, and Adaira mounted, settling in the saddle before him.

His arms wound tightly about her as she took the reins.

She rode through the city, a trace of fog in the streets. Once free of Sloane, Adaira diverged from the road, choosing to go by hill. The folk lent their aid, just as she hoped. Four hills became one, and fifteen kilometers became five. The eastern wind came behind her and Jack, blowing at their backs as if they were a vessel on the sea.

The horse was lathered by the time she finally saw Mirin's lights in the distance. Adaira let the mare walk to cool down. She took those precious minutes to mentally prepare herself for the meeting, to run her fingers through her tangled hair. She didn't know what she would find inside the house, but if everything played out as she had planned, then she had nothing to fear. She unsaddled the horse beneath an oak tree before she and Jack approached the house on foot with trepidation.

Jack's hand found hers, lacing their fingers together.

As they drew nearer, Adaira could discern figures standing in the yard. Breccan warriors. They had the cottage surrounded, and off to the side toward the byre was a ring of them, illumined by torches. Adaira slowed her pace. The East Guard and the watchmen must have been overcome, and while she didn't see any bodies lying on the ground, she sensed they were all held captive.

"Halt," a voice commanded her, breaking the tense silence.

Adaira returned her attention to the yard gate and stopped. Two Breccans aggressively stepped forward to meet her, but as soon as they saw her face by moonlight, their stances changed, softening.

"It is her," one of them said, lowering his sword. "Let her pass to the door."

She resumed her walk, drawing Jack in her wake. She felt the Breccans' gaze on her shoulders, on her hair, as tangible as the wind. All too soon, she reached the front door, and her hand shook as she touched the iron handle.

It swung open, and Adaira stepped into the firelight.

She was overwhelmed by the sight that greeted her. A sea of blue plaids. Mirin and Frae cowering in a corner. Torin on his knees with a dirk shining at his throat.

Innes wasn't present, and it soon became clear that a scar-faced Breccan with matted blond hair was in charge.

"Cora," he said to her, granting her half a bow. "It is good of you to come."

Adaira stared at him coldly. "Where is your laird?"

"She's not here. We've come to settle this matter with you, since word has spread that you are holding our heir in your dungeons."

"I won't settle anything with you," Adaira said. "Call your laird. She is the one I will speak with."

The blond smiled. His upper teeth were rotten. "Come now, Cora," he crooned. "This will be a simple exchange, one that we can do without bloodshed."

She was silent. From the corner of her eye, she watched as Jack knelt with Mirin and Frae in the corner.

"Your brother is intent on seeing you home safely," the Breccan continued. "If you will release him from the dungeons and follow him into the west, we will bring the three Tamerlaine lasses back to you."

Torin winced. Adaira glanced at her cousin. She could read the defeat in his face as a small tendril of blood began to stain his throat. She had never seen her cousin vanquished, and the sight alarmed her.

"I won't negotiate with you," she said, returning her gaze to the Breccan. "Summon your laird. I will only make an arrangement with Innes."

"If you refuse to settle with us," he said, waving his hand toward Torin, "then we'll slit the captain's throat."

"Then you would be slitting the Laird of the East's throat," Adaira said calmly. "And I will see to it that Moray's head is sent back to the west by sunrise."

The Breccan paused, brow arched. The realization dawned on him, and his smile deepened. Adaira had given up her power, which meant she must not plan to stay in the east. He turned to one of his men and said, "Ride to the west and bring our laird back with you."

The warrior nodded and slipped out the door.

The period of waiting felt like a year. The silence roared, but Adaira didn't move or speak. She remained rooted to the floor, waiting for her mother to arrive.

At last, the door creaked open.

Innes stepped into the house, dressed for war.

"What has happened here?" the laird demanded, but the frown on her face eased when she looked at Adaira.

Their gazes met. Everything around them melted into obscurity as Adaira studied Innes and Innes studied Adaira, the emotion rising like a wave coming to shore. Adaira swallowed it down, holding it deep in her chest as she began to see all the features she had stolen from her mother. Her hair, her sharpness, her eyes. She wondered how she hadn't noticed it before, when they met on the northern road.

"Did you know?" Adaira whispered, unable to help herself. "Did you know who I was when I saw you last?"

Innes was quiet, but a flicker of pain passed over her expression. "I knew."

Things came together in Adaira's mind. She now understood why Innes was so quick to apologize for the raid. Why she had brought the Elliotts' winter stores back, including an overpayment of gold. She had known Adaira was her lost daughter, and she had sought peace with her.

"Then you also knew that Moray was stealing Tamerlaine daughters?" Adaira dared to continue. "That your son was kidnapping and holding innocent lasses in the west while their parents mourned for them in the east?"

Innes's frown deepened. For a moment, Adaira was terrified of her as the laird's gaze swept the room, landing on the scar-faced Breccan. "I was not aware of this. Is this true, Derek?"

Derek seemed to shrink as he said, "It is, laird. Moray sought justice for you and your family. For our clan."

Innes's hand shot out to strike him. Her leather bracer caught Derek in the mouth, and he stumbled back, blood drooling from his lips.

"You have acted without my permission," she said in an icy tone, glancing around the chamber at the other Breccans. "All of you have let my son lead you astray, and you will pay for these crimes in the arena." Innes paused, bringing her attention back to Adaira. "I apologize for this pain. I will see it rectified."

"Thank you," Adaira whispered. "I would also ask to see the blade removed from the throat of the Laird of the East."

Innes glanced at the Breccan holding the dirk at Torin's throat. Her shock was only noticeable for a split second before her expression became pointed, and the warrior released Torin with a slight shove. It took everything within Adaira not to rush to her cousin and help him to his feet. She could only watch as Torin stood and limped across the room, coming to stand behind her.

"You wrote to me of a settlement," Innes said.

Adaira nodded. "Moray trespassed yesterday morning with the intent to steal another lass. He has committed crimes against the Tamerlaine clan, and although he is your heir, the east will want to hold him in chains to pay for his sins."

"I understand," Innes said in a careful tone. "But I cannot return to my clan empty handed."

"No," Adaira agreed. She could feel the perspiration dampen her skin as she prepared her next statement. She hadn't spoken of it to anyone. Not Torin. Not Sidra. Not Jack. It had come to her the moment she had ripped apart her old shawl. She didn't need counsel; she knew what she wanted, and yet it still was difficult to acknowledge aloud. "If you will see that the three Tamerlaine lasses are safely returned within the hour, then I will follow you into the west. You can take me as a prisoner if you prefer, or as the daughter you lost. I will agree to remain with you and serve you and the west, so long as Moray remains shackled in the east. He won't be harmed in his time of service, but the Tamerlaines will be the ones to determine how long he is to remain imprisoned, and when he is to walk free again."

Innes was pensive, her gaze on Adaira. Adaira waited, uncertain if she had just insulted the laird or if she was genuinely considering her offer. The silence deepened. It was the hour just before dawn, and a chill had crept into the room. But at last Innes reached out her hand.

"I agree to those terms. Take my hand, Adaira, and we will seal this agreement."

"Laird!" Derek protested. "You can't give our heir up to the east, leaving him to be shackled like an animal."

Innes's eyes riveted on him. "Moray acted without my permission. His fate is of his own making."

Derek drew his sword. Adaira felt Torin grab her arm and haul her backward as Innes responded, unsheathing her blade. The laird was quick; the firelight flashed on the steel as she effortlessly dodged Derek's cut, granting him a mortal wound in return.

Adaira watched in cold numbness as Derek gasped, falling

to his knees. The blood poured from his neck, staining Mirin's rug, as he succumbed to the floor.

"Are there any others who defy me?" Innes taunted, looking at Moray's warriors. "Step forward."

The Breccans were still, watching Derek breathe his last.

Adaira could hear Frae crying in the corner, and Jack's hushed whispers as he comforted her. She stared at the pool of blood on the floor, wondering what sort of life awaited her in the west.

"I agree to your settlement, Adaira," Innes said again. With one hand, she held her sword, but she stretched out her other. Speckled with blood and waiting for Adaira to take it.

"You don't have to do this, Adi," Torin murmured. His grip on her arm was like iron.

"No, but I want to, Torin," she softly replied. She wasn't sure where her home was anymore. She wasn't certain where she belonged, but she knew she would find her answer once she had beheld the west. The land of her blood.

Torin reluctantly released her.

Adaira stepped forward. She held out her hand, but just before her palm could touch Innes's, she said, "I would like for there to be peace on the isle. If I come with you into the west, I would like the raids on Tamerlaine lands to cease."

The laird studied her with eyes that suddenly looked old and weary. Adaira wondered if peace was only an illusion, and if she was naïve to still hope for it.

"I can make you no promises, Adaira," Innes said. "But perhaps your presence in the west, where you belong, will bring about the change you dream of."

It was the best answer Adaira could have expected in the moment. She nodded, and her heart quickened as she took her mother's hand. Firm and strong, scarred and lean.

Years had been lost between them. Years that could never

be regained. And yet who would Adaira be if she had never left the west? If her birth parents hadn't surrendered her to the forces of the isle?

She caught a glimpse of herself, marked in blue and blood. Cold and sharp.

Adaira shivered.

Innes noticed.

Their hands fell away, but the world had changed between them.

The laird's demeanor was collected as she looked at Moray's warriors. But Adaira heard the catch of emotion in Innes's voice when she said, "Return the lasses to the east."

CHAPTER 28

Sidra knelt in Graeme's yard as the sun rose. The wind was silent that morning. Only the light strengthened, burning away the last of the mist. Sidra savored the stillness as she watched the world awaken around her. But her heart soon grew heavy as she beheld the garden. The glamour was gone, and she saw the damage she had wrought weeks ago.

She began to gently uproot the weeds and broken stalks. She would have to replant, and she was preparing the soil for new seeds when she heard a distant sound. It was Torin's voice, calling her name.

"Sidra?"

She rose, searching for him. She was alone in the yard, although the front door to Graeme's cottage was open, and she could smell the first aromas of breakfast as he cooked.

"Sidra!"

Torin's voice was louder now, and she walked through the garden, slipping past the gate. She arrived at the crest of the hill and looked down toward her lands.

Torin was walking up the path, Maisie on his hip.

A sound escaped from Sidra. The break of a sob. She covered her mouth with her dirt-streaked hand just as Maisie caught sight of her. The girl flailed and kicked, eager to be free of her father's hold, and Torin set her down.

Maisie began to run up the winding path in the heather. Sidra rushed to meet her, falling to her knees and opening her arms.

"Oh, my darling," Sidra whispered as Maisie embraced her neck. She caressed the child's curls, breathing her in. She wondered if she was dreaming and said, "Let me look at you, my heart."

She leaned back to study Maisie's face, rosy from the chilled morning. Her eyes were still wide and brown, full of light and curiosity. She had lost another tooth while she was away, and Sidra didn't realize she was weeping until Maisie solemnly laid her palm to her cheek.

Sidra smiled, even as her tears fell. She held her daughter close to her chest, hiding her face in Maisie's wispy hair. She could sense Torin's presence as he reached them. He slowly lowered himself to the ground, his warmth seeping into her side.

"Don't cry, Mummy," Maisie said, patting her shoulder.

Sidra wept even harder.

The girls returned home on a blue sky day.

The southern wind was warm and gentle, and the wildflowers bloomed in the fullness of the rising sun. The heather danced on the breeze with violet abandon. The tide was low on the shores, the lochs glistened, and the rivers flowed. The hills were quiet, and the roads were like threads of gold in a green plaid as Adaira rode with the guard, bringing Catriona home to her parents on the coast, and Annabel home to her parents in the vale.

She sat on her horse and watched with a smile as the families were reunited. There were many tears and kisses and much laughter, and Adaira felt a weight slip from her shoulders. This is how it should be, and she hoped the isle would find balance once more.

The parents thanked the guard for bringing their daughters home safely, but they didn't even glance at Adaira. It was as though she had already departed from the east, and Adaira tried to swallow the hurt she felt. She reminded herself that, if not for her, the lasses would have never been stolen to begin with. In some deep way, she faulted herself for the pain of the clan, even though she hadn't known the truth.

She wondered if Alastair and Lorna ever planned to reveal to her who she truly was. Part of her thought not, since they had carried the secret to their graves. Adaira tried to cast away the feelings of betrayal and sadness. Today was a day when she needed to be as composed as one of Jack's ballads. She needed to follow the notes she had laid down for herself without emotion getting the best of her.

The guards escorted her back to the castle. She had until noontide to restore order, officially pass the lairdship to Torin, and pack. Innes was to meet her by Mirin's river, and the exchange would then be complete.

Adaira stood in her chamber, inwardly lost. She glanced at the bed, unmade and rumpled from her lovemaking with Jack. The window was still open, the breeze sighing into the room. Though she didn't know what to take with her, she slowly began to pack a leather bag. A few dresses, a few books. She was halfway done when a knock sounded on her door.

"Come in."

Torin stepped inside, trailed by Sidra and Maisie.

Adaira dropped her bag as Maisie dashed to her. She had

seen Maisie briefly when the girls were returned, but now Adaira had the chance to scoop her up in an embrace, warmed by how fiercely Maisie held to her, as if she didn't care who Adaira was now. Maisie's arms wrapped about her neck, healing a fracture in Adaira's heart.

"Maisie!" Adaira said with a smile. "The bravest lass in all the east!"

Maisie smiled, loosening her hold a bit. But her excitement faded when she said, "Mummy says you have to go away."

Adaira's smile froze on her face. "Yes, I'm afraid so."

"To the west?"

Adaira glanced at Sidra and Torin, neither of whom offered any guidance on how she should answer. They were all taking this hour by hour, moment by moment. None of them knew what the girls had experienced in the west, even though they appeared to have been treated gently. "Yes, Maisie. So I need you to look after your mum and da for me while I'm gone. Can you do that?"

Maisie nodded. "I have something for you." Her little hand shot out to Torin, and he set a battered, coverless book on her palm.

"What's this?" Adaira asked in a hushed tone.

"Stories," Maisie said. "About the spirits."

"Did you write them, Maisie?"

"It was Joan Tamerlaine's book," Torin said, drawing Adaira's eyes. "My father gave it to me, and we thought . . . we want to give it to you. He claims the other half is in the west. Perhaps you will find it there?"

Adaira nodded, suddenly overcome. She hugged Maisie close and kissed her cheeks. "Thank you for the book. I will read it every night."

"Elspeth will like the stories too," Maisie said, wiggling.

Adaira released her, wondering who Elspeth was. But she didn't ask, and Sidra stepped forward next with a handful of vials.

"For wounds," she began, holding up a glass brimming with dried herbs. "For sleep." Sidra held up another. "For your headaches. And for cramps."

Adaira smiled, accepting all four. "Thank you, Sid."

"If there's anything else you need while you're there," Sidra said, "let me know and I'll send it to you."

"I will."

Sidra embraced her, just as fiercely as Maisie had, and it was all Adaira could do not to cry.

"The clan is gathering in the hall for the announcement," Torin said, clearing his throat. "I'll wait for you there."

Adaira nodded as Sidra released her to gather Maisie in her arms. The girl waved to Adaira just before they slipped out the door, and Adaira was thankful for the silence again. Holding the broken book and the herbs, she cried.

She was wiping her tears, setting the gifts into her bag, when she heard the unmistakable click of a wall panel opening. She stiffened. She had left Jack at Mirin's, thinking he needed to be with his mother and sister in the wake of the Breccans' invasion of their home.

"Jack?" she said, afraid to turn and see that it might not be him.

"Should I bring the old, twisted harp or not?" his voice sounded, wryly.

Adaira spun to see him holding a bag. "What are you doing?"

Jack stepped into her room, shutting the secret door behind him. "What does it look like I'm doing? I'm coming with you."

"You don't have to do that," she protested, even as her heart softened in relief.

He walked across the floor to reach her, eventually coming to a stop when only a breath was between them. "But I want to, Adaira."

"What of your mother? What of Frae?" she whispered.

"They're both strong and shrewd and have lived a number of years just fine without me," he said, holding her gaze. "I'll miss them while we're away, but I'm not bound to them. I belong to you."

Adaira sighed. She wanted him to come with her, but she also had a strange, restless feeling about it. Something she couldn't name, echoing like a warning in her mind.

"You think you're dragging me away from a life here," he said, tracing her jaw with his fingertips, "but you forget that the west is also mine by half."

His father was there, Adaira reminded herself. Jack had roots on the other side of the clan line, just as she did. Of course, he would want to explore them.

"All right," she breathed. "You can come."

Jack's smile crinkled the corners of his eyes, and she thought he had never seemed brighter. She saw a flicker of light in him, like a flame burning in a dark night, just as his lips found hers.

The hall was overflowing, waiting for her.

Adaira didn't want to draw this out. She wanted to say her piece and leave, and she hoped the Tamerlaines would listen to her now that the girls had been safely returned and Moray Breccan was shackled beneath their feet.

Torin waited for her on the dais. She walked to her cousin, Jack close behind her. She stood at Torin's side and surveyed the sea of faces who watched her.

"My good people of the east," Adaira began in a wavering tone. "The story you heard on the wind is true. I was born to the Laird of the West but was brought in secret to the east as a bairn. Alastair and Lorna raised me as their own, and I didn't know the truth of my heritage until Moray Breccan revealed it to me yesterday.

"As such, I am no longer fit to lead you, and I pass the lairdship to one who is worthy of you. Torin has proven himself as an exceptional leader and will guide you now. I have all faith that he will continue to lead the clan to better days.

"In parting, I reached a settlement with the west, an agreement which I hope will bring peace to the isle. Moray Breccan is to remain shackled in your prison for kidnapping the daughters of the east until you deem him fit to walk free again. Because he is in the east, I must go to the west. I leave you all today, and I want you to know that I will continue to hold each of you dearly in my memories and in the highest regard, even if I am never afforded the chance to walk among you again.

"May you continue to be prosperous, and may the spirits bless the east."

Murmurs wove through the crowd. Adaira could hardly bear gazing at her old friends. Some of them looked sad, others were nodding in relief. Once, she had been great among them. Beloved and adored. Now she was regarded in various shades of sorrow, disgust, and disbelief.

So much had changed in a day.

She had spoken her last words to them, and the ring of power was on Torin's hand. Her cousin walked with her across the dais, escorting her through one of the secret doors. Jack was on her heels, but before they could slip away, one of the people shouted, "What about Jack? The bard is ours now. Is he staying?"

Adaira hesitated, glancing at him.

Jack's eyes widened. His surprise was evident, but he turned to look at the clan. "I go where she goes."

"Then you'll be playing for the west?" a woman called in anger. "You'll be playing for our enemies?"

"Don't answer that, Jack," Torin warned under his breath. "Come, let's go."

But Jack stood on the threshold and said in a clear voice, "I play for Adaira and Adaira alone."

Adaira was still reeling from his response by the time they emerged in the courtyard. Two horses stood tacked and ready on the moss-spangled flagstones.

"Can you send word to me when you arrive safely?" Torin asked once she was settled in the saddle.

"Yes, I'll let you know," Adaira replied, gathering the reins. She didn't know how to say goodbye to Torin. She felt like a part of her was being ripped away, and she drew a deep breath when he squeezed her foot.

"I'm sorry, Adi," he whispered, gazing up at her.

She met his stare. Her head was throbbing from all the tears she had swallowed. "It's not your fault, Torin."

"You will always have a home here with me and Sidra," he said. "You don't have to stay in the west. When Moray Breccan is released one day . . . I hope to see you return to us."

She nodded, but she had never felt more adrift in her life. As much as she longed to catch a glimpse of her future, the path ahead of her was murky. She didn't know if she would remain with her blood, if the east would one day draw her back, or if she would leave Cadence altogether.

She urged the horse forward, and Torin's hand fell away. She didn't say goodbye to him.

Torin had never liked farewells.

With the sun reaching its zenith in the sky, Adaira and Jack took to the eastern hills one last time.

Innes Breccan had yet to arrive by river.

Adaira and Jack dismounted from their horses, then decided to wait for the laird inside with Mirin and Frae.

The rug that Derek had bled to death on had been rolled up and removed, but Adaira could still taste a trace of death in the air. Mirin had opened all of the shutters, welcoming the southern breeze.

"Would you like some tea, Adaira?" Mirin offered. Her face was haggard and ashen, and her voice rasped like a ghost's. She looked worse than Adaira had ever seen her, and it sent a pang of worry through her.

"No, but thank you, Mirin," Adaira replied.

Mirin nodded and returned to her loom, but she seemed hung in a web, unable to weave. Frae was clinging to Jack's legs, and Adaira was trying not to watch them as Jack prepared his sister for a long absence.

"I don't want you to go," Frae cried. Her sobs filled the cottage, slipping beyond the windows, a contrast to the bright sunshine and warm summer day.

"Listen to me, Frae," Jack said gently. "I need to be with—"

"*Why* do you have to go? Why can't you stay here with me and Mum?" Frae said, her words smudged by her tears. "You *promised* me you'd be here all summer, Jack. That you wouldn't leave!"

Her wails were painful to listen to. Adaira suddenly couldn't breathe. The walls were closing in on her, and she slipped out the back door, panting. She closed her eyes, steadying herself, but she could still hear Frae ask, "When will you be back?" and Jack reply with a hesitant, "I'm not sure, Frae." Which inspired another round of weeping from the girl, as if her heart had broken.

Adaira couldn't bear it. She walked through the gate and sat in the grass, her legs trembling. She had been so certain just an hour ago that Jack should come with her. But now that she had seen Mirin's deterioration and Frae's distress . . . Adaira thought she should convince him to stay. The clan wanted him and his music. His family needed him.

She would be fine on her own.

She was absently staring at the distant forest when Innes and a trio of guards appeared. Their horses splashed through the river and onto the bank, approaching at a walk.

This is it, Adaira thought, rising. *This is the end and the beginning.*

Her heart was beating vibrantly in her chest as her mother's horse came to a halt on the hill. Innes's eyes swept over her, as if she could see the tears and the heartache that Adaira hid beneath her skin.

"Are you ready to come with me?" the laird asked.

"Yes," Adaira replied. "My husband Jack would like to accompany me, if you approve."

Innes arched a fair brow, but if she was annoyed at the thought, she hid it well. "Of course. So long as he knows life in the west is far different than it is in the east."

"I do know, and I go willingly," Jack said.

Adaira turned to find him standing in the garden, his bag slung across his shoulders and his ruined harp tucked beneath his arm. Mirin and Frae remained on the threshold to see him off, the lass weeping into her mother's skirts.

Jack moved forward to stand beside her, and that's when Adaira noticed that a change had come over Innes. The laird was regarding Jack with cold, narrow eyes.

Adaira's breath caught. Did Innes know that Jack was the son of the keeper? The son of the man who had given her daughter away? Suddenly, those earlier feelings of foreboding returned, like a strong tide rushing around her ankles. Adaira didn't know if Jack would be safe if the Breccans came to know of his true heritage. She was a moment away from drawing

Jack into a private space, to tell him to keep his paternal link a secret, when Innes dismounted.

"I would like a word with you, Adaira," the laird said. Her tone was reserved but heavy. Adaira felt herself bend to its command, and she saw the storehouse, a few paces away.

"We can speak there," she said, and Jack shot her an uneasy look as she led Innes into the small, round building.

The air was warm, dusty. Once, not long ago, Adaira had stood in this very place with Jack.

"Your husband's a bard?" Innes said tersely.

Adaira blinked in surprise. "Yes, he is."

Innes's brow furrowed.

Jack knew something was wrong.

He had felt it the moment Innes Breccan had looked at him, scrutinizing the harp in his hands.

He knew something was wrong, and yet he tried to keep his mood calm and expectant as he paced the yard, waiting for the laird and Adaira to emerge from the storehouse. Eventually, Innes stepped out and strode to her horse without granting him a second look. Adaira motioned for Jack to join her. Setting down his harp and dropping his bag, he walked to meet her inside the storehouse.

She shut the door behind him, enclosing them in the quiet space.

"What is it?" he demanded. "What's wrong?"

Adaira hesitated, but her eyes still held a trace of shock when they met his. "Innes just told me that music is forbidden in the west."

The words rolled off Jack. It took him two full breaths to comprehend them. "Forbidden?"

"Yes. No instruments, no singing," Adaira whispered, glancing away. "Bards haven't been welcomed among the Breccans in over two hundred years. I . . . I don't think you should—"

"Why?" he countered roughly. He knew what she was about to say to him, and he didn't want to hear it.

"She said that it upsets the folk," Adaira replied. "It causes storms. Fires. Floods."

Jack was silent, but his thoughts churned. He knew magic flowed brighter in the hands of mortals in the west, to the spirits' demise. The opposite of life in the east. He thought about how playing for the folk here had cost him threads of his health. He had never considered what it would be like to play for the spirits on the other side of the isle. Not until this moment, when he realized he could strum his music and sing for the west without cost. What power would spill from his hands.

"Then I'll leave my harp," he said, but his voice sounded strange. "I can't rightly play it warped anyways."

"Jack," Adaira whispered, sorrowful.

His heart turned cold at the sound. "Don't ask me to remain behind, Adaira."

"If you come with me," she said, "you'll have to deny who you are. You'll never play another instrument or sing another ballad. Not only would you have to surrender your first love, you would also be separated from your mother, who looks so frail I worry about how long she has left to live, and your sister, who is devastated to lose you and who might end up in the orphanage. The clan also longs for you to remain, and I'm sure that Torin would be—"

"The Tamerlaines don't know I'm Breccan by half," he said sharply. "I'm sure their opinion of me and my music will change rather quickly when that truth comes to light."

"And yet you might encounter far worse danger in the west, if the Breccans discover whose son you are."

Jack was silent.

Adaira sighed. She looked so weary and sad; she leaned on the wall, as if she couldn't stand upright on her own. Her breaths flowed fast and shallow, and Jack softened his voice, gently drawing her to him.

"I made a vow to you," he said, caressing her hair. "If you ask me to remain in the east while you are in the west . . . it will feel as if half of me has been torn away."

A sound escaped her; Jack could feel how she trembled.

"I worry that if you come with me," she said after a tense moment, "you will soon resent me. You will long for your family, and you will ache for your music. I'm unable to give you everything you need, Jack."

Her words struck him like a sword. Slowly, his hands fell away from her. Old feelings flared in him, the feelings he had carried as a boy, when he had felt unclaimed and unwanted.

"You want me to stay here then?" he said in a flat tone. "You don't want me to come with you?"

"I *want* you with me," Adaira said. "But not if it's going to destroy you."

Jack stepped back. The pain in his chest was crushing his lungs, and he struggled to breathe. He was angry at her, for her words held a faint ring of truth. He wanted to be with her, and yet he didn't want to be away from Mirin and Frae. He didn't want to surrender his music, all those years of discipline on the mainland going to rot, and yet he couldn't imagine surrendering Adaira.

Agonized, he met her gaze, and he saw that she was composed, just as she had been the first day he had seen her, weeks ago. Her guard was in place; her emotions were tamed. She had accepted this separation, and the distance suddenly yawned between them.

"As you wish then," he rasped.

She stared at him a long moment, and he thought she might change her mind. Perhaps she wasn't as firm in her beliefs as she sounded. Perhaps she could also taste the sour tang of regret and remorse that would haunt them from this decision, for years to come.

He watched as Adaira opened her mouth, but with a gasp, she caught her words, turned, and fled the storehouse, as if she couldn't bear to look upon him.

The sunlight poured in.

Jack stood frozen within its warmth until the pain boiled in his chest. He strode from the storehouse, looking for her.

Adaira was on her horse, following Innes and the western guards down the hill. Soon, she would melt into the woods and shadows. Jack fought the urge to chase after her.

He paused in the grass, waiting for Adaira to glance behind. To look at him one more time. If she did, he would follow her into the west. His heart was beating in his throat as his eyes remained fixed on her. The long waves of her hair, the proud posture of her shoulders.

Her horse stepped into the river. She was almost at the woods.

She never looked back.

Jack watched her disappear into the forest. His breaths were ragged as he walked down the hill. He came to a gradual stop in the valley. The river lapped at his ankles when he stepped into its currents. He stared toward the west, where the sun illumined the Aithwood, catching the rapids of the river.

He knelt in the cold water.

It wasn't long before he heard footsteps splash behind him. Small thin arms came around him in an embrace. Frae held him as he grieved.

The lush green of the hills turned into withered grass. The bracken was tinged in brown, the moss like patches of amber, and trees beyond the Aithwood grew crooked, bent to the south. The wildflowers and heather flourished only in sheltered places, where the wind couldn't break them. The mountains rose, cut from unforgiving rock, and the lochs were low and stagnant. Only the river ran pure, coming from a hidden place in the hills.

Adaira rode at her mother's side, into the heart of the west. The clouds hung low, and it smelled like rain.

She gave herself up to a hungry land where music was forbidden. The place where she had taken her first breath.

A gust rose, drawing its cold fingers through her hair.

"*Welcome home,*" the north wind whispered.

Acknowledgments

I remember February 22, 2019, was a cold bleak day. It was also the day when I sat down and began to write about an enchanted isle and the people who called it home. I was writing for the first time in *months*, at last breaking what had been a long, miserable creative drought, and I had no idea what this story was destined to become. I owe my eternal gratitude to the people who each invested in my work and in me, and who lent their magic to make *A River Enchanted* what it is today.

To Isabel Ibañez, for reading this book chapter by chapter as I wrote it, for spending hours with me brainstorming, and for encouraging me when I felt like giving up on it. Without you, this book would still be a messy draft on my laptop. I will always be so thankful for your friendship and the tough love you give to my stories.

To Suzie Townsend, agent extraordinaire. Remember when I sent this manuscript to you and I said, "I have no idea what this is?" You didn't bat an eye, and even as we strove to discover where this story needed to be, you believed in it and helped it find the perfect home. To Dani Segelbaum and Miranda Stinson, for helping behind the scenes and making my publishing journey run smooth and seamlessly. To Kate Sullivan, who read this manuscript at its first draft. Your incredible insight and notes were instrumental in bringing out the best of this story and gave me the confidence I needed to take this book from YA to adult. To the dream team at New Leaf—thank you for all the support you've given to me and my books. I'm so honored to be one of your authors.

To Vedika Khanna, my inimitable editor. Words can't even describe how honored and happy I am that this book found you, and that you saw all the ways in which it could grow into something fierce and beautiful. Thank you for believing in Jack, Adaira, Torin, Sidra, and Frae, and for helping me find the heart of their individual stories.

A huge thank-you to my amazing teams at William Morrow and Harper Voyager: Liate Stehlik, Jennifer Hart, Jennifer Brehl, David Pomerico, DJ DeSmyter, Emily Fisher, Pamela Barricklow, Elizabeth Blaise, Stephanie Vallejo, Paula Szafranski, and Chris Andrus. I am so honored to have your expertise and support in bringing *A River Enchanted* to life. Thank you to Cynthia Buck for copy editing and helping me polish this manuscript. To Yeon Kim, who designed the stunning cover. It's truly everything I could have ever dreamt of for this book. To Nick Springer, for creating the gorgeous map. To Natasha Bardon and my incredible Voyager U.K. team—I'm so thrilled to partner with you all and see this story take flight across the pond. Thank you for giving my novel the perfect home in the U.K.

When it comes to worldbuilding, there were many books I read for research and inspiration, and I am deeply grateful for the following authors and their works: *The Scots Kitchen* by F. Marian McNeill, *Scottish Herbs and Fairy Lore* by Ellen Evert Hopman, *The Complete Poems and Songs of Robert Burns,*

The Crofter and the Laird by John McPhee, and *Tree of Strings: A History of the Harp in Scotland* by Keith Sanger and Alison Kinnaird.

To the lovely authors who read early copies and provided words of encouragement and support—you have filled my creative well on the days when I have felt empty. Thank you for your kindness and time, and for sustaining me with your stories.

To my readers, here in the U.S. and beyond. I know some of you have been with me from the very beginning and some of you might have just discovered my books. Thank you for your support and all the love you have given to my stories.

To Rachel White, for taking my author photo on that very cold, windy day. You are someone I deeply admire, and I'm so thankful for you and your friendship.

To my family—Dad, Mom, Caleb, Gabriel, Ruth, Mary, and Luke. You are my people and my safe haven, and there is no way to measure my love for each of you.

To Sierra, for always inspiring a dog in my stories. To Ben, for believing in me even when I don't, and for carrying me through the hard days. You have kept my lamp burning on the darkest, longest of nights, and I love that my life has been woven with yours.

To my Heavenly Father. I would have lost heart had I not believed that I would see your goodness in the land of the living.

Soli Deo Gloria.